Sometime Around Midnight

a novel

By Stephanie Pass

For the girls who think they're unlovable—the quiet ones, the loud ones, the ones who've been told they're too much or not enough.

For the girls who've been left on read, left behind, and left wondering what's wrong with them.

You are not cursed.

You are not broken.

You are not too late.

You are not meant to be alone forever.

This is for you.

May you feel seen. May you feel worthy.

May you one day believe the truth: You are so deeply lovable—exactly as you are.

Content Warning

This novel contains sensitive material that may be distressing to some readers. Themes and events explored in this story include:

- **Death during pregnancy and childbirth**

- **Grief and complicated mourning**

- **Suicidal ideation**

While every effort has been made to handle these topics with care and emotional honesty, your well-being comes first. If you are in a place where these themes may be difficult for you, please read with caution—or wait until you're ready.

You are not alone.
You matter.
And it's okay to pause.

* * *

Sometime Around Midnight Playlist

"The Prophecy" - Taylor Swift
"Tidal" - Noah Kahn
"Nobody" - Mitski
"One of Those Days" - Joshua Radin
"Communicating" - Bad Suns
"Kiss Me Slowly" - Parachute
"Afterglow" - Taylor Swift
"Drag" - Day Wave
"Delicate" - Taylor Swift
"Apology" - SafetySuit
"Heaven or Las Vegas" - Cocteau Twins
"Greek Tragedy" - The Wombats
"Dance the Night Away" - Dua Lipa
"Part of Me" - Noah Kahn
"Waking Up in Vegas" - Katy Perry
"Someone Who's Trying" - The Band

Camino
"*Blame It*" - Jamie Foxx, T-Pain
"*Running Back to You*" - Matt Wertz
"*Ankles*" - Lucy Dacus
"*Renegade*" - Taylor Swift, Big Red Machine
"*The Last One*" - Maisie Peters
"*This is me trying*" - Taylor Swift
"*Back to December*" - Taylor Swift
"*Stay*" - SafetySuit
"*Gravity*" - Sara Bareilles
"*Bottom of the Deep Blue Sea*" - MISSIO
"*Marry Me*" - Bruno Mars
"*Bullet from a Gun*" - The Script
"*Sad Beautiful Tragic*" - Taylor Swift
"*Everybody's Changing*" - Keane
"*Single Ladies*" - Beyonce
"*Sometime Around Midnight*" - The Airborne Toxic Event
"*Meant to Be*" - Parachute
"*Sextape*" - The Deftones
"*Speechless*" - Dan + Shay
"*Grow As We Go*" - Ben Platt

BOOKS BY STEPHANIE PASS

0.5 THE ALCHEMY OF US
Available Now

1 TROUBLE OF THE MOST WONDERFUL
KIND
Available Now

2 SOMETIME AROUND MIDNIGHT
Available Now

3 THE BEACH HOUSE
September 2025

CHAPTER ONE

Darci

Why was I shoving a dozen trash bags filled with hacked-up couch parts into the back of my SUV at midnight on a Saturday? Because I thought I was rescuing a piece of curbside gold. Instead, I adopted a loveseat that smelled like it spent the last decade chain-smoking in the back of a dive bar with no ventilation and a jukebox that only played sad country ballads.

Lesson learned—never trust free furniture. I don't care how nice it looks from the street. If it's on the curb, it's there for a reason—and that reason probably has something to do with regret, lingering spirits, and at least three kinds of mold not recognized by science.

I'd been house-sitting for my best friend Claire while she and her fiancé Edison were off in Galveston, visiting her parents and being all annoyingly in love. My job? Water the plants. Grab the mail. Don't burn the place down.

But on my way out of their neighborhood yesterday, I spotted a couch on the curb—dark, paisley, and full of potential. Jackpot, right?

Wrong.

I should've known better when the owner stumbled out in socks and cargo shorts, a half-dead cigarette glued to his bottom lip.

"Lemme help you with that," he slurred, already dragging one end toward my car like we were in a buddy movie montage.

The stale smoke aura. Little cigarette burns peppering the armrests. The fact that he called it "Ol' Girl." There were so many red flags. But did I listen to the tiny voice of reason in my head? Nope. I let him hoist it into the back of my SUV like it was a treasure and not a cursed relic.

Thank God I had the sense to decline when he offered to come inside and "look around." I mean, I'm all for making bad decisions. But I'm not murder documentary bad.

It wasn't until I dragged it into my apartment, by myself—sweaty, smug, and proud of my curbside treasure—that the nightmare really began. I let it sit overnight like I hadn't just welcomed the ghost of a thousand Marlboros into my home. And when I walked into the living room the next morning, the smell hit me like a punch to the face.

Not a whiff. Not a suggestion. A full-body assault of old cigarettes and something worse—like decades of broken dreams filtered through nicotine and bad life choices. My eyes watered. My soul recoiled.

I scoured the internet like I was researching an exorcism. Baking soda? Dumped it on like I was trying to marinate the thing. Febreze? I used half a bottle. The couch smelled worse. I washed the cushion covers. Left it on the balcony all day like a naughty dog.

As a last resort, I sprayed it with bedbug spray. Why? Because some rando on a Reddit thread said it "neutralized toxins." It didn't. It made it smell like chemically enhanced despair.

That's when the panic set in. Because this wasn't just bad. This was invasive. This smell was going to creep into my walls, my clothes, my pores. I was going to wear that smell forever—like a tragic couch witch sentenced to haunt thrift store furniture with a cloud of stale cigarettes and broken dreams trailing behind her.

And the kicker? My lease had an iron-clad no-smoking policy. Management sent out monthly passive-aggressive emails about it, complete with grainy ring cam screenshots shaming people caught in the act and threats of fines. I might've seemed like the carefree, bad-decision type, but I was a rule-follower at heart. Always had been. Even as a kid, I once ratted myself out for stealing a single Skittle off a teacher's desk.

I needed that loveseat gone. Tonight. But it was Saturday, it was late, and management had a weird obsession with guarding the dumpsters like sacred shrines. There were signs in Comic Sans—Comic Sans, for god's sake—warning us not to even look at the dumpsters if we needed to dump anything larger than a grocery sack. Like that would trigger an alarm and a drone strike. It would not surprise me if they pulled out a stockade for offenders and made an example of them in front of the leasing office.

So tossing it straight into the dumpster was out. Fire was too suspicious. And I was out of options.

I flopped onto the floor, stared at the ceiling, and muttered to no one in particular,

"What the hell am I going to do?"

I was just a hair under five feet tall, so basically fun-size, like a candy bar. How in the hell was I supposed to get rid of an entire loveseat? I was running on iced coffee, total panic, and zero plan, so this needed to be simple. Because I was desperate and out of options.

It was me versus that goddamn couch. And I was *not* losing.

And that's when I sat up and had a brilliant idea. My one last Hail Mary. I could tear that motherfucker apart and hide all the evidence in trash bags, which *could* go in the dumpster. It was pure genius! No one, including management, would be the wiser.

Minutes later, I was hunched over my laptop, deep in a YouTube rabbit hole full of furniture disassembly tutorials. Apparently, taking apart a couch was a thing. Who knew?

The only issue? Every single video required power tools. Electric saws. Drills. At one point, I think someone used a blowtorch.

All I had was the tiny pink "Do-It-Herself" toolkit I bought when I moved into my first apartment—and a serrated bread knife.

But I had heart. I had rage. And I had nothing to lose at this point.

It took me all afternoon and most of the night, but I broke that loveseat down to the frame using a screwdriver, a hammer, and an unholy amount of determination and spite. I pried, unscrewed, and beat the hell out of it until it collapsed in a heap of defeated upholstery and splinters.

Then I shoved the remains into trash bags like I was cleaning up after a crime of passion.

Only the cushions were left. I took that bread knife, muttered an apology to it, and hacked them into neat little chunks like I was prepping for some demented upholstery tapas platter.

When it was all over, I stood there, sweaty and triumphant, surrounded by garbage bags full of carnage. I'd done it.

Was it unhinged? Absolutely. But I'd never felt more powerful in my life.

It was after midnight when I finally filled the last of the garbage bags to hide the evidence. By the time I was done, there were at least 10 bags lined up at my front door. Half a dozen were shoved in the backseat and trunk of my SUV, and I put the rest on the roof of the car. Then it was time for a midnight ride to the dumpster.

I was past exhaustion and more than a little pissed off as I tossed trash bags left and right. The sooner I was done, the sooner I'd be standing in a hot shower rinsing the years of cigarette stink off me.

Then, I saw him.

"Oh, for fuck's sake," I muttered.

Sweatpants riding low on his hips, barefoot, and wearing a faded, too-tight A&M T-shirt that hugged every muscle. I spun around quickly, pretending the dumpster was fascinating. As he came closer, I raked a critical glance over him.

He wasn't that tall, maybe a few inches above me. His jaw was sharp enough to cut glass, but the messy red hair and scattering of faded freckles instantly brought to mind a mischievous, carrot-topped little boy. Yet when his eyes locked with mine, even in the darkness, they seemed lit from within—a startling, electric shade of pale blue. Heat rose to my cheeks, and I quickly forced my gaze away, shaking off the unexpected reaction with an annoyed flick of my head.

Definitely not my type, I decided firmly. Maybe I was delirious because I took one more look and thought he looked… well… fucking delicious. Or maybe I was just telling myself that because he looked entirely too good compared to my walking disaster.

I was into super masculine guys. Give me the tall, dark, and hairy guys usually covered in tattoos. The ones who could pick me up and toss me around on the bed. And was there anything better than a beard burn between your legs? And if that beard played a little guitar, it was even better.

As he approached, he stared at me like I'd just crawled out of the sewer and asked for a hug. His expression shifted from surprise to amusement. I looked down, remembering I was still wearing the Well Hung Winery T-shirt with the Nutella stain on the chest and the hole near my belly button. I ran my hand through my tangled pixie cut, trying unsuccessfully to tame it. I wondered who would walk to the dumpster in the middle of the night to toss a single grocery bag.

I just had this feeling he had seen me down here and was so desperate to know what stupid thing I was doing this late at night that he grabbed whatever he could throw away so he wasn't too conspicuous.

He was nearly at the dumpster when I realized it was Alex. We'd met a few times at some mixers the apartment management held. He was a doctor, a nurse, or something over at the hospital across the street.

He stood a few feet away and smirked, his eyes full of delight as he asked, "Dumping the bodies tonight?"

"Um, sure… something like that," I murmured.

I turned back to my SUV to pull out another couple of trash bags. He followed me as I heaved two more bags in my hands and turned toward the dumpster. I let out a sigh and slowly slid my gaze to him, waiting for whatever he was going to say next.

"Need any help?" He came close and peered over my shoulder into the trunk with one eyebrow cocked. His cologne or aftershave wafted towards me, and it was nice—something spicy that made me want to inhale deeply.

I closed my eyes as I set the two bags down and pulled the trunk lid closed, even though there were more bags still inside.

I turned to face him, trying to keep my face as neutral as possible when I wanted to scream. My voice flat I said, "No, I'm good."

He inclined his head. "You sure? It looks like you've got a few more." That smirk still on his face, "I'd be happy to help."

"I don't need help. I can do it myself. Thanks."

I rested my elbow on the trunk, hoping he would get the hint and walk away. He didn't.

He looked over his shoulder, surveying the area when he asked, "So... what's in the bags, Darby?"

I narrowed my eyes and looked at him, certain he knew my name. I guess we were going to play that game.

I blew out a breath. "Look, *Alan,* as you can see, I need to finish up what I'm doing. I've got an early day tomorrow. So if you would..." I trailed off, waving my hand back towards his apartment building. Maybe he'd get it this time.

"If you don't show me, I'm just going to hang around

until you're done and open the bags myself."

I grimaced. "You want to crawl around in that dumpster?"

He raised both eyebrows, that goddamn smirk on his face. "Try me," He shrugged.

"Ugh, fine." I stared at the ground, feeling the heat crawling up my neck. I lowered my voice to almost a whisper. "It's a… couch."

"What?" The side of his mouth quirked up.

This was taking entirely too long. I ripped open the top of one of the bags to let him see the broken wood frame and the destroyed foam cushions.

I glared at him as I said, "It's. A. Couch."

He looked at me quizzically, walked closer to peer in the bag, and then abruptly jumped back with a look of disgust, pinching his nose.

"Man, that stinks." He looked up at me, blinking rapidly. "Jesus, my eyes are watering. Are you…Are you smoking in your apartment? It's a really bad habit. You should quit."

I ignored him as I re-tied the garbage bag before swinging it into the dumpster.

I turned, hands on my hips, an eyebrow raised. "Do I look like a smoker to you?"

He leaned a little too close and wrinkled his nose. "You definitely smell like one."

I tugged my t-shirt up, bringing it to my nose, unintentionally exposing my stomach. I reeked like an ashtray. But as I glared, his eyes flicked downward, and I caught the movement.

I muttered, "This is a fucking nightmare." I threw my hands up in the air as I stomped back to the trunk of my car.

"Wait, wait, wait." He chuckled. "Do you even live here, Darlie? You could just be illegally dumping these bags here." He nodded, satisfied with his detective work.

"What?! Of course, I live here." I gestured wildly over to my apartment. "I live right over there. Are you serious? You know me. We've both attended those stupid mixers in the rec room, *Alex*. I can't believe you don't remember my name. I sure as hell remember you. You're the guy who showed up to that potluck with a can of spray cheese and a box of saltines."

I crossed my arms, giving him my best go-to-hell look.

He gave me a smug look as he said, "I am pretty unforgettable."

I rolled my eyes and flicked my hand to shoo him. "Can you just… go away? Please."

He just stood there and shrugged. He shrugged!

He grinned and said, "You're clearly about to do something illegal, and I'd hate to miss it."

I heaved out a sigh. Ignoring him was my best course of action. I went back to the car, grabbed the last two bags from the trunk, and headed toward the dumpster. He just stood there watching me, still holding his itty bitty trash bag.

I stopped and turned to stare at him, dropping the bags on the ground with a thud as I pointed at him. He wasn't going to get away with this. I was too pissed.

I practically *snarled* as I took a step towards him. "Do you want to know what I've been doing all day?"

He interrupted, "Not really."

I kept walking until I was toe-to-toe with him. "Well, too bad because you're gonna. I've literally spent all day and night destroying this cigarette-infested couch I stupidly picked up on the side of the road. I had no idea it was infused with eau-de-Marlboro until I woke up and realized the stench had permeated my entire living room."

My chest was heaving. "And I tried everything." I started listing things off my fingers. "Febreeze, baking soda, the washing machine, even bed bug spray!"

I threw my hands up in the air. "And now? Now I smell like a two-week-old ashtray! So everything is just peachy for me, *Alex*."

He cocked his head, "You have bed bugs?"

I spat out, "Fuck! No!"

I took in a breath and let it out slowly before I leaned down, picked up the bags, and turned to toss them into the dumpster before I opened the side door to get the last trash bags out.

He dropped the smirk and held up his pointer finger, looking a little concerned. "Uh... do you want me to call someone?"

I whirled around on him. "What!? Goddamit! I'm not crazy!" I took another cleansing breath so I could calm myself down. "No, I don't want you to call anyone. Just leave me alone. Go... do whatever it is you do... please." I waved my hand dismissively at him.

His voice softened as he started to say, "I didn't mean...," but he drifted off, not finishing the sentence as our eyes locked, and I felt something stir deep in my belly.

Well, that was weird.

I sighed and said, "It's fine," before turning to throw two more bags in.

I glanced back at him, and he nodded. "Okay. Have a

good night, *Darci*."

That motherfucker. Yeah, real funny, dude.

I caught the twinkle in his eye as he gave me a little wave before tossing his trash bag and heading back to his apartment.

God, that man was infuriating. I kept my eyes on him, standing by the trunk of my car, as he walked back to his apartment. He looked over at me, something flashing across his face I couldn't decipher, just before he walked inside. As soon as his door was shut, I tossed the rest of the bags as fast as I could.

Back in my apartment, I mopped the floor with bleach where the couch had been. Then I cried as I threw my favorite clothes in double trash bags and left them by the front door. I wasn't making another trip to the dumpster tonight. I scrubbed myself clean in a scalding hot shower, washing my hair three times to make sure any trace of cigarette was permanently gone.

I put on my second favorite pair of pj pants with the cat heads and a tank top, climbed into bed, and cracked open a book. But no matter how hard I concentrated, I couldn't stop thinking about his smirk or the color of his eyes before drifting off to sleep.

CHAPTER TWO

Alex

"That woman is pure chaos," I muttered, giving her one last look over by the dumpster.

Why had she reacted to me so strongly? Of course, I knew Darci's name. I hadn't been able to forget her since we met at that mixer a couple of months ago. I was just giving her a hard time. I thought maybe we were flirting, but quickly realized she was in no mood for that. Or maybe she just wasn't in the mood for me.

I hoped this smirky, devil-may-care guy would eventually stick, and I'd feel something again. But it had been three years. Three, entirely too long, years since I lost Jenna and Savannah Jean, and it still felt like yesterday. I was so tired of feeling numb. You would have thought an ER doctor like me would care enough to seek out help and get my mental health in check. I'd given countless patients that very same advice. But nope, not me. I could handle it all on my own.

Walking back into my apartment, I grabbed a drink from the fridge and popped it open. The cold liquid slid down my throat, a temporary respite from the shame of my interaction with Darci. Running my hand over my face, I mulled over the ridiculous things I had said.

What was wrong with me?

I should never have walked out there, but I couldn't help myself. It had been almost comical watching her struggling with those giant trash bags. I just had to know. *What the hell was in those bags?* And why were there so many?

I'd taken out my trash this morning before my shift at the hospital, but I couldn't resist the urge to investigate. I looked around, gathering any trash I could find — mainly my dinner, which wasn't much. I knew she would figure me out, especially walking out in the middle of the night. I couldn't stop the smile spreading across my face as I thought about her reaction. She'd been so angry, like a little spitfire. It was almost… cute.

She must have gone through a lot today, trying to get rid of that couch. Sheesh.

I peeked out my window, watching her drag the last bag to the dumpster from her car. I should have been nicer. I should have insisted on helping her. A wave of guilt washed over me as I slumped into my favorite chair, reclining it with a groan that sounded suspiciously like an old man. But that's exactly how I felt, like I'd aged a decade or more after… everything from the last few years.

I could barely pay attention to whatever I'd put on the television. My thoughts just kept going back to Darci. I remembered meeting her at that first apartment mixer after moving in. How could I forget?

She had this whole sexy goth thing about her — dark lipstick, boots that could crush a man's ego, and that black dress she wore? It was still burned into my brain. The way it hugged her curves should've been illegal and dipped just low enough to make conversation a challenge. The sleeves were sheer, the fabric clung like a second skin, and she wore it like she didn't care who noticed—like she already knew she was the most magnetic person in the room.

She was exactly my type—bold, sharp, untouchable. The kind of woman who usually wanted nothing more than a good time and a clean exit.

But with Darci... I wasn't so sure. Something about her made me think she wanted more. And worse—I couldn't stop thinking about giving it to her.

With her dark chocolate brown hair in that short hairstyle I think they called a pixie cut, she looked like she wasn't even five feet tall. Being on the shorter side myself, I've always had a thing for smaller women, and Darci was perfect.

At our first introduction, I remembered how her features were delicate, almost elfin, with long dark lashes that brushed against her cheeks when she looked down. And her eyes were stunning. They were my favorite thing about her—light brown, almost golden, like whiskey. She seemed to always be in constant motion, fluttering around like a fairy, like some dark-haired version of Tinkerbell.

We practically lived across the parking lot from each other, and every time I caught a glimpse of her, something shifted deep inside me. Nearly every morning, she'd step out onto her porch, book in one hand, coffee in the other, settling into that old grandma rocking chair like she'd always belonged there. There was a quiet comfort in seeing her like that, as if the day hadn't truly started until she'd taken her place.

Noticing Darci—really noticing her—felt like a betrayal somehow. Paying attention to another woman when my wife's memory still lived in every corner of my heart… it was new. Strange. A little terrifying. I hadn't felt much of anything in years—not since I lost her. Grief had wrapped itself around me like fog, numbing everything. Every now and then, it broke open without warning—sharp, brutal—as if she'd only just left. As if the ache was fresh again, no matter how much time had passed.

Jenna and I met in middle school. Her family had moved to town that summer. I know it's a cliche, but I knew back then she was it for me. We were best friends, but it took me until college to finally ask her out. We didn't try to start a family until I got through med school, but Jenna struggled to get pregnant. When it happened, I was over the moon. I couldn't wait to be a dad and have our little family.

When we found out Jenna had placenta previa 20 weeks into her pregnancy, I wasn't too worried. Savannah Jean was our first baby, but lots of women developed placenta previa. It's easily managed with a c-section. Sure, it can have complications, but I was a doctor. We would be prepared.

After the diagnosis, Jenna was constantly monitored and saw her doctors and specialists every week. When she hit 30 weeks, they did an MRI, which was traumatizing. Stuffing her giant pregnant belly into an MRI tube brought out claustrophobia she didn't know she had. But she was strong and made it through everything they threw at her, and that's when we found out it was worse than we thought. It wasn't just placenta previa. It was placenta increta, possibly percreta. Her placenta was bulging in the images, which meant it was growing through the uterine wall. They suspected it was moving into her bladder.

Things moved fast. We decided to deliver our baby girl early, at 35 weeks, to give them both the best chance. And this was going to be a big production with about 25 people in the delivery room. There was going to be four doctors, including our ob/gyn, another ob/gyn, a urologist and a gynecological oncologist working on Jenna. When we first heard "oncologist" we worried there was more to this than we thought. Still, our ob assured us it was because he was so good at making the necessary repairs to her bladder and any other organs damaged from the placenta.

This surgery was a big deal. It was the first time they would perform it at this hospital. There were weekly meetings between the doctors, nursing, and surgical staff, so everyone was prepared. They assured me they had everything under control.

But things... changed. A week before the surgery, Jenna began to bleed. For weeks, they told us if there was any sign of blood to run to the nearest hospital. So that's what we did. The nearest hospital was not the hospital where we were delivering. It was the hospital where I worked in the emergency room.

I thought things would be okay, but the OB on call had no experience with placenta increta. Our doctor had been called. But... there was no time to transport Jenna. Things took a turn, and it all descended into chaos.

I begged to go back with her, but I didn't get the chance. It was pure chaos. She had to have general anesthesia so they could get the baby out fast. To try to prevent hemorrhage, they had to remove Jenna's uterus with the placenta still attached. It was bittersweet because this meant a permanent end to Jenna's fertility.

I walked alongside the stretcher as they wheeled her to the operating room. When it was time to say goodbye, I kissed her, brushed her blond hair out of her face, and said, "I love you."

I held her hand until they wheeled her away and couldn't help myself when I shouted, "I'll see you on the other side, darling," as the double doors swung.

I watched through the window as she held up a thumbs-up as the doors swung shut. That was the last time I saw my wife. I had no idea the other side would be so, so far away.

Now I was no longer a husband and never got the chance to be a father. It had been three years, and I still missed her and the sweet baby I never held in my arms every single day.

I'll never forget the look on the doctor's face when she walked into the waiting room. You know it's bad when they take you to a more private waiting room.

Her voice was somber, "I'm sorry, Alex. I'm so sorry."

I fell to my knees right there. Her eyes told me everything I needed to know before the words left her mouth. My parents had just arrived moments before. It was my dad who held me up when I thought I was going to die from the devastation. I probably would have done something foolish without my parents by my side for those first few weeks.

As the doctor continued, I sobbed openly. My mom ran a soothing hand over my back.

"Jenna had a double whammy against her during the surgery. We put stents in her femoral arteries to mitigate blood loss. Still, she went into a delayed anaphylaxis due to the anesthetic the radiologist used to numb her legs for the procedure. It happened on the table just before they were putting her under."

I looked up at the doctor. "She was never… allergic. Anaphylaxis?"

She nodded. "Lidocaine. It took a long time to stabilize her from that reaction. There was just too much blood loss, and she went into hypovolemic shock. We were pumping all the blood we could into her, but it was just coming right back out. Her heart couldn't keep up." She touched my arm, "I'm so sorry."

I whispered, "The baby?"

She shook her head. "Jenna's uterus spontaneously ruptured when the bleeding started at home. The baby never had a chance. She was already gone by the time we got her out."

All I could do was cover my face, leaning into my mom. The doctor murmured something to my father, but I didn't hear it. I didn't care. My world was gone.

I became a doctor to help people, and the two people who needed my help the most, I couldn't save. After their deaths, I took a week off and then went right back to work. Everyone thought I was crazy, but I had nothing without them, nothing but my work.

I needed something to focus on to get through the pain and the grief. The only silver lining to my tragedy was my refusal to lose a patient. Sure, it happened, especially in the ER, but I was good. Damn good. I busted my ass to give the best care I could to every single patient I saw, and I saved more people than I couldn't. I got really good at looking for the zebras, not the horses.

I became a workaholic. If there was an open shift in the ER, I took it. Sometimes, I'd work double and triple shifts. Anything was better than being at home, wallowing in my grief with their ghosts all around me.

It was hard at home. I'd swear I saw Jenna walking into a room or heard her call my name. I'd hear baby cries in the house. After three months, I was either going to go insane or I had to move. So I sold our house and rented an apartment close to the hospital. Besides, what's the point of a big house in the suburbs when there's no family to fill it?

But it wasn't enough. The entire town reminded me of her. I still had to drive by our favorite restaurant, the bridge where I asked Jenna to marry me, and the place where she told me she was pregnant. Every morning, I had to drive by the school where we became best friends.

It was just too much.

If I wasn't working, I was at the local bar getting shit-faced. I couldn't stand to be alone with my thoughts. They were too dark. I'd get blackout drunk, take an Uber home, and sleep it off until my next shift. I did that for two years until one day, I showed up drunk at work, soaking in alcohol, and nearly gave a patient the wrong drug. That was my wake-up call. I faked illness, went home, and called a therapist.

Therapy helped… I think. If I actually went and didn't cancel half my appointments. I could be alone with my thoughts, which weren't so dark anymore. I didn't drink much anymore.

My therapist, Dr. Matthews, suggested moving somewhere new and getting a fresh start, so that's what I did. Six months ago, I left the hospital, left my hometown, and moved three hours away to Denton. It helped. The memories weren't constantly in my face. I could forget, even just for a little while, and take a deep breath again.

I was tired of being lonely, tired of my self-imposed solitary confinement. It had been a long time since I even cared. I was beginning to believe I could start over here, but hope like that felt dangerous. So yeah, maybe therapy was making a dent in this thick skull of mine. And maybe the man I used to be could make a reappearance.

CHAPTER THREE

Darci

I was lying across my broken-down couch reading a book on Sunday afternoon when my phone rang.

As soon as I saw it was Claire, I answered immediately. "Hey, girlie! How's Galveston treating you?"

"Darci! It's been amazing! I had forgotten how much I loved the water."

"How's Bandit taking it?"

Edison and Claire rarely went anywhere without their Boxer dog in tow. He was basically their child.

"Bandit's in heaven! We go for walks on the beach every morning, and he loves to play in the surf." She chuckled, "He's a real beach dog now."

I laughed. "Now, I need to see that. Take a video and send it to me."

"I've already got tons. I'll send you some when we get off the phone."

"Can't wait!" I moved to find a more comfortable spot on the couch because a spring was poking me in the butt. "So… how'd it go with Edison and your parents?"

I could hear the smile in her voice. "They love him. When Sonny walked in and saw my dad's bookshelf, they instantly bonded over their favorite books. And my mom can't stop feeding him. They're even excited about the wedding. I wasn't sure if they would want to go, but they can't wait to see Vegas."

"So you were worried for nothing."

Before the trip, Claire had been bracing for impact— convinced her parents would stage an intervention and declare it far too soon after the divorce for her to be thinking about wedding bells again.

She laughed. "Yeah, I guess so. It seems my mom's mellowed out a lot." She paused. "It's a little bit… weird. My mom's been… suspiciously pleasant, like maybe she's saving her passive-aggressive comments for a group text later."

I laughed. "Maybe she's playing the long game. Act sweet now, and unleash the guilt trip when you least expect it—probably seconds before you walk down the aisle."

Claire let out a dramatic sigh. "God, I hope not. If she starts with the guilt-tripping, Sonny and I are eloping."

"Well… either way, I'm still your maid of honor, and I love a good party. So… if you need help with anything, anything at all, I'm your girl. You are going to love the bachelorette party I've got brewing when we get to Vegas."

"Just… don't plan anything," she said, lowering her voice to a whisper, "illegal."

I laughed. "Me? When do I do anything illegal?"

Claire snorted. "Um, that flight to Denver? When you casually slid mini vodka bottles into your purse every time the cart rolled by? I'm pretty sure the flight attendant was scared to make eye contact."

I huffed. "First of all, they were just sitting there, begging to be taken. Second, you thoroughly enjoyed that questionable margarita in the hotel room later."

Claire laughed. "Okay, fair. But only because you mixed it with Sprite and desperation."

We both giggled.

I continued in a sing-song voice, "Just remember, 'what happens in Vegas...'" I trailed off as I put the phone on speaker and set it on the coffee table. "It's going to be epic. We're drinking all the cocktails and going clubbing to dance our asses off. Maybe we'll get a lap dance or two from some hot male strippers?"

Claire barked out a laugh. "Oh my god, Darci. I can't wait, though I'm not sure how crazy I am about some male stripper rubbing his junk on me."

I laughed. "Oh, please, you'll love it, and if you don't, I'll be happy to take your place and let him rub it on me."

She cleared her throat, suddenly flustered—like someone had walked in or maybe she just realized what she'd said out loud. "Well, um, I'm definitely going to need some help planning this wedding."

I squealed with delight. "I'd love to help. I don't just love a good party. You know I'm also great at planning them."

"Cool, you can help me plan when we have downtime at work."

"Totally." I hesitated before asking, "Do you need to go? Because I am dying to tell you what happened to *me* last night."

I heard a door close. "Nope, I'm free. My mom's at a

quilt meeting, and Sonny's in the garage helping my dad fix… something with a lot of wires."

"Well, well, well. Look at him, turning into the perfect son-in-law."

I loved to tease her about Edison. He was a great guy and the ideal match for Claire. I was happy for both of them. I just wished I could find someone who made me feel like those two did for each other.

Claire said quietly, "But right when I said that thing about the strippers, they both walked into the kitchen for a drink. I had to flee to the bedroom."

I tried to contain my laughter. "Of course you'd accidentally activate the hot guy summoning spell." With mock seriousness in my voice, I said, "Teach me your ways because every date I go on is a disaster. Maybe I'm just destined to be alone."

"Oh, babe. That's so not true. One day you'll find him where you least expect him."

I sighed, "If you say so…"

"So was it another one of your crazy dates?"

"Nope, I think I need to take a little break from dating."

"Really?"

"God, yes. I cannot go on another date like capture the flag guy or footie pajama guy. I need someone… better. Someone… normal."

"I'm telling you, there is a guy waiting for you, for the right moment. But what happened?"

"Well, I was at your house picking up the mail and watering the plants. I saw a loveseat on the curb a few streets over as I left. It looked nice, so I got out to look at it. The owner came out and helped me put it in the car."

"Was it Mr. Crenshaw? Older guy, bald on top?"

"Does he smell like an ashtray?"

She giggled. "Yep, that's him, usually has a cigarette stuck to his lip. He's always putting stuff on the curb." She added sarcastically, "The HOA just loves him." Worry crept up in her voice, "But I refuse to get his furniture because he's a hoarder and smokes like a chimney."

"Yeah… now you tell me." I chuckled dryly. "So, I got the loveseat home, and by the next day, I could physically feel the lung cancer entering my body. That thing was soaked in cigarette smoke."

"Oh no. What did you do?"

Claire used to live in my apartment complex. She knew precisely what a disaster this could be since with that ridiculous no-smoking policy. I swear even the hint of cigarette smoke sent the management into overdrive.

"You know how insane the property manager is."

"Cyndi?" She laughed, "Remember when she was obsessed with everyone learning to spell her name?"

"Don't get me started on her."

"I'm so glad I don't have to deal with her anymore."

"We should all be so lucky," I said as I rolled my eyes. "Just the other day, I saw her putting up flyers at the dumpster threatening fines if anyone put furniture in it. So I couldn't just haul it over there, and it was a Saturday night. But I was desperate to get it out of my apartment, so the only thing I came up with was to rip it apart with my bare hands."

"What?" Claire sounded both horrified and amused.

"Well, not just my bare hands. I did have a screwdriver, a hammer, and a bread knife."

Claire laughed. "Oh my god! You're serious? What did you do?"

I took a breath in. "I literally deconstructed that bitch down to the frame. It took me hours, but by the time I was finished, I'd even cut the couch cushions into bits with the bread knife and put everything in about a dozen trash bags, and drove them to the dumpster."

Claire laughed hysterically, trying to catch her breath. "Oh my god, Darci… I wish I'd been there."

"I know. It was ridiculous, and I was so pissed off about the whole thing. But man, was it cathartic."

Through her laughter, Claire said, "I'm so sorry we weren't there to help you."

I waved my hand in the air like Claire could see me. "I mean, yeah, Edison's truck would have been real convenient, but it's fine." I let out a sigh. "You won't believe who showed up while I tossed the bags in the dumpster."

"Who?"

"This guy who lives across from me. Maybe you met him during one of those stupid apartment mixers? Alex? He came out of his apartment to throw a tiny bag of trash away at midnight and practically interrogated me about what I was doing."

Claire hummed as if she was trying to remember. "Oh, wait. Alex? Red hair and freckles? The ER doctor?"

"He's a doctor?"

"Yeah. I think he's fairly new."

"Whatever. He was such an ass. He pretended he didn't remember my name."

"Really? That doesn't sound like him. He was so nice to us."

"Us?"

"Me and Sonny? I didn't tell you about this? Weeks ago, I had to take Sonny to the ER. He's allergic to bees.

We were doing yard work, and he got stung and didn't realize his Epi-Pen was expired. We went to the ER, and Dr. Alex was so good with him."

"Dr. Alex?"

"That's what he introduced himself as."

I let out a sigh. "I guess he just hates me then." Great.

"Oh, who knows? Maybe he was just having a bad night. Adjusting to a new job and a new city can be super stressful. Try to be nice to him. It's hard to be the new guy."

I hesitated a moment.

"I guess you're right. I'll try giving him the benefit of the doubt." I sighed, "Oh, I wanted to ask you something about the wedding." I smirked, "Can I bring a plus one?"

In a teasing voice, she said, "Have someone in mind? Maybe... Dr. Alex?"

"Uh... god no. He's totally not my type. I just... wanted to know if by some miracle I met someone I could bring them."

"Of course."

We talked a few minutes more, but when I heard Edison in the background, I said goodbye.

I laid back on the couch, and as my mind drifted, going right back to last night when Alex walked over. Those low-riding sweatpants and the way his eyes had been practically electric.

I was tired of being single. I wanted a built-in plus one, a best friend who'd cuddle and watch movies, play board games, and go on adventures—someone who'd hold me at night and knew just what to say when I was upset.

I found myself looking out the front window toward his apartment. He was sitting on his patio, barefoot in a pair of shorts. His hair looked like he'd raked his hands through it a million times. He was leaning back in a chair, looking incredibly sad. It made my heart ache for him. I thought about going over and seeing if he was okay. But I just felt it was the last thing he wanted right now.

His hand went across his face, rubbing his eyes. Was he wiping tears away? He leaned over, his forearms on his knees, with his hands covering his face. Maybe he was an asshole to someone else and they finally hurt his feelings.

A moment later, he raised up and looked this way as if he could see me through the blinds. *Fuck.* I ducked, hoping he didn't see me staring. I peeked over the couch, and I swore he was still looking straight at me, his eyes narrowing before he got up and walked back into his apartment. *Great.* Now he thinks I'm a serial killer and a peeping tom.

For the rest of the afternoon, I couldn't stop thinking about the look on his face. Something tugged at my heartstrings seeing him so upset. I regretted not going over to check on him. That was just the kind of person I was. I was that girl in school who took the new kid under my wing or hugged the crying kid. Even now I tended to seek out the people who were sitting alone somewhere.

My mom repeatedly stressed empathy when I was growing up, but sometimes, I wondered if it made a person weak. She was such a pushover when it came to my dad. He was a musician, always on the road, so he wasn't around much. But when he was, their dynamic drove me insane.

Even as a kid, I could see how unhappy she was when he was home, but she stayed. She stayed until I graduated high school, and the literal day after my graduation, she packed her bags and left. My dad's career had slowed by then, so he was home more. But he seemed shell-shocked when she left. He couldn't do anything himself. She'd been the one to take care of the house and the bills, clean his clothes, make his dinners, and make all his doctor's appointments. He was lost without her.

For a while, I was angry she left. But she made sure she stayed in my life, even though it felt like she didn't just leave him. She left me, too. I was on the cusp of spreading my wings and about to go off to college. Seeing him so helpless, I couldn't leave. I ended up tethered to home, giving up a scholarship so I could attend college in town, and I could take care of him.

Truthfully, I was furious with both of them. If he hadn't been such a domineering jerk, maybe she would have stayed, and I wouldn't have gotten stuck as the go-between. I could have been having the time of my life in college.

He never treated me like he did Mom. Sure, he looked scary with his big muscles and tattoo sleeves, but he was my teddy bear. I was undeniably a daddy's girl. I'd had that man wrapped around my finger since birth. He'd always tried to give me the world.

Then, I'd lost him so unexpectedly a few years ago—heart attack, a year after I graduated college. The doctors had called it a "widow maker," but it was more like an "orphan maker."

On the good days, I thought of it as a blessing in disguise. If she hadn't left, I would have never had that time with him. And I still missed him. On the bad days, I just steeped in my anger, hating that I'd been trapped here.

My relationship with him was probably why I was so drawn to guys like him—the big, tall, bearded musicians covered in tattoos. But no matter how hard I tried, it never worked out.

I felt a hot flush up my neck just thinking about the embarrassing dates I'd had the last few months. I could write a book on what not to do to find your soulmate. And that was precisely why I was giving myself a dating break.

I shifted on the couch, unable to resist another glance out the window. Alex was down in the parking lot, about to get in his car, when he looked up at me, waving in a way that wasn't exactly friendly. I froze. What. An. Ass. I still had this urge to ask if he was okay, but why did I even care?

I leaned against the couch, sighed, and opened my favorite app, Lost Connections. After reading the posts looking for lost love or someone they saw across a room, I always felt a little thrill. That was my desire, my deep, dark secret I had never told a soul—though I had a feeling Claire had figured it out. I just wanted someone to feel that way about me. To be so mesmerized by my presence, they had to find me again.

I still remember the knee-jerk reaction I had when I found Edison's post about Claire and showed it to her. It set things in motion that were destined in the stars for those two. It was a goddamn fairytale. I was thrilled for my best friend, but a twinge of jealousy reared up.

Would something like that ever happen to me? I wanted my Cinderella moment more than anything. Would love ever find me? Maybe I was just... destined to be the sidekick, the best friend, the background character in everyone else's happily-ever-after. Maybe I was just unlovable.

CHAPTER FOUR

Alex

I stormed back into my apartment, slamming the door behind me with a force that echoed my frustration. The last thing I needed was a neighbor to witness my vulnerability across the apartment complex. Crying on the patio had not been on today's agenda. Usually, when memories of Jenna and the baby reared up, I could keep it together until I was in the privacy of my own home. But today... Today was our wedding anniversary.

Instead of crying alone on the patio, I should have whisked my wife away to somewhere special. I should have made love to her in the early morning, holding her against me, whispering how much she meant to me until our toddler joyfully bounded in, filling our home with the delightful noise of a happy family.

I wasn't supposed to be left here alone without them. Moving away from Patterdale had been a step forward, but on days like today – our anniversary, her birthday, Savannah's due date, the day they left this world—it was still so fucking hard. I had been making progress, but this morning, when I saw the date, the pain just slammed into me. For every step forward, each harsh reminder sent me two steps back.

I needed to make peace with this new life. *My life.* I needed to start living again.

I just needed a moment to breathe. I had hoped sitting on the patio would let me dwell in my memories alone, in peace. I went back inside when I saw her silhouette across the way through the blinds. I didn't need someone judging me.

I had to get out of here. The weight of my grief was suffocating inside this apartment. I went to the closet, yanking off my athletic shorts for a pair of jeans and swapping my worn-out t-shirt for something a bit more presentable. I had no idea where I was going, but I needed somewhere to forget—just for an hour, a moment, anything—for even a little while.

This would have been the perfect time to drown my sorrows until I was blackout drunk, numb myself against the pain, but that wasn't me anymore. At least, I hoped it wasn't.

Taking the stairs two at a time, I descended to the parking lot. The Hickory Street Bar came to mind on my way to the car. I'd been there a couple of times. It was always crowded, and today was one of those days when I wanted to be surrounded by people, even if I didn't talk to a single one, to dull all this pain. I could even grab a bite from the food truck outside. It seemed like the perfect escape.

Glancing at Darci's window again, I could still see her dark shadow peering at me. Irritated, I shot her a curt wave as I climbed into my car, determined to put distance between me and her prying gaze. Couldn't she just mind her own fucking business?

The bar greeted me with a surprising emptiness, a handful of people nursing their sorrows across the dimly lit space. It made sense. After all, it was early on a Sunday evening. At this hour, only desperate souls sought comfort in a place like this. I opted for a seat at the far end of the bar, several stools away from anyone else, and signaled the bartender for a double gin and tonic, my one drink for the night. I went to the kiosk and ordered a burger and fries from the food truck.

My attention shifted to the television on the wall with what seemed like the most boring baseball game ever played. I let myself get lost in its monotony. I wasn't much of a sports guy. In reality, I couldn't care less. Of course, admitting any of this would probably result in my man card being taken away so I half-heartedly followed basketball and football just enough to chit-chat with the guys at work.

Give me a video game or the pleasure of watching someone on Twitch tackle one, and I'd be in my element. Vampire the Masquerade or that latest iteration of Baldur's Gate. Those were more my jam.

"Hey there."

I slid my gaze to the right. A blond woman in a light pink sundress stood next to the seat by me. I grunted and went back to the game. Hopefully, she got the message that I wasn't interested. I kept my attention fixed on the lackluster baseball game.

She persisted, "Tough game, huh?"

I glanced briefly at her, trying to keep my response curt yet polite. "Something like that."

She smiled, seemingly oblivious or undeterred by my lack of enthusiasm. "Mind if I join you? It's always better to suffer through a boring game with company, don't you think?"

I hesitated, not eager to engage in conversation, but I gestured to the empty seat. "Suit yourself."

Whether I liked it or not, my evening at the bar was about to take an unexpected turn. She settled into the seat beside me, bringing a surprising warmth to the otherwise cold atmosphere. I continued watching the game, stealing occasional glances at her. It became apparent that she was genuinely trying to strike up a conversation.

"So, are you a baseball fan?" she inquired, trying to find common ground.

I chuckled dryly. "Not really."

She nodded, "Yeah, me either."

Despite my resistance, her easy-going nature started to wear down my defenses. We began chatting about everything from favorite movies to guilty pleasures. The more we talked, the more I realized I craved the company.

An hour into our conversation, she leaned in, her hand on my thigh, and her offer hanging in the air. "You know, we could go back to my place. It might be a better way to spend the evening than drowning in this baseball-induced coma."

I found myself shrugging in agreement. "Sure, why not?"

Maybe an emotionless fuck was exactly what I needed to forget today. She lived a block down above a taco restaurant. We made our way to her apartment, the quiet tension overshadowed by the anticipation of something different. Once inside, she gently pulled me onto the couch, initiating a passionate kiss. It seemed like an easy escape. I just wanted to forget the memories, and the alcohol I'd nursed for over an hour sure didn't seem to make a dent in them.

Yet, as she unbuttoned my shirt, a wave of regret crashed over me. I didn't want this. This wasn't what I needed—not with a stranger. Just as I gently pulled her away, ready to tell her I couldn't do this, Darci and those whiskey eyes popped into my head. It was a little odd, but the thought lingered. Before I could say anything, my phone buzzed, breaking the moment entirely.

It was an urgent message from the hospital. There had been a massive 30-car pileup on the freeway, and with the surge of injured patients, they needed all hands on deck. I quickly apologized, explained the situation, and hurriedly left her apartment.

As I jogged back to my car, I realized that the unexpected call had been a timely intervention in stopping me from making a decision I knew I would have regretted. As I headed to the hospital, I couldn't help but wonder if fate had a way of steering us in the right direction, even when we least expected it. But why was Darci constantly in my thoughts?

The walk from the parking lot allowed me to compartmentalize my emotions. Sure, it'd been a shit day, but now I needed to focus on patients, giving them my best. I had always been good at saving lives. It's one of the reasons I went into emergency medicine. I was empathetic, but I had always been able to tuck my own emotions deep into my pocket while I was at work. I quickly slipped into clinician mode by the time I'd made it inside.

I clipped my badge to my shirt, and as soon as I rushed into the bay doors, a nurse handed me gloves and a mask and helped me put on a gown as we waited for the first ambulances to pull up. We were the only Trauma 1 facility in the area, and according to dispatch, we had eight critical cases coming in. As I heard the sirens coming closer, I took a deep breath and let it out. I grabbed a gurney with a resident and two nurses, and we headed outside, ready to go. I had a feeling it would be a hell of a night.

It was nearly one in the morning when I finally pulled into the parking lot of my apartment. I was in hospital-issued scrubs after my clothes ended up covered in bodily fluids. I threw them in a biohazard bag at the hospital, knowing I didn't want to take them home and try to get all that mess out.

I had saved two people tonight and was still reeling from the high. It felt good, really good. One was a 45-year-old father of four. His truck had been rear-ended, shoving him into the back of an 18-wheeler. He came in with blunt force hemothorax, causing cardiac tamponade, blood pooling in his lungs and around his heart. We worked on him for over an hour, getting his heart going again before handing him off to the cardiothoracic team.

On the way home, I stopped at the grocery store and grabbed a case of root beer and a gallon of vanilla ice cream. Root beer floats were my celebratory snack after a night like this one.

All the good parking spots near my building were taken, so I had to park next to the building across from mine. When I got out of the car, instinctively, I looked up at Darci's apartment. Her lights were still on.

Without thinking, I climbed the stairs to the second floor and knocked on her door. After a few minutes, I realized how crazy it was to knock on someone's door this late and started to walk away when she cracked open the door.

"Alex?"

I smiled, feeling a bit foolish. "Hey, sorry. I didn't realize how late it was." I held up the root beer and ice cream. "I was going to see if you wanted a root beer float."

Darci's eyebrows shot up in surprise, and she looked at the offering in my hands. "You wanted to make *me* a root beer float? At this hour?"

I chuckled nervously, rubbing the back of my neck. "Yeah, I know, it's a bit random. But I had a sudden craving on the way home from the hospital, and there's plenty. Thought I'd offer to share my late-night indulgence. What do you say?"

She studied me for a moment before breaking into a grin and nodding.

"Well, who can resist a root beer float, even in the middle of the night? Sure, why not?"

Relieved, I asked, "Here? Or do you want to come over to mine?"

She opened the door wider, "You can come in."

I smiled again and handed her the ice cream as I walked through the door carrying the case of root beer.

As I followed her to the kitchen, I felt a strange anticipation. It surprised me because I hadn't been genuinely interested in getting to know a woman in a long time, not since I lost Jenna. I didn't know what to think about that. It made me... nervous.

I tried to shake off these new feelings, reminding myself this was just a friendly late-night offer of root beer floats. Yet, deep down, I couldn't help but wonder what it meant. Could I finally let myself live my life again instead of staying stuck in the past?

She set the ice cream down on the counter and pulled a giant scoop from a drawer. I put the drinks on the table, and she motioned me to grab some glasses from a cabinet.

"So… you were at the hospital?"

I opened the box and pulled out two cans of root beer, setting them down next to the ice cream as she dished it.

"Yeah, there was a big wreck on the freeway tonight."

She looked over at me with surprise and concern. "Really? I noticed a lot of sirens tonight."

I nodded. "Yeah, it was a big one, multi-car pileup."

She covered her mouth. "Oh my god, that's awful."

"We're a trauma one facility, so we take the worst cases. They called everyone in to help."

"Wow. How bad was it?" She cocked an eyebrow and winced.

I nodded, sinking deeper into the couch. "Had to do CPR on two patients tonight. Didn't lose either of them."

She let out a soft, slightly impressed sigh. "Okay, hero. That's good to hear."

We were curled into opposite ends of her couch, root beer floats in hand, knees angled toward each other like we were accidentally building a fort. The TV played some mindless crime show in the background, but Darci had my full attention.

"Yeah, kind of why I brought this over," I said, tipping my glass toward her. "Dumb tradition. After a bad night, I make a float. Helps me reset."

She gave a slow nod. "When I have a bad day, I make a cocktail, watch murder shows, and talk back to the screen like I'm qualified to solve things."

I smirked. "You work at the library, right?"

"I do. Children's librarian. Obviously qualified to crack cold cases and judge bad alibis."

God, she was sharp. Her humor didn't soften—didn't shrink itself. It leaned in with elbows out, unapologetic. She wore a soft gray T-shirt and pajama pants covered in little stars, hair tousled in that long pixie cut that somehow made her look both soft and like she could verbally destroy someone in under ten seconds.

"And what exactly does a 'bad day' look like there?" I teased. "A toddler meltdown over The Very Hungry Caterpillar?"

She rolled her eyes dramatically. "They probably don't compare to your life and death drama," she said, deadpan, "but we do have our own battlefield, thank you."

I raised an eyebrow. "Oh, I'm sure."

"I'm serious."

"I don't doubt you," I said, grinning. "I just doubt the books fought back."

She glared over the rim of her glass like she was calculating exactly how hard she could throw it without staining her couch. "You want examples?"

I shrugged. "Entertain me."

She took a long, exaggerated breath, eyes sparkling. "A few days ago, two kindergarteners pushed every book off an entire shelf. Alphabetical order? Gone. Picture books everywhere. It was carnage."

I laughed—full, loud, real. And there it was. That flutter in my chest I didn't want to name.

Shit. I liked her. Like… actually liked her.

She was brilliant and snarky and more alive standing in her kitchen than most people were in a room full of spotlights. And watching her grin into her float like she hadn't just completely rearranged the chemistry in my bloodstream? It hit me right in the gut.

"I take it back," I said, shaking my head. "You've seen things."

"Thank you," she said with mock pride, as she poured the root beer over the ice cream.

"I'm just saying, next time I'm elbow-deep in someone's chest, I'll think of you—dodging picture books like a combat medic."

She snorted. "You're lucky this float's good."

I smiled, watching her stir one of the floats with a spoon. She had no idea what she was doing to me. And for the first time in a long time, I didn't want to be anywhere else.

"Oh my god," I said, halfway laughing. "So what did you do... about the kids?"

"I told them we have to treat the books like friends," she said, deadpan.

"Jesus. Where were their parents? Buying popcorn and enjoying the chaos?"

She rolled her eyes and stuck a straw into each float like she was trying not to stab the glass. "They were there. Just one row away. But children move fast. Like little demolition teams in sneakers."

She handed me my glass and gestured toward the couch. We tucked in at opposite ends, her legs folded underneath her, barefoot and casual like this was a Tuesday night routine instead of an impromptu float therapy session. She angled her body toward me, all warmth and sharp wit, and I couldn't look away if I tried.

"The moms apologized about a dozen times," she said, settling in. "They offered to have the girls help me re-shelve everything, but that would've just made it worse. I told them not to worry about it and sent them on their merry way."

"Girls?" I blinked. "Really? I was totally expecting it to be boys."

"Nope. Girls." She grinned over the rim of her glass. "In glitter boots and pink tutus. Looked like they were heading to ballet and decided to riot first."

I barked a laugh. "Classy."

"Oh, absolutely. I caught one of them trying to lick a book about germs."

"That's poetic. And deeply concerning."

She gave a solemn nod. "I've never sanitized something with that much personal rage before."

"Well, that sucks," I said.

She shrugged and started stirring her float, swirling the ice cream into the root beer like she had all the time in the world. Then she held it up and wiggled her eyebrows.

"Behold. Emotional alchemy."

I chuckled. "That your official librarian term for it?"

"No. That's what I call a blended float."

I shook my head as I took a bite of ice cream.

"It's pretty good. You should try it sometime."

I grinned. "Next time. We can both have a blended float."

She smiled. "Sure… next time. At your place."

I gave her a wink before staring into the glass as it fizzed.

She took a long drink. Neither of us said anything as we demolished our floats, like it was some unspoken competition. She finished first, of course—drained the last of it with a loud slurp, then froze, eyes wide like she'd just caught herself mid-crime. Her gaze flicked to mine, then away, and I saw the blush creep back into her cheeks.

I couldn't help but grin. It was cute. Stupidly cute.

She set her glass on the coffee table and muttered, "Sorry. I'm kind of used to eating and drinking like a goblin in solitude."

I raised an eyebrow. "No judgment here. Honestly, you looked like you were living your best life."

She snorted. "I was until I remembered I wasn't alone and probably looked like I was trying to inhale dairy through a straw."

"Worked for me," I said with a shrug. "Passion is attractive."

She gave me a look. "Okay, calm down, Shakespeare."

"I'm just saying," I said, leaning back into the couch, "if slurping root beer floats with enthusiasm is wrong, I don't want to be right."

Her mouth twitched, trying not to smile. "I can't tell if that's charming or tragic."

"Bit of both," I said. "But mostly charming."

Her mouth curved into a slow, knowing grin. "So you're into girls who inhale ice cream and talk about feral toddlers?"

I took another sip of my float. "Maybe I am."

She leaned back, resting her elbow on the arm of the couch and giving me that look—the one that said she was about to go in for the kill. "Good to know. I'll file that under deeply questionable taste in women."

I laughed. "Hey, it's not my fault you've set the bar so high."

She raised an eyebrow. "That was almost smooth."

"Almost?"

"You get points for delivery. But if you're trying to flirt, you're going to have to work a little harder."

I smirked, heart beating a little too fast.

Challenge accepted.

I let my eyes wander around her living room—soft lighting, mismatched throw pillows, a shaggy pink rug that looked like it had its own personality. The bookshelves were stacked with romance novels, some with dog-eared pages and cracked spines. Photos of her and a curly redhead—Claire, maybe—were tucked into colorful frames. A shadowbox on the wall held pressed flowers and tiny scraps of paper covered in careful handwriting.

And on the kitchen table? An explosion of bamboo skewers spread out on parchment paper next to a can of gold spray paint. A crime scene? A spell? Or maybe just a Pinterest fever dream?

I caught her watching me, eyes narrowed in amusement.

"What?" I asked, giving her a crooked smile.

She lifted an eyebrow. "Just waiting for the moment you finally ask about my murder project."

I laughed softly. "I was trying to guess if it was some kind of cult ritual or an avant-garde kabob."

She grinned, tucking her feet under her as she leaned back on the couch. "Please. If I were starting a cult, you'd know. I'd send out matching robes and snacks."

I smiled despite myself. Being around her was... easy. Too easy.

But then she tilted her head and said, more gently this time, "Alex... are you—?"

I tensed. *Here it comes.*

"Is everything okay?" she asked. "I saw you earlier on

your patio. You looked… upset."

I forced my face into something neutral. "I'm fine."

She gave me a look that said yeah, right. "You sure?"

"Yep," I said sharply. I shifted on the couch, hoping the sarcasm would chase her off the topic. "Were you watching me?"

That hit. She blinked, startled. "I—I wasn't spying or anything. I just looked out my window and saw you there. You looked… sad."

I turned away. "It's none of your business."

Her brows drew together. "I'm trying to be a friend, Alex. Your friend."

"I don't need friends," I snapped, heat rising in my chest. "I didn't ask for your concern."

She drew back like I'd slapped her. "Wow. Okay."

She stood, gathering her empty glass and reaching for mine with stiff fingers. Her jaw clenched, but I caught the flash of hurt before she shoved it down.

Why the hell did I say that?

This wasn't how tonight was supposed to go. I came here to make things right after the other night, not torch what little ground we'd gained. But I couldn't let her see me cracked open. I couldn't risk it.

"Darci, I…"

She didn't turn around. "It's late," she said coolly. "You should go."

I hesitated. I should've apologized. Said something. But instead, like the complete idiot I am, I doubled down.

"Fine," I muttered as I stood. "I don't need your pity anyway. Keep the ice cream and the drinks."

That did it. She turned fast, her eyes blazing. "Alex, I don't pity you," she said, voice low and cutting. Then she let out a sharp, humorless laugh. "I just think you're a fucking asshole."

And then she walked away—calm, collected, like I hadn't just sliced her open and confirmed every reason she probably had for not trusting people.

And me? I just stood there, like the goddamn coward I was, and let her go.

Watching her walk away, I couldn't believe I'd let myself get into this situation again. I clenched my jaw. I wasn't angry at her. I deserved her words, but my anger towards myself was almost unbearable as I left her apartment.

When I got home, I went directly to the bathroom, stripping off my scrubs. I turned the shower on and got in, attempting to let the water wash away the anger. The shame. The regret.

What the hell was wrong with me?

As the hot water cascaded over my body, I repeatedly replayed tonight, cringing at my defensiveness and dismissive attitude. I wanted to apologize, turn back time, and handle things differently. I had finally let my guard down, and then I just pushed her away.

I stepped out of the shower and dried off before slipping on a fresh pair of boxers, but the regret lingered. I laid down in bed, staring at the ceiling as I contemplated whether I should reach out to her to try to make amends again or just let it go.

We were neighbors. Could I really avoid her forever? I didn't want to. Something about her stirred something in me—something I hadn't felt in a long time.

Had I just fucked it all up with someone who could have finally brought some much-needed light into my dark world?

CHAPTER FIVE

Darci

"What a fucking asshole," I muttered just as I heard the door snick shut.

Why did he show up offering root beer floats just to turn into a jerk? Why did I even invite him in and entertain the notion? I should have known. God, sometimes I was just so stupid.

I shook my head as I walked through my apartment, turning off all the lights. As I leaned over the lamp next to the couch, I couldn't help but look out at his apartment across the way. His blinds were open, and the lights flicked on as he entered. I followed him with my eyes as he walked through his apartment to the bedroom, a faint light turning on. He went into the bathroom and shut the door. Damn, I was hoping for a little… skin.

I laughed as I flopped down on the couch. What was wrong with me? What was it about this guy that kept me so intrigued? It was ridiculous. I was not into him in the least. He was so not my type.

I pulled my phone out and opened the Lost Connections app, scanning the posts. Maybe some late-night reading could help, but nothing caught my eye tonight.

I sighed and headed to the bathroom. After brushing my teeth, I went to bed and slunk under my 1000-count Italian silk sheets. They were one of the few luxuries that I couldn't live without.

My mom always told me, "Good sheets, good towels, and good makeup." Now that she was older, the woman was crazier than a cat riding a skateboard in a tornado, but occasionally, she spouted some pretty decent advice. The hard part was determining which weird tidbit was worth paying attention to.

I settled into bed when a sharp object poked my side. *What the...?*

I reached down, feeling for it. It was a book. I yanked it out of the covers, holding it up in the light streaming in from the window. It was *Book Lovers* by Emily Henry.

I sat up, flicking on the bedside light. How in the world did that get into my bed? I didn't own a copy, so it wasn't mine. Maybe it was Claire's? But... she hadn't been here in a few weeks.

This was weird. Really weird.

I flipped through the book, seeing all the handwritten notes. "Ah... this had to be Claire's. I guess she left it here a while ago." It still seemed odd that it wound up in my bed tonight of all nights, but whatever.

I lay back down and started to read, but it felt like the book resisted me—like the pages had grown heavier, unwilling to turn. I couldn't explain it. So I set it beside me, and that's when it started flipping open on its own —page after page rustling like caught in a breeze that didn't exist. The ceiling fan wasn't even on. *How in the hell was this happening?*

My heart pounded as I scrambled out of bed, never taking my eyes off the book. I was scared to touch it again, but needed it off my bed. I looked around the room, keeping one eye on the book. I didn't trust that thing, like it might suction itself to my face like some alien movie.

Now, how was I going to get it off my bed? And more importantly, what would I do with it once I did?

I reached for a pillow, hesitating, before grabbing it. With a deep breath, I swung the pillow at the book, knocking it onto the floor. It landed with a soft thud, and I exhaled in relief, already halfway to crawling back into bed—until it snapped open, pages flipping in a sudden, furious blur.

I looked down at the book and noticed something strange. It was practically glowing, a faint, ethereal light emanating from the pages. Curiosity overcame my fear as I reached down and hesitantly picked it up. As I did, the pages settled down, and a wave of warmth ran up my arm. A small handwritten note in the upper corner jumps off the page.

Don't judge a book by its cover...

This book? Then my next thought was Alex. When he showed up at my door tonight, I thought we were becoming friends. He seemed a little nervous and shy when I answered, which was cute. I thought maybe I'd misjudged him, that perhaps this weird thing between us might go somewhere.

But then I asked one wrong question, and he flew off

the handle. Maybe I'd pried too much, and he was just... scared.

I bobbled my head. "This does seem rather... fitting," I murmured as I set the book on my nightstand.

But it was late, and maybe this little "message" was pure coincidence. I was probably just reading too much into it. But laying back down, my mind wandered back to Claire and how she and Edison just found each other again, and it was all because of her strange, magical books.

I huffed out a breath. Maybe I needed to heed this little message. Something told me there was more to Alex than met the eye.

A few days later, I had the day off. I was lying around, reading for most of the day, when the phone rang.

"Guess what, bestie? We're home!"

"Finally. I was starting to consider recruiting the UPS guy for Murder Night."

"Hold up—did you watch ahead without me?"

"What? No! I would never betray the sacred oath of Murder Night."

"Good. Because Crimebrarians stick together. These past two weeks, I've had to resort to true crime TikToks with no context."

We both laughed.

"I've missed you, Darce. I can't wait to get back to work, back to our lunches, and see everybody else."

"Me, too, girlfriend."

"How about we do a Murder Night sometime next week, maybe Thursday next week? It'll be perfect. Come over, we'll stuff ourselves, and you can help me make wedding plans."

"Only if I can bring the cocktails."

"Isn't that what you always do? One of these days, I'll make you bring something healthy like a veggie platter." She teased.

"In your dreams, babe. But I'll see you tomorrow at work. I have so much to tell you."

"Oh really?"

"Yep."

"Does it have anything to do with a certain doctor?"

"How do you even know that?"

Claire laughed, "I have my ways."

"Hmm, I bet."

"I'll never tell." She said. "Anyway, I'm so glad to be home in my own house with my own bed. There's nothing like trying to be intimate with your fiancé when your parents are in the next room."

I cackled, "When I still lived at home with my dad, I was already working at the library, but my dad had a sixth sense for knowing when I had sneaked a man into my room."

She chuckled, "Sounds like a nightmare."

"You think?"

She let out a tired sigh, "I love you, but I'm going to shower, wash the travel grime off me, and then sleep like the dead until work tomorrow."

"See you tomorrow."

When we hung up, I sank further into the couch, finding my place in the book I was reading. I couldn't wait to see my best friend. Two weeks had felt like an eternity. But I wondered... how she knew anything about Alex and me.

On Friday, I arrived at work early. Every week, we had a storytime class for toddlers and preschoolers on

Mondays and Fridays. On Fridays, we offered the class early in the morning, and I had just minutes to prepare before they showed up. I went to the storage room and selected puppets, a few large story books, an overhead projector for the songs, and a basket of silks. I had to make sure we had enough silks for every child to hold one while dancing, or chaos would ensue and tears would fall.

While putting the supplies in the program room, I heard Claire calling my name. Walking out, I nearly ran right into her.

"Oh my god. You scared me."

She was practically glowing as she dropped her giant tote bag and grabbed me into a big hug.

I pulled back to get a good look at her. "Look at you! You're so tan!"

Claire was usually porcelain-skinned, but her freckles were darker, and she had a healthy tan on her face, arms, and chest.

She giggled. "I know. I just love it." She let out a sigh. "If I could live there..."

I gave her a playful pout. "You'd leave me?"

"Well, no, but I feel this strange pull to the ocean. Every time I visit my parents, I feel like I can't wait to return." She rolled her eyes. "But then I remember my mother lives there, and we can't live within 100 miles of each other."

We both laughed.

"Walk with me to the teen room so I can set my stuff down. I need to hear about Dr. Alex."

I heaved out a sigh. "There's not much to tell. He's kind of an asshole."

"That's not what I hear."

"Who is telling you this stuff?"

She mimed zipping her lips and throwing away the key.

I gave her a pointed look.

She grinned. "Oh, it's just my old next-door neighbor, Patsy."

"Patsy? The gambling addict? With the little dog?"

Claire laughed and waved her hand. "She's not a gambling addict. She's just... obsessed with bingo at the Catholic church and maybe watching everyone in the apartment complex."

"Sure..."

After setting her stuff down at her desk, Claire checked her watch. "We don't have a lot of time. Storytime is fast approaching. What happened with Dr. Alex?"

I raised my eyebrows. "Well, he knocked on my door at nearly one o'clock in the morning the other night."

She tilted her head, a smirk playing on her lips. "Did he now?"

I shook my head. "It's not like that."

She raised an eyebrow. "Sure, Darce."

"I'm serious. He knocked on the door and asked if I wanted a root beer float. He had a tub of ice cream and a 12-pack of root beer. I stupidly invited him in, and we talked as we drank our floats," I sighed, "until I asked the wrong question. Then, he got all pissy and left."

"I see."

"Earlier in the day, I saw him on his patio, and he looked like he was crying. So when he was at my apartment, I asked if he was okay."

"Oh."

I shook my head. "He immediately shut me down."

She nodded slowly and then lowered her voice, "I heard he lost his wife and child a few years ago."

I gasped, "What? How?"

She shook her head, shrugging. "I don't know. That's just what I heard."

"From who?"

"Patsy."

"How does Patsy know everything?"

"I honestly have no idea, but she seems to know everything about everybody in that apartment complex."

I looked away and murmured, "I wonder what she knows about me."

Claire chuckled, "Well, she knows about footie pajama guy."

I snapped my head toward Claire. "Uh… did you tell her that story? How else does she know about him?"

Claire put her hands up in surrender. "It wasn't me."

I looked at my watch, "I've got to go get ready for storytime. Talk more at lunch?"

She nodded. "Yeah. See you then."

At lunch, I found Claire in the break room. I pulled my salad from the fridge while she heated a glass container.

"That smells delicious. What'd you bring?" I asked.

"Chicken enchiladas." She inclined her head. "From my mom. When she hands you leftovers, you can't say no or else."

"Or else what?"

"She gives you a guilt trip you won't forget. It's easier just to take them home."

"Yeah. My mom creates a box of stuff she keeps at the front door to send home with me whenever I visit. And it's the weirdest stuff. Why do I need 12 packets of taco seasoning or a case of washi tape?"

A bubble of laughter escaped Claire as she sat at the little table. Why they had a table that only fit four when there was a staff of 20 was always a mystery to me.

She gave me a conspiratorial smile. "So I was thinking… about taking a weekend trip to Vegas to scope out everything for the wedding. Want to go?"

I grinned. "Are you kidding? Like a Girls' trip?"

She nodded as her smile widened.

I shifted uneasily, my fingers fidgeting with the edge of my sleeve. "Um, is Edison going with you?" I sat up straighter, "It's not that I don't want him… to come on the trip," I began, hesitating. "But I also don't want to be…" I let out a sigh, "a third wheel."

Claire was quiet for a moment, then let out a soft laugh. "You don't have to worry about that. He wants to stay home—he's sick of traveling after we visited my parents for two weeks." She shook her head, amusement flickering in her eyes. "What was I thinking, staying there for two weeks?"

I let out a breath I hadn't realized I was holding, giving her a small smile. "Yeah, that sounds exhausting."

Claire groaned dramatically. "You have no idea."

And just like that, the tension eased between us.

My smile widened as I stood up. It was nearly story time.

"Well then, as the maid of honor, I think I have to be by your side. When were you thinking?"

"I thought we could do a long weekend around the 15th of next month. Sound good?"

I nodded, pulling my phone out of my dress pocket and adding the date. "Yeah, I can do that."

Claire stood up and wrapped her hand around my shoulder. "Just you and me, babe. We can order room service and drink champagne in our pajamas."

I laughed, "Sounds perfect. But maybe we could... check out the clubs for your bachelorette party?" I wiggled my eyebrows at her.

She grinned. "Of course. But I have a list of things we need to do. We have to find a bakery for the cake, a florist for the flowers, and visit all the weird wedding venues."

"Still thinking about that Elvis wedding?" I giggled.

She laughed. "I don't want to rule anything out just yet."

As we finished lunch, Claire pulled out her phone and made a few notes in her calendar. She also mentioned we had an appointment in two weeks to visit the local bridal shop for dress fittings. Seeing how busy she was with wedding plans, I offered to check flights and hotels for our girls' trip when I got home.

After swinging by a drive-thru and picking up tacos, I set them on the coffee table and turned on my laptop before running off to change into leggings and an old boyfriend's sweatshirt I had stolen years ago. I climbed onto the couch cross-legged and set the computer on my lap.

As it finished loading, I grabbed a taco and moaned at the delicious flavors mingling in my mouth. I opened the blinds to let some more light in, but Alex was again on his patio when I looked out the window across the way. He was leaning against the railing with a beer in his hand. He caught my eye, raising his bottle in a toast. After our last exchange, it took me by surprise, but I raised my taco, like an idiot, back at him, giving him a cheesy smile. His lips quirked up as he gave a little nod in acknowledgment.

He was such a conundrum. One minute, he was a seemingly ordinary nice guy, and we could be friends, but at the drop of a hat, something might set him off out of nowhere. I couldn't figure him out, and to make matters worse, for some stupid reason, my body liked him, gravitated toward him. He had this energy I seemed to recognize subconsciously, but my head told me to be... wary. And I planned to listen to my head regarding Dr. Alex Dixon.

CHAPTER SIX

Alex

Saturday afternoon was unseasonably hot, and I was sweltering. Even with the air conditioning turned down to 68, I was still sweating. Gazing out the window, I thought about how refreshing a dip in the pool would feel. There were just a few people out there, but only one was in the pool. The others were lying on the pool chairs.

I quickly put on my swim trunks and slathered myself in sunscreen before grabbing a towel, slid on my flip-flops and sunglasses, and headed out the door. This was my first summer here, and I hadn't had a chance to try out the pool until now. When I walked through the gate, I was shocked at its size. It was huge, like Olympic size, with lanes for swimming laps and a hot tub off to the side. Nice.

I walked over to an empty chair and noticed the fluffy white towel on the chair next to it. I laid my towel down, slipped my flip-flops underneath the chair, and found the stairs to the pool. The cool water embraced me, a welcome relief from the scorching sun.

A dark-haired figure was swimming this way, probably headed to the stairs to climb out. As soon as I made it waist-deep, they popped up. Darci was in a midnight blue bikini that left little to the imagination. She reached up, slicking her hair backward, and I couldn't take my eyes off her curves. As I swept my eyes down, I noticed her pebbled nipples straining against the fabric of her top. Instinctively, the tip of my tongue darted out of my mouth, licking my lips. Her eyes went wide when she recognized me.

"Alex?"

"Hey, Darci. I guess I'm not the only one who needed to cool off in this heat." I smirked.

"Uh… yeah."

She looked around the pool, not really hearing me, but then she came closer, almost nose to nose. This was… different. My dick twitched.

She let out a long sigh and lowered her voice. "Um, listen, can you help me with something?"

I wrinkled my brow. "I'll try. What is it?"

She inclined her head to the left. "Um, do you see that guy back there? The one in that chair up in the grass?"

I started to turn my head. She reached out, grabbing my forearm, hissing, "No! Don't look!"

My skin broke out in goosebumps where she touched me. "Okay. But… how am I supposed to see him if I can't look?"

She leaned even closer, her hand still on my arm. Her breath was warm against my cheek. I had this sudden desire to… kiss her.

"Just be nonchalant about it."

I whispered back, "Okay…"

"Do you see him?"

I tried to look as casually as possible as I slunk down in the water and quickly turned in a circle before standing back up. I could see a young guy, maybe a teenager, with a bright blue beach towel draped over his legs.

"Yeah, I see him."

She stood up on her tiptoes, whispering against my ear, "He's jerking off."

I pulled back, startled, "What?"

She looked around again. "Yeah, he's…" She moved even closer, our bodies nearly touching as she made an obscene gesture with her hand against her belly, then raised her hands in a shrug.

"You're sure? How… how do you know?"

She gave me a pointed look. "Oh, I'm definitely sure. He's been doing it awhile."

"Okay," I grimaced. "How did you want *my* help?"

"Go to tell him to stop."

I took a step back. "What? Why me?"

"Because you're the only other guy here."

My eyes darted around the pool. Huh, I was the only other guy at the pool. *Fuck my life.*

I shook my head. "I don't think I want to do that."

The last thing I wanted to do was confront some guy masturbating in public, even if he was a teenager.

"Please? What if a kid walks in here and sees that?" She gestured in his direction.

I hesitated, thinking it over. This might just get me back in her good graces. "Fine."

She smiled. "You will?"

I let out a heavy sigh as I rolled my eyes. "Yeah, I'll do it."

"I really appreciate it," she said with a saccharin-sweet smile as she leaned back and began to float, keeping her eyes on me.

I watched her flip over and start swimming again before I slowly walked over to the ladder on the other side of the pool and climbed out. What the fuck was I going to say to this guy? *Hey man, could you put your dick up?*

I was dreading this. As I approached him, I decided to say as little as possible. That was probably the best move. I walked up into the grass and couldn't help but glance in his direction. The towel was moving in a jerky motion. *Seriously, what the fuck?*

I stood in front of him, trying my best authoritative doctor voice. "Hey, man. You need to stop."

He looked up at me, his hands clearly under the towel. "Stop what?"

Really? I cocked an eyebrow and narrowed my eyes.

"Just. Stop."

He let out a sigh. "Whatever, man."

"I mean it. Just. Stop. Now."

He huffed out a breath and mumbled, "Fine. Sorry."

Now that we both had been humiliated, I turned back towards the pool. As soon as I got to the edge, I jumped in, swimming underneath for as long as I could hold my breath, nearly to the other side.

When I came up, the water was too deep to touch, so I treaded water before swimming to the side to hold on to the edge. Darci swam up next to me, and I had the urge to reach out and touch her, wrapping my hand around her waist. But I just white-knuckled the side.

"Well?"

I shrugged, "I told him to stop."

She looked over her shoulder. "He's leaving."

I sighed, turning my head as we watched him wrap the towel around his waist and walk towards the gate. "Thank god."

She laughed. "You have no idea. He'd been doing that for at least 30 minutes before you arrived."

My eyebrows shot up. "30 minutes? Jesus." I leaned my head back.

She touched my forearm and genuinely smiled, "Really. Thanks for doing that."

I found myself smiling back, swimming towards her. I wanted to take her in my arms. But before I knew what happened, she quickly darted under the water and swam off to the far edge like some little water nymph.

I kept treading water, watching her, the corner of my mouth hitching up. She dunked her head under the water, using one hand to push her hair back as she slid on a pair of goggles lying on the edge of the pool. She pushed off and swam freestyle laps in the middle lane. I let myself fall completely under the water, cooling off from the sun's sting.

When I came up for air, I swam over to the side, climbed out, and went to the hot tub. I sank down, and the combination of the heat and bubbles from the jets was almost intoxicating. I could feel sweat forming on my neck, but this was like a soothing massage. Settling into one of the seats, I closed my eyes and leaned my head back, savoring the sensations along my body.

A moment later, I felt the water shift as someone else stepped into the hot tub. I looked up, the sun's glare forcing me to squint.

Darci smirked at me. "Enjoying yourself?"

I smiled and nodded. "Yeah, this is nice."

She settled in the seat across from me. Through the bubbles, I could see her legs floating up towards the surface. Her toenails were painted bubblegum pink.

Realizing how close they were to me, she squeaked out, "Sorry," and pulled her legs down, but it forced our legs to brush underwater. I was surprised at the subtle jolt I felt through the warm currents. I liked it.

Darci must have read it on my face because she smirked again, her eyes sparkling mischievously.

"So, any *hot* plans for the rest of the day?"

As our toes occasionally brushed together, I chuckled, playing along. "Well, this *hot* tub is pretty much the highlight so far. But who knows, maybe something else will come up?"

What in the hell was I even talking about?

Shock flashed across her face before it melted back into that smirk as she shifted closer. I wasn't sure if the flush rising to her cheeks was from the heat or something else entirely.

But then, she said, "Oh? Do you need help finding that something else…?" Her voice trailed off.

The hot tub became a catalyst between us. Relaxing together in the warm water, our conversation flowed easily. Her laugh was infectious, and I was saying anything ridiculous just to hear it again and again. I couldn't stop staring at her, drawn as if by some invisible force. I caught the flicker of desire hidden in her eyes. It was subtle but impossible to ignore.

Before I knew it, the conversation had taken a definite flirtatious turn. The afternoon sun bathed us in its warmth, and for the first time in a long time, I wanted this unexpected encounter to be something… more.

She asked, "So, any secret talents I should know

about?"

"Well, I can juggle three marshmallows without dropping one."

Her laughter bubbled up, and she raised an eyebrow. "Mini or full size?"

I nodded. "Both."

"Impressive. But can you do it blindfolded?"

I tilted my head as if considering it, my eyes crinkling as I grinned. "I've never attempted it, but I could try."

She leaned back, resting her head, and I traced the slope of her neck with my eyes, wondering what it would taste like.

She murmured, "I'd like to see that."

As the sun dipped lower, casting a sultry glow over the poolside, I mustered up the courage to take our conversation up a notch. I hadn't really done this in quite awhile, but there was just something about her. I needed… more. I settled next to her, our thighs almost touching.

"This hot tub is amazing, but how about we continue this conversation somewhere a little more private?" I threw in a playful smile, hoping she'd catch the hint.

She cast me a sidelong glance, that desire in her eyes now unmistakable. "And what kind of conversation were you thinking?"

I scooted even closer, the scent of sunbaked skin and sunscreen stirring something in me. I lowered my voice to a conspiratorial whisper against her ear as I placed my hand across her belly. "Something that involves fewer bubbles and even less… clothing."

I nipped at her earlobe. Her giggle echoed in the warm air.

"You're not wasting any time, are you?"

I shrugged, offering a sheepish smile. "Life's too short to beat around the bush, isn't it? Though I wouldn't mind if that's what you needed."

It was ridiculous how strongly I felt this attraction to her. I wanted to be all over her. I was tired of fighting it. I needed her out of my system.

Darci's smile widened, and she playfully nudged me as she stood up.

She held her thumb and index finger together and said, "Hmm, well, you could beat around the bush… a little bit." She reached her hand towards me and said, "Lead the way, Alex."

The warmth of the afternoon seemed to intensify as we left the pool. I reached for her hand. We grabbed our things, and our fingers intertwined as I led her across the parking lot and up the stairs, ready for whatever the afternoon had in store. Unlocking the door, I felt nervous and turned towards her.

"I know we haven't exactly gotten off on the right foot, so if you've changed your mind…" I trailed off.

She touched my cheek, letting her hand brush my scruff as she walked past me into the living room. "I haven't changed my mind."

I felt the heat rising in my cheeks and anticipation swirling in my belly. We were really doing this. I shut the door as she surveyed my apartment. I'd been here for months and had barely moved in. Boxes were still sitting on the shelves, waiting to be unpacked. Nothing was on the walls. Considering it through her eyes, I felt slightly embarrassed at how plain it was.

She nodded before turning to face me, giggling. "I like what you've done with the place."

She dropped the plush white towel she'd had

wrapped around her. It puddled around her feet. My cock twitched as I walked toward her, grabbing her hips and pulling her against me. That strange jolt again.

I couldn't help but smirk and roll my eyes. "Yeah, I was going for... minimalist."

She laughed, quick and full of energy, as her hands came up against my chest.

She leaned close and whispered, "I think you nailed it."

I couldn't look away from her beautiful eyes. This close, I could see flecks of gold in them.

"Good," I murmured.

I wasn't sure which one of us made the move first. Our lips touched, and a shock of desire coursed through me. She bit my lower lip, and I groaned, taking her mouth like I owned it. She tasted so... good, like cinnamon and peaches. I wanted more.

Her nails dug into my shoulders as her lips widened, and I ran my hands down to her ass, grabbing handfuls and hauling her against me, pulling her up against my hardening length. She wrapped her legs around my waist as I carried her to the bedroom. I leaned over, tossing her gently on the bed, and stalked towards her.

"We're going to get this bed soaking wet."

I grinned. "I plan on it."

She chuckled, "No, I meant... our swimsuits."

I laughed, standing up and shucking mine off to the floor.

"Better?"

Her eyes traveled down my body like a caress, pausing when she saw the evidence of just how much I wanted her. Her breath hitched, and that little flicker of a smile told me—she loved what she saw.

She licked her lips and said, "Definitely."

She untied her straps with quick, confident fingers, stripping off her top and tossing it to the floor without a second thought. I drank her in—every inch of flushed, bare skin, every curve I'd been aching to touch. My tongue swept across my lips, already imagining the taste of her, the heat of her against my mouth.

She saw how I looked at her—starved—and grinned like she was ready to be devoured. Then she hooked her thumbs in the ties at her hips and gave a slow, deliberate tug. Her bottoms loosened, sliding down her thighs, and she let them drop with a soft whisper of fabric.

She didn't flinch. Didn't cover herself.

She lay there like a gift she knew I wouldn't dare refuse.

I couldn't stop my eyes from roaming. She was small, tight, and utterly mouthwatering—like some wicked little pixie conjured just to tempt me. The thought of getting my hands and mouth on every inch of her made my balls tighten with need.

I moved towards her again, climbing across the bed and caging her in. She widened her legs as I settled between them. I wanted her... badly. I couldn't remember the last time I had craved a woman like I did now, not since my wife. I stiffened as a sudden twinge of guilt raced through my blood. I swallowed and tried to push it down.

"We don't have to do this if you don't want to. Just say the word, Tink."

She wrinkled her nose, "Tink?"

I breathed out a little laugh. "You just remind me a little bit like... Tinkerbell." I could feel my cheeks flushing.

She giggled.

"You're sure about this?"

"Oh, I want to."

I smirked, "You do?"

Her hand reached for my cock, stroking me as she murmured, "You have no idea."

That was enough talking for me. I leaned down, licking and nipping at her neck as she continued stroking me. With her other hand, she tugged my sack, gently pulling down as she stroked. God, if she kept doing that, I was never going to last.

I slowly kissed my way down her body, forcing her to let go of me. Her hands went to my shoulders as I flicked my tongue over one tan nipple, pinching and rolling the other as I sucked the first one into my mouth. I could do this for hours. Her breasts were the perfect handful.

I moved to the other nipple, licking and nipping and sucking as I played with the first one. Her chest flushed, and she made these little mewling sounds. Her hands came up to hold my head. My hand migrated down, finding the heat of her core as I cupped her. I slipped a finger into her folds. She was so wet, practically on fire as I circled her clit with my thumb as I continued to suck her nipple.

I licked down under her breast toward her belly button, and she readily opened her legs wider, guiding my head down to exactly what she wanted. But I needed to tease. I wanted to hear her beg for me.

I kissed down her pelvic bone, stopping just above those dark curls. I moved to her inner thigh, licking and kissing and nipping right up to her pussy before blowing across it as I moved to the other thigh. I chuckled softly at the frustrated moan she let out as she tried to guide my head right back.

I sat up on my forearms. "What do you want?"

She looked down at me, lust in her eyes. "You know what I want."

I smirked, "Tell me."

She tried pushing my head back between her legs, but I resisted.

"No. Say it."

She let out an exasperated sigh, "My pussy."

I smirked, "Your pussy, what?"

"Oh my god, Alex. Eat my fucking pussy."

"What's the magic word?"

"Dammit, Alex. Please! Please eat my pussy. Please."

"Good girl."

I held her open, taking a long lick from her entrance all the way up to her clit. She tasted like honey. I couldn't get enough. I pressed my tongue inside her, tongue fucking her before tracing slow circles around her entrance as I stroked her clit with my thumb.

"Oh fuck..." She let out a loud gasp, grabbing my hair and writhing under me.

I hadn't had this much fun in bed with a woman in a long, long time. I thought this was going to be a one-night kind of thing. Get her out of my system, but I suddenly had this awareness. I knew. I was going to need her again. She could turn into an addiction.

She let go of my hair and pressed my face into her core. Breathing could come later. I needed to get my fill of her. I sucked and nipped at her clit, flicking it over and over. I slid a finger into her, pumping in and out, slowly at first and increasing my speed. Over and over,

I finger fucked her as I sucked her clit. She squirmed and writhed, her breath coming faster and faster.

"Oh god, Alex… Alex, fuck. So good. I'm going to…"

She couldn't finish the thought, instead flexing her hips upward. Goosebumps rose along her thighs as her chest turned red. She screamed my name, and I dove back in and sucked her clit, pumping through her release. I licked and sucked along her lower lips as she slowly came down from her euphoria.

When her breath had calmed, she smiled at me and said, "I think… I just had… a religious experience."

I huffed out a laugh as I crawled up her body, stopping to pull and suck each nipple before finding my way to her lips and kissing her deeply, letting her taste herself on me.

My cock pressed against her thigh, and she murmured, "Condom?" into my mouth.

I pulled back. "Yeah…"

I leaned over to the nightstand, opened the drawer, grabbed a foil wrapper, and ripped it open with my teeth while staring into those whiskey eyes. She grabbed it from me, rolling it down my cock. I nuzzled and licked up her neck before nudging her entrance.

She kissed my chin and then bit my neck hard. "Take me," she whispered against my throat, "Hard."

I whispered in her ear, "You sure, Tink?"

There was a desperation in her voice, "Please. Don't hold back. Fuck me. I need you. Inside me. Right. Now."

She didn't have to tell me twice. I pushed in slowly, and in one deep thrust, I filled her to the hilt. She gasped as I groaned. She felt good. Too good. Perfect. I began to move, thrusting in and out. How long could I last?

"Harder."

She flexed her hips against me, begging for more, and I was going to give it to her. I wrapped one arm around her waist, my other reached up to the headboard for leverage, and I slowly pulled out to the tip and then slammed in deep. Again and again. Her hands found my ass, pulling me into her.

"Yes, yes, yes. Just like that. Fuck, Alex. Oh god. I need to come so bad."

She clenched around me as I continued to pump harder and faster into her. I reached down, pressing firm against her clit with my thumb. Three more pumps, and she was screaming my name again as she clenched so tight I thought my dick might break in half. But it felt so damn good. I lasted a few more strokes before I couldn't hold on any longer. I let go, cursing in satisfaction as I released. I kept pumping in and out, feeling a second release just seconds later, my hips jerking uncontrollably.

That... had never happened before. It was exhilarating.

I rolled off her, both of us catching our breath. I felt her gaze on me, and I turned towards her, our eyes locking. We both raised our eyebrows, no words exchanged, but she had to have been thinking the same thing I was—that was fucking amazing.

It shocked me when I realized I wanted her to stay. Since Jenna, my encounters had been limited to one-night stands, few and far between. There had never been a relationship, nothing lasting more than a night. I was always okay with them leaving. Usually, I hinted at it so I could be alone and drown in my guilt and despair. A few times, I practically bum-rushed them out. Yet, I didn't feel any of that, and I didn't want Darci to leave.

For some inexplicable reason, I didn't want to be alone, and I really didn't want this beautiful, dark-haired pixie to go. I wanted to hold her in my arms. I wanted to tangle our legs together as we fell asleep.

What was happening here? Most of the time, I never even bothered to learn their names. I was that asshole, yet, I'd already given her a pet name. She was a wild card, a force I hadn't anticipated. The moment I met her, I knew she'd bring chaos to everything she did, but it was... refreshing, like she could shake things up.

She could shake *me* up, and that was just what I needed. I needed her.

Whatever I was doing alone wasn't working. My life had been stuck on pause for three years. I was tired of it, tired of feeling miserable, tired of being alone. I wanted to move on and be happy again. Deep down, I knew if I allowed it, this woman would push me outside my comfort zone in the best way possible.

Taking a deep breath, our eyes met, and I uttered a word that surprised even me, "Stay."

CHAPTER SEVEN

Darci

Uh, come again? Did he just ask me to stay?

I could have sworn I saw a flicker of vulnerability flash across his face, but it vanished instantly. His eyes softened as he lay facing me, watching me closely. Did he want to cuddle?

I hesitated, searching his face for a sign, momentarily forgetting all the animosity between us. I thought about how it would feel to let him hold me in his arms. I wanted it. I craved it. But... this was a bad idea.

I ignored him. I had to get out of here. *What had we done?* As quickly as possible, I sat up, leaning off the bed to reach my swimsuit top.

I tried to act casual. "Well, that was... something." I grinned as I looked over at him. He furrowed his brow in confusion. I let out a sigh. "I mean, that was amazing. You have a real gift, kind sir."

He raised an eyebrow, "Kind sir?"

I didn't reply as I slid my top over my breasts, tying the straps behind me.

"Really. You can stay. I won't bite, Tink." He swallowed audibly.

I smiled briefly before wincing as I stood up, pulling my wet bikini bottoms on, wiggling them back into place.

"I think it's best if I go. And…" I trailed off before snapping, "Don't call me that."

He stood up and slipped on a pair of boxers, following me into the living room as I looked for the towel I had dropped earlier. He got to it first, picking it up and handing it to me. I wrapped it around me as I walked towards the door. We both stood there just staring at each other.

"Don't go," he pleaded. "You don't… You don't have to go. I don't want you to leave like this."

Jesus, was this guy clingy or what?

I shrugged, "It was just sex, Alex. I think I should go." I nodded like I was telling myself as much as him—*just go, don't stay.*

He smirked, "I see how it is. You just wanted my body, and now you're done with me."

I rolled my eyes, shrugging. "Yep, that's what I'm all about. Love 'em and leave 'em. That's me."

He laughed, and my lips twitched.

I turned around as I walked out, giving him a coy smile I knew he couldn't decipher. "See you around, Sunshine."

He followed me out the door. I never turned around, but I could feel his eyes on me the entire walk back to my apartment.

As soon as I shut the door, I slumped against it, exhaling a long, unsteady breath. *What the fuck was that?* I had no idea how I let that happen—how any of that happened—but I sure as hell hadn't been expecting it. And yet, my body was already buzzing, my mind spinning with one reckless thought—*how could we do it again?*

I went to the bathroom and took a long, hot shower, scrubbing myself with copious amounts of body wash. As soon as I was dressed, I picked up my phone and immediately called Claire. She answered after a gazillion rings.

She sounded slightly out of breath. "Hey, what's up?"

"Oh my god, Claire. You are not going to believe what just happened."

"What? Are you okay? What's wrong?"

"Nothing's wrong, but can you come over? Can we move Murder Night up to tonight?"

"Yeah. Hang on a sec." I heard some muffled murmuring between Claire and Edison, but I couldn't quite make it out. "Okay, give me 20 minutes, and I'll be there."

"Wait, wait, wait. Were you and Edison... uh, busy?"

She laughed nervously. "No, it's fine. Don't worry about it. I'll be over soon. I just need to... get dressed."

"Oh my god, you were. You two were totally doing it, and I interrupted. Why did you answer the phone? You don't have to come. Stay home. Finish what you started."

"Darci, it's fine. We, um, finished before I answered. Okay? Now I'm hanging up, and I'll be there in 20 minutes."

"Okay."

Eighteen minutes later, Claire knocked. When I opened the door, she had a chocolate cake in one hand and a bag with three bottles of red wine.

I ushered her in. "I'm sorry I interrupted your fun time. I'm having a bit of a… crisis."

She handed me the bag of wine, shaking her head, her cheeks pink. "Darci… It's fine."

I took it and said, "Babe, you always know just what I need."

She followed me back to the kitchen. I set the bag on the table and grabbed what we needed. Claire popped open the plastic container holding the chocolate cake, making a noise that would wake the dead. I sat across from her and got to work on a bottle of wine, pouring us each a glass as Claire dug into the cake.

Her eyebrows were nearly in her hair as she asked, "What happened?"

I grabbed the other fork, spearing a giant bite of cake, and shoved it in my mouth. She sipped her wine and waited, her eyes narrowing and her mouth tightening as she watched me, clearly annoyed that I didn't tell her immediately. But I needed to build up to it. This was humiliating.

She rolled her eyes, giving up and taking another bite of cake.

I took a deep breath, looking away, saying, "I slept with Alex."

She nearly choked on the bite as she looked at me, her eyes wide as saucers. "I thought you guys hated each other?"

I shrugged, "Yeah, we did…" I looked away, wrinkling my brow, "We do? I don't know how it happened. I was swimming, and he came out to the pool. He helped me get rid of this kid who was jerking off in the bushes."

She had just held her wine glass up to take a drink

when she stopped as her eyes slid to me, "What?"

I let out a chuckle. "A kid was jerking off…"

She interrupted. "No, I heard that part. But how did you two go from doing that to doing… each other?"

I stuck my fork in the cake again, dragging it through the fudge icing before popping it in my mouth. I looked up at the ceiling.

I sighed, "I don't know… We got in the hot tub, and one thing led to another. And next thing I know, I was in his bed having the most amazing sex of my life."

"Well, it sounds like you had quite the day."

I huffed out a laugh before taking a long drink. "I guess so."

"So what happened?"

"Don't get me wrong, it was good. Really good. But afterward, I just kind of… left."

"What?"

I threw my arms up, grimacing, "I freaked out and didn't know how to handle it, so I left. Okay?" I huffed out a breath as I eyed the cake for a perfect bite. "It was more than I… expected."

She narrowed her eyes as she said, "Did he make you leave?"

I shook my head before shrugging as I slid my fork into the cake for another bite, "No. He asked me to stay."

Her eyebrows shot up again, "Really?"

I nodded, "But I had to get out of there."

"Jesus, Darci. What are we going to do with you?"

"Please." I gave her a pointed look, "Do you remember the shit you and Edison went through?"

She blushed, looking away, as she took a sip of wine.

I shook my head again, "This was a one-time thing. It's not going to happen again."

"Keep telling yourself that," she murmured as she stared at the cake, looking for the perfect spot to devour. "So what are you going to do?"

I gave her a puzzled look, "What's there to do? I said it was a one-time thing, didn't I?"

"Yeah, but… aren't you going to… I don't know… see each other around? You're just going to pretend it never happened? Pretend he doesn't exist?"

"I don't know." I shrugged.

She took another bite and swallowed, "Wait. If it's just a one-time thing, then why are you freaking out?"

"I guess… I was surprised at our… chemistry. He's just been so hot and cold with me. One minute, he's nice and friendly. The next, he's a total asshole. So when we accidentally brushed against each other in the hot tub, I was shocked at the instant desire that spread like wildfire. He was very upfront with what he wanted, and I couldn't say no when he invited me to his place. I didn't want to say no. We walked into his apartment, and he was all over me."

I looked at Claire wide-eyed and feeling slightly dazed. I was still processing it myself. "I mean, Claire… he picked me up and threw me on the bed. Like a caveman." I let out a breathy laugh, shaking my head as I lifted my wine in a silent toast to the absurdity of it all. "It was fucking hot, and I felt…" I wasn't sure how to describe it.

She nodded for me to go on. "You felt…?"

I made a frustrated, unintelligible sound, and Claire laughed. I had never kissed someone and felt something so intensely, so instantly. Was it electrifying? Exhilarating? A little… terrifying?

"A jolt to your system?"

I smiled, thinking about that kiss again. I sighed, "Yeah. Like he jump-started something I wasn't even aware of."

She laughed before sipping her wine, "Darce, you're in so much trouble."

I nodded slowly, looking up at her as a small smile played on my lips, "I know! That's why I had to get out of there. What do I do?"

"You just need to figure out what you want and take it from there," Claire said before taking another bite of cake.

I sighed, contemplating her words. "Fuck." I took another bite of chocolate cake. "I don't even know what I want."

Claire grinned knowingly. "That's the million-dollar question, isn't it?"

I looked at her, "He's not even my type."

"If you say so." She eyed the cake before setting her fork down. "I'm feeling a chocolate overload." She let out a burp, and we both laughed. "But Darci, you say that, but the guys who are 'your type' never seem to work out, do they? Why not give him a chance?"

I rolled my eyes, "I don't know…" I whispered, "There's definitely something there, but… he can be such an asshat sometimes."

She shrugged as she stood up with her wine glass. "Want to watch a serial killer documentary to get your mind off everything?"

"Abso-fucking-lutely!"

We took our drinks to the couch and settled in for a true crime Murder Night. But as the night wore on, my thoughts drifted back to Alex and this afternoon. I couldn't stop thinking about the sex—that unexpected thrill. The flashbacks made me involuntarily press my legs together, and I wanted more. *I wanted him.* How did I go from hating him to not getting enough of him?

After emptying all three bottles of wine, we were both a bit tipsy and giggly. As soon as I entertained the idea of knocking on Alex's door for another round, I knew it was time to start drinking water. A little while later, Claire called Edison to pick her up, and it wasn't long before he knocked on my door.

He was so sweet to her. That's what I wanted. I watched from the porch as he held a wobbly Claire tightly against him, helping her down the stairs and into his old red truck. She was wildly gesticulating as she loudly told him and the entire apartment complex that I had slept with Alex that afternoon. So that was lovely.

After getting her in the truck, he raised his eyes to me and mouthed, "Sorry."

I smiled and gave him a shrug before walking back into my apartment.

Standing in my living room, I sobered up seeing our mess. There was spilled wine and smeared chocolate cake all over the coffee table. I thought about leaving it until the morning, but who wants to deal with day-old hardened chocolate frosting? I groaned as I grabbed some wipes from the kitchen and cleaned the table.

When I reached down under the table to collect the wine bottles, there was a book under them.

"Oh god, not another one," I muttered.

Flipping it over, it was *The Hating Game*. I loved a good romance novel, but... Wait a minute. *Another Enemies to Lovers book?* Really?

I picked it up. This wasn't mine either. Was it Claire's?

Maybe it fell out of her bag. I flipped through it, seeing all the notes, remembering when Claire showed me her box of magical books last year. Like this one, every one was full of all annotations. It was fascinating but a little... creepy.

I settled on the couch and started reading the book. When I finally looked up to check the time, it was hours later, and I was halfway through the book. I had stayed up way too late. At some point, I stopped reading the actual book. The handwritten notes were too enticing. What were the stories behind them? Did Claire write them? What made someone write in all those books? So many of the notes were about love or losing love.

There was one note that stuck out to me. It was written along the edge of the page, deep into the novel, in careful print. I couldn't help but run my finger across it, feeling the indentions of the pen.

He's not the want but the need,
a broken key to unlock destiny.

Unlock destiny? A broken key? Claire told me stories of people falling in love when they found one of her books. Hell, Edison found her again because one of her books went missing and ended up practically in his lap. I believed her, which suddenly gave me pause. Could she have left this book for me? Because of Alex? Maybe to help me find love? Would she do that without telling me?

I sighed. Truthfully, I needed all the help I could get. My dating life was a total joke. How could one person go on so many bad dates?

I closed the book and set it on the coffee table,

stretching with a yawn as I sank deeper into the couch. But the moment my body relaxed, my mind betrayed me—flashing back to the afternoon. *Alex on me. Over me. Inside me.* A slow heat curled through me, and I pressed my legs together. God, I wanted him… again. *Right now.*

My gaze drifted to the window, straight to his apartment. How stupid would it be to throw caution to the wind and knock on his door? Would it be so bad to wake up tangled against his warm body?

I exhaled, suddenly drained, my limbs too heavy to move. Maybe I'd rest my eyes for a second—then I'd decide. I pulled the quilt from the back of the couch and tucked it around me, but as sleep crept in, my thoughts snagged on that note.

…not the want, but the need.

My stomach twisted. Could that be about me? No way. It was just a book. Just a coincidence. Right?

I was overthinking it. Maybe I'd hit my head at the pool or something.

Still, as my mind faded into sleep, it wasn't the note I fixated on—it was Alex. And one lingering thought settled in my chest: How stupid was I to end up in Alex Dixon's bed?

More importantly… *How could I do it again?*

CHAPTER EIGHT

Alex

I took as many extra shifts as they'd let me take for the rest of the week. I even stayed and slept in an empty hospital room for a few of those nights. I told myself it was so I could help more people.

But the truth was ridiculous. I didn't want to be in my bed, her scent lingering on the sheets. It kept me up at night, remembering. Fantasizing. Wishing. And I certainly didn't want to be anywhere we would accidentally run into each other. I humiliated myself in front of her, begging her to stay, and she practically laughed at me as she walked out. *What the fuck was I thinking?*

Darci. Somehow, she'd gotten under my skin. She was all I could think about, constantly popping into my thoughts every second of the day. I'd even dreamed about her, and I never even dreamed about my wife. I couldn't stop thinking about the way Darci kissed me. The way she tasted. And I craved her. I wanted more, so much more. The softness of her skin, the way she felt against me. It made me want to tear my hair out. *What the fuck was I doing?*

With every other woman, I always lost interest after the first encounter. There was never a second time. Every time the guilt would come, the feelings of betrayal. But being with Darci had been... something else, something... more.

She reminded me so much of Jenna, but at the same time, she was also so different. I couldn't explain it, but I wanted a second, third, fourth time with this woman. Would I ever get her out of my system? *What the fuck? How could I do this to Jenna?*

None of it mattered now. We weren't doing that again... ever. She would stay on her side of the complex, and I would stay on mine. We were never going to be friends. We were certainly not going to be lovers. It was all just a mistake—a terrible, stupid mistake.

I even thought about breaking my lease and moving somewhere else, but I quickly threw that idea away. That was a little dramatic. I liked living practically across the street from the hospital. I wouldn't let one lousy mistake with that little vixen run me out of my apartment. I liked it here. She wasn't going to ruin that for me.

It was five in the morning, and I was getting ready for my shift at the hospital. I peeked out the blinds, hoping she wasn't out there. It was over an hour before the sunrise, and I couldn't remember seeing her out on her porch this early. I let out a sigh of relief before heading to my office. I needed to pay some bills before leaving for work.

I opened the drawer, looking for my ancient checkbook, when I saw the photo. I had only kept the one photo of Jenna, tucked into my desk's top drawer. It was still so painful. It had been years, but every time I saw her smile, that wound ripped wide open. I carefully picked it up, sitting in my desk chair and sighing heavily.

As I held the photo to my chest, memories of our life together flooded back like waves crashing over me again and again. I took one last look, seeing her beautiful smile frozen in time. I remembered taking the photo. We'd just discovered she was pregnant and drove to the coast to celebrate. We'd been trying for two years, and it had been a miracle.

I carefully set the frame down on the desk. Jenna's eyes seemed to pierce through the photograph. She had once colored my whole world. There wasn't a time I could remember when she wasn't in my life. We were supposed to grow old together. The ache in my chest grew as I traced the outline of her face with my fingertips, lost in thought. What I'd give to kiss her again, touch her… just be in her presence.

What would she think of me now? I knew without a doubt she wouldn't like the workaholic I'd become. Would she hate me for the one-night stands? Would she want me to let her go and find happiness? Move on without her? Or would she see it as a betrayal?

I wished so much to talk to her again. She always had the right words to help me, to soothe me. I wished I could turn this photo into a portal to our past. For just a moment, I wanted more than anything to have a conversation with her, to find comfort in her spirit.

I wanted to believe she wouldn't want me to be alone. She'd want me to be happy, but the guilt ate at me. I hadn't been ready. I hadn't saved her. I'd let her just… die. I should have been more prepared. If I'd just done things differently…

I sighed, frustrated, as I slid the frame back into the drawer. I quickly made out a check and slipped it into the envelope to drop off in the night drop on my way out this morning. I took a quick shower and threw on my scrubs before grabbing my messenger bag on the way out.

After locking the door, I instinctively glanced at Darci's apartment. It took me a moment to realize she was sitting on the patio in a rocking chair, a book in one hand and a mug in the other. It was my first time seeing her since we'd been… together. Our eyes locked, and I felt my stomach knot. A mixture of guilt and desire began to burn through me—that was new.

She offered a hopeful smile and waved, but I hesitated, panic washing over me. I'd been too vulnerable, too open. Asking her to stay had been a mistake, a reckless impulse born from a moment of weakness. But why had she said it would be a bad idea?

I turned and jogged down the stairs, her hopeful expression frozen in my mind. I could feel her eyes burning holes in my back the entire time as I drove out of the parking lot.

I'd always kept everyone at arm's reach, retreating into myself, the one to end things before they could ever get off the ground. So why did it bother me so much that she was the one to push me away? I should have been relieved. Maybe she'd regretted it because her reaction this morning seemed like an olive branch, but here I was running away from her.

When I got to the ER, I pushed Darci out of my mind and went on autopilot for the next few hours. Work kept me busy. I'd had the typical runny noses, but there were more complex patients who needed stitches, a toddler with ten popcorn kernels shoved up his nose, and a construction worker with a broken arm.

By the time lunch rolled around, I was starving and needed a break. Javier, another new ER doc, jogged up as I walked to the cafeteria. We both were new hires around the same time, so we became fast friends. We seemed like complete opposites. He looked like a scary biker, with a sculptured beard and sleeves of brightly colored tattoos on his arms and legs.

His typical work attire was a fitted Henley with the sleeves pushed up and scrub pants that hung on his hips. The ladies loved him. Some even requested him. In contrast, I was a head shorter and looked like Mr. Nice Guy with a clean-shaven face, neatly combed hair, and loose scrubs. But we had a lot in common. We both loved live music, especially punk and new rock. In the last few months, we had regularly caught small venue shows together.

"Hey, do you want to see Dish Rag Swill at Andy's on Friday night?" He asked as we walked into the cafeteria.

I nodded as we waited in the line. "Yeah, sure."

He looked relieved as he said, "Great. I went ahead and got tickets. We can just grab a bite on the square before the show. There's that new pasta place. Have you tried it?"

I slid my eyes to him and shook my head, pinching my lips. "Nope, but I've been craving a burger from The Meat Market. Let's go there."

He nodded slowly. "Sounds good. I'll *meet* you there. Ha!"

I deadpanned, "Hilarious, Javi," before I broke out in a grin.

We didn't talk again as I looked over the line, wondering what the special was today. Surprisingly, the food was decent. One of my favorites was their pizza by the slice.

I grabbed a tray and smiled at the woman behind the counter. "Hey, Ariana! What's the special today?"

"Oh, baby, you know it's Taco Tuesday."

I laughed. "Yeah? I completely forgot. I'll take three."

"Steak or chicken?"

"Hmm," I cocked an eyebrow, giving her a smirk, "Can I get both?"

"Of course you can, baby. Two steak, one chicken?"

I winked. "You know exactly what I like."

She winked, "Sure do, baby."

She handed me a plate piled high with rice, beans, and tacos a moment later. It smelled amazing. As I paid, I saw Javier wasn't far behind me. I went to a table and inhaled an entire taco before he arrived.

His eyes widened when he took in my plate full of food. "I don't know how you do it, but Ariana always gives you more than anyone else."

I laughed. "Really?"

"Uh, yeah. Look at my plate."

He leaned back, spreading his arms. My tacos were noticeably fuller. I chuckled, shoving another one in my mouth.

"Sorry, dude."

He cocked an eyebrow. "You gotta teach me your secrets."

"No secrets. I'm just that guy."

He rolled his eyes, chuckling as he shook his head. "Whatever."

Without much conversation, we shoveled the food into our mouths. There was never much time for lunch in the emergency department, so we ate fast. But I wasn't ready to get up yet.

Javier pushed back from the table and looked me up and down.

"Okay, man, what gives? You seem… off today."

I shrugged. Javier and I were friends, but I'd never really opened up to him. I wasn't sure I wanted to start now. I dug a chip through my beans before popping it in my mouth.

He shook his head. "Dude, something is eating you. You're never this quiet. You barely said two words since we started eating."

I sighed, balling up my napkin as I took a drink. "You're not wrong."

"Okay… so what is it?"

I took a deep breath. I really didn't have anyone to talk to about any of this. "I… slept with someone."

"And?"

I'd never told him about my past. But he'd seen me take women home for the night a few times when we went to shows. We both had.

I swallowed. "I'm a one-night kind of guy. And…it wasn't anything like that."

He nodded. "Yeah. I get it."

"I can't get her out of my head."

"Have you told her?"

"No."

"Why not?"

I shrugged.

Javier gave me a pointed look. "What's so bad about it?"

I let out another sigh. "I was… married before."

He nodded. "Bad divorce."

"No." My voice cracked, "She… she passed away."

That was all I was willing to say. I didn't think I could tell him everything, not right now.

"Man, that's rough. I'm sorry. I'm real sorry about that."

I swallowed as I nodded. "It's just that I feel a lot of guilt."

"How long's it been?"

"Three years." But it felt like yesterday.

"Therapy?"

I scoffed. "Yeah, but I don't know how much it's really helping." It would probably help if I kept the appointments. Before therapy, I didn't even have one-night stands. Two years without sex nearly killed me.

Javier leaned in, his expression filled with empathy. "Look, man, grief is a hell of a thing. It doesn't follow a schedule or make sense." He took a drink of his tea. "But your wife would want you to be happy." A faint, knowing smile ghosted across his face. "And... you can't control when someone comes into your life and shakes things up. If she's consuming your thoughts, maybe it's worth exploring." He shrugged.

His eyes softened. "If you were gone, and she was the one left behind, you wouldn't want her to be alone, would you?"

"No, of course not."

"Exactly. You've been through a lot. That pain never goes away, but... it gets better."

I let out another sigh.

Javier paused, his gaze sincere. "You can't punish yourself for moving on."

Oh, but I could. I was good at it. I'd been doing it for years.

He continued, "You deserve happiness. She'd want

that for you. If this woman makes you happy, talk to her. Life's too short to dwell on what ifs."

"Thanks, man. I appreciate it more than you know."

"Anytime, just don't ditch me. I need my concert buddy."

"Absolutely." I laughed as I cleaned up my tray, and we walked to the trash together.

He nudged me as we walked back to the ER. "So what's her name?"

I smiled and looked down, heat creeping up my neck. "Darci."

"Wait." He stopped and faced me. "Tiny with short, dark hair? Librarian?"

"Uh, yeah? You know her?"

We kept walking as he bobbled his head. "We hung out... once."

"When?"

"It was... several months ago. I met her online and invited her to meet me at the park. There was a capture-the-flag thing going on."

"You took her on a first date to 'capture the flag?'" I laughed. What the hell was he thinking?

He wrinkled his brow, getting defensive. "Yeah? What's wrong with that?"

I shook my head. "Nothing. Absolutely nothing." I couldn't stop laughing.

He shrugged, "Well... halfway through, she disappeared on me. We had found the other team's flag and were figuring out who would get it, but when I looked around she was nowhere to be found. I tried texting and calling her, but she never responded. Haven't seen her since."

My laugh quieted down to a chuckle. "I can imagine."

He stopped, his hands on his hips. "Okay, man, what's wrong with capturing the flag?"

I smirked, "Nothing… if you're ten years old."

He raised his eyebrows to his hairline. "Fine, what's your idea of a good first date?"

We started walking towards the ER again. "That gamer bar on Hickory. Have you been?" Javier shook his head. "It's pretty cool. They have shelves and shelves of board games. I think it'd be a great way to have a drink, play a game, and get to know one another."

He nodded, giving me a sheepish smile. "Yeah, maybe that is a better idea." He leaned closer, his voice low, "And maybe you should take Darci out on that date."

I considered it as we got back to the department. Grabbing my computer, I realized I felt lighter, better than I had in weeks. Maybe confessing my secrets to a friend was a good thing.

CHAPTER NINE

Darci

It'd been nearly two weeks since Alex and I had had our little rendezvous. I hadn't seen him at all until a week ago. He was never on his patio anymore. He wasn't at the pool. Even his car was missing most days. Was he avoiding me?

About a week after the "incident," as I liked to call it, I couldn't sleep. I'd been tossing and turning all night when I decided to just get up for the day. It was nearly 5:30 in the early morning. I threw on a pair of leggings and a T-shirt, made some coffee, and took my book outside to my rocking chair. I loved reading in my rocking chair. I was prepping for my little old lady years.

I had just gotten comfy with my book when I saw him walk out his front door. He stepped out, a leather messenger bag over one shoulder. He was in black scrubs, the pants tight across his thighs. Heat washed over me. His ass looked amazing. It gave me flashbacks when my nails were pressed into his flesh as he pumped into me.

After locking his door, he turned to start down the stairs, and our eyes met. He stumbled, and I smiled and waved. He hesitated before completely ignoring me as he jogged down the stairs to his car. He paused at his car as if debating something before finally getting in and leaving. I wasn't sure what to make of it.

Did he regret what had happened between us? It sure felt like he was avoiding me. Honestly, I still wasn't sure if I regretted it. Our chemistry was just so... unexpected. I was kidding myself if I didn't crave another taste of him.

But we could barely stand each other half the time. Maybe we were just too explosive together. I swear I was often my worst self when he came around. Why did he attract me one minute and repel me the next?

After work, I headed to the home improvement store. One of my favorite hobbies was DIY-ing designer home decor. And by *hobby*, I meant buying supplies for some cool project I saw online—only to never actually make it. Or worse, start it, get frustrated, and abandon it halfway. My coat closet was a graveyard of half-finished DIYs.

Watching DIYers on social media was my second favorite pastime—right behind crime documentaries. *How did they make it look so easy?*

This time, I had a feeling I was going to be successful. This one video I watched was a beautiful but ridiculously expensive chandelier made from chains. The actual version cost nearly 50,000 dollars. Are you kidding me? 50k on a chandelier? That's some batshit crazy right there.

But the video I saw made it look so easy to recreate,

and it would look amazing in my living room. How hard could it be? Maybe this would be the first time I'd finish a project. I crossed my fingers as I walked into the store.

It took me much longer than expected as I wandered the store, but I finally found the chain in blue, orange, and red. I decided blue would look best with my decor, so I hit the button for someone to cut it. A few minutes later, a cute guy wearing an orange apron with dark curly hair peeking out of a beanie came over. His t-shirt was tight on his biceps and revealed a scrawling tattoo. The dimple on his left cheek peeked out when he smiled at me, sealing the deal.

In a deep voice, he asked, "How can I help you?"

"Oh," I looked at his name tag—Jason. "Well, Jason, I need some chain."

His smile widened, that dimple deepening. "Which one and how much?"

"The blue one, and um, how much? Huh, I hadn't really considered that."

"Well, what do you need it for?"

I raised my chin proudly. "I'm making a chandelier."

He bobbed his head. "Cool."

"Yeah." I smiled up at him. A light bulb went off in my head as I pulled my phone out of my pocket. "Hang on a sec..." I searched for the saved video. "Oh, I found it!" I raised my eyes to him, "Can I show you this? Maybe you can help me figure out how much chain I need?"

"Sure..." He came closer, leaning over my shoulder to watch. He smelled amazing, like laundry soap and spearmint.

I leaned back nearly against his chest, holding the

phone. We watched the entire thing together. When it was over, I turned around, looking up at him expectantly.

"Well," he rubbed the back of his neck, "I think you'll need about 12 feet and a few other things." He shrugged, "I can show you if you want."

I smiled up at him through my lashes. "I'd love that."

Ten minutes later, I had a shopping cart full of what I needed: rechargeable globe lights, ceiling brackets, work gloves, and duct tape. Jason's number was also tucked safely in my phone. He walked me up to the checkout.

He squeezed my arm and said, "It was very nice to meet you, Darci. Give me a call if you need help making that chandelier or…" He raised an eyebrow. "Just to hang out."

I blushed and said goodbye. As I approached the checkout, I saw a huge pallet of drinks. I grabbed a 12-pack of grape soda. When I got to the register, I tossed gummy worms, cheese curls, and barbecue potato chips in with the rest of my supplies. I required some serious junk food reinforcements to prepare myself for this project.

They only had one checkout open, so the line was pretty long. I opened my book app and picked up where I had left off in my latest romantasy. The high Fae demon was about to ravage his offering.

"Moving to kidnapping now, Tink?" A familiar voice whispered against the shell of my ear.

I shivered from his hot breath against the nape of my neck and whirled around. My eyes went wide before they narrowed when I saw Alex's smirk.

"And here we go again."

That lazy smile drove me insane.

"Looks like a bonafide do-it-yourself kidnapping kit going on in that cart." He nodded his head towards all my supplies.

I shot him a dry look. "Because nothing says 'let's commit a crime' like globe lights." I rolled my eyes. "It's just a little DIY project, Alex." I broke out in a dark grin. "Besides, if I were planning a murder, do you think I'm dumb enough to buy everything in one place?"

He arched an eyebrow. "I haven't forgotten the trash bags from a few weeks ago."

I let out a frustrated sigh. "I showed you the ripped-up couch cushions."

"Who knows? Maybe that was just the one bag. Maybe all the others were body parts." He wiggled his eyebrows as he burst out laughing.

"You're quite the comedian," I muttered. "If you must know, I'm trying to DIY a chandelier I saw online that costs more than I make in a year."

He bobbled his head, still smirking. "Likely story." He stepped closer and lowered his voice, "So... did you know that guy?"

I wrinkled my brow. "What guy?"

He jerked his head toward the aisles. "The one leading you around the store."

"Were you following me?"

He flinched, his expression shifting to defensive. "Uh, no. Why would you think that?" His Adam's apple bobbed as he swallowed. "I just saw you with him when I walked in." He rolled his eyes, a hint of mockery in his tone. "You seemed to be... enjoying his company."

I snorted. "Oh, please. He was just helping me find supplies and stuff."

His lips curled into that infuriating smirk. "And

stuff?"

"Well... he did give me his number," I muttered, avoiding his gaze.

Alex's expression flickered—something unreadable darting across his face as he turned slightly away. But when he faced me again, the smirk was firmly in place.

"Darci," he said, his voice dropping, no hint of teasing in his tone, "you're beautiful. Anyone with half a brain would want to date you."

I felt the flush rising to my cheeks. I didn't know what to say. He thought I was beautiful? I was never the beautiful one. I was always the cute one, the feisty one, the sidekick.

He gave a short nod as if he'd decided. "You should call him."

One minute, he calls me beautiful, and the next, he pushes me to call another guy. What was I supposed to do with that? I mean, we'd slept together, for heaven's sake.

"You think... I should?"

A muscle twitched in his jaw before he shrugged. "Sure."

I looked down at my cart and took a deep breath. I wanted to clear the air between us, tell him it was a mistake I'd left so abruptly that afternoon. It felt so overwhelming—the chemistry, the sex, the feelings that had bubbled up from nowhere.

I started slowly, "Listen, Alex, about what happened..."

Just then, the clerk said, "Next," looking at me impatiently. I looked back at Alex, but he just looked resigned.

"Go ahead," he said. "You were here first."

I hesitated. *Was he brushing me off?* I glanced back at him, a pang of sadness in my heart. And then, as if to emphasize the point, the clerk called out, "Next!" again, louder this time.

With a sigh, I turned back to the clerk, set my things on the conveyor belt, and checked out. As she handed me the receipt, I felt Alex's warmth as he slid up beside me, his presence unmistakable.

When had that pine-and-cedar scent of his become so intoxicating? The urge to breathe him in was almost unbearable—but I sure as hell wasn't about to do it where he could see me.

He lifted my bags off the counter and placed them in my cart. His warm breath brushed my ear when he whispered, "Be safe, Tink."

He knew damn well I hated that nickname. But when I turned to look at him, he winked with that panty-melting smirk still on his face, and a bolt of heat shot through me. *Dammit.*

"Uh… thanks?"

God, why did I ask it like a question? He gave me a curt nod as he swiped his card and made small talk with the clerk.

I huffed out a breath, pushing my cart toward the exit. The last thing I needed was for him to see what he was doing to me. How did he get under my skin so easily? My nostrils flared. *What the hell is happening to me?*

Slipping my receipt into my purse, I turned the corner toward the door—and despite myself, I slid my gaze back to him. I wasn't expecting what I saw. He was watching me with a genuine smile stretched across his face. When he caught my eye, he lifted a hand in a casual wave. Before I could stop it, a smile spread across my lips, warmth creeping into my chest as I stepped outside.

I was still lost in thoughts of him as I loaded my bags into my SUV, until I heard the car beside me unlock. *Alex.* I felt his eyes on me. I sneaked a glance as he opened the driver-side door, tossing his purchase in the passenger seat. I continued loading my trunk when I felt him behind me.

"Hey, Darci?" Alex's voice cut through the sounds of cars driving by.

I turned around. "Yeah?"

He fidgeted, his hands tapping his legs, like he was nervous. "Got any plans for Friday night?"

A slow, calculating smile crept across my face. "Why? Need help planning a murder?"

His lips curved as he chuckled, a nervous flicker in his eyes.

"Not exactly. But Dish Rag Swill is playing at Andy's on the square," he offered.

"Sounds like fun."

"Would you… want to go… together?"

I was so confused. A concert? With Alex? What was happening? My stupid heart did a double-take.

"What time?"

He shrugged, "I think doors open at seven, and the show starts at eight."

Was he asking me out? I loved concerts. A slow smile spread across my face. "Like a… date?"

He shrugged, "Do you want it to be?"

This time, I was the one smirking. "Maybe I do."

His face brightened, and the tension in his shoulders melted away. He was so adorable. "Then, it's a date."

Oh shit, I just remembered I have to work late that

day. "But I'll have to meet you there, since I work late."

"Yeah, sure. That's fine."

"Great. It's a date." I grinned.

He breathed out, "Okay… yeah," still smiling as he walked backward to the driver's side, almost tripping over his feet.

I chuckled. I watched his car pull away and disappear down the street. A warm feeling spread in my belly. But… what the heck? One minute, he told me to call another guy, and the next, he asked me out on a date. Men were weird.

After a quick stop to pick up a pizza, I sank into my shitty couch. I flipped open the lid and picked up a slice while I tried to tame the whirlwind of emotions I was experiencing. I reached for my phone, the corners of my mouth pulling up as I dialed Claire's number. It was time to spill the tea.

"Hey, Darci. What's up?" I heard the soft clink of dishes—Claire was probably making dinner.

I didn't even say hello. "He asked me out," I blurted.

"Who?"

"Alex? He asked me out. On a date. To a show at Andy's on Friday night." I let out a squeal of delight. *Jesus, what was wrong with me?*

"He did, did he?" I could hear the smirk in her voice and the gears turning in her head.

"Claire… I can hear your scheming through the phone. Do not show up at Andy's on Friday with Edison in tow."

"What? I would never…"

"You're forgetting I know you."

"Seriously, I wasn't going to do that. But…"

"But what?"

"Wasn't Dish Rag Swill that band with that hot pizza delivery guy?"

"Who?" I racked my brain, and then it hit me—the night we packed up Claire's apartment when she moved in with Edison.

"Oh yeah. I remember that." I took a bite of pizza, remembering Edison embarrassing the hell out of me by hitting up the pizza delivery guy that night.

I spotted the book I found on my coffee table. With my mouth full of pizza, I asked, "Hey, did you leave a book here the other day?"

"I don't think so. At least, I don't remember leaving a book, but you know they walk off sometimes. Which book?"

"_The Hating Game_? I found it under the coffee table when you left the other day. You were a little tipsy, and Edison had to carry you down the stairs. Maybe it fell out of your bag."

"True… I had a nasty hangover the next day. I don't think anything was missing in my bag, but hang on," I heard some loud rummaging before she returned. "It's not here, but I didn't bring it over. I know I never took it out of the box." Her voice softened, "Hmm…."

"What does that 'hmm' mean?"

"Maybe it's your turn."

"My turn? For what?"

"For the fates to help you find love."

"Are you serious? From a book?"

"I mean, one of them did bring me and Sonny back together. I've seen things, Darce. I've seen couples fall in love after finding one of these books."

"I know you've seen it, but I don't know. It seems a little woo-woo to me."

Claire made it sound like this was all perfectly normal, but it seemed far-fetched to me. But stranger things have happened. She and Edison only came back together because one of those books escaped and found its way to him, and that seemed pretty incredible.

Wouldn't it be nice if finding love was that easy? My belly fluttered, just thinking it might happen to me. But it wasn't going to be Alex.

"Maybe it's all coincidences?"

"Even Elodie, who was certifiable, knew about the books' magic."

"God, I can't believe you brought her up. That fucking witch." Even now, I sometimes looked over my shoulder, wondering what she was up to.

"Well, if you're finding the books, don't be surprised if you see her. She has a habit of turning up when one of those books comes into play."

"Great." Just what I needed. That crazy woman coming after me the way she came after Claire.

"Seriously, don't worry about her," Claire reassured me. "She seems to be minding her own business lately. But, what happened with the book?"

"Like I said, I found the book under the coffee table after you left. But I haven't been able to stop thinking about one of the notes written inside."

"Yeah?"

Boy, she was taking this in stride, like it was an everyday occurrence.

"It said, 'He's not the want but the need, a broken key to unlock destiny.'"

Claire breathed out, "Huh..."

Did Claire know something? Because I was baffled.

"What do you think it means?"

"Who knows? But it could be about you and Alex."

"What makes you say that?"

"Well… he's not the typical guy you usually go for."

"Ain't that the truth," I conceded.

"So maybe that's the 'not the want' part."

"So I need him?" I said dryly.

"You seemed pretty into him after you slept together. I nearly had to hold you down, so you wouldn't go knock on his door for round 2 that night."

"Yeah, not my finest moment. But… what about the broken key and unlocking destiny part?"

Claire chuckled, "I have no idea. I'm just speculating."

Sure, I couldn't stop thinking about him, and the sex we had was mind-blowing. But I wasn't getting my hopes up. When it came to relationships, nothing ever worked out. I was cursed to be alone forever.

"Are you ready for the Vegas trip?"

Thank god she was changing the subject. "Next Friday can't come soon enough."

"Just remember, we have a wedding to plan. Sure, we can go dancing and have a little fun in the casino, but we're going to be responsible. We are not getting shit faced and doing something stupid."

"Okay, okay, but we can have a little fun, can't we?"

She sighed, "Yes, but let's try to behave ourselves."

"Okay, okay."

"Hey, I need to go. Bandit's ready for his walk, and he's already grumbling. He'll throw a fit if I don't put my shoes on soon."

I laughed, "Okay, I'll see you at work tomorrow."

CHAPTER TEN

Alex

When I walked up to The Meat Market, Javier was waiting outside. This burger place was a gem for the locals. It didn't look like much, but they had the best burgers and cheese fries in town. It was also a heart attack waiting to happen. Surprisingly, there wasn't much of a line for prime dinner time on Friday night.

I chuckled as I held the door open for Javi, "I don't think they've cleaned the grease from these windows in 40 years."

He laughed. "It adds character."

This place looked like it was straight out of the 1970s, with its creaky wooden floors and a menu that had remained unchanged for years. The tables were scarred from years of abuse and cigarette burns, and the chairs were armchair-style with nailhead trim and busted naugahyde.

It looked like a dump, but the cold beer on tap, all-you-can-eat fries, and the seasoned pinto beans made this place one of my favorite places to eat. I couldn't tell you how often Javi and I had met for burgers here, but the staff knew our names and had our orders memorized.

When we sat down with our trays of food, I leaned in and said to Javier, "Hey, I invited Darci to the show. Hope you don't mind. She's not showing up until closer to 8."

Javier raised an eyebrow, a playful smile on his face, "Well, aren't you the spontaneous one? No worries. I'll be your wingman."

After dinner, we made our way to Andy's, pausing at the door that led up to Javier's condo so that he could stash away some leftovers. I barely touched my food tonight. For some reason, I was really nervous for this "date." I felt like a highschooler, and the last thing I needed was a stomachache from indulging too much.

Shoulder to shoulder, we navigated busy foot traffic on the square. This was a college town, and Friday nights were always like this during the school year—a chaotic symphony of laughter and music. When the sun went down, people went wild. Tonight was no different as we squeezed through the dense crowd to get a spot in the line before it wound around the building. It seemed the craziness was in full force when we saw a woman try to pee behind a bush on the courthouse lawn before she fell over, laughing with her friends.

Andy's was an interesting place. The nondescript building housed three completely different bars. Andy's was on the main floor, a small music venue typically for punk and hard rock shows.

The Basement was a bar down below, hidden away in the actual basement. If I had to pick a place, I liked it best. It had a good vibe and was chill in a laid-back way. The decor was a bit "dungeon-like," and on nights when there was a show at Andy's, the shelves full of liquor would swing and shake.

The newest bar was a speakeasy called Oliver's on the top floor with a hidden entrance. It was supposed to be a big secret. Truthfully, it wasn't hard to find, so the place was usually packed with a long wait cascading down the staircase. I had only been there once to check it out, but it seemed more like a cool college girl hangout.

Standing in line, I looked at my watch and realized we had a good half hour before the doors opened for the show.

I slid my eyes to Javi, "Do you care about being up at the front?"

He shrugged, "Not really."

"Want to head down to The Basement for a drink instead of waiting in line?"

It was a great place to waste time and play a card or board game with friends.

Javier chuckled, "You read my mind." We walked around to the side of the building to the stone stairway leading down into the bar.

The crowd tended to be hit or miss. Sometimes, it was full of musicians. Other times, couples were all over each other. And then, on some weeknights, lonely people were drinking their sorrows away.

There was a mix of people tonight, including a strange woman I couldn't take my eyes off. She looked like a time traveler straight out of the Victorian age. She was extremely pale but beautiful, with blood-red lips and dark hair cascading down under a pointed hat. Her tight black dress had huge puffy sleeves, and while it was modest, it still showed every curve of her body.

She was closely nestled into a big, burly guy at the

bar, murmuring in his ear with a seductive smile. But as soon as I walked in, her head snapped, and she made eye contact like she recognized me. Her eyes narrowed, but I had no idea who she was. A shiver ran down my spine. Luckily, someone approached the bar next to her, and she quickly looked away.

I stood at the bar as far away from her and ordered a gin and tonic. Javier ordered a fancy drink with a speared raspberry.

Glancing at Javier's drink as we made our way to a table, I teased, "Look at you, Mr. High Roller. Did they serve that with a side of monocle and top hat?"

He laughed along with me, shrugging, "What can I say? I like sophisticated drinks." He leaned in, a mischievous glint in his eyes, "Did you see the guy who came in today at the ER with the fish bowl on his head?"

"What?" I chuckled, taking a drink. "I must have missed that one."

He began recounting, "I got stuck with him. He smelled like weed and said he was attempting to understand a fish's perspective. It took us a good hour to free him without shattering the bowl. Never a dull day, I tell you."

I shook my head as we both burst into laughter. It was never boring when it came to the ER.

I finished my drink, feeling a little more relaxed. I glanced at my watch and asked Javi, "Ready to go upstairs?"

When we made our way upstairs, a decent number of people were already filling in the space. I grabbed some foam earplugs out of a box on the bar. Javier and I were about halfway to the stage, spreading out a little to hold a spot for Darci. I faced backward, watching the door, a nervous flutter in my belly.

When she walked in, I couldn't take my eyes off her. Neither could a few guys by the door. She talked animatedly with the man at the door taking tickets. She wore a tiny black dress that showed off her shoulders and laced up the front. My hands itched to undo those laces.

"Be right back," I said over my shoulder to Javi as I walked towards her.

She was standing in the back, searching the crowd.

"Hey," I said as I walked up with my hands in my pockets. A slow smile spread across my face. She seemed relieved to see me.

"Hi." Her cheeks reddened as she gave me a friendly smile before looking away. "I wasn't sure... I thought maybe..." She trailed off.

I quirked my head. "You thought what?"

She shook her head as she smiled again. "It doesn't matter."

I wasn't going to push it, but it did make me wonder. What kind of asshole did she think I was?

"A friend of mine is holding our place up closer. Is that okay?"

She nodded as I put my hand on her lower back and guided her through the crowd, wanting everyone to know she was with me. I felt her take a deep breath as we moved, slipping between people.

I murmured in her ear, "You look beautiful tonight."

She looked over her shoulder at me as if surprised by my comment before she grinned.

I saw Javier holding our spot, and I leaned closer to her ear and said, "I hope you don't mind. My friend Javier is here."

I stepped back so he could greet her. Her eyes widened when he turned and said hello.

"Hey, Darci. Nice to see you again."

She smiled, her cheeks turning red as she nodded. Turning back to me, she wrinkled her brow, "How do you know Javier?"

"We work together."

"Did he tell you he knew me?"

I chuckled and nodded, "He told me about the capture-the-flag date he dragged you on."

She rolled her eyes before shaking her head.

"I told him never to do that on a first date again."

She muttered, "Someone needed to."

I laughed, and she smiled.

We watched the band on the stage getting their instruments ready before she leaned over and asked, "So, do you know this band?"

"Nah, I just like to go to shows at small venues like this. But I think they're punk."

She nodded, and I couldn't help but watch her as she scanned the crowd. Every time she slid her eyes to mine, I'd smile, that nervous flutter returning. Why was I so anxious?

A few minutes later, she leaned over to whisper something to me. But before she spoke, the lights went down, and the crowd went wild as the first band took the stage. I raised my eyebrows, but she shook her head, a small smile on her lips.

Just as they began to play the first notes, I remembered earplugs, pulled them out of my pocket, and offered her a pair. She nodded and took a pair, pressing them into her ears.

Usually, I just stood there when I went to a show,

nodding to the music. At first, Darci seemed a little self-conscious. She was moving but not quite dancing. Slowly, she began to let go and sway to the beat. The next song was faster, and suddenly, she was getting into it—jumping, dancing, and shaking her ass.

I found myself watching her with a big, stupid grin on my face as I barely paid attention to the band. The sudden urge to touch her, reach out, grab her hips, and dance with her surprised me. I'd never been like that, not even with my wife. But I couldn't take my eyes off Darci, and before long, she grabbed my hand, pulling me in. I couldn't resist, and soon, we were both dancing and grinning, lost in the infectious energy.

I couldn't remember when I'd had this much fun or felt this free. Caught up in the moment, Darci was laughing, her cheeks flushed. Her whole body radiated joy. I glanced over at Javier, realizing I'd completely forgotten he was next to me, but he was bopping along with a knowing grin as he watched us getting into it.

When the band began to play a cover of a popular pop-punk song, she sang at the top of her lungs, throwing her hands up and jumping along with everyone else in the crowd. Before I knew it, I was completely drawn in, jumping, singing, and waving my arms with her and the crowd.

My heart beat frantically, not just from us jumping around, but because I wanted to feel this way every day. She was like a spark trying to re-ignite my world. The room faded, the music distant, and she consumed me. It was just the two of us. She looked up at me with those whiskey gold eyes and her wide smile, and I had this overwhelming need to kiss her, to claim her. As the song ended and everyone began to cheer, I was breathless but still caught up in only her.

Darci's laughter echoed in my ears, "Oh my god, that was so fun!"

I couldn't help but grin back. I slid my eyes to Javier, who still had that grin. He gave me a thumbs-up as he slowly backed up and disappeared into the crowd.

When the next band started their set, Darci tugged me closer, encouraging me to keep dancing. We moved together in a synchronized rhythm, my thigh between her legs, my arm wrapped around her waist as her skirt rode up higher. We lost ourselves in the pulsating music. Our connection grew stronger with every beat, and I couldn't deny the magnetic pull drawing me even closer to her. The heat of her core against my thigh was making my dick thicken.

I leaned in, letting her scent wrap around me. I couldn't stop myself as I pressed my lips to her neck and nipped up her jaw. She turned her face, capturing my lips with hers, swiping her tongue against my mouth, and I opened, hungry for her. But just as suddenly, she pulled back, a teasing desire in her eyes as she smiled up at me, bringing her thumb to my mouth and rubbing her lipstick off.

As the night wore on, we danced to nearly every song. After the encore, we cheered and applauded with the rest of the crowd. Soon, people began to filter out, but Darci and I stood there, exchanging secret smiles. Even if nothing more happened between us, I would carry this night with me for a long time.

She had this energy about her—something that made it so easy for me to want to enjoy life again. It had been way too long since I'd felt like this. It was refreshing to let go of some of the guilt, stop overthinking everything, and actually live in the moment.

We made our way outside, and the cooler air felt

good.

I turned to Darci and asked, "Where'd you park?"

She blinked a few times before furrowing her brow. "Oh," she pointed down the street. "Down there."

With my hands in my pockets, I lifted my shoulder in a casual gesture, offering my arm. "Can I walk you to your car?"

She nodded, a soft smile playing on her lips. "Yeah, thanks," she murmured.

Sliding her hand through my arm, she clung to me, fitting perfectly, like she was right where she was supposed to be as we strolled down the path. Tonight felt different, and I couldn't help but feel a sense of anticipation for what was to come. I wanted to ask her to come over and spend the night with me. I hadn't gotten her out of my head since we had that wild afternoon.

The city lights illuminated our path as we walked in comfortable silence, occasionally interrupted by the distant sounds of boisterous laughs and yelling from people walking out of the other bars.

Darci turned her head, looking up at me. "Tonight was fun."

I grinned. "Yeah, I had a great time."

She opened her mouth like she would say something more when, out of nowhere, a man carrying multiple bottles of wine collided with us. The bottles crashed onto the pavement, spraying red wine everywhere, all over me, Darci, and the guy.

Before I could think twice, I glanced at Darci and joked, "We were *so close* to a normal night, Darci. So close."

As soon as I said it, I realized the joke came out

harsher than I intended. Darci's cheeks turned red, and she looked at me with such hurt and embarrassment. Her dress was dripping red wine down her legs. The man shot me an annoyed look, clearly not in the mood for jokes.

She didn't take it lightly when she shot back, "Really, Alex?"

Before I could apologize or the man could react, Darci let go of me, turned to him, and said, "I'm so sorry about this. Let me help you."

While I stood there like an idiot, she quickly began picking up the shattered glass, her expression apologetic. She even offered to replace the wine, but the man reassured her she didn't need to do that.

She tossed the glass she'd collected in the nearest trash can as she stormed off, not looking back once, leaving me standing there feeling like a complete asshole. I ran after her.

"Darci... wait! Please! I'm... I'm sorry! I didn't mean-"

She didn't even bother turning around as she gathered the skirt of her dress and squeezed the excess wine from it. She lifted her hand and yelled, "Just leave me alone!" as she unlocked her car. Before she got in, she turned towards me. I stopped abruptly and was standing about 10 feet away.

"You know, Alex, I had a really nice time with you tonight. But there you go again, ruining it—every damn time. What the fuck is wrong with you?"

She made an exaggerated shrug as I gave her a pleading look, trying to find the right words to say. But she didn't wait for my answer. She got in the car, slammed the door, and drove away.

Why had I let a thoughtless joke ruin a fantastic

night? Guilt gnawed at me as I watched her go. I let out a heavy sigh, hating myself, as I walked back to my car.

A few minutes later, Javier called out as he walked towards me, my takeout box in his hand, "Hey, Dixon? Where's Darci?" He smiled, wiggling his eyebrows, and looked past me. "I thought you two were getting pretty cozy."

Deep in thought, I looked up, surprised to see him, still angry at myself. I stopped, rubbing the back of my neck to hide my embarrassment. I took the box from him and jutted my chin. "She needed to go."

He studied me for a beat before noticing the wine covering my jeans. "What happened to you?"

I rolled my eyes. "Oh, you know, just trying out a new fashion trend called 'Eau de Red Wine.' It's the latest thing," I replied sarcastically, grinning as I attempted to brush off the awkwardness.

The worst thing about being a redhead was blushing. I always looked like a tomato, and I could feel the flush creeping up my neck from the anger at myself and the embarrassment of the situation with Darci.

Javier nodded. "Gotcha."

I just wanted to go home and wallow in my stupidity alone. I pulled my keys from my pocket, turning towards my car.

I raised my hand in a wave. "I'll see you at the hospital. Thanks for tonight."

"Sure, man, sure. But if you need to talk..." He trailed off, his eyebrows raising.

His offer made me pause, and I looked over my shoulder at him just as I stepped off the curb. I nodded and gave him a small smile, grateful for the offer. "Yeah, I think I just need to be alone. Thanks for the offer. Just not tonight."

As I drove the short way home, I just kept replaying that last interaction Darci and I had over and over. We'd had so much fun tonight, and then I just fucking ruined it. Why was I always self-sabotaging around her? No matter how hard I tried, my stupid mouth always got me in trouble with her.

Tonight had been amazing, and I hated myself for how it ended. Before that mess in the parking lot, I was sure we'd end up in bed again. There was no denying we had chemistry—electric, reckless, impossible to ignore. But maybe we were just wrong for each other. Too sharp at the edges. Too volatile.

I should stop whatever this was. I should let it burn out before it got worse. But the truth was, I didn't even know what this was. All I knew was that she brought chaos into every room like it was perfume—unapologetic, magnetic, and impossible not to breathe in.

And God help me, I think I loved it.

When I got to the apartment complex, I saw her car in the parking lot, but her apartment was dark. I slowly climbed the stairs to my place. As soon as I was inside, I guzzled an entire bottle of water before showering and throwing my clothes in the washing machine. Hopefully, the wine didn't stain.

I might have ruined everything, but tonight was the first time I'd been out with a woman, and my mind hadn't immediately gone to Jenna. I hadn't even thought of her once tonight. Before this, I would feel instant guilt, like I was betraying her.

It dawned on me—I didn't feel that way with Darci. Was I finally ready to move on? Or was it just unconscious guilt now? *How the fuck was I supposed to get past something like that?*

When I finally crawled into bed, I stared at the ceiling, realizing how alone I really was. I tossed and turned until my mind drifted back to tonight, the way Darci's body felt swaying in my arms and the lingering taste of her lips as I finally fell asleep.

CHAPTER ELEVEN

Darci

It was Friday, and we were on our way to Vegas, baby —even if it took longer than a Celine Dion residency to get here. I nudged Claire's shoulder as we disembarked the plane, a mischievous glint in my eye.

"Finally, we've arrived!"

"Alright," Claire sighed, a weary smile on her face. "Let's just get to the hotel and hit the hay. We can worry about conquering Vegas tomorrow after some actual sleep."

"Sleep? Who needs sleep when there's a million flashing lights and buffets overflowing with questionable shrimp?"

I grinned, already picturing a plate piled high. I was starving after surviving off airplane pretzels for the last six hours.

"Girl, that shrimp can wait," Claire countered, her smile fading a touch. "Look, I know you're bummed about missing the clubs tonight, but that flight cancellation was brutal. We'll be zombies tomorrow, and I don't want to mess this up."

A dramatic sigh escaped my lips. "Fine," I conceded, dragging out the word for emphasis. "But tomorrow night, we are painting the town red! We deserve an epic Vegas show after that airplane torture."

Claire let out a genuine laugh. The sound was music to my ears.

"Deal. Now, let's find our ride and get to that hotel. I'm exhausted. My dancing shoes can wait until my eyelids don't feel like they're stuffed with cotton balls."

After our flight cancellation, I figured there was no way things could get worse. Boy, was I wrong.

The hotel lobby doors whooshed shut behind us, the cold air conditioning a stark contrast to the desert heat that clung to us. Claire fumbled with her phone, frustration etched on her face.

"Let me call Sonny," she muttered, dialing his number.

I slumped onto a bench, weariness seeping into my bones. This trip was turning into a nightmare.

"Hey, honey," Claire greeted Sonny, her voice strained. "There's been a bit of a snag."

I couldn't hear Sonny's voice through the speaker phone amongst the city noises, but Claire came over and flopped beside me.

"...gave away your room? What kind of place treats women like this?" He let out a frustrated sigh, "I should have come with you."

"It's fine. We're going to be fine. They said we could have our room tomorrow. We just need a hotel for tonight."

A flurry of clicks and typing filled the silence. "Alright, I found something a few blocks off the Strip,"

Sonny announced, relief tinging his words.

"Thank goodness," I breathed.

"It's a double room at the..." Sonny trailed off, deciphering something.

The luxurious names of Vegas hotels danced in my head. Maybe The Grand Flamingo? The Grecian?

"The Royale?" I offered, hopefully.

Sonny chuckled. "Not quite, Darce. But it's a place to crash for the night. The Golden Nugget Motel."

He rattled off the address, and Claire sighed after hanging up.

She held up her phone and said, "Fifteen-minute walk," dragging her suitcase along the sidewalk. "Beats waiting for another rideshare."

Fifteen minutes in the gleaming heart of Vegas might have meant strolling past designer stores and celebrity-chef restaurants. But here, on the outskirts, it felt like miles. The glittering lights of the Strip dwindled behind us, replaced by flickering neon signs and questionable people congregating in front of convenience stores. An unsettling mix of desperation and decay hung in the air.

"What kind of hotel did he book us in?" I muttered, eyeing a shadowy alley with suspicion. "One with an hourly rate?"

Claire offered a nervous laugh. "It can't be that bad," she insisted, then pointed across the street. "See? A Motel 6!"

But relief evaporated as we approached The Golden Nugget. The hotel looked like it hadn't seen a paint job since Elvis left the building. The lobby reeked of cigarettes and cheap liquor, like the carpet itself was hungover. We buzzed the bell repeatedly before a weary-looking clerk with suspicious white powder around his nose finally shuffled out from the back.

Claire whispered from the side of her mouth, "Uh, Darci? Is that…?"

I looked at her out of the corner of my eye, grimacing as I nodded. "Uh, yeah, it looks like it."

"Oh god."

I sighed. "Yeah."

His vacant stare did little to ease our apprehension. He stood utterly still, not saying a word for a full two minutes before he seemed to snap out of it. Things went downhill from there.

After we finally got the keys, with no elevator in sight, we lugged our suitcases up the creaky stairs to the third floor. Sure, there were two beds, but that was the only positive. The carpet had large burn marks and was mostly threadbare, and the wallpaper was practically peeling down the wall. This place was a total dump, and someone's clothes were still in the closet.

Remembering the Dateline specials we had seen as kids, we each took a bed and stripped off everything but the sheets. Pulling back the bedspread on my bed, I recoiled in disgust. Unmistakable bloodstains marred the mattress, visible through the sheets. A strange, vaguely sweet smell hung in the air, but we were too afraid to lift the mattress and investigate the source.

The pièce de résistance? A roach the size of a miniature dachshund scuttled across the bathroom floor, disappearing into a dark corner. To top it all off, the toilet wouldn't flush.

Claire shoved the desk chair under the flimsy doorknob with a defeated sigh. It was a feeble attempt at security, but it would have to do. We stripped down to our essentials, climbed into the (hopefully) unoccupied bed together, and vowed to escape this roach motel at dawn.

I was wide awake. Laying there, my mind immediately went to Alex. Since our disastrous concert date last week, I'd been actively avoiding him.

That night had started so well. The show had been good, and he was fun and sweet, not the jerk I'd built him up to be in my head. Then, boom! Wine guy incident. Total jerk mode activated. What. The. Hell? How could someone be so sweet one minute and a complete asshat the next? It was like Jekyll and Hyde.

Sometimes, I wondered if all my bad dates was because I was just unlovable. Or maybe I really was cursed as some bad luck charm. Dr. Jerkface and this trip were just more evidence that if something involving me could go wrong, it would.

Claire's tossing and turning pulled me out of my thoughts. She wasn't sleeping either.

"Can't sleep?" I asked her.

"Not really. It's just..." She sighed. "This is not turning out how I expected."

"I know. I'm sorry, babe."

"I was picturing a fun girls' trip in a nice hotel, like a sleepover with champagne. But this... this is like the beginning of some B horror movie."

"It's not that bad." I countered.

Even in the dark, I could feel Claire looking at me with her eyebrow arched to the sky. It made me laugh.

"Look, we've got two more days. It can't get any worse than this."

Claire deadpanned, "Famous last words."

"Seriously. Let's get some sleep. We'll go back to The Pinnacle and eat breakfast at that huge buffet, and we'll steal extra toiletries off the maid's cart when we get our room."

She let out a sigh. "I just wanted to make this work."

"Come on, girlie." I laid my head on her shoulder. "We're going to plan the hell out of your wedding so that you can marry the most amazing man in the world." I held up my thumb and forefinger, pinching them together, "And we'll have a little fun tomorrow night. Trust me."

She yawned. "Okay."

She rolled over, and I heard her breathing even out as she fell asleep. I was still wide awake, so I pulled out my phone and opened my trusty Kindle app for some smut reading to help me fall asleep.

For a moment, Alex came back to mind, that afternoon we spent together after the pool. I pressed my legs together, trying to concentrate on my book. But my mind continued to wander, and I felt my toes curl just thinking about the possessive way he felt wrapped around me last week at the show. I still couldn't figure out why he'd snapped and been such a dick at the end of the night. *Was it really me?*

I snuggled into the covers, returning to my book. It was better to live in book-boyfriend land and read about meet-cutes than wish for something that would never happen for me. I was just destined to be single. Maybe love just wasn't for me. I fell asleep wondering if I could be content just living vicariously through romance books and my friends.

When my alarm went off at 6:30 in the morning, we flew out of bed, threw on our clothes from the night before, and high-tailed it out of that room in minutes.

A man approached us as we walked the long hallway

back to the stairs. He was tall and gaunt with a mop of curly, bright green hair. He looked like he hadn't seen the sun in years. As he neared us, he had a big smile on his face. Claire and I looked at each other wide-eyed as he got close enough for us to read his shirt. In giant block letters, it said, "Show Me Your Butthole."

He stopped right before us, bowed, and said, "Top of the morning to ya, ladies."

We both gave him a polite smile, nodding and quickly speed-walked away, dragging our suitcases behind us.

"What. The. Hell?" Claire hissed.

I looked behind us warily, just to be sure, but he had already disappeared into a room. Then and there, I vowed to try my hardest to make this weekend a good one for Claire. "What? That's officially my new standard for Prince Charming."

We tossed the hotel keys on the desk and left. As soon as we were outside, we both cracked up laughing.

I sucked in air as I said, "Now that... was a literal... Twilight Zone."

"It really was..." She trailed off as she shook her head. Walking back to The Pinnacle, she glanced at me, "I don't know if I should tell Sonny about all this until we get home. Knowing him, he'd be on a plane in an instant."

I nodded, knowing how protective Edison was of Claire. "My lips are sealed."

I ran my fingers over my mouth as if sealing a zipper.

Claire gave me a genuine smile. "Mine, too."

Fifteen minutes later, we skidded to a halt at the front desk of The Pinnacle, suitcases clattering to the floor. Claire explained our frustrating night in a voice laced with exhaustion. The clerk, Alfonso, scanned our reservation with a wrinkled brow. Then, a smile broke out on his face.

"Aha! Here it is," he boomed, a warm welcome in his voice. "Let me make things right for you, lovely ladies."

Claire's shoulders visibly relaxed. A wave of relief washed over me as Alfonso started tapping on his computer. Before I knew it, he was announcing a room upgrade.

"Presidential suite, coming right up!" he declared with a flourish. "And don't you worry about a thing. Leave your luggage here. It'll be magically whisked away to your room."

Like a magician, he flicked his hand and revealed two cards for the restaurant down the hall for a complimentary breakfast buffet. Making our way there, the weight of the past night lifted. This, I thought, was going to be a whole different experience, starting with a free breakfast of all we could eat.

The restaurant entrance whooshed open, revealing a scene that stopped me dead in my tracks. Floor-to-ceiling fish tanks lined the walls, a mesmerizing kaleidoscope of colorful fish and coral swaying gently in the current. Hold on... were those sharks in the back tank?

"Whoa," I breathed, mesmerized.

A hostess materialized, a welcoming smile on her face. She gestured towards a seemingly endless expanse of food stations as she escorted us to our table.

"Omelets, waffles, pancakes, crepes, breakfast meats, pastries...oh, and did I mention the fresh fruit bar?"

I was starving. Last night's dinner was basically airplane pretzels, and my mouth watered. This had to be the motherlode of breakfast buffets.

When she left, I turned to Claire and declared, "Let's eat!"

We made our way over, and each grabbed a plate. Claire, a mischievous glint in her eyes, headed one way, and I found myself at the crepe station, soon walking away with three crepes generously stuffed with bananas and hazelnut spread. Across the way, I spotted Claire with a plate overflowing with a picture-perfect omelet, golden potatoes, and a side of berries. But that wasn't all. She was already balancing a second plate piled high with fluffy pancakes and a mountain of sausage links. I made a beeline for the bacon as Claire passed me by.

I laughed, piling crispy bacon on my plate. "Are you planning to feed the whole hotel?"

"Shut up, Darce," she countered playfully. "After last night, a girl deserves to indulge." She winked.

I spied the drink station across the room as we returned to the table and set my plate down.

"Want a drink?" I asked Claire.

"Yeah, coffee and orange juice would be great."

I immediately ran off. I turned my head, surprised at the number of people coming into the restaurant. Not looking where I was going, I collided with a wall.

CHAPTER TWELVE

Alex

The silence from Darci's apartment was deafening. It had been over a week since the concert fiasco, and there hadn't been a peep or even a glimpse of her on her balcony. I kept telling myself it was a relief. Dealing with her brand of chaos was exhausting. Her laugh, the way she was so damn enthusiastic about... everything. The way her eyes crinkled when she got flustered. Annoying. All of it.

Except... who was I fucking kidding? I couldn't forget her soft lips against mine, the warmth of her body pressed close, fitting perfectly against me, and the intoxicating scent of her shampoo. I missed seeing her out in her rocking chair and how she practically skipped to her car across the parking lot every morning. I just missed her energy, the chaos she brought, being near her. *I missed... her.*

That scene when we crashed into the wine guy still played over in my mind like a broken record every time I went to bed. I stared at the ceiling for God knows how long, and I hated myself for that stupid joke. Those shattered wine bottles on the sidewalk had morphed into shards of regret that cut me every day.

Slamming my fist against the windowsill angrily, I knew I had to get out of there before I did something stupid. Some food would clear my head. A greasy burrito from that little taco stand down the street sounded perfect. I grabbed my keys with a muttered curse and practically flew out the door.

The drive was a blur, my mind still reeling with regret and the tangled mess of emotions it had unearthed. By the time I got back to my apartment, a greasy bag of deliciousness in my hand, the ache in my chest had morphed into something unfamiliar – a dull throb of... hope. Would she give me another chance?

There was no sign of her coming or going. Unlike every other weekend, Darci's SUV hadn't moved in days. My mind raced. Was it that Vegas trip with her friend? The one she had mentioned offhandedly? I couldn't remember when she said she was going, and I let out a frustrated sigh, wishing I'd shown more interest.

A tiny voice in my head whispered, "Was she with someone else?" Had he picked her up tonight? Because, really, who, in their right mind, wouldn't be out on a Friday night?

These feelings I was having were absurd—we weren't even a thing. If I was honest with myself, I was nothing but a pain in her ass. Yet, a flicker of something ignited in my gut. I wasn't sure what it was. Maybe jealousy? It was a ridiculous notion, but with every passing second, the flicker grew into a steady green flame fueled by my stupid imagination—her out with someone else, someone like Beanie Hat from the home improvement store, who was probably touching and kissing her.

I trudged up the stairs back to my place, and the very thought of someone else with her sent a fresh wave of jealousy crashing over me, leaving me feeling exposed and vulnerable. As I sank onto the couch, the uneaten burrito forgotten on the side table, a terrifying thought echoed in my mind—*what if I'd already missed my chance?*

What the fuck was I doing? Why did I care anyway? Losing Jenna, losing our baby – that was a wound that never fully healed—the crushing weight of grief and suffocating loneliness. I refused to put myself through anything like that ever again.

As if on cue, my phone buzzed, snapping me out of my self-pitying spiral. A text from Javi flashed on the screen: **"Meet the guys at Jack's to watch the game?"**

It was a welcome distraction. A night with the guys was exactly what I needed to drown out the unwelcome emotions swirling inside me.

With a sigh, I grabbed my phone and typed a quick response: **"On my way."**

Hitting send, I slid the phone into my back pocket, grabbed the burrito, and put it in the fridge. Maybe a few beers with Javi would clear my head and help me sort through this tangled mess of emotions.

As I drove to Jack's, the image of Darci dancing and smiling at the concert continued to flicker in my mind. She was probably on her trip to Vegas. How long was their trip? Did she even tell me where they were staying? Shame pricked at me. I hadn't even bothered to ask.

As soon as I walked into the bar, the familiar buzz of chatter and laughter hit me, instantly putting me at ease. Javi was already perched at a long booth, a beer cradled in his hand. A group of guys from the hospital filled the rest of the space, their faces animated as they debated the upcoming game.

Sliding into the booth next to Javi, I forced a smile. "Hey. What'd I miss?"

The conversation immediately shifted, welcoming me into the fold. As the beers flowed and the game unfolded on the big screen, I laughed and genuinely enjoyed the company. For a while, at least, the nagging thoughts about Darci were pushed to the back of my mind.

But then, during a lull in the game, Javi turned and studied me for a moment, nudging me with his elbow. "So, what happened with Darci? You two seemed to be hitting it off the other night."

My stomach lurched as I hesitated, debating whether to lay bare the thoughts gnawing at me. Finally, I sighed, realizing I couldn't hide it anymore.

"Well," I started, wincing at the memory, "it wasn't exactly smooth sailing. Things had gone great at the show, but..." I trailed off, not sure I wanted to admit my total failure.

His eyes held a mixture of curiosity and readiness, waiting for me. "No judgment, man," he said.

I took in a breath and let it out slowly. "I was walking her back to her car. I was certain we were going home together when this guy barrels out of a store and runs into us hard. He had a few bottles of wine in his hands and dropped them. They shattered everywhere—on Darci's dress, on me, and the poor guy looked like he was about to cry."

I took a swig of beer, the bitterness on my tongue mirroring the memory. "Trying to lighten the mood, I made a bad joke." I shook my head, remembering how

Darci's face went from flushed to furious. "I... I humiliated her, and the guy just stared at me, jaw clenched. I felt like a complete douche."

Javi's eyebrows shot up to his hairline as I took another drink.

"Darci helped the guy, and without a word to me, she stormed off to her car and peeled out of the parking lot, leaving me standing there looking like a fool. She hasn't talked to me since."

Javi took a long sip of his beer, his brow wrinkled in thought. "Honestly, the answer's pretty simple. Apologize. Own up to your stupid joke. Tell her you were trying to lighten the mood, but it backfired."

"I know," I groaned, running a hand through my hair. "I...," I stammered, a knot of guilt tightening in my gut. "As soon as I said it, I tried to. But..." I trailed off, sighing, "This whole thing with Darci... it just brings up all this other stuff with my wife, you know?"

Javi leaned back, furrowing his brow, before he abruptly stood up, lifting his hand toward the bar. "Let's go grab another drink at the bar."

As I followed him, relief washed over me. I didn't want to expose the depths of my despair to the other guys.

Javi ordered bourbon for both of us. I took a drink, feeling the burn as I fought tears. It was hard, but letting this all out felt like a relief. Javi turned towards me, allowing me to continue at my own pace.

His voice was gentle, and he asked, "You meant guilt about your wife?"

Taking a deep breath, I was at a crossroads. I'd only scratched the surface when I told him about losing Jenna. But keeping it bottled up inside wasn't working.

Maybe Javi was right. I knew I needed to talk to Darci. But the guilt was a heavy weight on my chest, threatening to choke me.

"Yeah," I started, my voice low. "There's a reason I haven't... tried real hard with Darci or anyone really."

A beat of silence stretched between us, and then Javi nodded slowly. "Alright, Dixon. Spill it."

So I did. I told him everything about the pregnancy and the baby. The words tumbled out without thought, a torrent of grief and guilt I'd held inside for so long.

"I hate myself because I couldn't... save them..." My voice was hoarse as I trailed off, tears burning the back of my eyes.

Javi didn't say anything for a moment, just sat there absorbing my story. Finally, he spoke, his voice quiet. "Man, Alex," he said, "I'm... I'm so sorry. I had no idea... no idea it was that bad."

Someone finally knew. Javi wasn't judging me, just... understanding.

"There were times when I just didn't see the point of living anymore. I thought about ending things so I could be with them. The pain was unbearable."

He paused, then continued, "Have you... talked to someone about all this."

"Yeah, but I don't know how much it's really helped."

Javier's hand went to my shoulder and squeezed, a tangible anchor in my storm of emotions. "It's helping. You're still here."

I lifted one shoulder as I nodded slowly. "Yeah..."

"I can't imagine what that's like. But I'm glad you're here talking to me now. And if it ever gets unbearable, you can always talk to me, Alex, day or night. You have my number."

"I appreciate that, man."

I drained my glass before letting out a heavy sigh.

"Look, don't let your guilt stop you from living. I told you before, but it's true. Jenna… she wouldn't want you to be miserable. If anything, she'd want you to be happy again. And you know what? When I saw you and Darci at that concert the other night, you were happier than I've ever seen you. You were laughing and dancing. There's something there. A spark. Don't let it go to waste."

I nodded, a flicker of warmth igniting somewhere deep inside.

"Yeah, I want to," I admitted, the words tasting heavy on my tongue. "I just…" My voice trailed off, the familiar guilt constricting my chest. "How do I let her go? How do I move on without feeling like I'm… betraying Jenna?"

Javi didn't answer immediately, taking a thoughtful sip of his beer. "Look," he finally started, his voice gentle, "loving someone doesn't stop when they die. It changes, sure, but it doesn't disappear. Jenna will always hold a special place in your heart, a part of your story. But that doesn't mean you can't write new chapters. "

He leaned forward, his eyes holding mine. "Jenna would want you to laugh again, to love again."

"But it feels too soon."

Javi shook his head. "Maybe it's too soon, but maybe it's not. There's no right or wrong answer. Grief is a journey, not a destination. Live a life Jenna would be proud of."

His words resonated with me. Jenna came to my mind, her beautiful smile, but not as a specter of loss, but as a woman who had loved me fiercely, who would want me to find joy again. Maybe I could figure out a way to carry Jenna's memory while exploring this connection I felt with Darci, if she ever wanted anything to do with me again.

"You know," I confessed, a hint of a smile tugging at the corner of my lips, "Maybe..."

I trailed off, leaving it unfinished, a promise whispered into the air. There was still uncertainty, still a knot of guilt to untangle. For the first time since I'd lost them, I finally felt something, a glimmer of a future where I could see myself embracing the possibility of something new with someone else.

Javier regarded me thoughtfully, his words carrying wisdom and encouragement. "Have you told Darci about your wife and daughter?"

I leaned back in my seat, shaking my head. It had never occurred to me to bring them... together. I'd always felt that my life before and now needed to be separate.

He continued, "She's always struck me as genuinely kind and understanding."

I sighed, the weight of Javier's suggestion sinking in. "I just don't want to burden her with my baggage. How would she react?"

Javier leaned back, shrugging as he spoke. "Look, you won't know until you try. Darci deserves to know what's in your heart, especially if you're considering a relationship with her. Maybe invite her to go with you to visit their graves or something? It might be a way to share that part of your life with her and see how she handles it."

His suggestion struck a chord. The idea of sharing that sacred space with Darci made me pause. Would she even want to do that?

"You think she'd be okay with it?"

"From what I've seen, she's got a kind heart. She's a children's librarian, man—she lives in the land of glitter glue and storytime. Didn't you say she helped that guy when y'all ran into him and his wine bottles went everywhere? That says a lot. If she cares about you—and I think she does—she's not going to run when things get real. She'll want to know your past. She'll want to be there for you."

Javier's eyes lifted to the television on the back wall as I mulled over his advice. The thought of opening up to Darci about the most horrifying time in my life was daunting. But maybe he was onto something. Maybe if she came along, it would help me open up to her and not feel like I was betraying Jenna.

We walked back to the group, sliding into the booth. I stayed until the end of the game, but I didn't pay much attention. I just kept mulling over what Javier had said.

Grief was a long, winding road, but for the first time, I saw a glimmer of hope, a possibility of something new blooming in the wreckage of my past. Driving home, the city lights blurred past my windows, and I felt lighter, like a weight had finally been lifted.

CHAPTER THIRTEEN

Darci

A deep voice apologized, "Are you okay? I'm so sorry."

I felt large hands on my hips, steadying me. My hand shot out instinctively. Glancing up, I was face to chest with… a lumberjack. His hair was in a man bun. His dark brown beard was nearly to his chest. But it was his eyes that got me. They were startlingly aqua blue with flecks of bright green. They were fresh and playful, dancing with amusement as he looked down at me. I'm not sure I've ever seen eyes that color before, and I just wanted to look at them.

He chuckled, and after realizing I was staring, I quickly looked down.

"Everything okay?" He asked, dipping his head towards me.

Clad in snug dark jeans and a red flannel shirt that stretched over his broad chest, my eyes instinctively traveled downward, noting a conspicuous bulge. His sleeves were rolled up to his elbows, revealing a few ink lines on his right arm. I wondered if he had other tattoos. I wanted to see more.

A smile involuntarily graced my lips, and my cheeks flushed with warmth as I returned to those eyes.

I snapped out of it and said, "Better now. Your chest might be my new favorite place to land."

He chuckled, the deep rumble vibrating through his chest and into my hand, resting there unconsciously.

"Do you mind if I get my shirt back?" He smiled, a single dimple revealing itself on his left cheek.

A jolt of electricity shot through me as I realized I had his shirt in a death grip.

"Sorry."

I let go as if he'd burned me, my face flushing deeper with embarrassment.

He slowly let go of my hips, almost like he didn't want to, and I found myself yearning for those hands on my body again.

He nodded towards the drink station and said, "I'm just going to get a drink. Where were you headed?"

Maintaining my grin, I reply, "Oh, um, me too."

His smile widened, and he motioned toward the drinks, suggesting, "We can go together."

Like a complete fool, I nodded in agreement, "Sure."

What was wrong with me? I never got this flustered. As we walked, I found his presence... strangely comforting.

He glanced at the array of beverages and asked, "What are you in the mood for?"

Still wearing my goofy grin, I replied, "Surprise me."

He broke out in a smile, his dimple making an appearance again, and began filling a mug, occasionally stealing a glance my way. After a moment, he handed me the drink with a playful smirk.

"Hope this qualifies as a surprise," he teased.

"Thank you."

I took the cup and immediately took a sip, watching him over the mug. He seemed nervous as he watched me take a long drink. The hot chocolate immediately hit my mouth, and the flavor was warm, rich, and inviting. I closed my eyes and let out a moan.

What the fuck was wrong with me? Then it hit me. Oh god, I think I was in my very own meet-cute.

He nodded knowingly. "It's the cinnamon. I don't know what it does, but it takes hot cocoa to another level." He filled another mug, still stealing glances at me, and said, "I'm Blue. What's your name?"

I smiled, replying, "Darci."

"Darci." He repeated my name thoughtfully as if testing it out. Then, with a friendly grin, he inclined his head and asked, "Join me for breakfast?"

I really, really wanted to. I hesitated before replying, "I can't. I'm with a friend. It's a girls' weekend, you know?" He nodded with understanding, and feeling bold, I blurted out, "Do you want to join us?"

His eyes searched mine briefly before a slow smile formed. "I'm not imposing?"

"Oh, Claire won't mind." I smiled reassuringly. Excitement bubbling, I pointed to the table where she sat. "See that redhead? Meet me there. I just need to grab some coffee and juice for her."

"Meet you there."

I filled another mug with coffee and carried both mugs in one hand and two glasses of freshly squeezed orange juice in the other.

When I got to the table, Claire had already finished her omelet.

"Wow, you were hungry."

She nodded, closing her eyes. "It was amazing."

She picked up the coffee and placed it in front of her, swirling in sugar and cream.

"I sort of met someone at the drinks." I grimaced, raising my eyebrows. "I... invited him to eat with us."

Her brow wrinkled. "You what?"

"Be quiet! He's coming." I hissed, looking over my shoulder as Blue approached us with a mug and a plate. When I caught his eye, he gave me a big grin. I smiled and waved him over.

"I hope I'm not intruding..." He said as he came around Claire, setting his food down and sitting next to me. Claire turned to him, a warm smile on her face.

She waved her hand dismissively. "Oh, not at all. You're more than welcome."

After getting situated, he held out a hand to Claire. "I'm Blue."

She gave him a warm smile and shook his hand over the table. "Claire."

He picked up his fork and stabbed his eggs, looking between us with an amused look. "So, girls' weekend, huh?"

I took a long sip of my cinnamon hot chocolate as Claire set down her fork and nodded.

"I'm getting married here in Vegas in a few weeks." She tilted her head towards me, "Darci's my maid of honor. Doing some wedding planning this weekend."

"Don't stay too busy and miss all the fun."

I laughed, glancing at Claire as I held my finger and thumb up, "We plan to have fun this weekend. But what about you? Visiting from somewhere?"

He had a thoughtful look as he popped open a yogurt

cup and mixed some of the fruit on his plate into it. "I just moved here."

Claire raised her eyebrows. "Really?"

He glanced at me before giving Claire a big smile. "Yep. New job. I work in... um, contemporary entertainment services."

What the hell is contemporary entertainment services?

She nodded slowly. "Oh... ok."

Her eyes darted to me like she was trying to communicate something. Maybe she knew what that meant.

I couldn't help myself as I touched the back of his hand, "So, is Blue short for something?"

His cheeks pinked.

"Oh, you know, it's just a nickname," He took a bite, "for my eyes."

"You do have beautiful eyes." I grinned at him, watching him stir his yogurt. *Did I say that out loud?*

I looked down at my plate, quickly taking a bite of bacon, and my cheeks flushed. I looked over at Blue's plate. He had an egg white omelet full of veggies and a pile of fruit. Mine? Not one single healthy thing on it. It was piled high with bacon, a waffle topped with whipped cream, and crepes filled with chocolate. I ate like a toddler.

We talked with Blue about Claire's plans for the day, and he seemed genuinely interested. He even recommended another wedding venue on the outskirts of town.

As I cut a bite of a crepe, I asked him what he meant by contemporary entertainment services.

He chuckled, "I'm basically a salesman," he said before shoveling at least a third of his omelet into his mouth.

"Okay…" *Well, that was vague as hell.* "So… where did you move from?"

He looked over at me. "I'm from Oregon. Portland, to be exact. And you're from… let me guess… Texas?"

I breathed out a laugh. "Is it that obvious?"

"Maybe," He winked. "I have friends in the Dallas area that I visit quite often. I recognized the accent."

"Oh." I felt a flush rising up and looked away.

He finished his omelet and looked at his watch. "Well, ladies, it was nice sharing a meal with you. I need to go get ready for work." He tossed his napkin on his plate with the silverware.

I gave him a hopeful smile. "Oh… well, have a good day. Maybe we'll see you around."

He winked as he stood up, and his gaze locked with mine. "Maybe you will."

Claire gave him a little wave. "It was nice to meet you, Blue."

I chuckled as he gave us one more wave before walking away.

Claire hissed at me, "Darci!"

I looked up at her wide-eyed. "Yes?"

She raised her eyebrows. "Go after him!"

I had a bite of crepe midway to my mouth. "What?"

"Go after him. He's totally your type."

"But it's your weekend. Are you sure?" I slowly stood up.

She laughed, "Don't worry about me. I saw the way he looked at you."

"Yeah?"

"Uh yeah," She gave me a big grin. "Go find him."

I took in a breath, nodding my head. "Okay…"

Just as I walked away to find him, I ran smack into that hard chest again. I heard a low chuckle as his hands stabilized me, and I relished the heat pouring into my body from his touch. My hands instinctively went to his chest, and I swear I felt him shiver.

"If we keep running into each other like this, somebody might get hurt."

My eyes widened as I looked up. His eyebrows were raised, but he looked... nervous. He let go of me, letting his hands drop to his sides. I wanted them back on me.

"I don't want to interfere with your girls' weekend, but... I'd kick myself if I didn't ask. Can I take you to dinner?"

I couldn't help the smile lighting up my face. I turned to look at Claire, who was nodding enthusiastically. She mouthed "Dinner" at me.

"Sure. I'd love to."

"Is a late dinner okay?"

I shrugged. "Yeah, that's fine."

"Cool. Can I get your number?" I nodded as he pulled out his phone and handed it to me.

I typed my number in, sending myself a text before handing him his phone back. I felt my phone buzz in my pocket.

"Meet me in the lobby around 10?"

I smiled and was oddly speechless as I said, "Can't wait."

Walking backward, he bumped into a chair behind him. He smiled sheepishly, his cheeks turning red as he shrugged. I grinned wider.

"I'll text you when I get a break."

He turned and quickly walked towards the entrance.

I walked back to the table to see Claire beaming at me.

"Well, that's exciting."

I sank down in my chair, feeling like I was on cloud nine, a big grin still on my face. I turned to look at the front of the restaurant and saw his red flannel quickly making his way across the lobby.

I grabbed my hot chocolate and took another long drink, looking at Claire over my mug.

"You sure it's okay if I meet him for dinner tonight?"

She waved her hand, shaking her head. "Totally fine." She wiggled her eyebrows. "Besides, I'll spend some quality FaceTime with Sonny while you're gone."

I rolled my eyes, grinning, wishing I had what they did.

"So... what are you going to wear?"

"Well, I did bring that little green dress. Just in case..."

She gave me a wry smile. "Really?"

"What's wrong with that one?"

Claire gave me a flat look. "Nothing... " she said, looking at her watch, "but why don't we go shopping and see what we find?"

Hours later, we were back from cake testing, and I was wrapped in one of the plush hotel robes, like a warm hug. Freshly showered and shaved, I slathered on lotion, a mindless ritual that grounded my nerves. Claire and I had spent all day on a whirlwind tour of wedding venues, bakeries, and everything in between.

Blue's off-the-cuff recommendation for this one particular wedding venue turned out to be a goldmine. Hidden Springs Ranch, a private farm outside the city. It boasted a stunning array of backdrops—an olive tree forest, a sprawling fruit orchard, a desert wilderness, and rustic woodland. Claire's heart melted at the sight of the orchard. There was just something about it that reminded her of Fireflower Farms, her special place with Edison. As for me, the highlight of the ranch was the on-site animal sanctuary, especially the ridiculously cute donkey that seemed to crave endless cuddles.

They offered an all-inclusive package, taking the stress out of wedding planning. Rooms, photographers, musicians, decorations—they had it all covered. Best of all, Claire's dream date was still available. It was like the wedding gods were smiling down on us.

The only thing left to check off the list was the cake. Tomorrow, just one more cake tasting, and then it was time to plan the hell out of Claire's bachelorette party. This wedding was going to be unforgettable, and I couldn't wait to be a part of it.

Walking out of the bathroom, the hum of the television from Claire's absent-minded channel surfing filled the room. It was a calming backdrop as I prepared for my date with Blue. I glanced at her, sprawled across the bed like a starfish, her eyes glued to the screen.

"You gonna watch every channel before the night's over?" I teased, tossing my last pair of earrings onto the other bed. I winced at the mess I was making, excitement and terror churning in my stomach. Tonight felt like something... big.

"You going to behave?" Claire's voice cut through my thoughts. "I don't want to have to bail you out of a Vegas jail cell."

I rolled my eyes. "Relax, Mom, it's just dinner. I'm not planning on a bender."

She raised an eyebrow, "Says the girl who once downed four tequila shots in one go."

I laughed. "That was a different time, a different me."

"That was three months ago." She said, shaking her head with a smirk.

We broke out in laughter.

I went back into the bathroom to finish my hair and then moved on to makeup. A smoky eye seemed like the perfect balance of sexiness and understatement.

"Whoa," Claire whistled, her eyes widening as I turned to face her. "You look amazing!"

I grinned, pleased with the result. "Thanks."

She hopped out of bed and grabbed the tight, strapless dress we'd picked out earlier that day. It was deep emerald green, almost black. I slipped out of my robe and into the dress. It hugged what little curves I had in all the right places. The deep green made my eyes look brighter, like gold.

Zipping me up, Claire stepped back, her eyes wide with approval. "Damn girl," she breathed, "you're gonna blow his mind."

Sliding my feet into a pair of black strappy stilettos, I twirled in front of the mirror, feeling a surge of confidence.

"You really do look amazing. Blue is going to melt."

I spun around again, giving her a twirl. "Think so?"

She nodded vigorously, her hand flying to her mouth. "Like a million bucks."

A blush crept up my cheeks as I grabbed my clutch and slipped my phone and hotel key inside with my lipstick.

"Don't do anything I wouldn't do," Claire called after me as I opened the door.

I turned to see her smirking and grinned, "I see what you're doing."

She laughed.

I gave her a playful wink. "Don't wait up."

With one last glance at my reflection in the mirror, I stepped out into the hallway, the promise of the evening stretching out before me like a trail of stardust—shimmering, magical, and filled with possibilities. I had a feeling this was going to be a night to remember.

CHAPTER FOURTEEN

Alex

Saturday morning, I had work, and the ER was a maelstrom of noise, with the steady beep of heart monitors competing with the frantic voices of patients and families. A woman was wheeled in, her face pale and drawn, clutching her abdomen. A silent prayer escaped my lips as I assessed the situation.

A miscarriage, the triage nurse had said. She was 12 weeks along.

Just being in the ER seemed to amplify the tragedy unfolding before me. I moved with practiced efficiency, giving her hushed condolences, knowing this feeling all too well. As I assisted in stabilizing her, my thoughts drifted to Darci. Did she want children?

Why was I even thinking this? She practically hated me. But I couldn't stop.

I wondered what she was doing and who she was doing it with. Most likely, she was sound asleep. She probably spent last night laughing with Claire somewhere in a neon-lit casino, or some guy had picked her up in a bar, the city's lights a vibrant backdrop to their carefree night. Maybe she spent the night in his hotel room. Who knows? Maybe she ended up getting married by Elvis to that guy in some drunken idiocy.

Why was I thinking about any of this? This was crazy.

A pang of jealousy shot through me. Her energy and zest for life were infectious, and I knew someone else would be drawn to her before long. The memory of the concert popped into my head for the millionth time. Her laughter as we danced, so bright and unfiltered, was something I couldn't get out of my brain. I shook my head, refocusing on the tasks at hand as I sat at a computer and discharged another patient.

A three-year-old toddler was brought in a while later, his chin covered in blood, eyes wide and glassy with fear, cheeks still damp from tears. My heart twisted with empathy—such a little guy.

"Hey, big guy, what happened here?" I asked, my voice soft, aiming for distraction as I examined his face.

His mother, a woman on the verge of tears herself, managed a choked, "He fell off the couch face-first into a wooden toy."

"We're going to fix you right up with a cool scar to show your friends, little man," I promised, my voice light. "And when we're done, you can have an ice pop for being so brave. How does that sound?"

His lower lip trembled, but a spark of curiosity ignited in his eyes.

"Can I get a purple one?" he whispered.

A surge of warmth spread through me. "Sure, buddy, we can get a purple one."

The nurse and his mother helped me lay him snugly

into the papoose. As I cleaned and numbed around the wound, his tiny body tensed, but soon he relaxed as I began to suture it closed.

I worked quickly and efficiently, but Savannah Jean popped into my head. She would have been around his age, full of boundless energy and a contagious laugh. What would she have looked like at three or four? If she were anything like me at that age, we would have probably had a trip to the ER for some stitches by now.

Sadness hit me in the gut, a sharp reminder of the life that could have been. But it was fleeting, a ripple in the calm waters of my emotions. I focused back on the boy, plastering on a reassuring smile as I finished suturing his chin. A small part of me wished for the simplicity of his injury, a physical wound with a clear solution.

When I returned with the ice pop, his eyes lit up like a Christmas tree. It was a small victory, a tiny spark of joy in what was often the bleak landscape of the ER. As he sucked on the purple ice, I couldn't help but feel a sense of peace.

As the day wore on, a relentless tide of pain and suffering swept through. Yet, I couldn't stop thinking about Darci, like a beacon of light in my darkness. I wondered if she was thinking of me, if even a sliver of her carefree spirit could reach me.

Finally, we had a lull in patients by mid-afternoon, and exhaustion weighed on me. I slipped off to the doctor's lounge just to close my eyes for a few minutes, but the memory of Darci's laughter lingered, a bittersweet echo of everything I'd messed up.

When I got off work, I stopped to pick up some dinner —hot wings drenched in buffalo sauce, and the best queso fries on this side of town. Driving back home, I thought about what Javi said last night and wanted to fix this thing with Darci.

It was time to face the music, or in this case, Darci's front door. I had no idea if she was home, but after I had eaten dinner, I found myself walking across the parking lot and standing on her doorstep, my heart pounding against my ribs. I knocked, but no lights flickered through the blinds. The heavy silence was suffocating.

I knocked again, my knuckles echoing in the quiet walkway. No answer. A third knock, louder this time, followed by another moment of waiting.

Ready to give up, I turned to leave when a voice called out, "One sec!"

I groaned internally. Mrs. Whitlock, one of our elderly neighbors, appeared at the top of the stairs, her tiny dog, Arlo, straining at the leash, eager to investigate the intruder on his turf.

Groaning internally, I braced myself as she approached. I knew what was coming next— another plea to examine a suspicious mole or a worrisome rash. Not only did she corner me in the parking lot for medical consultations, but she was the biggest gossip in this place. Somehow, she knew everyone's business.

"Hello, Mrs. Whitlock," I greeted, offering a polite smile.

"Oh, Dr. Alex, please... call me Patsy," she replied, a twinkle in her eye. "Arlo, say hello to Dr. Alex."

Arlo, true to form, preferred sniffing my shoes. I prayed he wasn't going to lift his leg and pee on me.

"How are you, Patsy?" I asked.

"Me? Oh, I'm fine, dear. But, you know, Darci's not home. She's on that 'girls' trip' to Las Vegas with Claire," she said, air quotes punctuating the phrase.

Relief washed over me, followed by a surge of

disappointment. So it was the Vegas trip.

"Is she?" My voice cracked on the last word.

Mrs. Whitlock patted my arm with a knowing smile. "Didn't you already know that?"

I scratched the back of my neck, feeling a blush creeping up my cheeks. "Well, we haven't spoken in a while," I mumbled.

"And why is that, young man?" she asked, her eyes twinkling with mischief.

I opened my mouth to respond, but no words came out. The truth felt too raw, too vulnerable. I searched for the right words.

"Just a misunderstanding," I said, trying to sound nonchalant.

"Well, young man," she began, her voice maternal, "you need to be honest with her. Tell her how you feel. Women appreciate honesty."

I nodded. Maybe Mrs. Whitlock was right. It was time to stop playing it safe and just be honest.

"Thanks, uh, Patsy. I think you're right."

She patted my arm again, a knowing smile on her face. "Remember, sometimes the biggest risks lead to the greatest rewards."

With that, she turned and headed back towards her apartment, Arlo trotting happily beside her. I watched her go, and a weird sense of determination filled me after that little pep talk. But I noticed something flapping in the breeze under Darci's rocking chair.

As I crouched down, I realized it was a book. Had she meant to leave it out here? There was a strong chance of rain in the next day or so, and I would hate for it to get ruined. I picked it up as I turned to leave.

Crossing the parking lot back to my place, I flipped

open the book as my mind raced between the moment I finally had the nerve to ask her out, the fun we'd had together at the concert, and that goddamn stupid joke that came out of my mouth.

I needed to give her a heartfelt apology, something more meaningful than root beer floats in the middle of the night. Darci didn't seem like the type to be impressed with just a bouquet of roses.

But something in the book caught my attention, and I stopped in my tracks. I tilted my head to get a better look. There were so many handwritten notes in the margins. I'd never seen a book covered in so many notes. But… wait… Were the words moving?

When I looked again, they weren't moving, but I could have sworn some of them shifted in the corner of the margin, like someone or… something was actively writing them. Huh… Maybe I'd finally lost my mind.

There was one that just seemed brighter than all the other notes. I read it about half a dozen times after returning to my apartment. For a moment, I thought maybe something was trying to send me a message. It said:

> **Not a wish but a heart's desire,**
> **Something new to ignite the fire,**
> **A piece of soul to make amends,**
> **A work of art, as you begin.**

This was crazy. Why was I even trying to figure this out?

But after a minute of mulling it over, an idea hit me. I was good with my hands. I knew my way around a DIY project. The smell of sawdust and the hum of power tools was as familiar to me as the back of my hand. My dad was a master craftsman, always tinkering in the garage. I spent hours watching him as a kid, absorbing his every move. He'd patiently guide my hands, teaching me the nuances of every tool, from the gentle caress of a sander to the power of a saw.

Maybe my apology could be that chandelier she mentioned at the store. That afternoon we'd spent in the pool, Darci told me she had a habit of starting projects, only to abandon them halfway through. She'd confessed, her cheeks turning red, to having a closet full of unfinished masterpieces—half-painted canvases, abandoned knitting projects, and countless other half-hearted attempts at home decor.

Where did I even start? I tried to think back to what she had in her cart that day at the store. There were globe lights and… plastic chain. But there were other things, and I couldn't remember much else.

I pulled out my phone, and a quick online search revealed a staggering number of DIY chandelier options —chains, crystal, and even a wine bottle version. My head spun. Which one had she mentioned?

Finally, after getting sucked down a DIY rabbit hole on YouTube for longer than I was willing to admit, I was pretty confident I knew which chandelier she wanted. It was a $50,000 chandelier that some YouTuber purchased. I shook my head. Ridiculous.

I made a list of the supplies and headed to the store. Once there, I grabbed a cart, and my first stop was the chain. I hit the help button and waited for someone to cut what I needed. After standing around for fifteen minutes and hitting the button several more times, a bearded guy in an orange apron and a beanie appeared.

He smiled and gave me a quick, upward nod. "Hey,

man, what can I do for you?"

"Hi...," I looked at his name tag, "Jason. I need some chain cut."

"Sure thing." Walking towards the chain, he asked, "Which one?"

Shit. What color did Darci have in her cart?

"What color plastic chains do you have?"

"Blue, red, and... orange."

I was pretty confident she'd had blue in her cart. "Can I get 12 feet of blue?"

"Sure thing."

He began to unroll and measure. When he was done, he wrapped it up and attached a ticket.

"Here you go."

"Thanks, man." I took it from him. "Hey, do you know where these globe lights are?" I showed him my list.

He looked at the list, a thoughtful expression on his face. "Yeah, follow me."

As we walked, he looked over his shoulder and said, "You're the second person who's wanted these same supplies."

I chuckled, "Let me guess." I held my hand up and said, "Was she about this tall? Short brown hair? Full of energy?"

He laughed, "Yeah. I gave her my number, but she never texted." He raised an eyebrow. "You know her?"

I ignored his last question as a flash of bitter jealousy shot through me.

"Really?" I managed, my tone flat as my hand balled into a fist.

He chuckled, a self-assured smirk playing on his lips. "Yeah, she was something else. I was hoping she'd text or call, but it's been crickets." A smirk played on his lips.

I didn't know why, but a surge of satisfaction washed over me. I managed to suppress a triumphant grin as we walked down another aisle. He stopped abruptly, picking up a box.

"Here's the globe lights."

"Thanks, man. But, that's unfortunate, sorry she didn't call," I replied, my tone dripping with false sympathy.

He shrugged with a casual indifference, masking whatever emotions he might be feeling. "Oh well, there are plenty more fish in the sea."

I couldn't resist a final jab before I left. "Maybe you just weren't the catch of the day," I countered, a smirk playing on my lips.

CHAPTER FIFTEEN

Darci

My phone pinged with a text from Blue as I headed down the hallway toward the elevator. He was already waiting downstairs. When the elevator slid open on the main floor, I spotted him standing by the lobby doors—and my breath caught.

His dark hair fell loose around the shoulders of a perfectly tailored navy suit jacket, completely transforming him from the rugged, lumberjack vibe he'd had this morning. He looked... sharper. Debonair, even. A surge of adrenaline shot through me as our eyes met, and I swallowed hard, unable to look away. Who knew beneath this morning's rough charm was an even sexier version?

His smirk widened into a grin as I approached, but then his gaze shifted—darkening with something heavier as he took in my outfit. His smile turned slow and deliberate, laced with surprise and unmistakable desire.

"Darci... wow, you look... beautiful."

I couldn't help but blush. "Aw, this old thing?" I teased, giving him a playful spin.

He held out his arm, his eyes sparkling with anticipation. "Shall we?"

I slipped my hand into the crook of his elbow, feeling a flutter of excitement. "We shall," I replied, my voice coming out breathless.

Blue hailed a cab, and we were instantly whisked away.

"I made a reservation at Sucre," he explained, a charming little French restaurant tucked away in a quiet corner of the city. His eyes gleamed with anticipation. He said, "They're known for their desserts, but the food I've heard is amazing."

My stomach growled in agreement. "I'm starving," I admitted, my honesty catching me off guard.

He leaned closer and chuckled against my ear, a low rumble that sent a shiver down my spine. "Good, because I'm pretty hungry, too."

The restaurant was a little bistro, tucked away on a cobblestone street like we were in an old part of Paris and not a modern commercial monstrosity like Vegas. The soft glow of candlelight cast a romantic ambiance, and the clinking of silverware provided a soothing soundtrack. I couldn't help but steal glances at Blue while he hung his jacket on his chair before sitting down.

After we ordered, our conversation flowed like we were picking up where we'd left off in some other life. No awkward pauses, no polite small talk—just an easy rhythm, full of laughter and subtle glances that lingered a beat too long. My nerves melted into something warm and humming.

There was something about Blue that felt... inevitable. Maybe it was the wine, wrapping everything in a soft, golden blur. Or maybe it was how he listened—really listened—like every word I said mattered. I couldn't stop smiling. Or watching the way his eyes lit up when he talked, the way he leaned in just slightly when I laughed.

Our food arrived before I realized how close we'd drifted toward each other. I had the sole meunière, flaky and rich and gone too quickly. Blue's ratatouille was beautifully plated and somehow still cozy, and when he offered me a bite, I didn't hesitate. His fork brushed my lips, and my eyes met his as I tasted it—earthy, warm, undeniably perfect.

And then—Alex. His name fluttered into my mind like an errant spark. Uninvited. Unwelcome. I blinked and swallowed. I didn't want to think about him, not here, not now—not when Blue was looking at me like I was something rare.

I exhaled slowly and took a sip of water, hoping the moment hadn't shown on my face. Blue was saying something about how the city always felt too loud until you left it, and I nodded, even though my thoughts were buzzing with frustration. Why now? Why him?

The dessert menu arrived, thank God. I chose the crème brûlée, Blue went for the chocolate soufflé, and we both asked for coffee—though it seemed just like an excuse to linger a little longer.

As the waiter walked away, Blue glanced at me over the rim of his water glass. "So," he said, voice a little lower now, "how's it possible I've only known you a few hours, and I already don't want the night to end?"

I froze—not in fear, but in that breathless, damn-it-he-means-it kind of way.

When the waiter placed the dishes between us, the sugar on my crème brûlée was still warm, the top perfectly caramelized. Blue's soufflé had that just-baked wobble, rich and dark and utterly indecent.

He dipped his spoon in slowly, watching me from under his lashes. "Want a taste?"

I nodded, and he held the spoon out to me—not across the table like a normal person, but up close, like he wanted to feed me. I leaned in, lips brushing the edge of the spoon, and let the bite melt on my tongue. It was warm. Sinful. A little messy.

He watched me lick a smear of chocolate from my bottom lip like it was the most interesting thing he'd seen all night.

"Good?" he asked, voice just a little rougher.

"Too good," I murmured, the words thicker than I meant them to be.

Then I returned the favor, cracking the top of my crème brûlée with the back of my spoon and offering him a bite. He didn't hesitate. And when his tongue flicked over the curve of the spoon, slow and deliberate, I knew exactly what he was doing.

Our eyes met across the table, and something in the air shifted—warm, charged, and undeniably mutual.

Blue started talking again—something about small-town boredom and big-city dreams—but I wasn't really listening. I was watching the way his fingers curled around his coffee mug, the way he smiled at me like I was the best part of his day.

It was past midnight when we got a cab ride back to the Strip.

Blue turned to me, his eyes holding a question. "Want to grab a drink?"

My heart did a little flip. More time with him? Absolutely.

"Sure," I replied as I tried to contain my grin.

We stepped out of the cab, and Blue intertwined our fingers. The walk back into the hotel was short but felt like an eternity. My stomach was a whirlwind of butterflies and possibility. I didn't want the night to end.

He led me into Cassiopeia, one of the hotel bars, a dimly lit oasis of plush seating and soft jazz. It was late, but the bar was still busy for a Saturday night. We found a secluded table, a perfect spot to escape the main hubbub of the casino. I slid into the booth, and Blue came in right next to me. He seemed more relaxed, his eyes holding a mischievous glint. I wanted to run my hands through his hair.

"Let's do a shot or two," he suggested.

I nodded, my mouth suddenly dry. "Okay," I managed, my voice sounding too high.

When the server arrived, Blue ordered a round of shots and then opted for a whiskey and coke while I went for the most outrageously pink cocktail on the menu. Waiting for our drinks, something like hope pulsed through me. I hadn't had a date go this well in… forever. This was happening. It was real. And it was turning out to be… perfect.

Thirty minutes later, we were both giggling. I felt a buzz as we ordered another round, the liquid courage flowing freely. Soon, the world took on a rosy hue, the edges blurring into a comfortable… something. I was beginning to feel dangerously relaxed, a warmth spreading through me, chasing away my inhibitions.

Blue slipped off his suit jacket, the casual gesture

sending a jolt through me. As he rolled up his sleeves, revealing forearms corded with muscle and floral tattoos, I couldn't help but admire the transformation. His arm snaked around me.

"Want to walk through the casino?" he suggested, his low voice inviting.

The idea was tempting. "Why not?" I replied as he stood and pulled me by the hand.

I reached over and grabbed my pink drink to bring along. The casino floor was a dazzling spectacle of lights and noise, almost like a living, breathing entity. Blue was headed towards the tables, but a thumping bass line emanated from somewhere and drew me towards it.

"Is there a dance club here?" I asked.

He scanned the room, his eyes narrowing in concentration. "Uh, yeah... the Moonlit Lounge," he replied with a hint of excitement.

"Can we check it out?" I asked, my curiosity piqued.

A security guy opened the door, and we were standing in front of another set of doors painted black. As we entered, it was a sensory overload. Lights overhead pulsed to the beat. Bodies moved in a hypnotic rhythm to the music. I barely had time to set my drink on a counter before Blue grabbed my hand, pulling me onto the dance floor. His movements were fluid, confident, and surprisingly sexy. Women on the dance floor were openly eye fucking him, which sent a wave of green straight to my core. But he only had eyes for me. I let go, allowing myself to be carried away by the music, my body moving instinctively.

The world melted away as we danced into a blur of lights and sound and laughter laced with liquor.

Somewhere between the second round of shots and a neon cocktail I couldn't pronounce, I forgot how to care about anything but the thrum of the bass and the man against me. My pulse spiked when he growled low in my ear and pulled me tight against him, his hand gripping my waist when another guy wandered a little too close.

It was all a perfect storm of euphoria. I couldn't stop moving. Couldn't stop chasing the next delicious shiver as Blue held me like I was his and everyone else could go to hell.

Another shot. Another song. I laughed too loud, danced too hard, and kissed the rim of a drink he handed me like it might tell me a secret.

Time slipped sideways. The world was all rhythm and heat, all sweat and skin and bass that vibrated straight through my bones. And Blue—God, Blue—was right there with me, his hands on my hips, his mouth brushing my ear, his breath hot against my neck.

As the night wore on, my inhibitions were gone—burned away in a haze of flashing lights and too much alcohol. Somewhere deep in the back of my mind, I knew Claire was going to kill me, and I was absolutely going to regret this in the morning. But then he grinned at me like I was the only thing he could see. And in that moment, I didn't care.

The music pulsed through my veins, mirroring the pounding of my heart. Blue's body moved with mine like we'd done this a hundred times before. Our rhythm was a promise and a dare, and the look in his eyes—those wild, storm-colored eyes nearly swallowed in black—told me exactly where this night was headed.

And I was all in.

A slow burn had been building in my core all night, but dancing with him ignited a wildfire. The heat between us intensified. His hand slid from my waist to the nape of my neck, his fingers threading through my hair. His head dipped as his lips brushed against mine, a soft touch that quickly deepened. My breath caught in my throat as his tongue swept into my mouth, a taste of whiskey and smoke and something undeniably intoxicating. I responded instinctively, my hands finding purchase in the fabric of his shirt, pulling myself into him.

Desire consumed me and demanded to be unleashed. I pulled him closer, my body molding and grinding against his. His hard length pressed into my belly. His arms tightened around me, lifting me off the ground. I was weightless, suspended in a world of pure sensation for a brief, exhilarating moment. His lips trailed down my jawline, sending shivers down my spine.

"Let's get out of here," he whispered against my ear, his voice quiet and urgent.

And my only answer was, "Please."

I woke with a start, my head pounding. The room was unfamiliar, bathed in neon lights from outside. My body was sore, a dull ache that pulsed through my joints. As my consciousness returned, a wave of nausea came over me. I was... naked, tangled in sheets.

Panic surged as I tried to piece together the events that led me here. What happened? Where was I? What time was it?

Glancing over, Blue was beside me, still asleep, completely bare—his chest rising and falling rhythmically. Bits and pieces of the night came back to me—the nightclub, the drinks, that kiss... Watching him, he looked peaceful, almost angelic, with his hair splayed across the pillow, but there was a growing dread in my chest. Claire was probably convinced I was dead somewhere. I had to get out of there.

I swung my legs over the side of the bed, my feet finding the cool, plush carpet. I scanned the room, searching for my clothes. On the floor by the door was my purse, half the contents spilling out. I picked it up, shoving everything back inside, my fingers trembling slightly. Inside, my phone glowed with a string of unread messages, mainly from Claire, demanding updates on the night's events.

I stood up, whirling around to find my clothes had been dropped haphazardly on the way to the bed. I grabbed my underwear and quickly put them on. As I reached for my dress, my hand felt heavy. I held it up to see the glint of a gold band on my left ring finger. My heart skipped a beat. Using my phone to see, I pulled my hand closer, examining the ring in disbelief as it caught the light.

What had I done?

I turned back to Blue, his face still relaxed in sleep. His left hand was resting on his belly, and on his ring finger was a matching band that gleamed as I shined my light. My stomach churned.

I breathed out, "Please tell me we didn't... I didn't..."

I looked down at my hand again. *Fuck.*

The thought was so absurd, yet the evidence... How? How did I do something so stupid? *Fuck, fuck, fuck.*

I needed to get out of there, fast. I slipped on my dress. My movements were jerky as my mind raced. I grabbed my shoes, my heart pounding in my ears. One last glance at Blue, and then I was out the door, leaving behind a bunch of unanswered questions and a growing dread.

Bleary-eyed, I found the elevator and made it to our room, tiptoeing inside. Claire was asleep. I crawled into my bed, wrapped the covers around me, and sank into oblivion.

She sat up immediately and whisper yelled, "Darci!"

The next thing I knew, Claire was poking me in the back. It was like a physical manifestation of a mental ice pick digging into my brain. I groaned, the morning light seeping through the curtains forcing me to pull the covers tightly over my head like a fortress.

"Don't talk to me," my voice muffled.

"Darci!" Her voice cut through my attempt at denial. I peeled back the pillow, squinting. She held up the marriage license, her expression full of shock.

"What the hell is this?" Her voice rang out in a mix of disbelief and accusation.

I snatched the document from her hand, unfolding it as I scanned the unfamiliar words. I had desperately hoped it was just a bad dream.

"Melvin Hardick?" I questioned, my voice quiet.

A surge of nausea hit me, and I swallowed to counteract it. How had such a great date turned into... this catastrophic, life-altering mistake? God, I really was cursed.

"Are you serious?" Claire's voice was incredulous. "You married some guy named Melvin Hardick?"

"I don't know," I groaned, burying my face in my hands. "I think... it's Blue."

Claire's eyes widened, grabbing my hand to see the ring on my finger. "You married Blue?"

The situation finally sunk in, and I grimaced. A fuzzy flashback of a chapel and a wedding veil came to my mind. Blue stood next to me with a shit-eating grin, and... wait... *Did Michael Jackson marry us?*

"Fuck, I think so."

"Well, this is going to be a fun day," she muttered, a grim determination creeping into her voice. "We need to figure out how to undo this mess."

I turned and just *stared* at Claire. Said nothing. Just locked eyes with her like maybe if I looked hard enough, she'd erase the whole night for me.

Her eyes widened, and she stepped back like she'd seen a ghost.
"You do want to undo this, right?"

I swallowed and nodded, too overwhelmed to protest. "Yeah, whatever. Just let me sleep a little longer. My head feels like it's going to explode."

She rolled her eyes, but her expression had an underlying current of concern. "I can imagine. You're covered in... glitter and smell like a tequila factory exploded in your mouth."

Glitter? Why was I covered in... glitter? That was my last thought before I fell back asleep.

I'm not sure how much time passed, but my head was still killing me when sunlight streamed through the blinds, casting a harsh glare on my face. I groaned, pulling the covers over my head, but the noise of the television seeped through—a constant irritant. With a sigh, I rolled onto my back, shielding my eyes and squinting against the brightness.

The room was a mess. My clothes and shoes were strewn across the floor like confetti. And there, on my left hand, a stark reminder of last night's debauchery.

Nausea churned in my stomach as I tried to piece together what happened.

What had I done?

CHAPTER SIXTEEN

Alex

Once I was home, I tossed my shopping bags on the floor and collapsed onto the couch, a takeout box with a giant quesadilla in one hand and the phone in the other. I finished dinner and dove into the project. After an hour of scrolling through countless DIY tutorials, I found a video matching Darci's supplies. It was a monstrosity of plastic chains and questionable aesthetics. *Why would anyone want this hanging in their home?* But I was determined to recreate it.

The trouble with having an apartment was the lack of a garage, so the living room transformed into my makeshift workshop, with tools and materials spread across the floor. I wrestled with the plastic chains and hardware for hours. By the time I finished, it was late. I was glad I didn't have to be at the hospital tomorrow.

The floor was littered with bits of plastic chains and my tools. My fingers ached, but a sense of accomplishment warmed my chest. I had done it. I took pride in myself as I held up the hideous chandelier against my ceiling. It looked nearly identical to the real thing.

Darci's face and her smile went through my mind. What would her reaction be? Would she love it? Or hate it? I could only hope it would smooth things over so we could start fresh and make a go at whatever this attraction was between us. I was tired of fighting it.

I found an empty box in my closet and placed the chandelier inside. When I was done, I grabbed a piece of paper and wrote a note that told Darci how sorry I was for my stupid joke. I tucked it under the chandelier in the box:

"I know I messed up, and there's really no excuse. This is a small token of my apology and how much I regret hurting you. You deserve the world. Let me make things right."

I told myself I'd just drop it by her door tomorrow. No big deal. But the truth was, I just needed a reason to run into her. Maybe she'd be home.

Just as I was about to wrap it all up, my phone rang, the sharp sound jarring me out of my moment of triumph. It was the hospital. My heart sank as I answered.

"Dr. Dixon, we need you to come in," the voice on the other end said, the urgency clear. "We've got a multiple-casualty situation with an eighteen-wheeler rollover. It's all hands on deck tonight."

"On my way."

Adrenaline kicked in as I raced to gather my medical bag and throw on a clean pair of scrubs. *The chandelier.* I had no idea when I might be home. Looking around the room, I grabbed my bag and the chandelier box and dashed out the door. I placed it carefully on her doorstep, my fingers pulling the string bow tighter. I had no idea if she'd even like it, but it was all I could do now.

When I got to the ER, the air smelled of antiseptic and... fear. Patients flooded in, a wave of humanity caught in another undertow of disaster. I put Darci out of my mind and moved through the chaos with a focused efficiency, my mind creating a calm island in the storm.

A little girl, her face pale and drawn, was sitting on a stretcher with her mother. Her arm was at an impossible angle, and blood seeped through the hastily wrapped gauze on her forehead. Her mother smiled tenderly at her daughter, fear and shock still written on her face, but a black eye was already beginning to form.

I bent down beside the girl, my voice was soft and reassuring. "Hey there, sweetheart, we're going to take care of you," I said, focusing on her injured arm. As I began to assess the damage, I couldn't help but feel a surge of protectiveness.

"What... what about my mama? Her eye..."

I offered a warm smile, "Don't worry. We'll take care of your mama, too. We'll make sure she's okay."

I ordered a portable X-ray of the little girl's arm and a CT scan of her head, trying to reassure the terrified mother with gentle words as I caught her eye. "We're going to take good care of her," I promised, my voice steady.

A frantic call from Javi in the hallway interrupted my focus. "Alex, we need you in here!" His voice echoed through the ER, and his tone was urgent.

I rushed to Trauma Room 1, my heart pounding. A woman lay on the gurney, her face a mask of pain. She looked oddly familiar. Long black hair, matted with blood, and a dark purple Victorian dress, torn and tattered, told a grim story. Javi was already at work, his stethoscope pressed against her chest as the nurse cut the dress off her body.

I quickly assessed the situation, scanning her for signs of serious injury. Bruises were already beginning to form, dark patches against her pale skin along her belly.

"Her car," he swallowed, his eyes darting at me, "was under the semi," Javi said grimly, focusing on the patient.

She let out a soft groan before the machines went haywire—a sharp breath, followed by a strangled cry, and then silence. A cold dread settled in my stomach when the monitors flatlined.

Javi yelled, his voice a sharp command in the chaos. "Code Blue!"

The crash cart was wheeled into position, an island in a sea of panic. I joined the rhythm of compressions, my hands a blur of motion. With each pump, a silent plea for life escaped my lips. Adrenaline coursed through my veins, pushing away the fatigue.

Javi yelled, "Clear!"

I pulled back as he shocked her chest with the paddles. Her body convulsed. We waited mere seconds, but after what felt like an eternity, her heart fluttered back to life. A wave of relief washed over the entire room, but it was short-lived. The ultrasound tech confirmed internal bleeding from a ruptured spleen. She was taken up to surgery in a matter of minutes.

I stepped back, my legs trembling with exhaustion. My stomach surged as the adrenaline crash hit hard. I needed a moment, just a quick break, before I swept back into the chaos. Grabbing a bottle of water from the vending machine, I retreated to the lounge, dropping into a seat on the old leather couch. The cool liquid was a welcome relief, the plastic bottle cold against my sweaty palms.

Returning to the ER, I was met with a new wave of casualties. A middle-aged man, his face pale and drawn, was hobbling towards the reception desk, blood soaking through his left pant leg. Without hesitation, I grabbed a nearby wheelchair and rushed to his aid.

"Sir, let me help you," I offered. He nodded, his face a mask of pain. As I guided him into the wheelchair, I assessed the damage. His leg was shredded above the knee, and the blood loss was significant. His face was pale, and he was clearly in shock.

"What happened?" I asked gently.

"My knee was jammed under the dashboard when the car behind me hit, sending my car straight into the one in front."

How did he get here? Did he drive? My brows knitted together, "Did you drive here?"

"Uh… I don't… Wait. I… climbed out of my car, and another car came up and a man offered to bring me to the hospital. I think that's… how I got here."

"We need to get you in a room," I said, pushing the wheelchair toward the triage area. A seasoned nurse, Amber, was already on the move, gathering supplies. Together, we stabilized him, my hands moving with practiced efficiency before handing him off to orthopedics.

There wasn't a hint of the sunrise when I finally pulled into the quiet parking lot at home at almost five in the morning. I was past exhaustion. The ER had felt like a war zone, a relentless onslaught of trauma. The woman with the ruptured spleen had coded during surgery again and didn't make it, and I heard rumors the truck driver from the 18-wheeler had died of his injuries at another hospital.

One of the cops told me they suspected he fell asleep. He had left a trail of destruction in his wake, and I suspected the freeway would be closed for several more hours while they completed the investigation. We'd triaged nearly thirty patients, a blur of blood, bruises, and broken bones, and most likely shattered lives.

My gaze drifted towards Darci's apartment as I walked to mine. Was she home? The soft glow of a lamp spilled onto the balcony from her window. I had a clear view of her porch, and the package I'd left earlier was gone. A nervous hope flowed through my veins. *Had she opened it? Read my note?*

The pull to see her was strong, but the rational part of my brain won out. At this hour, there was no way I was knocking on her door. She was probably jet-lagged and needed rest, and so did I. With a heavy sigh, I trudged up the stairs to my apartment, the promise of sleep feeling far away.

CHAPTER SEVENTEEN

Darci

When I finally managed to pry my eyes open, Claire was perched on the edge of the bed, arms crossed, a deep crease between her brows as she stared down at me.

"Oh good, you're finally awake," she said, her voice dripping with sarcasm.

I groaned again, burying my face in the pillow. "Please, god. Too loud," I mumbled into the soft fabric.

She chuckled, a sound that grated on my already frayed nerves. "Well… I called Sonny."

My head whipped up like a horror movie reveal, hair sticking up in tragic directions. I squinted at her through one bloodshot eye, the betrayal sharp and immediate. "You *what?*"

"I didn't know what to do!" she said, hands in the air, all innocent panic. "You scared the hell out of me!"

"Great. Just great." I mumbled as I pressed my face back down into the pillow.

Her voice took on a serious tone. "There's a way to undo this. You can get an annulment. They should never have married you when you were drunk."

I felt a wave of relief, but it was tempered by disbelief. *We could just undo this?*

"An annulment?" I echoed, my voice muffled.

"Yep," Claire said with a long, suffering sigh. "I already printed the papers in the business center downstairs. But we'll need a notary and... Melvin Hardick to sign them."

"Blue?" I blinked, my brain tripping over itself as it tried to reboot. "I came from his room, but..." I rubbed my temples. "God, I don't remember the floor. Or the room number. Or how many shots I had before I apparently made the decision to become someone's wife."

She exhaled through her nose like a woman summoning supernatural patience. "Cool. Great. Love this for us."

I groaned, "Claire... I'm sorry."

"I know." She walked back over to her bed and nodded, her expression grim. "Let's just hope we can find him." She wrinkled her nose. "But first, you need to go take a shower."

After my shower, we headed downstairs.

They should recruit hotel desk clerks as spies because the one downstairs wouldn't tell us anything, even if you're the wife holding a marriage license. No matter how much I begged, they refused to reveal my husband's room number. And I tried everything— politeness, snacks, even bribery when I slipped a $20 bill in her hand, but she wouldn't budge. I had a feeling this would be more challenging than I thought.

We walked around the lobby and peeked into the buffet, but he wasn't there. My next dumb idea was to try every hotel floor, jogging my memory. I thought I might remember his room number, but no such luck. Finally, we walked out of the hotel and down the strip, hoping something might trigger my memory.

Another flashback hit me as we walked back inside The Pinnacle—the neon signs. They sparked a memory of dancing.

"Claire! I think I remember something." I grabbed her shoulder.

"Yeah?" She said dryly.

I nodded vigorously. "We walked around the casino, and then I think we found the dance club."

We made a beeline through the slot machines, weaving past blinking lights and the hum of jackpots. On the far wall, I spotted the sign for the Moonlit Lounge. We rushed toward the heavy doors—but they were locked.

Fuck.

A small sign mocked us from the glass: Opens at 9 PM. We'd be on a plane by then.

I pressed my forehead against the cool metal, frustration sinking into my bones. Claire stood beside me, arms crossed, clearly trying not to explode. I reached out, gently squeezing her wrist.

"Hey… I'm sorry. I don't know what I was thinking."

She let out a slow sigh. "Darci…"

I braced myself, waiting for the well-earned lecture. But it didn't come.

Instead, she said softly, "It's… okay. We all do stupid things."

I let out a breath and managed a half-laugh. "Yeah, but I feel like you'd never do something this stupid."

Her brows lifted. "I don't know… if Sonny and I had

that blind date here in Vegas, I could totally see us doing the same damn thing."

I blinked, surprised. "Seriously?"

She smiled, looking into the distance like she was rewinding a memory. "I don't think I ever told you how intense it was. By the second day, he was calling me my love, and I had to physically bite my tongue to keep from saying I love you to him."

I stared at her. "Wow. And here I thought I was the impulsive one."

Claire snorted. "You still win, don't worry."

I bumped her shoulder with mine. "Good. I'd hate to lose my title. But... for what it's worth, I get it now. Kind of."

She looked at me, softer now. "Yeah."

I pushed off the door, and we both heard my stomach growl.

She put her arm around my shoulders. "We'll find him and fix this." She squeezed me as she said, "Come on, let's go get something to eat."

We headed back to the buffet and filled plates with everything. I glanced at the dining room, and it was pretty packed. Did people ever leave this place, or did they just camp out?

At the drink station, Claire asked, "It looks pretty full. Want to eat outside? There's a patio out that door, and the weather's nice." She jutted her chin behind me.

I turned to look, and there were a few people outside. But there were plenty of shaded tables.

"Sure. I'll meet you out there."

Carefully balancing her plate in one hand and two drinks in the other, she made a beeline for the door.

A few minutes later, I found her at a table in a shady

spot. I had piled my plate high with greasy food—the best way to get over a hangover. I plucked a fried chicken leg off my plate and began to chow down.

"I think there's supposed to be some kind of entertainment out here?"

I wrinkled my brow as I looked around. "How do you know?"

"Look over there," she pointed towards a small stage.

I turned to see a sound guy putting microphones on the stage.

"Hmm. I wonder what the show is?"

"I don't know, but I'm going back for seconds."

Claire set her plate to the side and went back inside. Even though it was lunchtime, I had found bacon on the buffet, and I popped a piece in my mouth, groaning at the crunch and flavor. Claire returned with a salad in one hand and two steaks on a plate.

My eyes widened, "Damn, girl, where'd you find steak?"

She smiled. "They just set it out." She slid one onto my plate. "I got you one, too."

"You're such a good friend."

Her cheeks turned red, and she reached out, squeezing my arm.

I sliced into the steak, which was cooked perfectly medium, just like I liked it. It was so tender that it cut like butter. As I ate, I tried to remember what had happened last night, but I just kept coming up blank. There was a flash here and there, but nothing I could make sense of.

What the hell was I going to do if I couldn't find Blue? Just... go home a married woman? I'd joked about being cursed before, but this sealed it. This wasn't quirky or funny anymore—this was a nightmare.

Claire nudged me hard, her elbow digging into my ribs, and hissed a whisper, "Darci! Look!"

I rubbed my arm, trying to ignore the sharp pain. "What?" I mumbled, looking around.

She pointed towards the stage, her finger vibrating with excitement. My gaze followed hers, and my jaw dropped. Standing on the stage, bathed in the spotlight, was a man who could only be described as a budget-friendly Michael Jackson.

"A low-budget Michael Jackson impersonator?" I questioned, my voice filled with disbelief.

"No," Claire replied, her voice low, "behind him."

The sun was so bright I had to squint, trying to focus through the blurriness of my vision. And there they were, two men dressed in sequined jackets, their movements stiff and awkward. My heart skipped a beat as recognition clicked. One of them was… *Blue?* I stood up abruptly, my chair scraping against the floor.

"Oh my god! It's him!" I exclaimed, my voice echoing through the crowded patio.

My cheeks heated when I noticed several people turning to stare at me. I sat back down and leaned in close to Claire.

"What do I do?" I whispered to Claire, my mind racing.

She pulled the annulment contract out of her tote bag.

"Get him to agree to sign these," she said, pressing the papers into my hand.

I nodded, my heart pounding in my chest. I made my way to the side of the stage, weaving through the tables. Blue's head snapped in my direction. He waved, a sheepish grin spreading across his face. I waved back, feeling a surge of adrenaline.

As the impersonator wrapped up his performance, Blue appeared beside me, slightly breathless, a sheen of sweat glistening on his forehead.

"Hey," I called, raising my voice just enough to be heard over the music. "So... is this what you meant by 'contemporary entertainment services?'"

He looked at me, surprised, then chuckled, shrugging one shoulder. "Something like that."

A brief silence settled between us, slightly awkward, before he spoke up. "You disappeared on me this morning."

"Sorry," I said, a bit sheepishly. "I had an early... thing. Didn't want to wake you." I took a deep breath, "I'm guessing you noticed the gold band on your finger when you woke up this morning?"

With a sheepish smile and a hand ruffling his hair, he shrugged and said, "Yeah."

I cocked an eyebrow, "Do you remember getting married?"

With that same smile, he shook his head.

I chuckled, shaking my head, "Me neither." I let out a breath as I held up the papers. "I found out we can easily get this annulled, but we need to sign these papers before a notary. Are you done with the show?"

He grimaced, "No, we have one more set, but I can meet you as soon as we're done."

Tension melted from my shoulders, "Thank god. I thought I would have to fly home a married woman."

He laughed. "We're back on in a few minutes, so I need to go, but... wait for me?"

I nodded. "See Claire over there?" I pointed to her. "We'll wait for you over there."

He headed backstage, and I returned to our table, Claire's expectant gaze burning into me.

"So… he agreed?"

"Yeah, but we have to wait until their next set is over."

She tilted her head with a half smile, "At least we found him."

I chuckled dryly, "You're telling me. I was not looking forward to going home as Mrs. Melvin Hardick."

We both giggled.

About 45 minutes later, Blue sat down at our table.

"Thanks for staying."

I gave him a tight smile, "Didn't really have a choice."

"So… what do I need to do?"

I pushed the papers and a pen over to him. "Fill out your information, and while you do that, we'll call a mobile notary."

He nodded and got to work filling out the forms while Claire went upstairs to pack our stuff. Twenty minutes later, Blue and I headed to the lobby to meet Peggy Martin, a mobile notary I had found. Another fifteen minutes later, Peggy had left, and all our paperwork was filled out, ready to be filed.

We walked towards the elevators, "I appreciate you getting this done for us." He chuckled.

"Truthfully, it was Claire. That girl gets shit done. I was worthless today. My hangover nearly killed me."

"Well, I appreciate it all the same."

I nodded and looked up into those ice-blue eyes, "Um, Blue?"

"Yeah?"

"From what I can remember, I had a lovely time with you. I'm sorry we ended up… married." I said sheepishly, my cheeks heating.

He grinned. "You don't need to apologize. I'm just as much to blame as you are. And I had a great time, too."

He patted my shoulder and seemed to feel as awkward as I did.

I rolled my eyes, "Oh, come here," I said with a grin, opening my arms.

We hugged each other and said goodbye.

My eyes lifted to his, and I said, "If you're ever in Dallas..."

He nodded as he pulled back. His Adam's apple bobbed before he smiled and said, "Will do."

He stepped into the elevator, our eyes locking just before the doors sealed him away. There was longing in his face—unspoken, undeniable, and aimed straight at me.

For a split second, I wished things could be different. That we'd met somewhere else, closer to home, somehow without all the chaos and tequila and glitter-fueled bad decisions. But that wasn't real life.

This was a mess—a stupid, colossal mistake. And I was ready to put it behind me. A moment later, Claire popped out of another elevator with both our bags and led me to the hotel's business center. Jesus, this had come down to the wire.

"Ready to get unmarried?" She asked with a grin.

"God, yes."

I sat down at the computer and uploaded our documents and filed everything. And that, my friends, was the stupidest $272 I'd ever spent.

What had I been thinking? But that was essentially the problem. I hadn't been thinking a damn thing. I was always up to being the good-time girl, but how did I let it go this far? Usually I held my liquor pretty damn good. And, honestly, I don't know what I would have done if Claire hadn't been here.

Just as I closed the website, she said, "The car's here. You ready?"

I sighed and nodded as I tucked the documents in my tote bag, grabbing my suitcase and tote as we headed out of the lobby. I'd never wanted to leave a place so badly—or been so desperate to just get home.

CHAPTER EIGHTEEN

Alex

Sunlight streamed through the blinds, hitting me right in the face. A quick glance at my phone confirmed my suspicions: It was late afternoon, and I had slept like the dead, which was rare. Most days, I could only sleep four to five hours.

I stretched, my bones cracking. My body ached in protest from the familiar soreness after an intense shift. That or at the ripe old age of 31, I was getting old. I swung my legs over the side of the bed, the cool hardwood sending a chill through me.

I pulled on a pair of sweatpants. The best thing for my body aches was a short and sweet workout to shake off the remnants of last night's shift. I reached for the pull-up bar on my closet door. After three rounds, I was dripping with sweat, but my body felt better, more alive. A glass of milk and a much-needed coffee were next on the agenda.

Filling the coffeemaker, I glanced out the window and did a double take. *She was home.* My stomach flipped when I saw Darci was back on her balcony, sitting cross-legged, holding a book in one hand and a mug in the other as she absentmindedly rocked in what had to be her favorite chair. The morning sun cast a golden glow around her, making her look almost ethereal and fairy-like. She was a beautiful sight to behold.

Huge sunglasses swallowed her face. I couldn't see much of her expression, but she smiled softly while reading. She had a bright red scarf tied around her hair, loose strands poking out. A pang of longing hit me as I watched her, and something pulled at me to go to her. I guzzled my milk but skipped the coffee. Instead, I jumped in the shower and was dressed in less than ten minutes. Before walking out the door, I grabbed the book I'd found under her chair the other day.

My heart pounded as I approached her building. She was wrapped in a big, oversized black cardigan, which had to be a favorite since she wore it nearly every time I saw her reading. She was lost in her book and didn't notice me coming up. The smile on her face was comforting yet a little nerve-wracking, too. Had she seen my gift?

I cleared my throat, the sound echoing. "Darci?" My voice was hesitant.

She looked around until she spotted me down the stairs, raising her sunglasses to perch precariously on her head. A mix of surprise and wariness flickered in her eyes.

"Uh, hi," she replied, hesitating.

I took a deep breath, the weight of the past few weeks heavy on my shoulders. "Can I... come up?"

"Uh... I suppose," her voice was gentle.

I climbed the stairs, and my heart felt like it might

beat right out of my chest. The sun warmed my face on the landing, and I took a few tentative steps closer.

"Here," I thrust out the book. "I wanted to apologize the other day, but you weren't home. I saw this under your chair, and I didn't want it to get ruined from rain or something…" I mumbled, my voice dropping off the last few words. God, I sounded desperate.

She took it from me, raising her eyebrows before wrinkling them when she looked at the book. "Thanks…" She still hadn't really looked at me.

Her sweet, sugary scent filled my senses, and I shoved my hands in my pocket before I inadvertently reached for her.

"So, how was it? Your trip?" My voice was rough with nerves.

Our gazes locked.

"My trip? It was… fine." She nodded.

She closed her book with a decisive snap, narrowing her eyes. She took a long sip from her mug, keeping her eyes on me.

"Alex, what are you wanting? Why are you here? Need to humiliate me again? More fodder for your stupid jokes?"

Her words hit like ice water, sharp and stinging. I hadn't meant to hurt her—just thought a little humor might help the situation. But now a knot of shame twisted in my gut, leaving a bitter taste. I shifted uncomfortably, feeling more out of place by the second.

"Darci, I'm sorry." I took a breath. "I'm really… sorry." I murmured, my voice sounding strange, even to me. "Did you find a package on your doorstep?"

She arched a brow. "That was you?" Her tone stayed flat, but there was a faint lift at the end, just enough to reveal a hint of curiosity.

I rubbed the back of my neck, a small, sheepish smile slipping through. "Yeah... guilty as charged." Her expression didn't change, so I quickly added, "I just thought... well, maybe it'd make you smile."

She turned in her chair to face me fully. "Wait... you made that knock-off Flux chandelier I found on my doorstep last night?"

I couldn't stop the grin spreading across my face. "Yeah, that's the one."

Her eyes softened, a spark of curiosity in them. "You made that? For me?" Her voice dropped, a trace of disbelief threading through it.

"I did." I nodded, pride in my voice. "Took me all day, but it was worth it."

A genuine smile broke across her face. "It's beautiful," she said softly, surprise clear in her tone. "How did you..."

"Figure it out?" I smirked. "I went down a YouTube rabbit hole."

She laughed, her eyes lighting up. "No, I mean, how did you know what I was trying to make?"

"Oh... you mentioned a chandelier, so I just looked up DIY chain chandeliers and pieced it together."

She glanced away, shaking her head slightly. "I can't believe you did that."

I chuckled, the sound filling the small space between us. "I'm glad you liked it," I said. "I wanted to do something to make it up to you."

She tried to hide it, but a flicker of emotion slipped through—like my words had found a place she hadn't meant to leave open.

I felt heat creeping up my cheeks as I added, "I feel

awful about that stupid joke I made. I say dumb things when I'm embarrassed. I'm really sorry..." I knelt down beside her. "I've missed you."

She laughed, a soft, musical sound that softened the moment between us. "Alright, alright—you don't have to get on your knees. And... I missed you too," she murmured.

We both stood up, and she glanced down, her cheeks flushing, then slid her eyes toward me, a hint of a smile teasing her lips. "Did you..." She paused, her gaze flicking back to the floor. "Did you write that note I found at the bottom of the box? It wasn't signed."

I swallowed, holding her gaze as I straightened up. "Yeah. That was me."

She licked her lips, taking a step closer. I could feel the warmth radiating from her, and it was all I could do not to reach out. "You really want another chance?" Her voice was soft, her eyes searching mine.

I nodded. "I do."

She leaned closer, maybe without realizing it, our faces just inches apart. I moved to reach for her, but she pulled back abruptly, breaking the moment.

"Don't." She shook her head, her expression conflicted. "I don't think this is a good idea. We're... not good for each other. I bring out the worst in you."

I stepped back, stung. "That's not true. Remember the Dish Rag Swill show? I haven't had that much fun with anyone else."

She looked away, a faint smile breaking through. "But there's one thing you could do..."

"What do you need?" I asked, hopeful.

Her smile turned a bit sheepish. "Would you hang the chandelier for me? Even with my ladder, I'm too short to reach the ceiling."

I let out a quiet chuckle, relief mingling with guilt. This was my chance to show her I could do something kind, no strings attached.

"Yeah," I said, grinning, "I'd be happy to. Where's the ladder?"

She gestured back toward the door, her smile finally reaching her eyes. "Right this way."

It took forty-five minutes to hang the chandelier in her living room, though it wasn't because of the setup. She changed her mind at least fifteen times, directing me to move it an inch this way, then a bit that way, only to finally settle on the exact spot we'd started with. I swallowed down the urge to roll my eyes, keeping my face steady and calm as I waited for each decision, letting her take her time.

As I tucked the ladder back in her storage room, I heard her soft footsteps behind me.

Quietly, she asked, "What would we do... if I gave you another chance?"

I turned around, feeling like I was walking on eggshells, but trying for a hopeful smile. "I'd take you out."

She studied my face. "On a date?"

I cleared my throat. "Yeah... a real one." Then I raised my eyebrows, trying not to sound too eager. "Ever been to Una Notte di Luna?"

She crinkled her brow. "No..."

"It's this Italian place in Westlake, three stories tall. We'd have dinner on the rooftop, surrounded by twinkle lights and greenery everywhere—a kind of fairyland vibe."

Her eyes softened, widening just slightly as she

drifted closer, hanging on every word.

"Afterward, we'd go dancing," I continued, my voice lowering. "And I'd want to hold you close with you in my arms... until I couldn't wait another second to take you home and memorize every inch of you."

The words lingered in the air, my voice trailing into a whisper as her breath mingled with mine. Time seemed to stop. And before I knew it, her lips brushed against mine, her hands softly cradling my cheeks, guiding me as her mouth opened, inviting me in.

I didn't hold back, letting my tongue glide against hers, my hands instinctively finding her waist, then moving lower, pulling her against me until our bodies melted together. Her chest pressed against mine, and a low groan escaped me.

If we didn't slow down, this kiss would take us to her bedroom. I reluctantly eased back, watching her eyes flutter open, dazed and warm.

"So," I murmured, lifting a shoulder with a small smile. "What do you say?"

Her lips curved into a smile. "I say... yes."

Relief flooded through me, and I pressed my forehead to hers, closing my eyes, breathing her in. "Really, Darci. I'm so sorry. I want to be better for you."

She whispered back, "I know. But if you do something like that again..." She shook her head slowly, her gaze fierce before letting out a sigh.

CHAPTER NINETEEN

Darci

I fidgeted with the hem of my dress, nerves fluttering in my stomach. Was it too much? Not enough? I took another look in the mirror before glancing at the clock again—how could time be moving this slowly and still feel like it was running out?

I pulled out my lipstick and reapplied it for the third time. Like maybe if I got the edges just right, I could convince myself I was ready. That I deserved this.

Tonight wasn't just a maybe. Not another one of our not-quite, almost-there, casual hangouts. This was a date. A real one.

And Alex... God, Alex.

I didn't know if fate had been saving this moment or if I'd just imagined it into being. But either way, it was here. It was real. And my heart hadn't gotten the memo to stop racing.

What if everything changed tonight?

I'd spent the entire evening getting ready. I blew my hair out with a round brush, coaxing it into soft waves that framed my face. Typically, I was a wash-and-go kind of girl, but tonight, it fell into perfect, voluminous layers. My usual swipe of mascara and lipstick wouldn't cut it—I went all in, adding eyeliner, a touch of shadow, a hint of blush. I barely recognized myself in the mirror.

Then there was the dress—a little black number I'd accidentally stumbled on in the sample section while shopping with Claire for her wedding dress. Lacy and fitted, it hugged me just right, with a deep V in the back and a flirty, swishing skirt that made me feel bold. Nothing like the usual gothic boho dresses I lived in. I finished it with a pair of black stilettos, each ankle fastened with a delicate bow, the final touch to an outfit that whispered "fuck me" with every step.

A knock at the door pulled me from my thoughts. My heart kicked up as I smoothed down my dress. I took a deep breath and opened the door.

Alex stood in a tailored gray suit, a complete departure from his usual scrubs or athletic shorts. It emphasized his broad shoulders, the clean lines sharp against his frame, while the crisp white collar added a polished edge. His hair was styled neatly, but an almost irresistible urge stirred me to grab his collar, mess up that perfectly coiffed hair, and pull him close.

I wanted him—imagining the soft clink of his belt, the faint rasp of his zipper, as I pulled him out of that suit. Maybe we'd get to do that later.

When my gaze drifted up to his, I caught him watching me, his eyes tracing my figure with a slow, deliberate appreciation, a grin tugging at his lips. He held out a bouquet of dark red roses, their velvety petals nearly black. How had he known?

"These are for you," he murmured, his voice low and

husky.

I took the bouquet, breathing in the rich, heady scent of the dark red roses. "They're beautiful," I said, unable to stop the smile spreading across my face.

I gestured for him to come inside, retreating to the kitchen to find a vase—a welcome distraction from that nervous flutter in my stomach. As I arranged the roses, I stole glances at him, feeling his gaze on me. His eyes had a glow that made my breath catch. There was a thrill sparking between us, and something told me this might be a night to remember.

After setting the vase in the center of my small kitchen table, I turned back to Alex, meeting his gaze head-on.

"Ready?" he asked, his voice steady, though his eyes hinted something more.

I nodded, clutching my bag as he took my hand in his. It sent a spark up my spine, and I couldn't hold back a smile.

The drive to the restaurant passed in an easy silence, broken only by the soft jazz playing on the radio. Alex's hand rested on my thigh, warm and steady, edging my skirt higher until it brushed near the junction between my thighs. He hadn't moved beyond that simple touch, but somehow, it felt scandalously intimate, sending a slow, delicious warmth pooling in my belly.

Una Notte di Luna came into view as he turned down a winding, quiet road, glowing against the night sky. From here, it was stunning. I couldn't imagine what it would be like once inside. It was lit up from inside. Twinkle lights draped over a large rooftop pergola, casting a soft glow, while ivy climbed up the glassy facade. At the center of it all, a grand spiral staircase stretched in the center of the building up to the rooftop, adding an almost dreamlike touch.

When we pulled up to the entrance, a valet opened my door, his gaze skimming over me with quiet appreciation. Alex was already there, reaching past him with an outstretched hand. I slipped my fingers into his, and without missing a beat, Alex shot the valet a quick look before guiding me toward the entrance.

The hostess, dressed in sleek black, greeted us with a professional smile as soon as Alex gave his name. "Good evening. Your table is ready."

We followed her up the winding staircase until the top revealed a breathtaking view of the city skyline glittering against the night. We passed through an ivy-covered archway and stepped onto the rooftop—a hidden, magical world with the city lights before us. It felt like a place out of time, a lush garden oasis high above the bustling streets.

Stone paths snaked through a sea of greenery, leading to cozy, candlelit tables scattered across the terrace. The air was thick with the scent of blooming flowers, a delicate sweetness that mingled with the cool night breeze. Soft murmurs of conversation floated around us, underscored by the gentle notes of string music.

Our table was tucked into a quiet corner. It was secluded but offered a sweeping view of the city lights in the distance. As I settled in, the enchanting surroundings washed over me, and for a moment, it felt like I'd stepped right into a fairytale.

"So... what do you think?" Alex asked as he sat down, his eyes bright with hope and maybe a hint of nerves flickering beneath.

I let out a soft laugh, glancing around at the magical

scene. "What do I think?" I repeated, a touch of wonder in my voice as I teased him. "Color me impressed, Dr. Alex."

His grin widened, a bit of relief in his expression. "Glad you like it. They say the food's incredible." He picked up the menu, casting a quick look my way. "Anything catching your eye?"

A few minutes later, we'd ordered enough to fill the entire table. We started with cocktails—me with a Peach Bellini, because I was always up for a fruity cocktail, and Alex with a Negroni. He even ordered us a bottle of Merlot for dinner, braised beef with mushrooms for him, and chicken piccata for me. I could hardly wait for the prosciutto bruschetta appetizer to arrive.

After dinner, we lingered over coffee and shared a slice of tiramisu, watching couples sway together on the dance floor. I was itching to join them, but I wasn't sure if Alex would be up for it.

"Do you like to dance?" I asked, slicing off a small piece of tiramisu and offering it to him.

He chuckled, a glint of amusement in his eyes. "Yes and no."

Leaning forward, he took the bite, his lips grazing the fork, and I felt myself inching closer, tempted to taste him right then and there.

I raised an eyebrow. "I'm not asking for a miracle, just a willingness to pretend you're enjoying yourself," I said dryly.

"I can... dance," Alex said, his voice low, almost like he was trying to convince himself. "I just... usually do it where no one's watching. And definitely not to violins."

He paused, taking a slow sip of his coffee, his eyes

never leaving mine. "But I'll give it a shot."

I smiled, trying not to show how much that little confession undid me. The music played something soft and sweeping in the background, and for a second, I could swear the moment shimmered—just a little—like fate was holding its breath, waiting to see how this would play out.

I didn't give him a chance to reconsider. Standing up, I gently took his coffee from him, setting it aside, and tugged him to his feet.

"Good enough for me. Let's get out there and make the rest of these people question their life choices."

He laughed, threading his fingers through mine as we headed to the dance floor, choosing a spot a little off the side. His hand settled warmly on the small of my back, fingertips brushing my bare skin, while his other hand wrapped around mine. We swayed in time to the music, and my eyes drifted to our clasped hands before slowly meeting his gaze.

Everything else blurred, like someone had dimmed the world but left him in perfect focus. His eyes locked on mine, pupils dilated, something tender and a little uncertain flickering behind the slow curve of his smile. It felt like the universe had narrowed down to just the two of us—breath to breath, heartbeat to heartbeat— moving together like we'd been doing this forever.

I'd felt things for Alex before. That afternoon in his bed after the pool? I'd felt everything, maybe more than I was ready for. But this... this felt different, like something I couldn't quite name. His blue eyes held mine, and it was as if the world had shifted just slightly, leaving his arms as the only anchor holding me steady.

Part of me thought I should say something to break

the spell hanging between us. But I didn't want to. I wanted this moment, this feeling, to stretch out forever.

Then, another couple bumped into us, murmuring apologies, and the magic around us frayed. The song ended, and we stepped back, exchanging a small, knowing smile before returning to our table.

Alex paid the bill, then turned to me, his voice gentle. "Ready to go?"

A pang of disappointment hit me. I wasn't ready for the night to be over.

"No," I confessed.

He stepped closer, his eyes searching mine. "You don't...want to leave?"

I picked up my clutch, meeting his gaze. "I'm not ready for this... to end."

A slow smile spread across his face, and he closed his eyes briefly as if savoring my words.

Leaning in, his breath warm against my ear, he whispered, "Then, let's not let it."

I felt warmth bloom in my cheeks as I looked up at him, everything in me aching with hope. "I was hoping you'd say that."

He pressed his palm against the small of my back again, his hand searing against my skin as we left. He didn't move it until we reached the valet stand. The valet brought the car around and opened my door with a wink and a smile. Alex took the key, arching an eyebrow at the guy, who gave him a tight-lipped smile and a slight bow before running off to get someone else's car.

Alex pulled out of the parking space slowly, only to steer us into a shadowed corner under an old, sprawling tree just outside the property. Before I could ask why, he leaned in, his mouth capturing mine in a hungry kiss. His fingers laced into my hair, tightening just enough to make my pulse quicken, and his tongue traced my lips, coaxing me to open for him. I did, letting him tangle with mine in a rhythm that left us both breathless.

He kissed his way down my neck, his lips warm against my skin, then trailed up along my jaw, every touch igniting something deep and unsteady within me.

He rumbled against my ear in a low voice, "Come home with me, Tink. I can't stop thinking about the last time you were in my bed, and I..." He let out a growl before saying, "I fucking need you."

I swallowed, barely able to contain myself, and squeaked, "Okay."

He nipped my earlobe before pulling back, and our eyes met again. Those electric blue eyes were nearly swallowed in black as he leaned in again and kissed me hard.

On the ride back, we didn't talk. Alex could barely keep his eyes on the road, and his hand was like fire against my thigh. He was slowly rubbing his thumb further up my leg. The edge of my panties was on display, and my skirt was nearly at my waist. I was sure there would be a wet spot when I exited the car. Hopefully, it didn't ruin his pristine leather seats.

He pulled into his usual spot, then turned to me with a small smile. "Hold on a sec," he said, his eyes gleaming with something unreadable.

He hopped out of the car and swiftly opened my door, offering his hand to help me out. The moment I stood, he guided me back against the car. His lips crashed against mine, his hands gripping my waist as he pulled my leg over his hip, pressing himself against my core. His hand found its way under my skirt circling around my thigh to my ass.

When we came up for air, he nuzzled my neck, his other hand tracing the low neckline of my dress.

"Let's go inside. I need to take these off," he said as he snapped my panties with his fingers.

I licked across his lips, and he growled, taking my mouth in a frenzied kiss. Before I was ready for it to end, he pulled back, grinning, and grabbed my hand, leading me up the stairs. I pressed my body against him, my hands roaming as I kissed the back of his neck while he attempted to unlock the door. His hand slid around my waist, dragging me inside. As soon as we crossed the threshold, he kicked the door shut, pushing me against it, kissing me again before he spun me around so my back was against him and my ear was pressed to the door.

He searched for zipper on my dress, chuckling as he muttered, "Where the fuck is it?"

He finally found it on my side and slid it open, then pushed my dress down until I was standing in nothing but heels and fishnet panties.

The warmth of his body slipped away, and I glanced over my shoulder to find him stepping back, sliding off his suit jacket with slow, deliberate ease. His gaze swept over me like a touch.

"Damn, Tink," he said, voice rough and reverent. "You look fucking delicious."

I let out a breathless laugh as I turned to face him. I was wearing underwear, technically, but the sheer fabric left little to the imagination. I was practically bare to him, and he ate every inch.

He reached for me, fingertips brushing mine, then tugged gently, guiding me toward the bedroom as he walked backward, never breaking eye contact. He laid me down on his bed and pulled my underwear off in one move. I'm not even sure if they were still in one piece. And I didn't really care.

He looked ravenous—eyes dark, jaw tight—as he dropped to his knees between my thighs. There was nothing gentle in the way he moved, just raw need as he hooked my leg over his shoulder like he couldn't stand the distance a second longer.

I reached for the buckle of my heel, but his hand shot up, gripping my wrist hard enough to make me freeze.

"Don't," he growled. "Keep them on."

His palm slid rough and possessive up my thigh, his breath hot against my skin like he was already devouring me. I smirked as I lay back down, and he began to kiss up my inner thigh.

The heated anticipation of a man teasing before he feasted on you was unlike anything. I could barely hold still. My orgasm was building as I let out a whimper.

When he began to nibble and nip my lower lips, I moaned, arching my back. My clit pulsed with my heartbeat. I reached out, trying to guide his head right where I needed him. He dodged me, and with a flat tongue, he took one long lick from my opening straight to that little bundle of nerves. I nearly flew off the bed. He continued with downward strokes from my clit to my opening before coming back to my clit, sucking and biting and licking me into a frenzy. When he slid two fingers inside me as he suckled, I let out a long moan. His fingers curled as he pushed in and out, slowly increasing his speed.

"Oh fuck. Right there. Right. There. Don't... don't stop. Please." I begged. I was close to shattering, and in a strangled voice, I said, "Alex... Fuck... I'm going to come."

His voice gruff, he said, "Come for me, Tink. I want your come all over my face."

He dove back in, circling my clit with his tongue before sucking it between his lips hard, and I screamed his name. I probably woke the neighbors. A powerful squirt shot out of me. *What the fuck?*

Amused, he said, almost to himself, "Holy fuck, you squirted!"

I was out of breath, but he didn't stop. He continued sucking and biting, his fingers still pumping until I came down.

"That... that's never happened before. Um... sorry?"

He stood up, "Fuck, baby. Don't apologize. That was hot."

Euphoria was still coursing through me, but a lick of heat rolled straight to my belly as I sat up, still out of breath. I unbuttoned his shirt, kissing his chest as I went. He smelled so good.

He unzipped his pants, pushing his pants and boxers down and kicking them off. He stood at attention so fucking hard. The velvety head of his cock was purple, with a drop of pre-cum glistening at the top. I didn't waste a second before my thumb went to the head, rubbing his pre-cum around. He leaned his head back, groaning as I stroked.

"Darci... fuck... that's so damn good."

My other hand traveled down to his balls, and I gently tugged them as I continued stroking. A moment later, his hands stilled mine. His eyes came back to me.

"Get on your stomach, ass up."

I shifted, my heel slipping loose. He caught it, slid it back on with maddening patience, his fingers trailing fire up my calf. His voice was a smirk wrapped in gravel. "These stay on. You have no idea what that does to me."

He ran his hand all the way up to my core, spreading my wetness. I heard the rip of a condom wrapper. I smirked as I looked behind me, watching him slide it on. The memory of the last time he was inside me came back, and my hips gyrated with need. I couldn't wait for him to fill me up.

He caressed my ass with one hand as he slowly guided himself in. God, that initial stretch and burn felt so good. I pressed back on him until he seated himself completely. He paused, but without thought, my body began to stroke him, trying to get him even deeper.

"Still like it hard?"

I looked behind me and grinned, "Pound me, baby."

He chuckled, "As you wish…"

He pulled out to the tip but slammed back into me, slow at first, but then he began to fuck me faster, harder, our skin slapping together.

I moaned and whimpered and made noises I'd never made before before mumbling into the sheets, "Oh god… Alex… So good… so fucking good."

I felt the coiling deep in my belly. His hand ran up my spine to my shoulder. He grabbed on, allowing himself to thrust even harder against me, his pubic bone slamming against me. His balls were swinging into my clit, teasing me into a frenzy. I clenched against him from the buildup.

I screamed, "Don't stop… Please… Oh god…"

He gritted out, "Not stopping, Tink. I'm going to… pound you… into oblivion."

"Yes," I screamed, clenching tighter around his cock, my body convulsing with ecstasy as I pushed back against him one more time before I went boneless as the orgasm took me.

"Oh fuck… Yeah… That's it… I'm almost…" He let out a growl that sounded almost inhuman as he came, and I clenched around him.

He fell on top of my back. We were both out of breath. A moment later, he rolled off of me, pulling me against his chest. My limbs were like a rag doll as he nestled me against him. His heart was racing, and I wasn't sure I had ever felt this satiated, this complete.

He stroked my hair and kissed my forehead. "Wow, Tink… just wow…" The last words dropping to a whisper.

He sat up on the edge of the bed, and I began to sit up, too. But he leaned over, his hand on my cheek, and his thumb tugging my bottom lip.

"Stay with me… please. Don't leave."

I lifted my gaze to his, and his eyes held such vulnerability. I turned my face into his hand. "You didn't even have to ask."

One corner of his mouth hitched up, "Promise?" His eyebrows raised.

I nodded. "I'll stay."

He smiled, his eyes crinkling, as he stood and said, "Be right back."

I must have fallen asleep because I woke with a start a few minutes later as he pressed a warm washcloth between my thighs, and a tendril of warmth flickered in my belly.

He came back to bed, lifting the covers. "Come up here with me."

He smoothed the pillows, then looked at me with a tenderness that seemed to reach straight through me, and my heart practically melted. I slipped out of my shoes and climbed up, sliding beneath the covers as he followed, wrapping his arm around me and pulling me close. His hand rested gently on my stomach, our legs entwined as if they'd always fit this way. I felt the warmth of his breath before his lips brushed the sensitive spot behind my ear, a kiss that lingered.

My eyes grew heavy as sleep began to pull me under. For the first time in a long damn time, it felt like I was exactly where I was supposed to be.

Muffled against my neck, he said, "Good night, sweetheart." And then I swear I heard him thank me. For what, I wasn't quite sure.

As I drifted off in his arms, I last remembered whispering, "Good night."

CHAPTER TWENTY

Alex

Dawn crept into the room, slow and golden, and there she was—Darci—tangled against me, and it made it hard to breathe. Like the world had paused so that I could memorize her like this. I traced down her arm with my finger. Our legs were intertwined like puzzle pieces. I hadn't slept that well in a long damn time.

I leaned down, my lips brushing against her shoulder. A small constellation of freckles dotted the back of her shoulder, a perfect replica of the Big Dipper. She stirred, stretching her limbs languidly. A sleepy smile graced her lips as she turned her head towards me.

"Hi," she murmured. Her velvety voice held a sleepy charm that made my heart skip a beat. I couldn't help but lean in and kiss her.

"Morning," I whispered back.

She yawned, covering her mouth. Her cheeks reddened, and she lifted her eyes to mine. "What time is it?"

I chuckled. Our phones were on the nightstand, out of my reach.

"I have no idea," I replied, grinning. "But it's definitely morning." I tilted my head. "Why? Do you have somewhere you need to be?"

She chuckled, "No, just curious. Do you?"

"Nope," I said as I pulled her against me, "And this is exactly where I want to be."

"Me, too," she said sleepily, snuggling against my chest.

She exhaled, eyes closed, and I watched her for a beat, just breathing her in. The closeness buzzed under my skin—quiet, but all-consuming. After last night, something had shifted. I couldn't explain it, only that it felt... right.

Somehow, we both drifted back to sleep, and when I woke again, the sunlight was brighter and warmer than before. Darci stirred beside me, letting out a soft groan as her eyes fluttered open, still heavy with sleep. She blinked a few times, her gaze unfocused, then slowly came to life, a sleepy smile tugging at her lips.

"I've got to pee," she said, sliding out of my embrace and slipping off the bed.

Just as she shut the door to the bathroom, her phone went off with a text. I didn't move until it went off a dozen more times. Maybe something was wrong.

I stretched my limbs and leaned over the bed, reaching for her phone on the nightstand. The notifications were on the lock screen—someone named Blue. The first message was just a greeting, but they sent several messages in a row. They were coming into town and wanted to get together for dinner or drinks while they were here. I had the distinct impression that this was a guy.

Who the fuck was Blue? When did she meet him? Were they seeing each other? Was she fucking him, too? A cold dread seeped into my bones.

I sat up on the edge of the bed, digging through my dresser for clothes. When Darci returned, she had my T-shirt on and a seductive smile, but her smile dropped when she saw me dressed and leaning over to slip on my shoes.

Hesitantly, she said, "Uh, what's up? I thought you didn't have anywhere to be?"

Without looking up, I said, "Change of plans."

She took a step closer. "Did the hospital call?"

I ignored her, tying my shoes.

"Did I... um, do something wrong?"

I straightened up, avoiding her gaze, turning around and grabbing my wallet and keys and slipping them in my pocket.

She stomped over to me like an angry little fairy, her hands in fists. "Are you for real? You're just going to ignore me?"

I took a deep breath before I faced her. I ignored her questions and patted my pockets, ensuring everything was there. I searched the bed and nightstand for where I had left my phone.

She followed me, sitting on the bed and picking up her clothes from the floor. "Alex? What's going on?"

I found my phone on the floor next to the nightstand and stood up as I pocketed it. I cocked my head when I looked at her. "I don't know, Darci. Who the fuck is Blue?"

Her eyes widened. "Wh- What?"

I pointed to her phone, now lying on the bed. "Blue

wants to know if you're free next week for 'dinner or drinks.'" I used air quotes for the last words.

She turned her head to look at the phone on the bed, her eyes narrowing. "You were looking through my phone?"

"No, of course not." I shook my head. "Your phone went off a bunch of times, and I was worried something was wrong. I just glanced at the notifications on the lock screen."

"Oh." She looked down, a blush creeping up her neck. Quietly, she said, "I met… um, Blue when Claire and I went to Vegas. He, uh, ate breakfast with us."

"Just breakfast, huh?"

She waved her hands around. "It was very spur of the moment. I ran into him face-first at a breakfast buffet. We got to talking. He was alone and invited me to eat with him, so I asked him to eat with Claire and me"

"What else did you do with *Blue*." I drew out his name like he was some pretentious ass. What kind of name is Blue anyway?

"Um, we… had dinner together…" Her voice trailed off. She bit her lip again, her cheeks reddening.

I prompted her, "And then?"

She looked away. "We went to a nightclub."

I narrowed my eyes. "That was it?"

She swallowed and fidgeted with her hands. "Yeah, that was pretty much… it."

I turned to leave before looking over my shoulder at her. "You should text him back and let him know. I hope you have fun with… *Blue*."

She shook her head and chuckled. She teased, "Oh my god. You're jealous." A smile played on her lips.

I guess we were doing this. With my hands on my

hips, I scoffed, "Why would *I* be jealous?" I rolled my eyes, waiting for her response.

She arched an eyebrow, seeing through my attempt at indifference. "Oh, come on, Alex. It's just dinner with a friend."

"Does he see it that way? Because he seems very interested in… *dinner*," I retorted, gesturing towards her phone. I took a deep breath, trying to dispel my anger.

She shrugged casually. "It's not a big deal. I'll tell him I can't make it." She let out a sigh. "Please don't leave."

My frustration intensified. "It's a big deal when he's asking you out."

"I think you're overreacting."

Unable to contain my irritation, I snapped, "Maybe I am." Without waiting for her response, I headed towards the door, my mind buzzing with anger and hurt.

She came up behind me quickly and sighed, "Alex, please. Wait…"

I whirled around. "What, Darci? What else is there to say?"

She took a breath, and her eyes lit up with fire. "Really?" Her chest was heaving. "Are you fucking serious? What exactly are we doing here?" She gestured between us. "Every time I get close to you, you turn into an asshole. I don't even know why you're mad at me." In a whisper, she asked, "Do you even want this?"

I sighed, closing my eyes and pinching the bridge of my nose. "I'm sorry." I sat down in the armchair by the door and sighed heavily. "I don't know what I'm doing."

She slowly walked towards me, shaking her head. "Join the club." She let out a hollow laugh. "Before you, I hadn't made it past a single first date in years."

Staring at the floor, I quietly said, "Before you, there was only my wife."

A soft gasp escaped her, drawing my attention. When our eyes met, hers were filled with a warmth that caught me off guard. I hadn't planned on telling her like this—it had just slipped out. I held my breath, hoping Javi was right, that this was the right thing to do.

"Divorced?"

I shook my head. "No, she… she died."

"Oh…" She swallowed. "I'm so sorry, Alex. I had no idea."

I mumbled, "No one does."

She sat almost tentatively on the arm of the chair and murmured, "What's her name?"

I huffed out a shaky breath. "Jenna."

Her fingers brushed my arm gently. "Tell me about her?"

I took a slow, deep breath, feeling the weight of the words pressing against my chest. My heart hammered as I looked at her, searching her eyes. I saw something like understanding, but I wasn't sure how to do this. I tried to find the right place to start.

"We were kids." I shrugged. "She moved in down the street when we were in middle school. I had the biggest crush on her. But we were just friends for a long time. It wasn't until we ended up at the same college that I finally got the nerve to ask her out. I thought she was it for me. We married right after graduation." I swallowed hard.

Her reassuring smile and nod encouraged me to continue, but I looked away. I chuckled, remembering how Jenna had told me she was pregnant.

"She couldn't wait to be a mom. She got pregnant

soon after I finished my residency. We would go to this bar and play Scrabble. One night, I don't know if she cheated or what, but somehow she managed to spell 'positive,' 'pregnancy,' and 'test' as we played."

I looked over at Darci as she grinned.

"She sat there with the biggest grin just waiting for me to figure it out as we played." I shook my head, laughing, "I don't want to admit how long it took me to realize it."

A laugh bubbled out of Darci, "Wow, I love that!"

"It was a girl." My smile faded, "But there were complications. Her placenta grew through her uterus into her bladder." I didn't miss it when Darci flinched. "It's a rare complication but very dangerous. If the placenta detaches early, the mother can bleed to death. So we planned to deliver the baby at 35 weeks for the best chance."

My voice shook as I continued, "But a week before the scheduled c-section, she started bleeding. Her placenta spontaneously ruptured. I was home and rushed her to the hospital, but it was… too late." The words caught in my throat before I could fully utter them. "… for both of them."

My chin dropped to my chest, and the hot tears rose. Darci eased down into the chair next to me, wrapping her arms around me and drawing me close. And I let her cradle me as I gave into the sobs. I couldn't remember when I let someone hold me like this. I was surprised at the unexpected comfort I felt with her.

I took a few deep breaths, attempting to regain my composure. The emotional grip began to loosen with each breath.

Sensing the change, Darci murmured, "What'd you

name her?"

I gradually pulled away to look at her, sniffling and wiping my face as a faint smile played on my lips. I replied, "Savannah Jean."

She smiled warmly, "That's a beautiful name."

Wiping away the remaining tears, I managed a shaky but grateful smile and nodded.

Darci reached back around, pulling me into her again. I wrapped my arms around her and buried my head into the curve of her neck, closing my eyes and breathing in her comforting scent.

I didn't want to let her go, ever. Somehow, she knew what I needed. I didn't have to tell her. I'd had something similar with Jenna, but it felt like a distant memory. It had been so long since I'd had anything like this—I missed it, wanted it, needed it.

Slowly, Darci unfolded herself from me, standing up and offering her hand. She guided me back to the bedroom. I kicked my shoes off as soon as we walked in. Neither of us said a word as she pulled off my pants and shirt. She lifted the covers, silently inviting me to slide in. Still, in my T-shirt, she joined me, scooting close. She traced soothing, lazy circles on my chest as I pulled her tight against me, leaning down to plant a tender kiss on her head.

As I drifted off, Darci whispered, "I'll be here when you wake up."

I didn't reply, and I didn't fight it as I fell asleep wrapped in her warm embrace.

CHAPTER TWENTY-ONE

Darci

We'd slept until nearly the afternoon. I guess we both needed it. Alex looked so peaceful. I was hesitant to disturb him. I was curled against him, my hand resting on his stomach. When I lifted my head, drool glistened on his chest. I must have been in a deep sleep. Mortification washed over me as I swiped it off his chest, my cheeks burning with embarrassment.

He stirred, his eyes fluttering open. A lazy smile spread across his face.

"Hey," he murmured, his voice deep and husky.

I grinned. There was a sense of comfort in this moment, a sense of belonging that felt familiar and new.

"Hi," I said shyly.

My stomach rumbled, a loud and insistent protest against the quietness of the bedroom. Alex chuckled, his eyes twinkling with amusement.

"Hungry?"

I nodded, my embarrassment momentarily forgotten. "Starving," I corrected.

Sitting up, he said, "Let's go get something to eat."

The familiar scent of fried food filled the air as we pulled into Morning Glory's parking lot, one of my favorite places to get breakfast any time of day. They were famous for their waffles—savory, sweet, dessert—all kinds of golden, fluffy deliciousness. My stomach growled in anticipation. Luckily, there was no wait this late in the afternoon.

I didn't even need to glance at the menu. My go-to order was always cinnamon roll pancakes covered in cream cheese frosting. My mouth watered just thinking about them. Alex had never been here before and needed a minute with the menu. He opted for savory waffles topped with eggs and potatoes.

Our meal came out in minutes, and I wasted no time digging in. The first bite was pure bliss, with the sweet, fluffy waffle melting in my mouth.

I was halfway through my second waffle when Alex cleared his throat.

"Can I talk to you about something?" he asked, voice a little too serious.

I paused mid-bite, lowering my fork as something twisted low in my stomach. Not panic exactly… but a flicker of that old, familiar unease.

I gave him a half-smile I didn't quite feel.

"Yeah?" I said, keeping my voice light, even though part of me was already bracing for impact.

He hesitated, his eyes searching my face. "I know this might be sudden, but I'd like you to come with me to see Jenna and Savannah Jean, um… at the cemetery."

My heart skipped a beat that he even asked, but I hesitated, considering the implications. This… this was a big step, an invitation to share a deeply personal part of his life.

I offered him a small smile. "You really want me to come with you?"

He immediately replied, "I do."

He'd been shouldering this grief all on his own for years. He needed someone to lean on and was reaching out to me. I nodded slowly, trying to process the unexpected request.

"I'd like that," I replied, my voice low. "Did you mean today?"

He nodded, his expression serious. "We can go today or another day, but I'd like you to be there."

I reached across the table and squeezed his hand. "Should we go today? Do you need that?"

His shoulders relaxed as he smiled, "Okay, yeah, I'd like that. Let's do it. We can stop and get some flowers."

After our late lunch, we stopped at a flower shop. It was bursting with color, a rainbow of blooms filling the space. The sweet scents overwhelmed my senses. Alex stood beside me, his brow wrinkled in concentration.

"What do you think?" he asked, holding a bouquet of white lilies.

It was a classic choice, but I shook my head. The delicate petals were lovely but not quite right. My eyes scanned the buckets, finally landing on a cluster of sunflowers. Their bright yellow faces seemed to radiate warmth and optimism.

"Those," I said, pointing to the sunflowers. "They're perfect."

Alex nodded, selecting a few stems and handing them to the florist.

As we waited for her to wrap the bouquet, I had a thought. "We should get something different for

Savannah Jean. Don't you think?"

A thoughtful expression came over his face, and he nodded with a small smile. "Okay. What did you have in mind?"

I walked right over to the lilacs and grabbed a cluster of them. They made me think of youthful innocence, which seemed fitting. The decision was easy, a sense of peace washing over me as I selected the blooms. I laid them on the counter as the florist finished with the sunflowers.

"These are perfect."

Alex watched me with a gentle smile, his eyes filled with a quiet admiration. "You have a good eye," he said, his voice low.

I turned to face him. "There's a language to flowers, you know? It's important to choose the right ones to convey what you want to say," I replied.

With them clutched in my arms, we began the drive to his hometown. The drive to Patterdale was mainly a journey of silence, punctuated only by quiet music and the occasional glance shared between us. The landscape gradually changed from the city skyline into rolling hills and sprawling farmlands.

As we exited the freeway and went down a two-lane road to the small town, Alex said, "I thought I'd never leave this place," his voice tinged with nostalgia. "It's changed a lot, but some things never do."

I turned to face him, curious. "Like what?"

"The feeling of peace," he replied, his eyes distant. "It's like the world slows down here."

"I get it. I'm from a small town a little ways outside of Denton."

He glanced at me, "Do you see your parents often?"

I shook my head. "My dad died soon after I graduated college. He retired when I started college. He was in one of those big 90s rock bands for most of my childhood."

He cocked an eyebrow, "Really? Which one?"

"Slicing Dolls? He played bass."

He grinned, "Are you for real?"

I nodded.

"My dad loves them. He'd play their music in the car all the time. He still does."

The next thing I knew, he broke out in the chorus of their biggest hit, "Ghost of My Heart," a surprisingly strong and clear voice.

"Ghost of my heart, haunting the night, electric soul, a blinding light. Lost in the shadows, a fading desire, burning passion, a funeral pyre!"

Surprised and amused, I laughed as he finished with a flourish, looking at me expectantly.

I shook my head in disbelief, another burst of laughter escaping my lips.

"I can't believe you actually know the lyrics."

"Like I said, my dad's a big fan."

I grinned, shaking my head.

"What was it like growing up with a rock star?"

I shrugged, sighing softly, "I don't know. He was never home, always on tour. It was just my mom and me. And then… when I graduated high school, she took off, divorcing him."

His eyes flickered toward me as they widened, "That sounds rough."

I shrugged, "Yeah. It sort of forced the band on a permanent hiatus. He tried to win her back, but she was done. I felt like I needed to stay home and take care of him. So I gave up my scholarship and lived at home, attending the local college. And then…"

His eyes briefly met mine, "And then?" He prompted.

"A little while after I graduated college, he had a massive heart attack. By then, I was already working at the library. I… came home one day after work and… found him."

"Oh god, Darci. That's awful. I'm so sorry."

I slowly nodded, "It is what it is, you know?" I looked over at him, and he inclined his head in agreement. "But at least it was sudden. The doctors said he probably didn't even know what hit him."

I shrugged and continued, "My mom refused to help with his arrangements and stuff. His manager and his lawyer helped me get everything done."

I murmured, "She and I… don't talk much now."

"I guess I was lucky. My parents helped with everything when I lost… Jenna and the baby. I don't know what I would have done without them."

My heart ached for him, and I reached for his hand, squeezing it.

"I'm glad they were there for you. It's so important to have a support system. I wished I'd had that. It was hard. I felt so alone, but it helped shape me into who I am. But now I have a good group of friends, especially Claire. She and Edison have really become my family now."

He stole another glance at me, his eyes softened with empathy.

A sign flashed by the window: Patterdale, 5 miles. Alex's demeanor shifted. It was subtle, but I could see a shadow pass over his face. The energy in the car shifted, like a heaviness pulling everything down. My eyes darted to him, and his knuckles were white as he gripped the steering wheel and let out a heavy sigh.

We drove in silence—the kind that didn't ask to be filled. The tires hummed against the road, and for a while, that was enough. Then we turned onto Chillingham Court, and something about the name snagged in my chest. *Chillingham.*

It sounded like a ghost story you'd only tell in a whisper, like the name itself had teeth. Whoever named this place and decided, "Yeah, you know what belongs here? A cemetery," clearly had a flair for the dramatic. Probably also the type who thought clowns were charming and black licorice was a personality.

Up ahead, the cemetery came into view—wide and sprawling, dotted with weathered tombstones like bones pushing through skin. It was beautiful but quiet and orderly, and it just felt like a place with so many things left unsaid.

The gravel crunched beneath us as we followed the winding path deeper in. Trees arched overhead, filtering the sunlight into fractured pieces. By the time we stopped near the back, the world felt far away, like we'd slipped into some in-between place where time bent and breath slowed.

Alex didn't say anything at first. Just sat there, staring out the windshield, shoulders tense like he was preparing for a battle. When he finally looked at me, there was something raw in his eyes. Not a crack—more like a door had opened, just a little, and what was behind it was aching.

I wasn't sure what he needed from me. Maybe nothing, maybe everything. But the grief was there, thick in the air, curling around us like smoke. It clung to him, silent and heavy, and I could feel it without him saying a word.

I looked at him again, and I didn't care what came out of his mouth—even if it cut, even if it burned. I just knew I wasn't going to let him carry it alone.

"Still want to do this with me?" he asked, his voice low.

I nodded as I gathered the bouquets and met him in front of the car. Alex's footsteps were heavy as we navigated the rows, his silence a palpable presence between us. I squeezed his hand, offering a silent gesture of support. He squeezed back, his grip firm and reassuring.

But when we stopped in front of two side-by-side graves, the names Jenna and Savannah Jean carved into the cool marble, Alex dropped my hand like a hot potato.

Shame flushed hot under my skin. What had I expected? Comfort? A moment that wasn't about them? His wife. His child. His loss. Still, I felt like a third wheel, and I couldn't stop the ache that bloomed where his touch had been, couldn't shake the ridiculous, selfish sting.

He faced the graves, his shoulders hunched as he knelt down, his movements slow and deliberate, pulling weeds around Jenna's grave marker. I followed suit, placing the bouquets to the side.

My gaze lingered on the inscription:

Jenna Dixon
Wife Mother Beloved
1987-2021

Beside it, a smaller stone etched with a delicate butterfly:

* * *

Savannah Jean Dixon
Our Little Light
2021-2021

The silence between us felt heavy as we worked, but Alex's focus was intense. He seemed lost in his own world, and I didn't want to disturb him. I wanted to respect his need for solitude if that's what he needed.

I worked on the weeds around Savannah Jean's gravestone. I removed the dead flowers in their vases and replaced Savannah's with the beautiful lilacs and Jenna's with the bright yellow sunflowers. When he finished, Alex stood up, brushing the dirt from his hands, and I gathered the weeds and dead flowers, wrapping them in the tissue paper from the one we brought, and waited.

"I haven't been here in a while," he said quietly. "The weeds had really taken over."

I nodded, understanding the things he couldn't say. His pain was too deep for words. I reached out to squeeze his hand, wanting to give him some silent comfort, but he stepped away. Not harsh, not even deliberate. Just... enough.

Right. No big deal. It didn't mean anything. I told myself that twice. But my chest still went tight, and I folded my hand behind me like I could hide the shame there.

He stood in front of the graves and took a deep breath. And I just stood back, quiet and still, reminding myself this wasn't about me.

"Hey, Honey," he began, his voice low. "I'm sorry I haven't been here in a while. The weeds really took over.

But I cleaned it all up for you."

Then, just for a second, he paused and glanced back over his shoulder. Quick. Barely a flicker. But it landed square in my chest. Was it regret? Guilt? Nothing at all?

"This is my friend, Darci. She came and helped me clean up your spot today. She picked out sunflowers for you and lilacs for Savannah Jean." He let out a sigh, "I hope… you like them, and they make you smile."

I hadn't expected him to say my name, especially not *here*. Not standing in front of them. It caught me off guard, hit me low in the ribs like a breath I didn't realize I was holding.

I wanted it to mean something. Like I wasn't that third wheel or the temporary distraction he hadn't figured out how to shake yet. But I knew better than to build stories on single sentences.

Grief makes people reach. It doesn't always mean they want to hold on. Still... I couldn't help how my heart leaned forward, even as my head screamed to stay still.

He continued, his voice thick with emotion. "I know you're watching over me. I miss you both every day."

A lump formed in my throat as I watched him. His grief came off him in waves, impossible to ignore. He wasn't crying, not exactly, but it was in the way his shoulders curved inward and his voice faltered. There was something so raw about it, so unguarded, I felt like I was intruding just by being near.

Something told me he needed space for this, without an audience, to say whatever he needed. So I stepped back quietly, giving him distance without making it feel like I was leaving. I wandered toward a shaded stone bench tucked beneath a sprawling oak. On the way, I tossed the weeds into a nearby trash can.

When I sat down, my mind was a storm of thoughts I couldn't hold still. The contrast between last night and now was sharp enough to cut. The warmth of his hands, the softness of his kiss—it all felt so far away now, like something I dreamed and woke up too soon from.

I didn't think he meant to drop my hand earlier. But he had. And even if it wasn't intentional, I felt the bruise bloom anyway. Still, I understood. Grief has its own gravity, which he struggled to pull away from. You don't just walk out of mourning and into someone else's arms, no matter how badly you might want to.

Lost in my thoughts, I hadn't noticed his approach. He just appeared beside me, quiet, but close enough to shift the air.

"Darci, I'm sorry," he said, voice soft and hesitant. He was staring at the headstones when he said it.

I turned toward him. "I know this isn't easy for you. I just wish…" But the rest caught in my throat. It wasn't the time. Not here. So instead, I said the only thing I could. "I'm not going anywhere."

He glanced over, eyes meeting mine with a small, tentative smile. "I just didn't want…" he started, then trailed off. A sigh. A tiny shake of his head before he let out a breath. "I'm glad you're here with me."

I reached for his hand and gently squeezed it—and this time, he didn't pull away. "Alex, it's okay."

We sat in silence, just breathing, the weight between us softening.

And when the sun began to fade, I finally spoke. "Take your time… I'll be right here."

CHAPTER TWENTY-TWO

Alex

On the drive back, we barely spoke. Darci's gaze seemed fixed on the passing landscape. Was she mad at me? Giving me time to process?

I'd invited her in a desperate attempt to share my world, but now doubt gnawed at me. Maybe this wasn't something I could share with someone else. Maybe I'd dragged her into something she wasn't prepared for. Was it too much? Had she regretted agreeing to come?

It wasn't like I dealt with this very well, either. Every visit to the cemetery was followed by a long, fitful sleep, a desperate attempt to shed the clinging weight of grief. It was a pattern I couldn't break, a cycle that left me drained and disconnected. Even now, after sleeping much of the day away with Darci, I could feel the need for sleep calling to me again. I wanted it to be over. I was tired of this endless cycle.

I looked over at her, feeling a strange sense of relief settle inside me—something about her being there today lifted some of the weight pressing down on me, easing the grief and the loneliness that had wrapped around me for so long.

She hadn't asked for anything. Hadn't tried to fix it. She just... stood beside me.

And now, with the quiet between us soft and steady, it should've felt like peace. But instead, something twisted low in my chest. Because how the hell could I feel lighter? After all this time, after everything I'd lost—how could a single day, a single person, start to soften what had hardened in me for years? And worse—what did that say about me? About my love for Jenna? For Savannah Jean?

What would people think if they saw me like this—with Darci? *What would Jenna think?*

The guilt hit fast and sharp. I gripped the steering wheel tighter, jaw clenched. I could feel it rising, that old instinct to cut and run—to say something cruel before I got too close and let her in too far.

The words came fast, ready to launch like reflex. "You don't have to pretend you care, you know." That's what I almost said. But I bit it back, hard.

Because she did care, she was the one who showed up, helped me clean up their spot, picked sunflowers and lilacs, and didn't once ask for thanks. I glanced at her again, and the tension in my chest shifted—not gone, not even close, but not as loud.

She didn't deserve something like that. Not this time. So I kept driving, the words burning in my throat, and let the silence settle again.

Still, doubt scratched at the edges. She'd come today without hesitation, stood next to me while I tried to make peace with ghosts I still didn't understand how to carry. What if I'd asked too much? What if being there was the thing that finally made her pull back? I didn't want to wait until I eventually said something stupid that would push her out of my life.

A few minutes later, I pulled off the freeway, spotting the familiar glow of a fast-food sign. Without thinking too hard, I flipped on the blinker and eased off the freeway. She turned to look at me, but I kept my eyes on the road.

I just… I needed to talk to her. Really talk. Even if it scared the hell out of me.

Darci didn't say anything, just slid into a booth by the window like she somehow knew I wasn't ready to talk until we were seated.

The vanilla milkshake soothed my jumbled nerves as I took a sip, watching Darci across the table. She was slowly savoring her double chocolate cherry shake, a perfect match for her vibrant energy. I chuckled at the perfect reflection of us—her with all these decadent layers of chaotic sweetness and my simple and steady plain vanilla. I opened my mouth to say something, but the words tangled like a knot in my throat.

I sat across from her and picked up the menu again. "I, uh…" I cleared my throat, suddenly hyper-aware of how dry it felt.

She raised an eyebrow, but didn't push. "You okay?" she asked after a beat.

I nodded too fast. "Yeah. No. I mean…" I let out a breath and dropped the menu on the table. "I just—I wasn't sure if it was too much to ask of someone."

She tilted her head slightly, watching me. I couldn't tell if she was annoyed or just letting me dig the hole on my own terms.

Her gaze lifted to mine, steady and searching. "Coming with you? To the cemetery?"

I nodded, feeling the comfort from earlier slipping away.

"No," she said softly. "Not at all. Everyone deserves someone beside them in moments like that. I'm glad I came. Glad I could be there for you."

A deep breath escaped me, words spilling out before I could stop them. "I don't want to lose you."

A flicker of surprise crossed her face, then softened into something close to worry.

I blurted out before she could say anything, "I know I've been a mess, but I'm trying. I want to be better for you, for us."

She reached across the table and took my hand. "I know."

I stared at the table. "I want this... you and me. I want to see where this goes."

My eyes rose to hers. A flicker of sadness crossed her face, a fleeting cloud shadowing her bright eyes.

"I... I don't know," she replied, her voice barely a whisper.

My heart sank. This wasn't the response I'd been hoping for. It was ridiculous, but a pang of jealousy shot through me as her eyes drifted towards the soda fountain, where a waitress crafted a banana split. I wanted to be the one she was focused on.

"What don't you know?" I pressed, my voice laced with hope and desperation.

Her pointer finger traced the rim of her glass, a nervous tic that made me want to reach across the table.

"We've had fun," she began, her voice soft, "but..."

That one word stretched between us like an abyss. "Would this ever work out?" she continued, her gaze meeting mine. The question was like a punch to the gut, knocking the wind out of me.

"I want to support you," she pressed on, "but at the cemetery... It was like I was intruding."

"I... I know, and I'm sorry," I managed, my voice rough. "I just haven't talked to Jenna about any of this."

Her eyebrows shot up, a mix of surprise and disbelief in her expression. "Alex, Jenna can't hear you," she said gently, her voice dropping to a hushed whisper. "She's gone."

In the harsh light of reality, hearing those two words spoken aloud was a different kind of pain. Even three years later, it still made the world tilt.

"I know," I mumbled, my eyes stinging as I blinked back tears. "It just feels like... a betrayal."

She nodded slowly, her eyes filled with both compassion and understanding. "I get it. I do," she said, her voice steady. "And I like you, but how can we move forward when you're still stuck in the past? I don't want to feel like a consolation prize."

My hackles rose as the weight of her accusation settled on me. "I'm not living in the past," I retorted, my voice sharper than intended. The words tasted hollow, as if I was trying to convince myself more than her.

Darci's eyes flickered with surprise and then sad resignation. "But... aren't you?" she countered softly.

I let out a shaky breath, feeling the weight of it all bearing down, threatening to crush everything I wanted in the here and now. I didn't want to lose her, but it was so hard to let go.

"Let me try..." I swallowed. "Just give me a chance," I

pleaded.

Her gaze flickered, searching my face. A silent battle raged within her eyes between hope and doubt. She looked down at the table, her fingers tracing patterns on the placemat.

"And then?" she asked softly, her eyes holding a reluctant glimmer of hope.

"Then, you can kick me to the curb for good," I promised, my voice steady even as something tight pressed against my chest. I needed her to know I was serious and willing to risk it all—she was worth that risk. Her eyes met mine again, a flicker of something I couldn't quite decipher. "Please?"

She bit down on her bottom lip, a thoughtful expression crossing her face. Her fingers drifted along her jaw, pausing at her collarbone. It was as if she was weighing each word. Finally, with a small nod, she lifted her gaze, but I could still see some lingering doubt.

"Okay," she breathed out.

A smirk crept onto my face, a sense of triumph mixed with trepidation. "I'll win you over," I added, unable to resist a playful jab.

Her lips curved into a wry smile. "We'll see about that," she retorted, her tone laced with playful defiance.

Our burgers arrived, each a towering mountain of meat, cheese, and condiments. We both grinned at the sight of it all.

"Wow, this might be a challenge," I said, eying our plates.

"Watch and learn, Casanova," she said, her eyes glinting with mischief as she hefted up the burger in two hands and took a massive bite.

A glop of ketchup and mustard escaped the back of

her burger and splashed in slow motion right onto her chest. It raced down into her low-cut shirt, disappearing between her breasts into the unknown. Before she could set the burger down, red and yellow bloomed on her pink shirt, and her cheeks heated as she followed the mess with her eyes.

She muttered, "Fuck my life."

Our eyes locked, and I tried desperately not to laugh when I suddenly snorted. We both froze before she shook her head, laughing along.

"I should just wear a bib everywhere I go." She rolled her eyes. "Guess I'll go clean this up before it takes over my entire shirt," she muttered, heading to the restroom.

I smirked. "I'll save you a fry."

A few minutes later, she re-emerged from the bathroom, and the stain on her shirt was completely gone. But what caught my attention wasn't her shirt. It was a book in her hand.

She made a beeline for the waitress refilling ketchup bottles and held the book up, saying something I couldn't hear. The exchange was brief—the waitress barely looked up before moving on to the next table.

Darci returned and dropped the book on the table with a soft thump.

"Look what I found."

I raised an eyebrow at the shirtless man brooding on the cover. "A romance novel?"

She shrugged like it was nothing. "It was just sitting on the sink."

She flipped it open, scanning the pages, her gaze skimming until it snagged on something. Her finger stilled over a handwritten note tucked neatly in the margin beside a highlighted line. Her breath caught.

I leaned in, my tone light but curious. "Let me guess—true love conquers all?"

"Not exactly." She bit her lip, then looked up at me with a faint, unreadable smile. "It says something about love being a choice. Especially when it's hard."

I nodded slowly, turning the thought over. "Yeah... that's the thing, isn't it? Choosing someone, even when life's a mess. Even when it'd be easier not to."

We fell into a quiet pause, almost like we'd slipped into a pocket of stillness.

Darci glanced down at the book again, shrugging as she chuckled under her breath. "Well, she did say it was my turn."

I looked up. "Who? Your turn for what?"

She rolled her eyes and reached for her burger. "It's... dumb."

I leaned closer, lowering my voice. "Tell me."

She hesitated, then grabbed a napkin, fiddling with the corner before glancing back at me. "Alright," she sighed. "But you're going to think it's crazy."

She tapped the book lightly. "Last year, Claire got this box of romance novels—old, dog-eared paperbacks—and every single one was filled with these handwritten notes. Like this one."

She turned the book towards me, and I could see the scribbled margin again. I wrinkled my brow. "So... people writing in books. That's the big mystery?"

Darci shook her head, eyes sharp now. "Not just notes. Claire swears they're... enchanted, like the books are matchmaking people. Literally. She thinks they make people fall in love."

She met my eyes, watching for the moment I'd laugh or roll mine. I didn't.

I asked, "So... you think this one just showed up here for you to find love?"

"I mean… It is how Claire met Edison again…" She let out a soft laugh, uncertain. "You don't think Claire came out here just to leave it in the women's bathroom, do you?"

"I picked this place at random," I said slowly. "How would she even know?"

"I don't know…" She shook her head. "I don't know how to explain it."

The silence returned, not awkward, but with something neither of us could quite name. We both dug into our food, the conversation simmering just below the surface.

A few minutes later, as I pushed the last of my fries around my plate, I said, "Remember that book I found on your porch?"

Her brow wrinkled, and then she nodded. "I assumed it was yours. Why?"

I hesitated, feeling suddenly self-conscious. "It wasn't. Could it have been… one of Claire's magic books?"

Darci sat up straighter. "Why? Did something happen?"

I gave a slight shrug, trying to sound casual even as the memory prickled along my skin. "It was full of those same kinds of notes. And one of them—it kind of… glowed. I don't know how to explain it, but it felt brighter than the others. And… it read like a riddle. It's what gave me the idea to make you that chandelier."

She blinked. "Wait, what?"

"I know," I said quickly. "It sounds nuts. But I swear, the words were shifting, like someone was writing them as I read it."

Darci stared at me, her mouth parted slightly. "Why are you just now telling me this?"

I looked away, heat rising in my cheeks. "I don't know. I thought maybe I imagined it. It felt too weird to say out loud."

She went quiet, staring at the book in her hands.

Then she whispered, "Alex? Oh my god. That's kind of what happened to Claire and Edison. Books showed up for them, too."

I looked at her. Really looked at her. There was wonder in her expression, but something else, too—like we'd just cracked something strange and wonderful open right in front of us.

"Well then," I said, grinning slowly, "guess we'll have to see where this leads us."

CHAPTER TWENTY-THREE

Darci

I grinned as I tucked another clue behind a stack of picture books, imagining the squeals and gasps that would follow when tiny hands uncovered it. The scavenger hunt was nearly done, bits of mystery scattered like breadcrumbs across the children's department. This was one of my favorite things each month. It was the one thing I kept for myself and never delegated.

One last clue to go. I scanned the shelves, spotted the perfect nook, and dropped to my belly, the carpet prickling against my arms as I crawled beneath a bookcase, hoping I wasn't flashing the entire library. With one hand, I taped the final picture beneath the lowest shelf.

Behind me, I heard footsteps. I froze, half-tucked under the shelf like a secret.

"Darci?" Claire's voice startled me. "What in the world are you doing down there?"

I pressed the tape one last time and scooted back,

brushing my hands off like I'd just escaped an archaeological dig. How is it this dusty? What do they clean under here—with a prayer and a hope? At this point, I deserved hazard pay and a tetanus shot. Next time, I'm hiding the clue in a fake plant like a sane person.

"The monthly scavenger hunt?" I peered up at Claire with a smile as I started to stand up.

"What's the theme this time?" She quipped, raising an eyebrow.

I giggled, my amusement bubbling over. "Cryptids. They'll have to find Bigfoot, Mothman, and other creepy creatures."

Claire's eyes widened in excitement. "Oh, that sounds fun!"

Walking to my desk, I leaned my head against her shoulder. "I feel like we haven't talked in forever." I glanced away, feeling the heat in my cheeks. "You're not..." I swallowed. "You're not still mad at me about Vegas, are you?"

She grabbed my hand, "Darci, I was never mad at you. I was just... mad at the situation."

I chuckled dryly, nodding, "The situation *I* put us in."

She rolled her eyes and then laughed, "I suppose, but... I could never be mad at you." She squeezed my hand. "What matters is we fixed it, and you're back to being a single woman again." She chuckled, "I'm sorry I've been so busy. This wedding is taking over my life."

"That sounds like we need a Murder Night," I declared, the idea hitting me mid-eye roll. "It's been forever."

Claire's face lit up as she nodded enthusiastically. "God, yes. I need a break. Come to the house—I'll order

Thai. A night of pad see ew and vengeance sounds wonderful."

"A sacred gathering of the Crimebrarians," I said solemnly, placing a hand over my heart. "Justice and spring rolls await."

She snorted. "God, we're insufferable."

I grinned. "I'll bring the drinks."

"Perfect," she replied, a mischievous glint in her eye. "Sonny barely leaves his office. He had a big breakthrough with his latest manuscript."

I heard the hurt under the sarcasm. It was subtle but there. Claire didn't say things like "I feel forgotten" out loud, but I recognized the look—that quiet ache of being in the room with someone who felt miles away.

"I get it," I said. "It's hard when they vanish into something that doesn't include you. But he loves you. He'll circle back."

She paused, the air stretching between us. "I know it's important, I do. It's just…"

She gave a slight shrug, clearing her throat and brightening with effort. "Anyway—spring rolls or crab rangoon?"

"I say both," I grinned. A wave of excitement washed over me, but something tugged at the back of my mind. Was I forgetting something? There was… something, but I couldn't remember. I pulled my phone out of my pocket and searched the calendar. It was empty.

"Can't wait," I replied, my anticipation growing.

"Do you want to sleep over? Stay in the guest room?"

"I don't have to work tomorrow. Do you?"

She laughed, "Nope. I planned to spend the day putting together gift bags for the wedding. Want to help?"

I gave her a wry smile. "Of course, I'd love to. I just need to avoid another killer hangover like Vegas."

"Sure, Darce..." She rolled her eyes, laughing as she stood up and backed away. "I've got to run. Another appointment for a dress fitting. See you tonight!"

I waved as she turned and headed to the main office.

When I got home, I didn't even take off my shoes. I yanked a box from the closet and beelined to the pantry, tossing in whatever felt vaguely cocktail-adjacent.

Vodka since I was out of tequila. Some dried blood orange slices. A rogue can of coconut milk. It was less "recipe" and more "emotional damage, shaken with ice."

"Orange juice," I said, chucking it in. "Grenadine, for dramatic effect. This is about the vibe, not the accuracy."

The drinks weren't really the point. But if Sonny was too deep in his writing cave to see her, then fine. I'd show up. With citrus, chaos, and cocktails. A glance at the clock told me I had about thirty minutes to shower and get ready before driving over.

I'd just thrown on clothes when there was a knock at the door, cutting into my pre-party cocktail prep. I groaned inwardly, already guessing it was Alex. He'd finally switched to the day shift at the hospital, which meant we were now operating on the same schedule.

I hollered, "It's open!" as I walked into the bedroom to throw some pajamas into a bag.

It wasn't that I didn't want to see him. I did. But tonight? I needed a break from emotions with eyebrows and dimples. I needed true crime. I needed girl talk. I needed the kind of night where I could wear stretchy pants, mock my own dating history, and pour drinks without worrying about whether I snorted when I laughed.

A moment later, he startled me. "You shouldn't answer the door like that," he scolded, his voice laced with a hint of concern. "What if I were a stranger? Someone dangerous?"

A playful smirk crept across my face. "I knew it was you," I teased, my tone light. "Besides, I've got a black belt in badassery."

He raised an eyebrow, a silent challenge. "More like smartassery," he replied, his voice laced with amusement as he leaned against the kitchen counter, his arms crossed, casual confidence radiating from him. I couldn't help but feel a surge of attraction.

I backed up towards the hallway, "I'll be right back."

I went to the bathroom and fluffed my hair a bit. I threw a pair of shorts, jeans, and a T-shirt into the bag for tomorrow. When I walked back to the kitchen, my bag was slung over my shoulder, and I grabbed the box.

"Whenever you're ready…" His eyes scanned me quizzically.

"Uh, for what?" I managed to stammer out. A wave of panic washed over me as I set the box back down and fully faced him.

His eyebrows raised in amusement. "Dinner? The Ethiopian place?"

My heart sank. How could I have forgotten? The guilt was immediate and overwhelming. "Oh my god, I completely forgot," I exclaimed, my face flushing with embarrassment. I mumbled, "I was just on my way out to Claire's… for girls' night."

"You… forgot?" His brow wrinkled as he stepped toward me. "Well, this is just fan-fucking-tastic," he replied, his voice dripping with sarcasm. "I guess I'm just supposed to sit around and wait for you to remember I'm here."

I sucked in a breath, "Alex... I'm... I'm sorry. I didn't mean...." I wasn't sure what to say.

"You're flaking out on me," Alex accused, his voice low. Then he smiled, but it didn't reach his eyes, "Fine. Go have a girls' night."

"Don't be dramatic," I retorted, my voice rising. "I forgot. It happens."

His jaw clenched, his eyes narrowing. "And if I had forgotten?" he countered, his voice dripping with sarcasm.

He waited. Silent. Patient. Too patient.

I opened my mouth and then shut it again. What could I say? I'd be pissed too.

His nostrils flared—just slightly—and something flickered across his face. Frustration, maybe. Hurt. But then his jaw loosened, and the tension in his eyes gave way to something softer.

He let out a quiet sigh. "Just... forget it," he said, his voice even. "Go have fun with Claire. I'll call Javi, maybe grab a beer or something."

"Alex..." My cheeks burned. "I feel awful."

I reached for his wrist, but he didn't answer. He just stared at his feet.

"It's just—we haven't really hung out in weeks. And she sounded like she really needed this."

He nodded once. Dismissive, maybe. Maybe just tired. Either way, a knot twisted in my belly, low and aching.

"You're sure?" I asked in a whisper.

Another nod. This time with a smile. Not at all convincing, but softer. "Go. I'm fine. I'm just... being ridiculous."

"You're not," I said quietly. "This is all my fault."

He chuckled, a defensive edge to his laughter. "It's okay. It's just..." He trailed off like he was searching for the right words.

I raised an eyebrow, coming up and placing my hands on his chest. "Tell me," I prompted, my tone light.

He shook his head. "We can try the Ethiopian restaurant another time," he offered, his voice gentle.

"I know," I replied, a small smile gracing my lips.

But something was eating at him. He wrapped his arms around my waist as I nestled into him, his scent enveloping me.

Almost as an afterthought, he added, "How about a late-night sleepover when you get back?" His eyebrows raised suggestively as he brought his lips to mine.

"Oh," I murmured, "it was going to be a girls' sleepover," I confessed, "with all the cocktails and true crime documentaries. I might be too drunk to drive home."

"What about Edison?"

"He's on a writing binge to finish his manuscript. Claire says he barely comes out of his office."

He nodded, a hint of disappointment crossing his face.

"Okay..." he replied, his tone laced with a hint of skepticism.

I pulled back, "Alex, what in the hell is that supposed to mean?"

If he rolled his eyes harder, they'd disappear into his skull. "Forget it."

"No, tell me what you're implying," I said firmly. "Are you accusing me of something?"

"God, no, Darci. No. I'm just...," He murmured,

almost so softly I didn't hear, "jealous."

"You're jealous? Of girls' night?" I raised my eyebrows nearly to my hairline. "You'd probably hate it."

"What if…" he whispered, "I come pick you up if you can't drive home? Then we could have that sleepover," he offered, his voice soft.

"I don't know…" It was sweet, but was that a good idea?

"Come on, Darce. It's the least you could do." He smirked.

A flash of anger shot through me. "The least I could do? What is that supposed to mean?"

He lifted a shoulder. "I don't know. You forgot our date, and this could…" He looked away before meeting my gaze again. "Make it up to me."

"Make it up to you? Good god, I don't owe you anything. I just forgot, okay? It's not like we haven't been spending time together nearly every day." I swallowed. "I'm sorry, but I need to get to Claire's."

I backed out of his embrace, picked up my bag, and grabbed the box with my cocktail ingredients. As I turned to leave, he stopped me.

"Wait." He wrapped his hands around the box, brushing his fingers against mine, and I was startled by the jolt of electricity. "Let me help you to the car."

I jerked away. "No, I can do this myself."

He tugged the box against my grip. "Come on, Darci. Just let me help you."

With a swift movement, he snatched the box from my hands. Then, as if in slow motion, the box hit the floor, and the glass made a deafening crash. The shattered remains sparkled on the kitchen tiles. Orange juice, vodka, and grenadine slowly pooled at my feet, a sticky, iridescent mess. Our eyes met across the chaos, his face mirroring my shock.

"Darci... I didn't mean..." he stammered, his voice low.

I was too stunned to speak, racing to process the disaster unfolding before me. Anger, frustration, and a touch of disbelief warred within me. My movements were automatic as I grabbed the mop, broom, and dustpan from the pantry.

I murmured, almost to myself, "What the fuck?"

"It was an accident, I swear." He toed the rug under the kitchen table, which was bunched up. "I tripped. Look, I'll replace it all. I'm really sorry..."

I began to sweep up the mess. A moment later, he picked up the dustpan, but I grabbed it as he knelt down.

"I can handle this," I said, my voice steady despite the turmoil churning inside.

He opened his mouth to protest, but I cut him off with a stern look.

"Just... go," I managed, my voice steady, just barely. The last thing I needed was his help.

He hesitated, his eyes filled with guilt and frustration. Finally, he heaved out a breath and walked towards the front door, his steps heavy with defeat.

It took another half hour, but I swept up all the glass and mopped the sticky mess before running to the dumpster to throw it all away. I was only 25 minutes late to Claire's after making a quick pit stop at the Margarita Hut for a jug of ready-made strawberry margaritas.

It wasn't until I rang Claire's doorbell that I realized I

never changed clothes after the mess. I was a walking alcoholic sweet tart.

When Claire opened the door, she took one look at me and said, "Darci? What the hell happened to you?"

I offered a weak smile as she took the bags from my hands.

"Alex kind of... happened."

"Oh?" She looked over her shoulder as I followed her inside. "In a good way or a bad way?

I muttered, "Definitely bad."

"Well, that sucks. Are you two at each other's throats again?" Claire set the bags on the coffee table next to the takeout boxes of Thai food before she flopped down on the couch.

I set my tote bag over to the side and slid off my shoes. I tucked my feet under myself as I let out a long sigh, "Honestly, I don't know. One minute, he's perfect, and the next..." I rolled my eyes. "Goddamn, that man!"

I told Claire all about what happened with Alex.

"You should have canceled," she said, giving me a pointed look, "and gone out to dinner with him."

I took in a breath and slowly let it out. "Maybe..."

"And do you really think he threw the box on the floor? That seems a little aggressive. Maybe it was just an accident?" she asked.

"I don't know. He said he tripped on the rug in the kitchen. But... he was pissed I forgot our date. He was pissed I had made other plans. He was just pissed all around. Maybe he just wanted to punish me."

Claire asked, "And then try to help you clean up?"

I groaned. "I don't know," I shrugged. "He's just so... so frustrating!" I threw my hands up in the air.

"Or maybe, babe, he just tripped." She leaned

forward, taking the food out of the bags.

I murmured, "Maybe..."

I leaned forward, inhaling deeply. The food smelled heavenly. For the next few hours, I was more than ready to forget about Dr. Alex Dixon.

I continued, "But right now, I need a margarita and some of that noodle stuff right there." I pointed towards one of the containers Claire had just opened.

While she made our plates, I went to the kitchen and grabbed two glasses. I returned to the couch, filling them with strawberry margaritas. Just as I handed one to Claire and we clinked glasses, Edison padded barefoot into the room.

He smiled when he saw me. "Hey Darci, how are you?"

I held my glass up and said, "Pretty good, now. You?"

"I'm good." He looked at the drinks in our hands. "Um... how many of those have you two had?"

Claire set her drink down. "None. Why?"

"Well... I have a favor to ask." He gave us both a sheepish smile. "Can y'all add another to girls' night? I need you to go pick up my sister at the airport."

Claire wrinkled her brow. "Your sister? She's already here? But the wedding's weeks away."

He let out a sigh. "I know, and I'd do it myself, but..."

Claire set her drink down and went over to Edison and wrapped her arms around his waist. "I know, I know, Honey. You're on a roll, and we don't want to mess that up."

He chuckled, kissing her gently. "I'd really appreciate it."

I asked, "Wasn't she in Asia?"

They broke apart, and Claire slipped on her shoes and

grabbed her purse off the entryway table while I closed up the takeout containers.

"She was supposed to be in Vietnam with Devin, but..." He shrugged. "She called me yesterday and seemed... upset. Like she needed to come home, but didn't really ask. So I offered. And since she's been traveling for the last few years, my home is pretty much hers."

Claire's eyes softened as she looked at him. "Is everything okay with her?"

He cleared his throat and twisted his lips. "I don't really know. It's been a while since I've seen her."

"Okay, we'll get her. Don't worry," she ran her hand down his arm. "Just text me her gate number." She turned to me, "Well? Road trip to the airport?"

I slipped my shoes back on and said, "Heck, yeah. We can listen to that new murder podcast."

An hour later, Claire and I were helping Mallory load her bags into the trunk of Claire's car. Mallory looked wrecked in that post-16-hour-flight kind of way. Her eyes were rimmed red, her ponytail barely holding on, and she clutched her suitcase like it was the last thing holding her together.

"Thanks for picking me up," she said, voice thin and scratchy. "And for letting me stay."

Claire didn't hesitate. She just pulled her into a hug and said, "Our home is yours."

Mallory nodded, but didn't speak again. She didn't need to. The way she melted into Claire's arms said everything.

And I stood there, suddenly protective as hell.

Claire gently bumped Mallory's shoulder. "Besides, tonight's girls' night. Darci and I were just about to watch a serial killer documentary, eat Thai food, and drink strawberry margaritas until we can't see straight."

"Oh, that sounds exactly like what I need."

Edison met us in the garage as soon as we pulled in. He hugged Mallory, who seemed to melt in his embrace. Then, we all grabbed a bag and headed towards the guest room. After she had changed clothes, Mallory met us in the living room. I was already pouring fresh margaritas, and Claire was reheating the food.

When we all settled on the couch, Edison pointed a finger at us and said, "Don't corrupt my little sister."

We all laughed when Mallory said, "Bro, I'm 28 years old. If I've been corrupted, it's already happened."

He rolled his eyes with a smirk and headed back to his office.

I turned toward Mallory and Claire. "Well, now that he's gone," I thumbed back toward his office. I leaned toward Mallory, "So what's the deal? What happened?"

Claire had big doe eyes, but I could see the tiny smirk lurking on her face.

Mallory let out a long heavy sigh, "Well... let's just say Devin can go fuck himself."

Claire's eyes went wide as she took a long drink.

Mallory shook her head. "I found that... that fucker... in our bed with someone else."

My eyebrows shot up to my hairline. "In your bed?"

She nodded before taking a big drink of her margarita, mumbling into her glass, "And it wasn't the first time."

"Jesus, men can be such pricks," I said.

"Yep," Mallory muttered.

I flicked my eyes to Claire over Mallory's shoulder,

raising my eyebrows, as we both watched Mallory down her drink in one go. This was going to be a… night.

"Well, *I* forgot about a date Alex and I had planned for tonight. What about you, Claire? Anything Edison does that makes you want to kill him?"

She chuckled, "Well…"

My ears perked up. "Yes? Tell the class what Mr. Perfect does to annoy you," I gestured to the two of us sitting on the couch.

She sipped her drink and lowered her voice almost to a whisper, "He leaves the seat up."

I cocked an eyebrow, "Okay… and?"

She shrugged.

"That's… it? He leaves the seat up?"

In a small voice, she said, "I fell in. It was… cold."

Mallory let out a laugh that soon became contagious, and we were all giggling uncontrollably.

I wiped the tears. "Oh my god, Claire, if that's the most annoying thing, you are one lucky lady."

Between giggles, she agreed, "I know. But… It's still a cold shock in the middle of the night to sit down to pee and end up ass-deep in the water."

Three hours later, we were still sprawled on the couch, the remnants of our margaritas and noodles forgotten on the coffee table. Mallory's infectious energy was a welcome addition to our little party.

"Oh god, I've missed this kind of thing," she exclaimed, her voice muffled by a couch cushion. "It's been forever since I've just hung out with the girls."

Claire wrapped her arm around Mallory in a comforting embrace. "Well, you're always welcome to join the Crimebrarians," she replied, a mischievous glint in her eye.

I choked on my laughter, the word "Crimebrarians" coming out as a breathless splutter.

Mallory's eyes widened in amusement. "What in the hell is a Crimebrarian?" Her words slurred together.

"We're librarians who watch true crime," I giggled. "It's totally a thing."

"Yeah, it's a..." Claire hiccuped, "a thing."

Another wave of giggles washed over us. Mallory was going to be a perfect addition to our weird little club.

"Well, ladies, this was fun, and I can't wait to do it again, but..." Mallory took two tries to stand up from the couch. "I've got some serious jet lag. I'm going to bed."

"Goodnight, Mal," Claire said. "Just remember to check the toilet seat before you sit down."

Mallory's eyes widened before turning down the hallway. Claire snorted, and I couldn't stop giggling. A moment later, Edison came in with a big grin.

"Is the party winding down? I could hear your giggles in my office."

Claire yawned. "Yeah, I think so. I'm so...." She yawned again. "Tired."

She stumbled as she tried to stand up, but in two strides, Edison was there, lifting her in his arms. She wrapped her arms around his shoulders and snuggled her face against the crook of his neck.

"You smell so good, baby."

He chuckled and looked over at me. "You staying tonight, Darce?"

I sighed, stretching my legs on the couch. "I haven't decided yet, but I'm good." I jutted my chin towards

Claire, who was already snoring in his arms, "Just take her to bed."

"Alright, goodnight."

"Goodnight, Edison. You're a… a good guy. Thanks for always taking care of my best friend."

He gave me a small smile as he nodded and left the room.

CHAPTER TWENTY-FOUR

Alex

I woke with a start. The trill of my phone pierced the quiet of the night, jolting me awake, my heart racing. My eyes struggled to focus as I reached for it, the glowing screen revealing 2:57 AM.

Darci's photo flashed across the screen, and a wave of concern washed over me. Had something happened? Was something wrong?

"Darci?" I answered, my voice thick with sleep.

She laughed—bright and unguarded—and something inside me tilted toward her, like it always had. The sound shimmered in the quiet, familiar and brand new all at once. I found myself smiling before I even realized it.

"Alexxxxx..." she slurred, her voice sweet and seductive—a jolt of desire shot through me.

I sat up, trying to shake off the deep sleep.

"Yeah, it's me," I managed to croak out.

"Are we okay?" she asked.

"Yeah, we're good, Tink," I replied, trying to hide the

growing warmth in my body. "Are you okay?"

"I'm good, I'm real good. I'm at... Claire's," she giggled. "Everybody went to bed, and I'm lonely, Alex. You said you'd pick me up."

A surge of protectiveness ran through me. "I did say that, didn't I?"

She let out a dreamy sigh, her words slurring together. "I need you," she breathed out, her voice filled with a vulnerability that pulled at my heartstrings.

"Can you text the address?" My heart pounded in my chest.

"Yeah, hang on."

It took her a moment, but the text came through.

"I'll be there soon," I replied.

The drive to Claire's place was just a few minutes, but it was a blur of red lights and stop signs. I pulled up to the curb, my heart pounding in my chest. The street was silent, apart from the rustling of the trees. As I stepped out of the car, I took a deep breath, steeling myself for whatever this would be. The house was dark, except for a soft glow from the living room. I knocked softly, my hand hovering over the doorbell.

Scratching sounds came from inside the door. A few minutes later, the door creaked open, revealing Darci leaning against the frame, her eyes glazed over. A wave of concern washed over me as I took in her disheveled appearance.

"You came," she slurred, her voice barely audible. A playful smirk tugged at her lips as she stumbled forward, nearly losing her balance.

I reached out to steady her, my heart beating frantically as I looked around the room. I nodded, my arms opening to welcome her. She stumbled into my embrace, her body limp and yielding. The scent of alcohol and citrus candy filled my senses.

"Of course I came, Sweetheart," I replied.

"Aww... you called me sweetheart." She poked my chest, "You always just call me Tink." Her eyes had trouble focusing on me. She put her finger to her lips, "Sshhh. We have to be quiet," she whispered, her eyes darting around the room. "Mallory and Claire are asleep."

Mallory? I nodded, my focus on keeping her upright. "Where's your stuff?" I asked, trying to sound casual.

She pointed vaguely towards the living room. "Over there... somewhere," she mumbled, her voice growing more slurred by the second.

I looked where she pointed but found nothing.

"We can get it tomorrow. Let's get you home."

She nodded, her body swaying slightly. I tucked her against me, her face nestled into my neck.

Her voice muffled as she said, "How do you always smell like this? It's so... intoxicating. I hate it."

I chuckled, "Yeah, Tink, you can smell me at home. Ready?" I asked, offering her my hand.

As I was about to walk her to the door, Edison entered the living room in black boxer shorts. Wasn't he a writer or a professor or something? How did this guy look like a ripped athlete?

"Darci?" He asked, peering into the darkness.

"Hey, uh, Edison. It's me, Dr. Alex."

The tension in his shoulders eased, and he grinned at me, "Oh, hey man, I was just coming to check on Darci. I heard some noises."

My arm protectively wrapped around Darci. "She called me to come get her. Do you know where her purse is?"

He walked further into the room, grabbed her bag from under the coffee table, and handed it to me.

"Here it is. You need any help getting her to the car?"

I shook my head as I put her bag on my shoulder, keeping her wrapped into me with my other arm. "Nah, I think we're good. We'll get out of your hair. Goodnight."

He walked us to the door.

"'Night, Darci," he said.

She mumbled something into my neck.

I looked over my shoulder. "Night, man. Thanks again." He nodded and shut the door.

I tried to carefully walk Darci down the front steps to the car, but she stumbled repeatedly. Finally, I gave up, threw her bag over my head, and picked her up to carry her in my arms.

She was so light, like a feather. That feeling of protectiveness surged again as I carried her to the car. She seemed so small and vulnerable, and I had this overwhelming need to shield her from the world.

I grinned as I opened the passenger door, and she clung tightly against me. "Baby, just let me put you in the car."

"Okay," she sighed as she snuggled into the seat.

Once inside, I carefully buckled her in, making sure she was secure. Her head was against the headrest. I jogged around to get in, sliding into the driver's seat. As we pulled away from the curb, I glanced at her, her head resting against the window. She was asleep, her face serene in the soft glow of the streetlights.

The drive back was quick. When we arrived, I carefully lifted her out of the car and carried her to my apartment. I didn't want to leave her tonight.

I laid her down on my bed, pulling off her shoes and leggings and then tucking her in with a gentle hand. She stirred, her eyes fluttering open.

"Alexxxxx....." she murmured, her voice barely audible. With a sleepy smile, she said, "You saved me."

I brushed her hair off her forehead. "Did I?"

Her eyes widened just for a moment. "Are we having a sleepover?"

I smiled, leaning down to kiss her forehead. "We are. And you need some sleep."

She nodded, blinking slowly as a slow grin spread on her face.

"Dr. Alex?" She reached her hand out to me, and I laced our fingers together.

"Yeah?"

She giggled as her eyes closed again.

"Mmmm," She moaned, and I thought she was falling asleep until she said, "Your bed always feels so nice."

I sat beside her, still holding her hand, "I think it's pretty nice, too."

She giggled again before surprising me with her next question.

"Are you my boyfriend?"

I chuckled, feeling like I was in high school again, "I don't know. What do you think?"

Her eyes fluttered as she grinned and whispered, "Yessss..."

Her eyes closed as her head lolled to the side. She snuggled into the pillows, her breathing slowing as she drifted asleep. I waited a moment before I stood up and stripped down to my boxers, climbing into bed behind her. Her warmth settled next to me, easy and quiet, like it had always belonged there.

"Goodnight, Tink," I whispered.

She murmured something unintelligible in response. As soon as I was under the covers, she rolled over like a sleepy kitten, curling up in my arms.

"Sweet dreams," I replied, my voice filled with a tenderness I hadn't felt in a long time. This. This was where she belonged—in my bed, in my arms, every night.

The next morning, I woke to find Darci still curled against me, but with the sheets kicked off both of us. A glance at the clock confirmed my suspicions—it was already mid-morning. I smiled, the memory of the night before washing over me.

Drunk, giggly, and adorable Darci was a far cry from the sharp-tongued woman I usually encountered. I ran my hand gently along her side, needing to touch her. Darci groaned, shifting in her sleep.

Her voice was rough from sleep, so she asked, "What time is it?"

My arms tightened slightly against her, "Half past nine."

She stretched before wincing, her hand coming up to her head.

"How... how did I end up here?"

I looked down at her with a small smile, "You don't remember?"

She moved to shake her head but winced again, holding her head with her hand. She whispered, "Not really."

I kissed her temple, "Well... my sweet menace, you called me to pick you up at Claire's around three in the morning."

She pulled back to look at me, her eyes barely open, "I did?"

I nodded.

"You also asked me to be your boyfriend and told me I smelled good."

She cringed and covered her face with her hands.

"Oh god…" was all she said before nestling back against me, her head in the crook of my shoulder.

I couldn't help but grin when I felt her take a deep breath as if she were breathing me in. We lay there for some time. I think I fell back asleep, her rhythmic breathing lulling back into my dreams.

I woke again a while later and carefully untangled her from me as I stretched.

She snuggled into the pillows, her voice muffled as she said, "No… don't leave me."

I leaned over, running my hand through her hair. "Let me make you my hangover cure."

She opened one eye, peering at me, her voice still muffled, "Hangover cure?"

"I'll be right back."

I headed to the kitchen to make her my version of Hair of the Dog—whiskey, half and half, and honey, all over ice. It was an unholy marriage of ingredients, but it worked every damn time I've tried it.

A few minutes later, I returned with two glasses of my concoction, hoping it might cure my headache, too. Darci sat up with her hands over her face.

"Here you go," I said, handing her one. "I thought I'd drink in solidarity with you."

"It's a classic," I continued, taking a sip, trying to hide my wince. "Trust me, it works."

She brought it to her nose, sniffing it. "What's in this?

Whiskey?"

"Yeah, whiskey, half and half, and honey."

She squinted at the drink. "You're sure about this?"

I took another sip, "Absolutely. It's my go-to hangover cure."

"Okay…" she mumbled before bringing it to her lips and drinking the entire thing in one go.

She wrinkled her nose as soon as she was done, "Wasn't too… bad."

I chuckled, "You liked it?"

She tilted her head from side to side before shrugging. "Maybe?" She lay back down, looking a little green as her hand covered her forehead. "So, how long does it take?"

I lifted a shoulder. "I don't know. Maybe 30 minutes? An hour?" I took her glass and handed her the pain reliever and water I left on the nightstand. "Take these for now, and you should feel better soon."

I lifted the covers and gently tucked them around her as she snuggled back into the pillows.

As I turned to leave the room, Darci said quietly, "Alex?"

I turned back around, "Yeah?"

"Thanks for… taking care of me." Her cheeks reddened.

I grinned, "I… like taking care of you."

I could tell my response surprised her when her eyes widened for a split second. But she didn't respond other than nodding as she closed her eyes again and drifted back to sleep.

CHAPTER TWENTY-FIVE

Darci

I couldn't say exactly when things shifted between us. Maybe it was the night he opened up about his wife and baby, or when he took care of me after I drank too many strawberry margaritas at Claire's. All I knew was that I liked the way we fit together now.

Alex had slipped into my life and somehow stayed. Whether we were cooking dinner at my place or tangled up in each other at his apartment, each moment felt like a quiet, precious thing I didn't want to disturb. Saying it out loud felt risky, like admitting we were in a relationship might make it all fall apart.

I'd never felt this way, but he stirred something deep and unexpected in me. Was I falling for him? Was he feeling it, too?

A few days ago, I figured out his birthday was coming up. We went to another show at Andy's, and they always carded everyone. He pulled out his license and handed it to me, while he put my lipstick and keys in his pocket, so I didn't have to carry a purse inside.

Before I gave it to the bouncer, I noticed his birthday was just a few days away. He hadn't even told me.

I wanted to make it special for him, so I booked a table at Matteo's—a spot Edison and Claire had raved about, though somehow I'd never been. Claire dropped by to help me pick the perfect dress from my closet. After sifting through a few options, we settled on a yellow sundress that laced up the back. Black was usually my color, but the warm weather made it just right for tonight, and it hugged my waist, making me feel beautiful.

As I slipped on my wedge sandals, my phone buzzed with a text. I smiled, guessing it was Alex letting me know he was walking over. I hadn't told him what we were doing, but I mentioned that he should dress up.

When he arrived at my door, he looked like he had walked straight out of the pages of GQ magazine with his slim-cut dark blue suit. His tie matched his eyes, and I couldn't help but stare.

Desire tugged at me to wrap my hand around that tie, pull him inside, and forget the dinner reservations. Instead, I smiled and blushed when he told me how beautiful I looked. He waited near the door as I grabbed my purse, discreetly tucking the small present I had for him inside.

The scent hit me the second we stepped inside— garlic, butter, and something slow-cooked that made my mouth water on impact. The wooden floors creaked beneath our feet as we made our way to the hostess stand, where a white-bearded man greeted us with a twinkle in his eye and the energy of someone who knew exactly how good his kitchen was.

"Evening," he said. "How many?"

I gave him my name for the reservation, and he nodded, scooping up menus. As he led us to our table, he listed off the specials in a voice that could probably convince me to order anything: truffle risotto, bourbon bread pudding, yes, please.

Once we were seated, he handed us the drink menu with a wink. I leaned in, letting a grin curl at my lips.

"I'm Darci. Edison and Claire have been raving about this place forever, and now I get it. Everything smells amazing. I'm already halfway in love."

"It's so nice to meet you. I'm Tate. Any friend of Edison's is a friend of mine. He's like the son Noelle and I never had." He gave a big belly laugh. "And Claire? I knew she was the one the minute I met her. I can't tell you how thrilled I am they're finally tying the knot."

I nodded, giving him a big grin, "Me, too. I'll be there with bells on as the maid of honor." I gestured to Alex. "This is my friend, Alex."

Still grinning, Tate gave Alex a subtle nod. "Wonderful, wonderful. I'll make sure you both enjoy tonight."

Tate took our drink order before dashing off to the kitchen.

Alex leaned toward me, mischief in his eyes, "Well, now we know where Santa hides during the off-season."

I swatted his arm, "Oh my god. Shush! Before someone hears you."

"What? He said his wife's name is Noelle. He practically gave it away."

I rolled my eyes, "Sure..."

I looked around the room as I put my napkin in my lap. The atmosphere was romantic. The dining room was dimmed, lit by flickering candles on each table.

There were pale pastel flowers everywhere. A small bouquet of tiny pale pink roses was in a vase on our table.

Alex glanced at me, and I gave him a sly grin. "I know your secret."

He reached for my hand resting on the table.

"And what's that?" He quipped, a smile playing on his lips.

I beamed when I said, "It's your birthday."

His expression shifted, just slightly, before that familiar smirk took over. "How do you know?"

I gave him a slight shrug, "I peeked at your license when we went to the show at Andy's last weekend." I gave him a teasing smile and said in mock sternness, "And we're celebrating, whether you like it or not."

A waiter came by, holding a bottle of red wine and two glasses. He poured each of us a glass and then left the bottle.

"Wait, we just ordered a glass each?"

He turned and smiled at me, "Tate said it was on the house."

"Really? Please thank him for us."

"Will do."

When we first arrived, the dining room was nearly empty. But by the time our first course hit the table, the place had begun to fill in around us. I noticed a family tucked in near the corner, already finishing their meal. It struck me as unusual, seeing a young child in such a fancy, romantic restaurant. The little girl looked about four, white-blond hair topped with an enormous pink bow that matched the gauzy floral dress she wore like a tutu at a tea party.

Her feet stuck straight out from the chair, little black

Mary Janes wiggling in the air as she colored furiously, completely absorbed. Her parents laughed softly with each other, looking relaxed in that way people only do when their kid is either asleep or unusually well-behaved.

She was adorable—quiet, contained, but glowing with the kind of joy that comes from knowing the world is still safe and good. And for a moment, I let myself imagine what it would feel like to be her mother. Would I ever get that chance?

I glanced at Alex, wondering if now was the right time to give him his birthday gift, but he seemed far away—lost somewhere I couldn't reach. The candlelight danced across his features, softening the edges of his jaw, but his eyes were distant, hollow.

The little girl let out a giggle as a waiter came over and placed a single cupcake in front of her. She blew out the candle in one huff, her parents beaming. It must have been her birthday too.

Alex stared at them, unmoving, as if they were a reminder of the memories he never got to make. And never would.

I reached across the table for his hand, my touch delicate and tentative, as I brushed his knuckles. He pulled away, flinching as if I burned him, his eyes darting to me before focusing back on them. My smile faltered as I looked between him and the family, realizing his daughter would probably have been close to her age by now. I was sure that was probably going through his mind.

"Alex," I breathed out, my voice just above a sigh, "Come back to me."

His eyes locked on mine as his jaw clenched so tightly

that the muscles twitched. "They were supposed to be here," he rasped, his voice cracking with a pain that chilled me to the bone.

The little girl laughed, high-pitched, bubbly, radiating pure joy across the room. Her mother broke out in laughter with her. His eyes shot right back to them, drawn like a moth to a flame as the girl enjoyed her cupcake.

"They should be here," he choked out again. "At this table, laughing like that. My family. My wife, my daughter..." The words shattered on his tongue, replaced by a strangled sob.

"I know," I murmured.

Again, I reached my hand across the table, hoping a familiar touch could bring him back. But he jerked away. My heart slammed against my chest, trying to escape. I tried to think of the right words to bring him back.

"But they... they can't be here."

His head snapped towards me, his eyes glinted, accusing and ready to ignite with anger. "What?" He paused before he continued, "Why? Why shouldn't they be here?" His voice rose, raw and desperate, tearing through the restaurant's hushed chatter.

The entire restaurant stopped. The other customers around us stiffened, their smiles replaced by awkward discomfort. I tried to smile, but my cheeks burned with shame.

"Because life is never fair," I whispered, my voice shaking. "It takes, and it gives, and sometimes, it rips the most precious things away before you can even blink."

He scoffed with a harsh, bitter sound. "So this is supposed to be *my* birthday gift? Watching other people live the life I was supposed to have while I'm... stuck here with you?" He gestured between himself and me, his words dripping with self-loathing.

Tears welled up in my eyes as I stared at my lap. He was hurting. But couldn't he control it, just this once?

"Alex," I choked out, "I thought..." I drifted off, unsure what to say, but then I sucked in a breath and let loose, "You're here, you're alive, and you're breathing. You told me you wanted..." Should I remind him? Was this the wrong thing to say? I didn't know what to do. I just needed him to stop this. Maybe... "You told me you wanted to build new memories that could just be... ours."

But it was too late. My words were lost in the storm brewing within him. He pushed himself away from the table, his chair scraping against the floor like a mournful cry.

"Don't you get it?" his voice thick with fury. "Everything I touch turns to shit. I can't build anything new. All I have are memories. This," he gestured at that family, the other customers, at the world outside, "is a constant reminder of what I lost and can never have again."

Everyone was staring. You could have heard a pin drop. I could feel their eyes burning into us. And then whispers rippled through the room. Humiliation seeped into my skin, but his words were like shards of ice, piercing my heart. That's when I finally saw the truth in his eyes, a truth that felt too dark to acknowledge.

He had built his grief into a room, brick by brick, and chose to live there.

And with a slow, aching clarity, I realized what I'd been afraid of all along—he didn't want out. He wasn't waiting to be rescued—he'd made peace with the walls.

I wasn't the key or the chisel or whatever the fuck. I was just a flicker of light in a place he never planned to leave.

"Please, Alex," I whispered, looking down at my lap. "Please don't do this here. Let's go home and talk this out."

"Home? That's not my home." He hurled out with bitterness. "My home is with them, six feet under in a steel box."

Panic rose in my throat as I took a look around. Everyone was still staring.

"Alex, I think you might need some help. This isn't healthy for you... or for me."

He pulled back, a look of shock on his face. He looked around the room as if he'd just realized where we were.

"I'm trying," He pleaded, his voice breaking. "I'm really trying, Darci. I'm trying to move on, but it's like I'm stuck in quicksand, sinking deeper every time I reach for the surface."

"You don't have to do it alone," I said quietly, "But even if you don't want help, I'm here, anyway."

And then something in him shifted. Not big, not dramatic—no grand apology. Just a flicker. His shoulders sagged, just slightly, as he sighed, like he'd suddenly remembered not just where he was, but what he'd done.

I stood up and tilted my head toward the front. "Let's go home."

His eyes stopped darting and locked onto mine. And that's when I saw it—the exact second he realized he might've just blown it. The flush that rose up his neck wasn't anger this time. It was shame. And fear. When you finally understand what you've risked.

I headed towards the door, looking back to ensure he was coming. Our eyes met, and a wave of regret washed over him, followed by a silent apology as he followed me through the dining room.

Tate was at the hostess stand, and I gave him a sad smile and mouthed, "I'm sorry." He shook his head and waved, giving me a sympathetic smile in return. I had a feeling this night would go through the grapevine. I was already dreading the call from Claire that I knew that would be coming.

CHAPTER TWENTY-SIX

Alex

That family, their bright and mocking laughter, chased me into the car. Darci took my keys and drove us home while I stared helplessly out the window, watching the world pass me by. I'd been trying desperately to keep up, but it felt like I had been a few steps behind for years. And now it was slipping past me even faster.

I followed her into the quiet dark of her apartment, guilt clinging to me like smoke. She wrapped her arms around me before I had time to brace for it. The warmth of it caught me off guard—gentle, undeserved—and for a moment, it felt like it might burn right through the numbness.

I sank into the blue armchair I always seemed to end up in, like it had been waiting for me. Darci dropped onto the couch, kicked off her heels, and tucked her legs under her like she was trying to shrink herself small enough to disappear.

I leaned my head back, staring at the ceiling, the weight of it all pressing into my chest. That family at the restaurant—their laughter, their easy joy—it cracked something open in me. I hadn't expected it to hit like that.

And Darci... god, she was just trying to make me feel better. Trying to do something kind. And I'd shut her down. In public. Like an asshole. The regret curled in my stomach like a fist.

I'd spent so many nights begging whatever god might still be listening to give them back. But tonight, I'd been handed a moment of grace—and I'd thrown it away.

I felt her gaze, but a moment later, she stood up and walked off. I stayed alone in the darkness with the remnants of our shattered night haunting me. For weeks, I'd been so good at hiding everything, trying to be the good boyfriend, pretending everything was fine. But I had exposed myself tonight, and Darci... hell, the entire fucking world had recoiled in horror.

The worst part wasn't the judgment of all those strangers. It was knowing this was probably the final nail in the coffin. We'd agreed to one chance, and even though, right now, she was still here, I was sure this was it. This would be the thing that finally drove her away for good, and she was the one person who had dared to try to pick up the pieces of my wrecked soul.

I caught a flicker of movement and saw Darci standing before me, her arm outstretched with something in her hand.

"Here," she said, her voice even. "I got this for you. For your birthday."

My head pounded as I raised it and blinked, forcing my eyes to focus on what she held. It was a small package wrapped in glossy black paper, a dark red satin ribbon tied carefully around it. I glanced up at her, searching her face, but her expression gave nothing away. Dread churned in my stomach, the restaurant scene replaying in fragments.

I gently took it from her, my fingers brushing the smooth paper as she sat back on the couch, a weary sigh slipping from her lips.

"Thank you, but you didn't have to do this."

"I wanted to," She said quietly.

I delicately removed the ribbon before unwrapping the paper to find a small framed photo of the two of us at that first concert, our first sort-of date. I couldn't help but smile. We were both mid-dance and smiling at each other, oblivious that our photo was being taken. We looked... so happy, like we were having the time of our lives.

I swallowed, feeling like cotton was trapped in my throat.

"Where did you..."

"Javier took it. He texted it to me a couple of days later."

I stared at the photo, running my hand over the frame, wondering how I let everything get to this point.

"I love it."

"I'm glad." She smiled sheepishly, shrugging her shoulders. "But I think... we need to talk," she said, her voice tight, holding back a torrent of concern.

I dropped my head, staring at my lap and the photo. I didn't want to have this conversation, not yet. I looked up at her, blinking back tears.

"I... I couldn't help it," I choked out. The words rasped against my throat like rusted nails. "Seeing them, that family... it was like they were there to remind me of what I lost."

Darci stood up and crawled into my lap.

"I know," she said.

Her arms wrapped around me, a lifeline thrown into the churning abyss of my grief. But I stiffened like it was a betrayal, and I hated myself for that. How could I be hers if I were still Jenna's? She backed away, her warmth leaving me yearning for more.

"No," her voice thick with tears I couldn't bear to see. "Please don't shut me out."

I looked at her. Her eyes were glassy pools of sorrow.

"But how can I not?" I spat, the words full of bitterness. "They're everywhere, Darci." My voice broke, a ragged sob escaping my lips. "I see them everywhere. Hell, I moved out of my home, my town. I moved here to escape their ghosts, and they still haunt me."

She moved from my lap, sitting across from me on the coffee table.

"You're allowed to be happy and live your life," she murmured, each word a pinprick, drawing fresh blood from my despair. "But this... this isn't living. It's surviving. Barely. And I don't want that for you, Alex. Not because of me—because of you."

Her hands trembled slightly in her lap, but her gaze never wavered.

"You think holding onto the pain is some kind of loyalty. But it's not. It's just more loss."

She let out a shaky breath. Her words stung, cutting through the layers of denial I'd woven. But somewhere beneath the anger, a sliver of truth pierced deep. I was lost in the darkness, but she was holding a lifeline. Could I find it to save myself?

"What about us, Darci?" I whispered, my voice catching. "What does this mean for us?" The words scraped out, raw and vulnerable.

I'd fucked up tonight badly. But the thought of losing her twisted something deep inside me. I couldn't let her go. I didn't want to let her go. I'd come to need her more than I wanted to admit. It had been just a few months, and already she was woven into my life, a thread I couldn't just pull free.

Her voice shook, eyes glistening with unshed tears. "Is there really an us, Alex? Because I can't keep going in circles with you, feeling like I'm the bad guy whenever your guilt flares up. It's draining." She paused, searching my face. "I want a future with someone who sees me, who's ready for something real. I don't want to be the one you settle for."

She shook her head softly, a sad smile playing on her lips. "I know I might come across like some manic pixie dream girl sometimes, but I want more than that. Someone to build messy, beautiful days with. I want a life. A home. Maybe even kids."

She took a breath, steady but gentle. "I'm not saying that to pressure you. I just… I need to be honest about what I hope for."

Another breath. Softer this time. "Because I do believe I deserve that."

Everything felt too heavy—the room, my clothes, our silence. What happened at the restaurant seemed a distant echo now, replaced by the harsh reality of our crumbling future.

"You deserve that. You absolutely do." I nodded. "I don't want to lose you," my voice cracked. "But I don't know how to let them go."

"Let yourself heal, Alex," she said, her gaze steady. "Set their ghosts free."

I nodded as I closed my eyes, a battle raging within me.

Her tone was gentle. "I want to help you, really I do. But I can't let you tear me apart. I can't be the collateral damage."

My eyes snapped open.

"So what, you're just done?" I bit out, the words harsher than I meant them to be—but I didn't pull them back. "You're tired of me because I have someone who meant something to me?" I gave her a smug look.

She didn't flinch, just looked at me with that same maddening softness. That same patience I didn't deserve.

I could feel it—my anger thrashing around, not at her, not really. At myself. At the impossibility of moving on.

"Maybe you don't get it," I added, cold now. "Maybe you never could."

I sucked in a breath. I needed to stop thinking this was okay to do to her. I needed to apologize.

She took a deep breath, slowly letting it out, and suddenly stood up as if she had made a decision.

"Just go, Alex." She closed her eyes, shaking her head. "I can't... I just can't do this anymore."

She walked to the front door, waiting for me. All I could do was stare at her, shaken to my core. It hurt more than I ever thought it would.

I sighed, "Darci..."

She shook her head. "Don't."

She opened the door, staring at the floor. I stood up slowly, feeling like I had been beaten to the ground. I knew I had royally messed up, but when she finally looked up, and our eyes met, she looked at me like I was a stranger.

The framed picture of us dropped from my hand and landed on the seat cushion. I ran my hand through my hair as I walked out of her apartment. When I turned around, she had already quietly shut the door.

My stomach was a knot of regrets, and any hope of fixing this was swallowed whole with each step I took back to my apartment. It was like a slow-motion train wreck that I couldn't stop.

I felt more alone than I had ever felt in my life. I just pushed away the only person who truly knew the hell I'd been living in. I should have known from the beginning that this was doomed. How could it not?

As I climbed the stairs, the hallway light flickered before burning too bright and then burning out completely, plunging me into a darkness that reflected the depth of my despair. As soon as I was inside, I made a beeline to the liquor cabinet, filling a glass nearly to the brim with bourbon. I shambled over to the couch, falling into it, not caring that half the glass splashed all over my suit. I sat there, staring out the window, watching her turn out the lights in her living room before she closed the blinds.

I sat there a long time, alone. The ghosts hadn't gone anywhere—they never did. But the silence without her felt different. Not emptier. Just... lonelier. Like something good had finally left the room, and the ache it left behind didn't scream—it echoed.

The only way out of this mess was to face it, and I had to do it alone. Darci couldn't help me do it, even if I wanted her to. I had to climb out, one step at a time, even if it meant leaving behind pieces of my heart that would be lost forever.

I took a long sip, the alcohol burning all the way down. I pulled my phone out of my pocket and texted my therapist. I'd been avoiding Dr. Matthews for months, canceling appointments, thinking I was okay. But I wasn't. I was sinking into a deep, dark hole. And I needed help getting out. I just hoped he'd still take me back.

It was late, but if I waited any longer, I wouldn't do it. I'd lose the clarity I had right now.

Maybe I'd find my way out of this darkness, and Darci would be in the light at the end of that tunnel. Or maybe I was just destined to be alone with my ghosts forever.

CHAPTER TWENTY-SEVEN

Darci

Weeks had passed since I'd heard from Alex. I missed him. I missed his infectious laughter, that smirk, and the sting of his sharp wit. I really missed the warmth of his touch. Every corner of my apartment felt like a shrine to our shared memories.

Our time together had shattered into longing stares across the parking lot. I'd peek out the window, catching glimpses of him nursing a drink on his porch with dark circles under his eyes, like he hadn't slept in days. I'd immediately lower the blinds to shield my aching heart. If I was outside reading and he emerged from his apartment, I could feel his heated gaze before he retreated inside. A wave of loss would wash over me, leaving me with regret. *Had I made the right decision?*

In the first few weeks, I'd walk into my apartment and pause, expecting the familiar scents of dinner wafting through the air. It had become our routine. Alex should've been standing at the stove, apron tied haphazardly, with that stupid smirk as he handed me a glass of wine. Sometimes, he'd meet me at the door, teasing me about my day before pulling me into a kiss that made everything else fade away.

But now, the space was dark and quiet, the emptiness almost mocking. I dropped my keys on the counter and sank into the silence, aching for those nights when we'd curl up on the couch together. He'd laugh at the ridiculous reality shows I insisted on watching, but he never changed the channel. And later, when the world outside faded to nothing, he'd pull me into the bedroom and make me feel things I wasn't sure I deserved to feel, like it was something sacred. *Like I was something sacred.*

He'd never been my type. Not even close. I'd always gone for the charming tattooed disasters, the walking red flags in a leather jacket. But with him, everything had just... clicked. Like finding the right thread in a tangle—suddenly, the whole thing made sense.

So why had I cut him off? Was it self-preservation or more like self-sabotage? All I knew was an ache that now lived in his absence. I missed him in a way that made my chest feel hollow, like a puzzle missing the one piece that mattered most.

But honestly, I wasn't surprised it ended. What surprised me was how long it lasted. Two dates were usually my relationship limit. So maybe this was progress... if you could call it that. Still, I couldn't help but wonder—*was it me?* Was I just hopeless at navigating love?

If you got down to it, I was the common denominator. Maybe I wasn't built for forever. Maybe I was just so unlovable that I'd end up alone forever.

I picked up my phone and typed out a message to Claire:

* * *

Thinking of leaning fully into my cat lady arc. Gonna start by giving all my furniture names and talking to my toaster like it's my husband.

I hit send, hoping for a quick laugh. A meme. Something light to take the edge off the ache. But minutes passed. Then an hour. Nothing. When she finally replied, it was short:

You're not unlovable, Darci. Don't be dramatic. You'll be okay.

I stared at the screen, the words landing like a pat on the head. I know she meant well, but... Suddenly, I felt lonelier than I had all night.

I let out a shaky breath, determined to keep the tears at bay. Crying alone in the dark over a guy wasn't who I wanted to be. That just wasn't me.

I'd convinced myself it was for the best. I didn't want to be second place, not to anyone. But now, sitting on this couch surrounded by the echoes of him, of us, I wasn't so sure anymore.

Thank god Claire's wedding was almost here. Two months had passed since Alex and I fell apart, and I'd been moving nonstop ever since—burying myself in work, Claire's wedding plans, day drinking, and anything that kept me from sitting still long enough to feel it.

But now, with the wedding just days away, I could feel it creeping back in. I couldn't help wishing I were taking this trip with him. That he'd be beside me on the plane, sneaking peanuts from my tray. Reaching for my hand, pretending not to be scared of turbulence. If he were mine again, even just for this.

Nope. Stop that. This wasn't about me. This was for Claire.

She needed me—her maid of honor, her emotional support goblin, her chief bouquet wrangler—and I wasn't about to let some lingering heartbreak turn me into a ghost when she needed me most.

This wedding meant everything to her. I couldn't afford to get tangled in my own drama. The last thing I needed was Claire knocking on my hotel room door and finding me curled up in bed, mascara-streaked and ugly-crying into a decorative pillow.

Not happening. Not on my watch.

Tomorrow was her last day at work for a few weeks, and we were throwing her a surprise wedding shower at the library. Somehow, I had managed to keep it a secret, and Claire had absolutely no idea.

My trusty librarian assistants, Anna and Melody, were currently on their way to help me whip up a few DIY bridal decorations for tomorrow's little party. I'd invited Mallory, but she had a last-minute thing come up and couldn't make it.

I popped a casserole dish full of brownie batter into the oven and glanced at the clock. They'd be here in fifteen minutes.

Exactly on time, the doorbell rang, jolting me out of my thoughts.

"Coming!" I yelled, rushing to answer the door. Anna and Melody stood on my doorstep, their arms laden with stuff.

"Ready to get this party started?" Anna grinned, her eyes sparkling with excitement.

Melody nodded enthusiastically, holding three pizza boxes.

"I've got the pizza," she announced, kicking off her shoes and shedding her jacket.

"I've got the decorations," I added, gesturing towards the craft store bags scattered across the living room floor.

Anna jiggled her bags, "And I've got the drinks!"

As we ate, I explained my vision for the decorations, and then we spent the next hour creating a couple of centerpieces and weaving decorations to create a bridal shower haven. Tomorrow, we'd be able to string streamers quickly from the ceiling in the break room, with balloons floating in every corner. We even cut out props for an impromptu photo booth. When we were finished, my apartment was a kaleidoscope of color and excitement.

"Claire is going to be so surprised. I can't believe we got it all done," Melody exclaimed, stepping back to admire our handiwork.

Anna raised a glass of bubbly apple cider in a toast. "To the bride-to-be!"

We clinked our glasses together and giggled.

"Can you believe I've managed to keep my mouth shut about our little fête? I'm starting to think I have a future in espionage," I said with a sarcastic grin as I took a bite of my pizza.

Anna rolled her eyes as she smiled, grabbing another slice of pizza. "If anything, I thought Bert would surely tell her. That man cannot keep a secret for more than five seconds."

I chuckled knowingly. I was convinced he was the one who told everybody Claire had thrown Elodie out of the library a while ago.

"Okay, so one last thing," I said, "I'm going to run out at lunch to get the cake and balloons. Melody, you're bringing a fruit tray and a charcuterie board, right?"

She nodded, "Already in my fridge and ready to go."

"And Anna, what are you bringing?"

"Chips, dips, and a veggie tray."

"Okay, perfect. Anna, meet me in the break room at 1 o'clock, and Melody, you keep Claire busy with… I don't know, something."

She gave me a conspiratorial grin, "I've already got a plan because I'll be taking over her shift when she's on her honeymoon. I've got a list of questions that will keep her busy for at least an hour."

We all giggled.

I stood up, rolling my shoulders and struck a mock runway pose. "Okay, ladies—we're gorgeous, we're dangerous, and we are very on schedule."

The next morning, Claire and I pulled into the library parking lot within seconds of each other. I stepped out of my car just as she started walking toward me, and I had to bite the inside of my cheek to keep from grinning too hard.

Right on cue, Mallory slid out of the passenger seat.

I arched a brow, playing along. "Well, well. Look who's here. What a *surprise*."

Mallory shot me a knowing smile that Claire completely missed. "Freelance project," she said cheerfully. "Figured I'd tag along with Claire this morning and do some work."

Claire just nodded, distracted as she dug through her bag. "She brought coffee, so she can stay forever as far as I'm concerned."

I exchanged a quick look with Mallory, the excitement bubbling just under my skin. Claire had no idea what was waiting for her inside.

I sidled up to Claire as we walked in together. "Can't believe your big day is almost here," I said, my voice filled with excitement.

Her eyes lit up with anticipation. "I know, right?" Dreamily, she said, "I can't wait for our honeymoon."

I wiggled my eyebrows. "You sure Edison will let you leave the hotel room?"

She rolled her eyes. "You know what I mean." She sighed softly, "I still can't believe I get to wake up next to my… husband in Greece. It feels surreal, like how did this even happen?" She giggled and lowered her voice. "I still can't believe Sonny will be my husband on Saturday."

I winced internally but grinned, squeezing her shoulder, "Babe, that man has no idea how lucky he is."

When she beamed, it hit me right in the gut. It wasn't jealousy. Claire had found the love of her life, and I was truly thrilled for her. It was just my desperate wish to find what those two had together. I had thought maybe… with Alex, but that ship had sailed. Maybe I just needed to accept that I was born to play the sidekick.

I shook those thoughts away and nudged her playfully as I glanced at Mallory, "And tomorrow night? After the rehearsal dinner? You, me, and Mal? We're painting the town red."

"Just not… too red," Claire replied, a playful warning. "The last thing I want on my wedding day is a hangover and well… you know." She glanced between me and Mallory.

A mischievous grin tugged at my lips. "Relax—you'll be the only one tying the knot this weekend," I said, voice dripping with sarcasm. "No impromptu Vegas weddings. Just a few dangerously fruity drinks, some half-naked men, and maybe a little light clubbing-slash-dancing-on-a-table-if-the-mood-strikes."

Right on cue, Mallory leaned over, heels clicking, eyes already sparkling with trouble.

"Oh, the mood will strike," she said, slipping an arm around Claire's shoulders. "I've got bail money, lipstick that doesn't smudge, and zero shame. Let's make some memories you'll pretend not to remember."

Claire groaned. "Why do I suddenly feel like I should make you both sign a behavior contract?"

Mallory laughed, "Just kidding... I'll behave... maybe."

When we got inside, Mallory went to find a table to set up her work space, while Claire and I went to store our belongings in the work room.

As Claire headed toward the teen room, she said, "I'll see you at lunch," a hint of excitement in her voice.

I twisted my lips to keep from smiling, "Sorry, Babe, I've got some errands to run during lunch, but I'll see you after."

She raised an eyebrow, a silent question hanging in the air.

"Promise," I added, sealing the deal with a wink and a grin.

As the morning wore on, I swore time seemed to move at a glacial pace. Finally, my phone buzzed with a reminder from the bakery. With a surge of excitement, I slipped away from my desk. I sneaked a peek at Claire, but she was busy helping a patron in the stacks.

When I reached the break room, Anna and Melody were busy hanging a few last-minute decorations, but the room had been transformed for the most part.

Pale pink and white streamers and balloons adorned the space, creating a festive bridal atmosphere. Food and drinks were laid out meticulously, and a perfect spot remained empty on the table, just waiting for the grand finale.

"Oh wow!" I whisper-yelled. "You guys, this place looks gorgeous."

Anna twisted toward me and smiled. "We've been sneaking in here all morning to do a little work at a time."

"Well, it's amazing." I grinned. "I'm going to run and grab the cake, but Melody, as soon as Claire is done with the patron she's helping, go keep her busy."

She smiled and nodded as she climbed down from the step stool.

With a sense of purpose, I slipped out the back door, careful not to be seen. The party store and the bakery were just a few blocks away, and I arrived back at work in record time, the cake box tucked safely in both arms. I saw Claire and Melody animatedly talking at Claire's desk, so I hurriedly walked by with my back towards them.

When I entered the break room, Anna smiled and held the door. We carefully took the cake out of its box and placed it in the center of the table. It was a pale pink two-tiered cake beautifully decorated in swirls of delicate ivory buttercream flowers. It was perfect.

I grabbed Mallory to help with the balloons stuffed in my car and had Anna meet us at the back door.

Once we had the balloons set around the room,

everything was ready. A moment later, I sent a group text, summoning the troops. I couldn't stop fiddling with the decorations, my heart fluttering with every footstep down the hall. I just wanted it to be perfect — for Claire.

Bert was the first to arrive, his face a mask of curiosity. "Is it time?" he asked, his voice low.

I nodded, a conspiratorial grin spreading across my face. "We're about to pull off the ultimate surprise." I tilted my head, "You came up with a good excuse to get her over here?"

"Yeah, I got a good one. I'll ask her to look at a weird YA book we got in the returns."

I grinned, "I'm sure she'll come running for that one."

People started filtering into the tiny break room. When Melody came back, I turned to Bert. "Go get her."

He gave me a thumbs up over his shoulder as he ducked his head to leave the break room. I swear he was almost seven feet tall.

"Okay, everyone," I said, rubbing my hands together like a cartoon villain about to steal Christmas, "Bert's gone to get Claire. Get ready."

A few minutes later, the break room was packed with excited coworkers. Everyone buzzed with nervous energy as we waited for Claire's arrival. I glanced at my watch, my heart pounding in my chest.

Mallory sneaked in a moment later, coming to stand by me, she leaned in and whispered, "She really has no idea?"

I grinned and shook my head.

Just as I started to doubt whether Bert's plan would work, the door swung open, revealing Claire standing in the doorway. Her eyebrows raised in curiosity as she looked back at him, not realizing any of us were here.

"So what's this weird book?" she asked, amusement dancing in her eyes.

"Congratulations!" We all yelled in unison, and she nearly jumped out of her skin.

She walked in slowly, taking in all the streamers and balloons, transforming the break room into a festive wonderland. I watched her, a slow grin spreading on my face.

She cocked an eyebrow at me as she smiled, "Did you plan this?"

Someone turned on a love song playlist on the Bluetooth speaker.

"Guilty," I said as I practically bounced over to her. We grabbed hands and bopped around to *Marry You* by Bruno Mars as the rest of our co-workers watched and mingled, munching on the food.

"Darci..." Claire's voice was a hushed whisper, her eyes full of disbelief and joy. She blurted out, "I'm getting married... this weekend... I can't believe it. It's happening all so fast."

I squealed, my heart pounding with excitement. I bit down on a baby carrot. "Believe it, girlie. And you're going to be the most beautiful bride." I assured her, squeezing her hands.

Her cheeks reddened as she scanned the room. "I can't believe y'all did this," she whispered, her voice filled with gratitude.

"Oh, babe, you deserve this and so much more," I replied, pulling her into a warm embrace.

Anna, ever the practical one, began pouring champagne into small glasses, quickly handing them out.

"To the bride-to-be!" she announced, raising her glass.

We clinked our glasses together, a chorus of cheers filling the room. Claire's eyes filled with tears as she took in the scene.

"This is so sweet," she said, her voice trembling.

She handed me her glass and walked over to the cake. "Oh my god, Darci, this is beautiful."

"I got it from your favorite bakery." I leaned in close, my voice low, "It's buttercream on the outside, but the inside is your favorite—blackout chocolate."

She gasped, her hand flying to her heart, and blinked back tears. "I don't deserve you as a best friend," she said, her voice thick with emotion.

I hugged her as we rocked together, cheek to cheek, "You're truly the sister I never had. And you are going to make an amazing wife to Edison."

We pulled apart as I clapped my hands together.

"Now, who's ready for some cake? We need to get back to work soon or Daryl will kill us for leaving our patrons alone for too long."

Everyone laughed as we cut and served the cake.

Twenty minutes later, everyone was back to work, and it was like we'd never even had a party in the break room. The decorations were all down. The food was put up. The top tier of the cake was all that was left, now in the box in the fridge, ready for Claire to take home.

When it was time to go, I helped Claire as I carried two shopping bags of gifts to her trunk while she carried the cake and buckled it into the passenger side of her car.

"Now," she said, squeezing my hand, "I'll see you bright and early at the airport tomorrow. Don't forget your dress!"

I smiled, "I won't. Everything is already packed and ready to go."

"Well, color me impressed, Little Miss Organized. Unlike me, who is packing everything tonight, you've got it all together."

I waved her off, "Oh, you'll be fine. Besides, I had to figure out how to fit all the bachelorette stuff in my bags."

"Bachelorette stuff?"

"Yeah… It's a themed bachelorette party… of sorts." I snickered.

"And what's this theme?"

With a smirk, I said, "You'll see… tomorrow night."

Claire rolled her eyes before giving me a big smirk. "Please tell me we aren't dressing up like the cast of Jersey Shore or famous bald men."

In a sing-song voice, I said, "You'll just have to wait and see…" as I walked backward to my car. Her eyes widened, and I gave her a big grin as I unlocked it. "See you tomorrow! Bright and early!"

CHAPTER TWENTY-EIGHT

Alex

I walked into the ER this morning with a familiar dread. It was like putting on a heavy coat on a summer day. I knew I should shed it, but I was comfortable in my own miserable way. Since Darci and I had called it quits nearly two months ago, I'd been going through the motions, a zombie just trying to get through each shift. A shell of the ambitious, driven person I used to be.

One of the nurses said my boss, Charlie Rutger, the chief of the ER, was looking for me. My heart pounded. Had I made a mistake? Was someone complaining about me? I braced myself for the worst.

My stomach knotted as I followed him into his office. Something was off. I'd been coasting lately, phoning it in. This sudden summons couldn't be good.

Charlie shut the door behind us and gestured to a chair in front of his desk. I sat down, my heart trying to escape my chest. He looked at me, releasing a heavy sigh, his face etched with annoyance and relief.

"Alex, I've got a bit of a problem," he started, leaning

forward.

Oh god, here we go.

"I was supposed to be at an ER Physician conference in Vegas this weekend, but my wife just informed me her cousin is getting married on Saturday. Can't miss it, even if it's the fourth time down the aisle. You know how women are." He chuckled nervously.

I blinked, trying to process this. Why was he telling me this?

"Uh… that's… that's quite the predicament, sir. I'm sorry to hear it."

He grimaced. "I know it's last minute, and I hate to put you on the spot, but I was hoping you could take my place. I've already booked a suite at the hotel where the conference is. It's the Pinnacle. You'll love it. You could order room service, get a massage…"

Did he just wink at me? What was going on?

He continued, "Maybe do a little gambling, catch a show… What do you say?"

I blinked. Wait. What? Vegas? A conference? Me? I felt a surge of adrenaline. A free trip? A chance to clear my head?

"Of course," I blurted out, more enthusiastic than I'd intended. "I can do it."

A wave of relief washed over Charlie's face. "You're a lifesaver, Alex. I owe you one." As he stood up, reaching out his hand, I jumped up, grasping it as he shook my hand vigorously. "I'll have my secretary fix everything with your name on it. She'll have everything emailed to you by the end of today."

"How long is the conference, sir?"

He let out a deep chuckle, "Please, Charlie is just fine. The conference goes through Sunday. Are you on the schedule for Monday, son?"

I wrinkled my brow, trying to remember my schedule. "Well, I'm not quite sure... But I can make sure I'm here bright and early...."

Before I could finish, he interrupted, "How about you take Monday off and be here bright and early Tuesday? Sound good? Recover from whatever happens in Vegas? Hmm?" He laughed.

I nodded, chuckling nervously as I tried to hide my excitement. "That's very generous, sir... uh, *Charlie*."

Maybe this was just what I needed. A change of scenery, a little vacation, a few days of distraction. It sounded perfect.

Hours later, the clock on the wall blurred. It was almost shift change, and I was ready to ditch the hospital for the night. Just as I was about to slip out the door, Javi intercepted me with a wide grin.

"Hey, Alex, I've got two tickets at the Echo tonight in Dallas. Velvet Cage, that Slicing Dolls tribute band. You in?"

Perfect. A distraction before my Vegas flight tomorrow. I nodded, a smile creeping onto my face.

"Awesome! Pick you up in an hour?" He asked.

As we entered the parking garage, I said, "I'll be ready."

Two hours later, we were standing near the back of the crowd, the bass thudding through my feet like a second heartbeat. Around me, a sea of gray hair, leather jackets, and worn-out band tees nodding to the rhythm. The air was thick with the sharp tang of old cigarettes and the faint, unmistakable curl of weed—nostalgia and rebellion steeped into every breath.

I didn't quite belong here. This was my dad's era, not

mine. I felt like a fish in the wrong tank—but at least the music was loud enough to drown out everything else.

I took a long drink of my beer and let my gaze wander across the crowd. That's when I saw her—maybe. Just a flash of glossy dark hair, a familiar silhouette, the glint of a little black dress that clung in all the right places. My heart jumped. Could it be her?

I leaned forward, trying to get a better look, but the crowd swallowed her up again. It probably wasn't even her, but my pulse was already racing.

"I'll be right back," I told Javi, just before disappearing into the crowd.

I weaved through bodies, murmuring apologies as my eyes locked on where I'd last seen her. Nothing. No one looked anything like her, just a mass of sweaty strangers. Panic started to creep in. I turned in circles, scanning the crowd again, my gaze desperate. Had I imagined her? I ran a hand through my hair, feeling ridiculous.

"Did you see a tiny woman with short dark hair and a... little black dress?" I asked a couple of random dudes.

They stared at me like I was an alien. I tried a few more people, but the same blank stares met me.

Fuck. Was she haunting me now, too? Or was I losing my mind?

I stumbled back to Javi, my face flushed and my heart still pounding. He raised an eyebrow, a silent question hanging in the air. I shook my head, unable to find the words.

"False alarm," I managed to croak out, my voice a little too high, a little too hopeful. I took another sip of beer to cover it, but the damage was done. I could feel the heat crawling up my neck.

Great. I was probably blushing like a tomato. A sweaty, emotionally compromised tomato at a punk show.

"Thought I saw someone I knew," I added, trying to sound casual—like my heart hadn't just tried to stage a dramatic exit through my ribcage.

Javi shrugged, his attention already back on the stage as he nodded to the beat and sang along. I forced myself to focus on the music, but my mind was racing. Had I really seen her? Or was it just my mind playing tricks on me? The thought of running into Darci here, of all places, was both terrifying and exhilarating at the same time.

I took a deep breath, trying to calm myself. This was supposed to be a break from my shitty reality. I had to let it go. For now, at least.

We hadn't had time to eat before the show, so by the time it ended, I was ravenous. The neon glow from the gas station taco shop lit up our faces in ghostly green as I pushed the door open. The smell hit me immediately—grilled meat and something spicy-sweet that made my stomach growl.

Javi had sworn this was *the* spot—best tacos in the city, open twenty-four hours, no exceptions. Judging by the crowd, half the city agreed. The place buzzed with life—bartenders off shift, night owls, and people like us, chasing grease and comfort at midnight.

I tore into my carne asada tacos like they owed me money and, somewhere between bites, told Javi about Charlie's unexpected offer.

"You lucky bastard," he said, grinning. "Vegas, baby! Enjoy it," He wiggled his eyebrows, "the endless possibilities..."

I chuckled, shaking my head at Javi's enthusiasm. Vegas—the last place I'd imagined myself ending up. Yet something about it felt right, like maybe this was exactly the kind of thing my therapist had been pushing me toward.

Dr. Matthews had been nudging me to confront the grief that I'd let build walls around me, trapping me in self-punishment—the same thing Darci had said that night we ended things. He encouraged me to take risks and let myself enjoy moments without the guilt dragging me down. I'd been trying. Maybe this was another step forward.

"You're not betraying them by living, Alex," he'd said just last week, his voice calm but unyielding. "Your wife and daughter wouldn't want you to spend the rest of your life drowning in guilt. Living your life and being happy isn't a betrayal. Look at it as if you're honoring them.

I'd spent the last few years telling myself the same damn thing, but weeks ago, his words landed like a sledgehammer, cracking something open inside me. He was right—deep down, I knew he was—but knowing and truly believing it was two different battles. I'd held onto my guilt as if letting go meant losing them all over again. But a switch flipped one day when he said letting go didn't mean forgetting. It didn't mean I loved them any less.

Clinging to the past kept me from seeing a future— not just with Darci but with anyone. It was why I kept sabotaging the best thing that had happened to me in years. Darci made me feel alive again, and I'd convinced myself that was wrong, making me disloyal.

After Javi dropped me off, my thoughts wandered— just like they always did lately.

Always back to her. I couldn't stop thinking about her, watching for those blinds to shift, hoping for some small sign she might still be looking for me, too.

The urge to knock on her door, apologize, and see if there was any chance for us was overwhelming. But fear held me back. Had she already moved on? Was there someone with her tonight?

What if she hated me now? I'd said some pretty awful things the last time we spoke. But yet…

I shook my head, trying to clear the storm of thoughts. It was the middle of the night—hardly the right moment to show up and beg for her forgiveness. With a heavy heart, I dragged myself inside my apartment and found myself at the window, one hand braced on the cold glass, staring across the parking lot between our buildings. Her apartment glowed softly in the early evening light, curtains drawn halfway, shadows moving behind them like she was home.

She was close. Just there. And somehow, still completely out of reach.

I pulled out my phone, thumb hovering over her name, heart already racing like I'd hit send. I typed:

Hey. I've been doing the work. I just… miss you.

Backspaced the whole thing.

Tried again:

I know I screwed everything up. But I want to fix it. If you'll let me.

Deleted that too. I stared at the blinking cursor, desperate to do something. *Anything.*

I could see her windows. I could almost picture her on the couch, maybe curled up with a blanket, maybe not thinking about me at all.

I locked the screen and dropped the phone on the table. Not tonight. But soon. At least, I hoped she'd still be waiting when soon finally came.

I sighed heavily and walked to the bedroom, stripped to my boxers, and climbed into bed. The weight of the world pressed down on me. Sure, I was making progress. But was life ever easy? Why was everything always so hard? I just needed some peace. Fleetingly, I had thought I had found it, but it shattered right in front of me.

I sighed, "No, you did this to yourself. You fucking pushed her away."

My phone lit up on the nightstand, and I grabbed it without thinking—heart already halfway to hope. For a second, I let myself believe it might be her. A message. A sign. Anything.

But it was just the confirmation text for my ride to the airport. The letdown settled fast, dull but familiar. I stared at the screen a little longer than I needed to, as if it might still change. Then, with a sigh, I opened my alarm app, setting it early enough to pack. Because what else was I going to do?

I sank deeper into the pillows, mentally running through tomorrow's to-do list, but thoughts of Darci kept flickering through my mind, pulling me from it. I tried to push them away, grabbing my phone instead and opening the photos I'd taken of my wife just before I lost her. She was glowing, her smile radiant above the swell of her pregnant belly. The sheer happiness captured in those pictures only sharpened the emptiness I felt now. I swiped slowly through each image until exhaustion began to blur the screen. Setting the phone aside, I closed my eyes, but Darci immediately filled my thoughts again—her playful smile, the teasing spark in her eyes, the way she laughed as we danced. She was the last image in my mind as sleep finally took hold, and for once, I didn't feel guilty about it.

I jolted awake, suddenly aware I was behind the wheel of my car. Fuck. How long had I zoned out? Panic rose as I tried to piece together where I was heading. Wasn't I supposed to be on my way to Vegas?

I recognized the scenery on the way to Patterdale. I needed to see them again, talk to Jenna, and unburden myself from the tangled mess that had become my life.

I glanced at the passenger seat. Two bouquets were there—one lilac and one sunflower, just like the ones Darci had picked out when I brought her. I didn't even remember buying them. I'd probably need to weed their plots again. It'd been a while. I hadn't been there since I took Darci months ago.

Before I knew it, I was driving the small winding path closer to their plots. I killed the engine, but didn't move —just sat there, hands resting on the wheel, breathing like I had to relearn how.

Getting out of the car, it was strangely quiet. I stepped out of the car and started walking, the ground soft beneath my feet. The only sound was the whisper of wind—no birds or insects or trees. In broad daylight, it felt almost… eerie.

The calm came in quiet waves. It settled in—the ache, the guilt, thick in my throat. It wasn't just grief anymore. It was every mistake I'd made since. Every way I'd tried to numb it, outrun it, bury it. I could feel it —like a pressure in my chest—the shame, the confusion, the stupid choices that had filled the hollow space where my heart used to be.

Jenna would've hated what I'd become.

Looking down at their plots, the weeds had overtaken everything again. I couldn't figure out how. It hadn't been that long since I'd been here. Shamefaced, I knelt before the graves.

"Hey, you two," I mumbled, the words scraping raw against my throat. Silence stretched, broken only by a strong breeze rustling leaves. The flowers we'd left before were gone. I unwrapped the bouquets, sunflowers in the vase on my wife's headstone, and the lilacs in Savannah's.

"Sorry, I haven't been around much," I started, pulling a fistful of the stubborn weeds. My voice sounded rusty and unused. "Work's been crazy, and... well, you know."

You know. The unspoken truth hung heavy. My guilt tightened around me. I thought I'd gotten past this by now. I reminded myself that Jenna, always so understanding, wouldn't judge me for anything. But would she understand about Darci? How her fiery spirit had captivated me, the way her laugh echoed down to my core and chipped away at the walls I'd built around my heart?

I winced, pulling another weed with a snap.

"She's not a replacement, Jenna. You never could be replaced. But... she made me laugh again. It's been so long since I've done that."

My eyes started to burn. "I miss you both," I finally choked out, the words thick with grief and a burgeoning hope I couldn't quite name. "I miss... our life together."

A tear escaped, tracing a path down my cheek. I

wiped it away angrily, frustrated by my weakness.

"I just... I don't know what to do, Jenna. Maybe it's too soon..."

The sun dipped lower in the sky, casting long shadows across the cemetery. I carried the weeds to a nearby trash can, and when I returned, I was so tired. I sat down, leaning against Jenna's headstone. Maybe I could close my eyes for a minute or two before I drove back home.

I was startled awake as my head dropped. But when I opened my eyes... the cemetery was bathed in the twilight. How long had I been here? A movement at the edge of my vision sparked a jolt of adrenaline. I whipped my head around, my heart hammering against my ribs.

There, on the weathered wooden bench I'd sat so many times just a few feet away, was Jenna. Not a wisp of a memory but a living, breathing presence. Her long hair, the color of spun gold, shimmered in the gentle breeze. Ethereal and beautiful, she wore a smile that could light up a thousand nights. But something else snagged my attention. A baby was in her arms, cradled with a tenderness that brought tears to my eyes. Our baby. Savannah Jean, swaddled in white, with the faintest of cries escaping her lips.

Disbelief turned my legs to lead as I stood and took a tentative step towards them.

"Jenna?" My voice cracked. "What are you doing here? What is this...?" My voice trailed off.

She looked right at me. Her laugh, which had haunted so many of my waking moments, filled the air. It was the same laugh that could fill a room like sunshine, inviting everyone to join her.

"Goose," she said, her voice like a soft melody, "I've

been here the whole time, waiting on you."

I searched her face, one etched in so many of my memories. "On me?"

"Oh, Alex," she said, her gaze unwavering. "I've been waiting for you to tell me you found her."

My brow wrinkled, confusion clouding my joy. "Her?"

Her smile held a tinge of sadness. "The woman who can give you the life I couldn't," she said, her voice laced with a bittersweet tenderness.

My breath hitched, a strangled sound escaping my throat. "What?"

Jenna's smile widened, pushing a loose strand of hair behind her ear as she put the baby on her shoulder. "I knew the moment I saw her here with you." She nodded slowly, "She was the one."

"I don't... I don't understand."

"Stop," she said, her voice a gentle caress. "Stop feeling guilty for moving on."

"But... without you..." I let out a heavy sigh, "It's so fucking hard..."

Jenna stood up, rubbing the baby's back. She took a step towards me, her smile bittersweet.

"Goose, I know. I wish things were different. But they aren't." Her voice softened as she took another step towards me.

She was so close, and I desperately wanted to touch her.

"Stop punishing yourself. It wasn't your fault. You're a good doctor. But it wasn't in your hands." The baby cooed as Jenna tucked her closer. "My body... it just couldn't fight anymore. Don't let it define everything about you." Her blue eyes widened, "Live. Find love again. Fill your life with the happiness and the laughter you deserve."

She reached for me, pressing her palm to my face. "Go be happy, Alex."

I closed my eyes, turning into her hand, desperate for her touch, for a single ember of warmth to confirm this wasn't some cruel trick of my mind. But I felt nothing but the kiss of a cool breeze against my cheek.

She whispered, "You can let go…"

I opened my eyes, but in an instant, the sun flared, and I had to turn away. But when I opened them again, I was in my bed, tangled in the sheet, my alarm blaring as the sun peeked through the window.

I jolted upright, breath ragged, the sheets wrapped around my legs like they were trying to hold me in the dream a little longer. My hands skimmed the mattress, reaching for something I knew wouldn't be there—soft skin, a familiar weight, the faint scent of lavender.

Nothing. Just silence and the thump of my own pulse in my ears.

I swung my legs over the side of the bed, elbows braced on my knees, head in my hands. The dream clung to me—thick, vivid, my pulse still racing from the intensity. I could still see her standing there in the cemetery, the breeze tugging her hair across her cheek, her voice calm and sure.

Go be happy, Alex.

The words hadn't left me. Not when I'd opened my eyes. Not now, as I crossed the room and pulled my carry-on from the closet.

Drawer by drawer, I filled the bag without thinking, clothes folding on autopilot while my mind replayed what I'd seen and felt. The guilt was still there, in its usual place—but it has loosened its hold. And something else had slipped in next to it.

Something quieter. Lighter. Hope.

Steam curled around me as the shower pounded against my back, but it couldn't drown out her voice. *Go be happy, Alex.* It played on a loop in my head, soft and steady. I stepped out, dragging a towel over my face, the air cool against my skin. As I reached for my toothbrush, something felt… off.

I looked down at my hand. My wedding ring was gone.

My chest tightened. I turned my palm over, staring at the faint indentation that soft band of paler skin like a memory etched into flesh. I hadn't taken it off in the last three years — not once. Not even when I wanted to forget everything.

And yet there it was, resting quietly on the nightstand beside my watch and phone. I walked over, picked it up, and felt the familiar weight in my palm. The metal was cool. My fingers curled around it on instinct.

But something stopped me. Her voice returned, not loud, not forceful — just true.

You can let go.

I closed my eyes. Then, slowly, I set the ring back down. Not out of guilt. Not out of grief.

Out of love. And finally, the beginning of letting go.

CHAPTER TWENTY-NINE
Darci

I scanned the crowded gate and dropped into the seat beside Claire. It was eight o'clock in the morning, and this place was a zoo. Nearly every seat was filled, and people spilled over into the walkways. Vegas bound, the whole lot of us. I rummaged through my tote, pulling out a tiara with 'BRIDE' sparkling across it. I presented it to Claire, bowing my head with a grin.

"For you, my darling," I teased.

She snatched it up, a playful glint in her eye as she seated it into her fiery curls. Edison was lost in a book, but Mallory joined us, sitting cross-legged on the floor.

Leaning in, I whispered to Claire, "So, future hubby upgraded us all to first class?"

Her face flushed pink. "Yeah, he thought it would be 'fun,'" she said, air quotes.

I arched a brow. "Fun as in bottomless champagne?"

Her laugh was pure sunshine as she shrugged.

Dryly, Mallory said, "More like he probably just wanted the extra leg room."

We giggled quietly.

Mallory's eyes lit up. "We should play a game—'never have I ever' when we're on the plane."

Claire looked at her like she'd grown a second head. "Never have I ever played what?"

I couldn't believe it. "Claire, seriously?" I gasped. "Have you been living under a rock?"

She raised an eyebrow at me.

I waved dismissively. "Never mind. I forgot the whole I-was-married-as-a-teenage-bride."

"I wasn't a teenager… I was 21."

I gave her a flat look. "It's essentially the same thing."

Claire rolled her eyes. "I still had some… fun."

"Like what?" I asked.

She paused, clearly rifling through her mental file labeled *Mildly Rebellious Life Choices*. "One time, Pete and I snuck into the hotel pool after hours," she said, a little too proud of herself. "We didn't even bring swimsuits. We swam in our pajamas."

I blinked. "Wow. Living on the edge." Then I leaned in with a smirk. "Tell me—did you also steal a complimentary mint from the front desk? Or was that just too wild?"

Claire's cheeks flushed again, but she lifted her chin like she was proud of her pajama-drenched rebellion. "It was a big deal."

Before I could respond, Mallory pocketed her phone and leaned over. "Are we talking about Claire's wild phase?" she asked, sitting up straighter.

"Oh yeah," I said, nodding solemnly. "Apparently, it peaked with some after-hours pool splashing... *in pajamas*."

Mallory burst out laughing. "Claire, no."

Claire huffed. "Okay, fine. What about the time I made out with the pizza delivery guy in the back stairwell of my dorm?"

Mallory and I locked eyes. Claire just sat back, deadpan.

"Wait—what?" I asked, leaning forward. "You did what?"

She shrugged. "I ordered a pizza by myself, offered him a slice, and… one thing led to another. I was going through something."

Mallory let out a wheeze. "Claire Montague, you little pizza perv."

I shook my head, grinning. "Here I was thinking you were Little Miss Disney Channel—but no, you were like PG-13 Lifetime movie energy."

Claire gave a mock bow, then raised an eyebrow. "So, how does this game actually work? I feel like I'm about to be tricked."

Mallory jumped in. "No tricks. It's simple. Someone says, 'Never have I ever' done something. If you've done it, you take a drink."

My eyes sparkled as I rubbed my hands together. "I have a feeling this is going to be good."

We were giggling like schoolgirls as the boarding call came over the loudspeaker.

On the plane, there were four seats across—Edison and Claire on one side. Mallory and I on the other. We each had a glass of champagne in hand before take-off.

"To my brother and his beautiful bride," Mallory offered, raising her glass.

Edison blushed, staring at Claire as if she hung the moon. He clinked his glass to hers as their eyes met and gave her a chaste kiss. I clinked mine with Mallory's and downed it in one go.

When the flight attendant offered me another, I eagerly took it, settling back into my seat, my head against the headrest, and closing my eyes.

Mallory leaned closer, "Nervous flyer?"

We started to move, and I felt the heat rising up my neck. I murmured, my lips still on the rim of my glass, "Something like that."

I white-knuckled the armrests as Mallory said in a low voice, "Just breathe. In... out..."

I slid my gaze to hers and followed her instructions. Her eyes never left mine, saying the gentle mantra repeatedly, low enough that only I could hear until we flattened out, and I let out a long sigh.

When she hit the call button, the flight attendant was instantly there. Mallory asked, "Can we get another round of champagne or maybe just the bottle...?"

Once all three of us had a glass, Mallory said, "Let the game... begin!"

Edison leaned towards the aisle, a lazy smile revealing one of his dimples. "What are y'all up to?"

I chuckled as Mallory gave him puppy dog eyes and said, "We're just entertaining Claire." She pointed to the book in his lap. "You go back to reading. This is girl time."

He huffed out a laugh. "I see."

He whispered something against Claire's ear before cracking the spine and returning to his book. At least, I think he was reading. Maybe he was pretending and just listening to our crazy. Who knows.

Mallory cleared her throat. "Okay, here we go. Never have I ever... Googled myself."

I barked out a laugh and took a drink. Claire just

looked confused.

She leaned over, "If I haven't done it, do I take a drink?"

"Nope."

She nodded. "Okay."

"You're turn, Darci."

"Hmm, let me think. Okay… Never have I ever…" I winced as I said, "Been in love."

Both Claire and Mallory took a drink.

Mallory met Claire's gaze, "You're turn, Claire."

"Okay… Never have I ever… oh, this is hard… Never have I ever…" She smirked as she said, "Given a lap dance."

Surprised, I leaned back, fanning myself with my hand. "Your mind's in the gutter this morning, babe."

She giggled, surprised when both Mallory and I took a drink. I swear I heard Edison chuckle under his breath.

"Really?" Claire asked, "Who are y'all giving lap dances to?"

Mallory blushed, flicking her eyes toward Edison with cautious dread. She lowered her voice, "It was… a long time ago."

Claire's gaze turned to mine. Her eyebrows raised expectantly.

"Um… well…" My voice dropped almost to an inaudible whisper as I realized I had actually given quite a few lap dances in my day. "Let's see, there was Aiden, Gary, Jacob… um… Alex… a couple others, I think."

Edison's head snapped toward me, an amused glint in his eye. I cocked an eyebrow, staring him down. I was positive he was eavesdropping and had absolutely no shame about it.

Mallory went again, "Okay... Never have I ever sexted the wrong person."

We all looked at each other, and then Claire took a drink. I grimaced.

She shrugged as her cheeks reddened, "I was trying to send Sonny something... intimate, and... somehow it went to my mom."

Mallory groaned, "Oh, god."

Claire's eyes widened. "I was completely mortified."

"I bet," I said as I winked at her.

The more we drank, the less filtered we got—soon the game was just giggles, bubbles, and way too many confessions. It turned out that Mallory and Claire were both walking around with hidden ink. I'd pegged Mallory for it, but Claire? Not a chance of that. I'd been begging her to show me for the past half hour, my curiosity growing with her laughter-filled refusals.

Even Edison joined in on our little game, his admission of never having a one-night stand surprising us all. But my turn was the real pathetic showstopper.

"Never have I ever had a relationship last longer than a month," I blurted out, bracing myself.

Claire and Mallory choked on their drinks, their faces mixed with shock and disbelief. Mallory recovered first, squeezing my shoulder with a sympathetic smile.

"Oh hon, like ever?" Her voice was soft.

I pursed my lips and shook my head.

She leaned in, her eyes serious. "I have this weird thing, like a gut feeling about people. And I'm telling you, he's out there—your perfect match. Maybe he's even in Vegas this weekend."

I said with a hint of sarcasm, "Well, if he's out there, he needs to hurry up and find me already."

Once we landed in Vegas, the van ride to Hidden Springs Ranch was over in a flash—just twenty minutes outside the city, and suddenly, the hustle of the Strip was behind us. Check-in was smooth, with barely a pause, the staff moving like they'd done this a thousand times. The ranch was just as stunning as when Claire and I first visited, sprawling out in front of us like something out of a movie. I could already feel the excitement bubbling up inside me—I couldn't wait to find the petting zoo again.

The hotel had this effortless charm, rustic but inviting, with a cozy bar and a restaurant that practically begged you to come in and stay a while. Our rooms were all on one quiet floor. Most of the guests were trickling in tomorrow. For now, it was just the four of us—Claire, Edison, Mallory, and me. Later today, Claire's parents and Edison's groomsmen from college were showing up for the rehearsal.

Claire and Edison slipped off to their room when we got our keys. Mallory and I dragged our bags down the hall to our rooms, right next to each other. I barely made it through the door before I collapsed onto the bed, sinking into the mattress with a long, relieved breath. My eyes fluttered closed when there was a knock at the door. I let out a heavy sigh.

Mallory stood there, grinning like she had a secret. She leaned in a little, glancing toward Claire and Edison's room before whispering, "So, what's the plan?"

I blinked, still half-dazed. "The plan?"

Her grin widened as she came into my room. "Yeah, for the bachelorette party tonight."

It clicked, and I laughed. "Oh! Well, first, I was going to see if the wives of Edison's friends wanted to come along with us. A limo is picking us up after the rehearsal dinner, and there's plenty of room. But…" I went over to my suitcase, unzipping it to pull out a big tote bag. "First, we'll be playing Trucker Hat Roulette." I pulled a few hats out of the bag without letting Mallory read any of them before shoving them back. "Each of us is pulling one out randomly, and we're going to wear them all night proudly."

"Oh god," She giggled. "I can't wait!"

I grinned. "Me, too! Then, we're hitting the Strip. Maybe some clubbing. Definitely some drinking. I have a reservation at Hunk-O-Licious. Every bachelorette party needs half-naked men gyrating around."

Mallory burst out laughing, nodding in approval. "Now *that's* a plan. I came armed with singles and zero shame."

We spent the afternoon lounging on the bed, half-watching Hallmark romance movies while tossing ideas back and forth for the night ahead. It was easy and comfortable—the perfect downtime before everything kicked into high gear. Around 6, her phone chimed with a familiar alarm.

She groaned a little, then grinned. "Welp… time to get ready. Meet in the hallway at 6:30, and we'll head down together?"

I nodded. "Sounds good."

After she left, I unzipped my suitcase, carefully lifting out the maid of honor dress first, then my favorite little black dress for tonight, and hanging them in the closet.

At 6:30 sharp, hair fluffed, heels on, and my little black dress doing exactly what I needed it to do, I knocked on Mallory's door. She opened it almost instantly, looking like sin in a dark red backless mini that was made to ruin men's lives—and probably already had.

Her eyes swept over me, and she let out a low whistle. "Damn, Darci. That dress is illegal in at least three states."

I grinned. "Takes one to know one. You look like heartbreak in heels."

She laughed, grabbed her clutch, and linked arms with me like we were about to burn the whole night down.

We found Claire and Edison tucked into a corner of the bar with her parents and his old college buddies, everyone mid-laugh with drinks in hand. Claire's mom had the same vibrant, curly red hair, but it was her dad's warm, easy smile she'd inherited.

Claire looked like a walking daydream in a light blue corset dress, her hair swept up in soft waves that made her look like she'd wandered out of a love story and into real life.

Edison, in his usual rolled-up sleeves and khakis, looked slightly underdressed by comparison—but judging by the way he was watching her, like he still couldn't believe she was his, I don't think he gave a damn. His hand stayed on the small of her back, his eyes never far from her face. Every time she leaned in to whisper something, he looked like he might melt into the floor. Like he'd been holding his breath for years and finally got to exhale.

I watched them for a second longer than I meant to. I wanted that. I didn't even care about the fairytale—just someone who looked at me like that. Like I was the miracle.

I swallowed hard and forced a smile as Edison introduced us to his friends, Avery and Chase, and their wives. One of them, a petite woman with a gentle smile, was visibly pregnant. I asked if they were up for joining the bachelorette party later, but both wives politely declined, smiling as they shook their heads.

Mallory shot me a playful glance, and I shrugged. "Their loss," I whispered, already thinking ahead to the wild night we had planned.

Edison paused, checking his watch as a knowing grin spread across his face. "Time to head down," he said.

We nodded, a chorus of excitement and nervousness.

We made our way outside towards the orchard, and the air was thick with the scent of ripening peaches. The sun was setting, and it was just a picture-perfect setting —golden hour with the trees heavy with fruit, their branches almost brushing the ground. In the clearing, there was a hexagonal arch adorned with twinkling lights stood at the center. Tomorrow, it would be covered in wildflowers for the ceremony.

As we approached, the officiant, Carole, dressed in a cream pantsuit, greeted us warmly.

"Welcome, welcome," she boomed, her voice carrying over the soft rustling of leaves. "Anyone not in the wedding party can grab a seat."

Claire's mom found a spot in the front row while Avery and Chase's wives settled on a pew at the back. The rest of us gathered around Carole, forming a circle of eager faces.

"So," Carole began, "we have Claire, the blushing bride, and Edison, the groom-to-be." She gestured towards us, a playful twinkle in her eye. "And who are these lovely people?"

Claire stepped forward, introducing me as her maid of honor, Mallory as the bridesmaid, and lastly, her father. Edison followed, presenting Chase as the best man and Avery as the groomsman.

"Perfect," Carole replied, her smile widening. "Now, shall we have the girls walk down the aisle with escorts, or shall the guys wait at the altar?"

Claire and Edison exchanged a glance, and he inclined his head, giving her the reins.

She turned to Carole. "Let's have them line up at the front."

We watched Edison, Chase, and Avery take their positions, forming a line on the right side of the arch.

"Ladies, it's time for your grand entrance!" Carole sang as she turned to us. "Line up back at the trees."

Mallory and I exchanged a nervous glance before following Claire and her dad to the orchard, the trees framing the path ahead.

"She seems a little too enthusiastic," I muttered out of the side of my mouth.

Mallory's mouth twitched, trying to contain a laugh.

This far away, I couldn't make out Carole's words to Claire, but the urgency in her voice was intense as Claire motioned for her dad to join her. They followed the path, going further back into the orchard, hidden from view. I peered down to the front where the guys shifted impatiently as Carole spoke with Edison.

The next thing I knew, Carole's voice burst through the air like a firecracker, echoing all the way to the path where we stood. "Alright, everyone!" she called out, enthusiastically clapping her hands. "Let's do a run-through! I'm starting the wedding march, and we're practicing the walk!"

Her energy was electric, pulling everyone into her orbit, whether they were ready or not. She held up her phone, a determined look in her eyes as she hollered at us, her voice carrying a commanding cheer, "Alright, ladies, nice and slow! Ready, Mallory? And... go!"

Carole called out. "Step... step... step... good. And... two, three, four, Darci. Slow and steady, feet like confetti." *What?*

As I started down the aisle, I couldn't help but glance at Edison. He gave me a grin and a short nod, and I returned it with a small smile, trying to hide my nerves as I passed the first benches.

"Claire," Carole said, her voice filled with excitement. "You and your dad should make your way to the opening."

Where the trees parted, sunlight spilled through the branches like something holy—and then Claire appeared.

"Remember," Carole's contagious energy reached the trees. "Wait for the music to change. I'll call everyone to rise, and then you'll come down, nice and slow."

Carole changed the music to Fur Elise, waited a beat, and called for the audience to stand. A few seconds later, Claire and her dad started to walk down the aisle.

I swallowed hard, my throat tightening. A heavy weight pressed on my chest. My dad... We'd never... I took a deep breath in and slowly let it out.

Claire stepped into the clearing, her arm tucked through her father's. Her smile grew with every step, slow and sure, like the moment was unfolding exactly how it was meant to. Even from where I stood near the altar, I could see the light in her eyes—calm, radiant, almost impossible.

Her dad glanced at her, and his whole face softened, pride blooming across his features like he couldn't believe he got to walk her toward this.

It was just the rehearsal. No dress. No music. No bouquet. And still, my throat tightened. *God, she deserves this.* After all those years spent shrinking herself to survive a loveless marriage—she was finally walking toward a love that saw her. *All of her.*

I shifted my stance, pressing my thumb into the center of my palm. The ache was quiet but familiar. I'd never been that lucky in love. Maybe I never would be. But right now, I got to witness hers. And that was something.

And then… the way Edison looked at Claire stole my breath. His eyes locked on her with such raw tenderness that it felt almost intrusive to watch. There was something in his gaze, as if she were the only person in the world. Claire's eyes shimmered with emotion as her father leaned in, gently kissing her cheek. She offered him a tender, grateful smile before turning to Edison, who extended his arm, drawing her to his side. It was a moment so full of love that it left a lump in my throat.

I looked away, blinking back tears as a breath caught in my throat, and I felt the warmth of Mallory's hand on my back. Slowly, I turned to her, giving her a hesitant smile.

She whispered, "God, I hope I find that someday."

I swallowed hard and gave a quiet nod, unable to put into words the ache her words stirred in me.

Edison reached for Claire's hand, interlacing their fingers as they approached Carole.

Her voice rang out. This is when you'll both say your vows and exchange the rings." She looked between them, "Do you have the vows memorized or do I need to give them to you?"

Edison gave Claire a quick glance, then smiled. "I've had mine memorized since the night I wrote them."

Claire rolled her eyes, but the corners of her mouth twitched like she was trying not to melt.

She said, "I have mine, too."

"Perfect! Well... then," Carole grinned, "Next is the kiss!"

Edison wasted no time. He scooped Claire up in his arms, his lips brushing hers in a tender, lingering kiss. I swear a collective sigh went through all of us.

Carole's smirk widened. "Okay, okay... let's save that for tomorrow."

They pulled apart, their cheeks flushed.

"Now," Carole continued, "how do you want me to introduce you? Mr. and Mrs. Edison Wright? Edison and Claire Wright? Or something else?"

They exchanged glances, a silent conversation filled with unspoken love and excitement.

"Mr. and Mrs. Edison Wright," Edison said, his voice filled with pride.

Claire beamed. "Yes, I like that."

Carole clapped her hands. "Alright, let's run through everything one last time. Let the love shine through."

We ran through the ceremony again, and everything went off without a hitch. This time, I kept my emotions in check, mostly. Still, when Claire arrived at Edison and they exchanged a smile that held secrets just for them, something inside me tightened. A wistfulness crept in, uninvited, and I wondered if I'd ever have that.

Before I knew it, the rehearsal was over, and we were following the path back to the ranch house. This time we went to the restaurant, and I froze, my breath catching. A table stretched across the room, adorned with vibrant wildflowers spilling from centerpieces and flickering candles casting a warm glow. It looked like something from a hidden, enchanted garden, the kind you only dreamed about. The gentle murmur of conversation and soft laughter around us added to the magic of the moment, making everything feel like a fairytale come to life.

Claire gasped, her eyes wide with delight. "Oh, this is just beautiful!"

Edison pulled out her chair next to his at the end of the table, a gentle smile on his face. "Take a seat, my love."

My heart tugged at his affection for her. Weeks ago, I'd thought my relationship with Alex was blossoming into something deeper. But now? Would I ever experience the kind of adoration Edison had for Claire?

That night when Alex had picked me up at Claire's—just the memory made my stomach flip all over again. Even now, a rush of warmth crawled up my neck. Sure, he called me Tink constantly, a teasing nod to my size that usually made me roll my eyes, but Sweetheart? That had been different. No one had ever given me a pet name like that before, and it did something to me I couldn't quite explain.

Mallory passed by, sliding into her seat on the other side of Edison, but not before catching the ridiculous look on my face.

She smirked, her voice laced with curiosity. "What's got you grinning like that?"

Claire and Edison turned toward me. I blinked, suddenly aware of the wide smile plastered across my face. I took a breath, squared my shoulders, and gave my full attention back to the room.

Whatever this was—whatever Alex was doing to me —I had to stop it. Tonight was for Claire. For her joy, her second chance, her happily ever after. Not the man who'd turned my brain into mush with one word.

Stop it, I told myself. Biting the inside of my cheek, I forced myself to snap out of it.

Mallory nudged her brother, "Hey, can we play musical chairs?"

"Sure, Mal."

We all quickly switched seats so I was between Mallory and Claire.

Mallory leaned her head on my shoulder for a moment and whispered, "Is this okay? I just had a feeling you might need a distraction."

Was I that obvious? I swallowed hard as I dipped my head before glancing at her with relief. I mouthed, "Thanks," just as the server approached with menus in hand.

I looked around at everyone, realizing they were all coupled up except me and Mal. At least it wasn't just me, but still, I had to blink back the burn behind my eyes. I really needed to snap out of whatever this was.

I stared down at the menu, clearing my throat and put on a smile.

"Can I get anyone a drink?" The server asked.

"Lavender Strawberry Smash," I announced, my choice already made.

I loved anything sweet and tart, and right now, I needed to get a few drinks in me to stop being so stupidly emotional. Tipsy Darci was the happy, giggly girl, and that's exactly what I needed to project tonight.

Mallory and Claire ordered wine, while Edison and his friends opted for a local craft beer on tap. The rest of the group settled on a mix of iced tea and water.

I couldn't help but notice how incredible the food choices looked. "I didn't know the food would be this fancy," I whispered to Claire.

She grinned, her eyes sparkling. "I know, right? When I made the choices, I was just guessing. But now, I'm having a hard time choosing."

Scanning the menu, my stomach rumbled. The farm-to-table dishes were mouthwatering—Vine-Roasted Tomatoes, Bruschetta Ratatouille, Steamed Lobster were just a few of the delicious options.

"I'm leaning towards the lobster," I said, but still debating between the steak salad and seafood.

"I think I'll go with the lobster, too," Claire replied.

Mallory announced, "I'm getting the salmon. I just hope the butter sauce doesn't get all over my dress." She grinned, "I have a habit of making quite the mess."

I chuckled as the server set down my Lavender Strawberry Smash. Taking a sip, I savored the sweet, floral flavor and sighed. This was going to be a night to remember.

CHAPTER THIRTY

Alex

The phone alarm jolted me back to reality. I had ten minutes. I scrambled out of the shower, pulled on jeans and a polo shirt, and grabbed my bag. I had just enough time to make a cup of coffee, strong and black. With each sip, I felt a calming clarity settling into my mind. Maybe this trip wasn't just about attending a boring conference. Maybe it was about getting out of the rut I'd been steeping in for too long.

When my phone buzzed again—two minutes until the airport shuttle arrived—I was dressed, caffeinated, and ready. Stepping outside, I noticed Darci's SUV pulling out of the parking lot. A pang of something—longing, maybe?—shot through me. But then the van pulled up, and a surge of excitement took over.

My flight was completely uneventful, which put me in a good mood for once. The air-conditioned blast from The Pinnacle's lobby hit me like a wall the moment I stepped inside—cool, crisp, and smelling faintly of citrus. It was exactly the kind of place that didn't need to show off to prove it was expensive. Polished marble floors stretched beneath glittering chandeliers, and the soundscape was pure Vegas—slot machines chiming and laughter bouncing off the walls.

Check-in was smooth, the concierge charming, and my room? All sleek lines, soft lighting, and a view that could bankrupt someone. I dropped my bag, took one long breath of that chilled, perfumed air—then turned around and stepped back into the furnace of the Vegas strip.

I wasn't much of a gambler, so I wandered the Strip, dodging tourists as I avoided the relentless sun. Eventually, my stomach reminded me I'd only had that cup of coffee early this morning, and I spotted an old-fashioned burger joint. I slid onto a stool at the counter, the worn leather seat feeling surprisingly comfortable. The aroma of sizzling meat and grilled onions filled the air. But the fancy milkshake I ordered reminded me of Darci when we went to the cemetery.

When my food arrived, it was a Texas-themed burger topped with crispy onion rings, a towering masterpiece that dwarfed the plate. I dove in, starving, and it was a symphony of flavors.

By the time I finished eating, I was full—but wired. Restless in a way where sitting alone in a hotel room sounded like a punishment. So instead of heading upstairs, I veered toward the casino, drawn in by the buzz of lights and possibility. The roulette table called to me, all drama and chance, and I figured—why not?

Maybe I'd hit the jackpot.

At the very least, I'd have a story to tell.

I placed a small bet on red. The wheel spun, the ball danced, and finally, it landed on black. I chuckled, shaking my head. Luck wasn't on my side tonight. I stayed a little longer, watching the players around me. I glanced at my watch, realizing it was nearly six o'clock, and the conference opening remarks would start soon.

I found the escalator up to the ballrooms, which were bustling hubs of activity. A long line snaked around the check-in table, and I joined the queue, eyes scanning the crowd for familiar faces.

A woman tapped my shoulder, a playful smile on her lips. "This conference is going to be a snoozefest, isn't it?" she asked, her voice full of amusement.

I turned to face her, unable to look away from her bright green eyes.

"Absolutely," I replied, returning her smile. "I'm Alex, by the way."

"Sarah," she said, extending her hand. "Nice to meet you, Alex."

As we chatted, the line slowly inched forward. Sarah was a whirlwind of energy, her laughter infectious. I found myself drawn to her easygoing nature and quick wit.

"Hey," she said, nudging me with her elbow, "Want to grab a drink together at the social hour? I could use someone to talk to."

I grinned. "Sure, why not? People watching at one of these things is quite the entertainment."

Sarah laughed, her eyes crinkling at the corners. "Exactly. We can make the best of this conference, one cocktail at a time."

After checking in, the swag bag was heavy in my hands, filled with promotional items and freebies I'd probably never use. I spotted Sarah's thick, golden hair across the room, holding court as she gestured wildly.

Already with a drink in her hand, her laughter carried over the chatter.

"Hey!" I called out, waving her over. She caught sight of me and waved back, her smile widening as she approached.

"So much free stuff," she exclaimed, dumping the contents of her tote bag onto a nearby table. She set her empty glass down on the table.

"Yeah, they don't skimp on the swag," I agreed, setting my bag beside hers.

"I'm going to grab a drink. Want a refill?" I offered.

Sarah tilted her head in thought. "Espresso martini, please."

I grinned. "Coming right up."

I made my way to the open bar, a sea of people milling about, drinks in hand. I ordered two espresso martinis, the caffeine promising a much-needed energy boost, and turned around, taking in the scene while I waited. The DJ spun upbeat tunes, but the dance floor was empty.

The conference attendees ranged from young professionals to seasoned veterans. Some chatted animatedly in small groups, while others wandered, clutching their tote bags like life rafts.

Finally, the bartender handed me the drinks. I carried them back to the table where I left Sarah. She was already chatting with a woman in a floral dress.

"Here you go," I said, handing her the espresso martini. The other woman smiled and walked off.

Sarah took a sip, her eyes widening in appreciation. "This is exactly what I needed," she said, raising her glass in a toast.

I clinked my glass against hers. "To a great conference,

and hopefully, a few good stories to share."

Sarah laughed. "Here's to that."

We continued chatting as we sipped our drinks, the conversation flowing effortlessly. Sarah was a physician's assistant in the ER at a hospital in southern California. She had a passion for her work in emergency women's services. I found myself drawn to her energy and intelligence.

Just as we were finishing our drinks, the room began to empty. It was time to head to the auditorium for the keynote speaker. We set our drinks down, grabbed our tote bags, and walked together. Sarah and I found a pair of seats towards the back, offering a good stage view.

Before it started, I leaned in, "Are you staying for dinner after the next session?"

She quirked her eyebrow, a smirk on her face, "Rubbery chicken breast and cold fish? No, thank you."

A surge of courage washed over me as I chuckled. "Why don't we grab dinner together? I hear there's a great spot right here in the hotel."

Sarah's cheeks flushed a rosy pink. "I'd like that," she said, her voice soft.

As the keynote speaker droned on, Sarah leaned over. "I swear, this guy could put anyone to sleep," she said, a playful smirk on her face.

I huffed out a quiet laugh, nodding in agreement. "I'm starting to wonder if he's reading directly from a textbook."

The speaker finally wrapped up, and the audience erupted in applause. As people filed out of the auditorium, Sarah turned to me. "So, where are you headed next?" she asked.

"The seminar on the post-Roe emergency room," I

replied.

Sarah's face lit up. "That's a critical topic. I wanted to attend, but I'm going to the emergency obstetrics session instead."

We exchanged numbers and agreed to meet later tonight at The Sapphire Room downstairs. As I walked away, I couldn't shake the feeling of excitement. This conference was shaping up to be much more interesting than anticipated.

My session ended early, so I joined the crowd, weaving my way through the maze of displays in the exhibit hall. Topics ranged from the latest advancements in emergency obstetrics to strategies for handling complex patients and navigating mental health crises.

Time flew by, and before I knew it, it was 9:30. I rushed back to my hotel room, eager to freshen up before meeting Sarah. After a quick shower and change, I emerged feeling refreshed and ready to face the night.

The elevator took an eternity to reach the lobby. Finally, I stepped out and made my way to The Sapphire Room. The place was packed, the atmosphere electric. I found a seat at the bar and scanned the crowd for Sarah. Just as I spotted her walking over from the bathroom in a low-cut red dress, she saw me. A smile lit up her face.

"Took you long enough," she teased, sliding into the seat beside mine.

"Sorry, the elevator was slower than molasses. I nearly took the stairs," I replied, returning her smile.

Her eyes widened, "Down that many floors?"

I chuckled, "I'm only on the tenth." I raised my eyebrows, "Hungry?"

Sarah nodded, her eyes scanning the menu. "I'm starving."

I ordered short ribs, mashed potatoes, and a boilermaker, while Sarah ordered chipotle salmon and fries with a glass of wine.

We chatted about the sessions we each attended and our plans for tomorrow. Our schedules were similar, so we agreed to meet in the morning for breakfast.

As I dropped the shot of whiskey into my beer, the clink of the glass interrupted our conversation, and I glanced down as my beer sloshed dangerously close to the rim.

A familiar giggle pierced the air, and I froze. *Darci?*

Jesus Christ, she was everywhere. How was I going to get her out of my head?

CHAPTER THIRTY-ONE

Darci

Edison hadn't taken his eyes off Claire all evening. And honestly? I got it. She was radiant, the center of every orbit in the room, and he looked like a man who'd won the lottery and still wasn't sure he deserved it.

"So," I said, tipping my glass his way, "what kind of trouble are your groomsmen planning for your last night of freedom?"

Avery glanced at Edison and smirked. "Just the three of us heading to a cigar lounge on the strip," he replied.

"Let me guess... poker and whiskey?" I raised an eyebrow, feigning disappointment.

Edison shrugged. He leaned toward Claire, whispering something I couldn't quite hear, and she blushed as her eyes widened, glancing at him. He gave her a lingering kiss before she broke it off.

She nudged my arm, her eyes sparkling with mischief. "We should get going."

Edison narrowed his eyes and gave us that crooked grin as he asked, "Where are y'all going?"

I grinned, leaning in conspiratorially. "Wouldn't you like to know?"

Before he could protest, I grabbed Claire's hand and pulled her towards the exit, Mallory not far behind. My phone buzzed, letting us know the limo was waiting.

As we stepped into the night, I heard Edison calling after us.

I laughed, nudging Claire into the limo and nearly sending her sprawling across the seat.

"Hey!" Edison jogged toward us, eyebrows raised in playful suspicion. "Where exactly are you taking my bride?"

I spun around, flashing him my most innocent grin. "Relax, my guy. It's Claire's last night as a free woman." I winked at him. "Don't worry—I'll have her back safe and sound...just very, very late."

Mallory leaned forward, giggling as she poked her head out. "You heard her. See you tomorrow!"

Edison shook his head, chuckling despite himself. "Fine, but behave."

I blew him a teasing kiss. "No promises!"

Once we were all tucked into the limo, I asked, "Ready for more fun?"

I grabbed the bag of trucker hats, and Mallory giggled.

"What's this?" Claire asked.

I grinned. "Trucker Hat Roulette. We each pull a hat without looking and wear it for the rest of the night."

Claire giggled.

Mallory's eyes lit up. "I'm in!"

I held up the bag.

"No peeking," I warned.

Claire reached in, her hand disappearing into the

depths. A moment later, she pulled out a bright red hat.

She looked at it as she burst into laughter and slipped it onto her head. "This is perfect." It had a bright red brim and said, "Mayor of Titty City" across the front.

"Your turn, Mallory," I said, handing her the bag.

Mallory plunged her hand in, rummaging around before triumphantly pulling out a purple hat. Two giant fishing hooks dangled from the front, and the text read, "Master Baiter."

She grinned, slipping the hat onto her head. "I love it!"

"My turn!" I exclaimed as I closed my eyes and dug around in the bag before pulling out a black hat with the words, "I NEED A HUGE COCKtail." I put it on my head and grinned.

We collapsed into a heap of giggles. Claire wiped under her eyes.

She playfully pushed my arm. "I can't believe you're making us do this."

I shrugged and smirked. "Just keeping it interesting."

Mallory held up her phone. "Selfie time!" We leaned together, our trucker hats on full display. The night was young, and this little adventure was just beginning.

A thrill shot through me when the limo slid to a stop in front of the neon-pink glow of the Hunk-O-Licious sign. This was going to be good. The building was a spectacle, its facade a dazzling array of bright blue lights.

Inside, the theater was a sensory overload. A buff guy wearing nothing but hot pants and go go boots took my name and led us to a table near the front. The stage was bathed in a kaleidoscope of colors while smoke machines filled the air, creating a hazy, mysterious atmosphere.

It was mostly women of all ages who filled the room, from wide-eyed twenty-somethings giggling nervously into their drinks to groups of elderly ladies whooping loudly and waving fistfuls of dollar bills as the lights began to dim.

A trio of men dressed in assless chaps, cowboy hats, and g-strings took the stage. They were visions of sculpted muscles. The crowd erupted in cheers and whistles, their energy infectious.

Mallory stood up, removing her truck hat and waving it in the air as she whistled and began to chant, "Take it off!" with a group of women at the next table.

I giggled before joining her, but Claire's attention was elsewhere. She leaned in, nudging me with her elbow.

"Darci," she whispered, her eyes fixed on the approaching waiter. "Isn't that Blue?"

I followed her gaze and felt my stomach flip. Blue, dressed in tight black pants with his golden tan chest on display, was weaving through the crowd, a tray of drinks balanced effortlessly in one hand.

"Yeah," I murmured, trying to sound casual. "That's him."

Claire's eyes sparkled with mischief. "You should talk to him. Maybe ask him to be your date for the wedding tomorrow."

I hesitated, glancing around. "Now? We're in the middle of your celebration. I don't want to bail on you again."

"Aren't we headed to the casino next?"

"Yeah... but..." I hedged.

She squeezed my hand reassuringly, "Offer to meet him at the bar there, have a chat, and then find us afterward."

I took a deep breath, considering her suggestion. The idea of seeing Blue again stirred something in me, but the thought of walking away from Claire—again twisted a knot in my belly. I couldn't do that to her *again.*

I raised an eyebrow, "You sure you're okay with it?"

Claire beamed. "That's my girl. Now, let's enjoy the rest of this show before we head to The Pinnacle."

"Okay…" I breathed, but the words caught. I leaned in, needing to ask one more time. "Are you sure? Really sure you're okay with this?"

Claire turned toward me fully, her smile fading into something softer… deeper. She reached for my hand again.

"Babe," she whispered, "I want you to stop worrying about letting me down." Her voice cracked just the slightest bit as she added, "I want you to have this." She squeezed my hand. "So yes… go."

She turned back to watch the cowboys on stage. I tried to focus on them—but my eyes kept straying back to him.

Blue.

He moved so easily through the crowd, balancing that tray like he'd done it a hundred times. I waited for the right moment to catch him or wave him over. But before I could build up the nerve, I noticed something.

He was already headed straight for *our* table. Panic fluttered in my chest. My palms grew clammy as I whipped my head back toward the stage, pretending to be *very* interested in the cowboy currently doing unspeakable things to a chair. I tried to look casual. Cool. Like I hadn't just been shamelessly staring at the shirtless man about to walk up beside me.

I stole another glance as he crouched down next to me, that familiar smile tugging at the corner of his mouth.

"What can I get you ladies?" He asked.

"Blue?" I whispered, my throat suddenly dry.

He looked up, a flicker of surprise crossing his face before a grin spread across his face. "Darci? Didn't think I'd be seeing you here tonight."

I grinned right back as I leaned in, lowering my voice, "Claire." I hooked a thumb toward her, "It's her bachelorette party. She's getting married tomorrow."

He nodded toward Claire, who was chatting with a group of girls also having a bachelorette party next to us.

"Oh yeah, I remember now. Congrats!" he said.

"Actually… it's kind of perfect I ran into you tonight," I said, my eyes crinkling in amusement. "When do you get off?"

He glanced at his watch. "This is the last show. Why?"

"Can a girl just want to talk to her ex-husband?" I teased.

He rolled his eyes and chuckled, "Always for you, wifey."

I blushed, my heart a nervous flutter of excitement.

He leaned close, and I shuddered as his nose grazed my jaw and whispered, "Can you meet me at The Sapphire Room at The Pinnacle next door after the show?"

I nodded slowly, "Yeah… I can do that."

He took our drink order and disappeared into the crowd. A few minutes later, he returned with our drinks.

He squeezed my shoulder and whispered against the

shell of my ear, "See you after the show," before vanishing again.

Just then, one of the cowboys, wearing only his G-string and cowboy hat, approached Claire. "I think the Mayor of Titty Town needs a ride from this cowboy. Ready?" he asked, his voice dripping with fake Southern charm.

Claire's eyes widened in mock horror, but she played along, mouthing, "Oh my god" to me as the cowboy offered his hand, and she hesitantly took it. Mallory whipped her phone out, ready to record the whole thing.

The music blared as the cowboys danced on stage, gyrating all over Claire, who was seated center stage. Her cheeks were bright red as they stood her up, twirled, and dipped her. The crowd cheered, and I saw Blue clapping his hands and grinning.

At the end of the performance, one of the cowboys offered Claire his arm with an exaggerated flourish and led her back to our table. Still flushed and laughing, she let him guide her through the crowd. Once they reached us, he turned to face her, his movements suddenly slower, more deliberate. With a charming smirk, he dipped into a low, theatrical bow, sweeping off his hat with one hand and holding it out to the side. His gaze met hers for a beat longer than necessary—playful, a little smug—before he straightened and spun smoothly back toward the stage, disappearing into the haze of lights and applause.

She leaned over and whispered, "I can't believe that just happened."

I grinned, "Believe it, girlie." I tilted my head towards Mallory, "She has it on film."

Claire covered her face as she blushed, "Oh god. Do not show that to Sonny."

The lights went completely out except for what looked like a starry sky on stage as the next group of guys who took the stage were dressed as astronauts, each standing in front of a mobile stripper pole.

An hour later, the crowd spilled out of the theater. We made our way next door to The Pinnacle. Claire and Mallory were already plotting their blackjack strategy as we stepped inside, but I hung back near the entrance to The Sapphire Room.

Claire clocked it immediately. "Wait... are you not coming with us?"

I tucked my phone into my clutch, trying for casual. "I told Blue I'd meet him for a drink."

Claire stopped mid-step, her brow arching in slow, judgmental concern. "Darci..."

I held up both hands like I was under arrest. "Don't worry—I'm not doing *that again.*"

She didn't look convinced.

I dragged a finger across my chest. "Cross my heart. I just want to ask if he'll be my plus one tomorrow. Nothing more. Scout's honor."

Mallory snorted. "Were you ever a scout?"

I grinned. "Exactly. So you know I'm being sincere."

Claire gave me one last look, the kind that said I love you, but I swear to God, then let Mallory tug her deeper into the casino.

I spotted him across the bustling lobby. He was in navy dress pants and a fitted blue button-down, his sleeves rolled up on his forearms. I made my way through the crowd, weaving through groups of people.

When I reached him, I touched his stomach and said,

"You clean up nice."

He offered a small smile, the warmth of his hand pressing on the small of my back. "Ready to grab that drink?"

I nodded, feeling a lick of heat in my belly at his touch. The Sapphire Room was packed, the air thick with energy and excitement. I was already buzzed from the rehearsal dinner and the shots we did at Hunk-O-licious. We searched for a booth, but there were none.

We found two empty seats at the bar, and he asked, "What'd you like to drink?"

I giggled as I attempted to climb into the seat, tossing my sequined bag onto the counter. After my second try, Blue's hands came around my waist as he hoisted me into my chair like I weighed nothing. One of my heels fell off and hit the wood floor with a loud click.

"Oops," I giggled, realizing that the buzz I had earlier had turned into full-fledged tipsiness.

I scanned the room, a strange, sudden feeling like I was being watched.

His gruff voice caught my attention. "Darci?"

I snapped out of it and looked at him. "Oh, um, a drink? Something… fruity. Surprise me?"

He grinned. "Sure thing," he said, turning to catch the bartender.

After ordering, he scooted his barstool closer to me, wrapping his arm around my chair as his fingers traced slow, absentminded circles along my neck, sending a shiver down my spine.

Before we met up, I wasn't sure how awkward this would be, but Blue couldn't keep his hands off me. And honestly… I didn't mind. While it was a crazy night when we stupidly got married, I remembered how good our chemistry was.

"So…?" He asked.

"So…" I purred back, grinning.

"Why'd you want to meet?"

I raised my eyebrows. "Maybe I just wanted to see my ex-husband for old times' sake?"

He laughed, "Darci, we were married for five minutes."

I rolled my eyes. "I know." I willed myself to sober up and not seem as drunk as I was feeling. Maybe this was a bad idea.

I blurted out, "I was wondering…"

"Yeah?"

He leaned close, his lips within kissing distance if I just bent a little toward him. His arm dropped to my waist, his fingers wrapping protectively around my side. God, I liked how the heat from his body seeped into mine.

I cleared my throat. "I was wondering if you'd like to be my plus one tomorrow at Claire's wedding."

His eyes softened. "Oh." His eyebrows crinkled. "What time's the wedding? I have a shift next door tomorrow night."

I licked my lips, staring at his mouth, remembering his kisses. My body moved toward him on instinct. Was I this desperate?

I pulled back just slightly, looking left. "Um… It's like 2 to 5."

He had a thoughtful expression before he nodded slowly and said, "I'd be honored," his voice low and husky.

I smiled, feeling a rush of relief.

He stood up, walking backward. "I'm going to run to

the restroom. Be right back."

I nodded and reached for my drink, the glass cool against my fingers as I casually scanned the bar. Then a figure stepped up beside me, a looming presence that shifted the air. Their shadow fell over me, and instinct made me glance up.

My breath caught. "Alex?"

What the fuck was he doing in Las Vegas?

CHAPTER THIRTY-TWO

Alex

The sound of her name in another man's voice hit me square in the chest. I snapped my head around, scanning the crowded bar. I heard her laugh—*that laugh*, like a sucker punch to my chest. I'd know it anywhere. She was only a few seats down, wearing that dress she had worn on *our date*. The one that had driven me crazy.

I couldn't tear my eyes away as I picked up my drink and drained it, trying not to notice. He leaned into her space like he owned the air around her. And Darci—she smiled up at him like he'd just stepped out of one of her dog-eared romance novels and offered to carry her groceries.

What the fuck? Who was that guy? Tall, broad, long hair down to his shoulders like some shampoo-commercial Sasquatch who just wandered in off a mountain and discovered hair gel. If he ripped off his shirt and declared he only drank protein shakes and rainwater, I wouldn't have been surprised.

Sarah nudged my elbow, amusement in her voice.

"Thirsty? Another drink?"

I shook my head, my eyes drifting right back to Darci. She was oblivious, lost in conversation *with him.*

I dug into my food, eating aggressively. The flavors blurred compared to the churning in my gut. But I couldn't stop myself from watching her, completely ignoring Sarah. Just as I finished my last bite, I heard her laugh again and glanced over to see Sasquatch's hand wrapped around her waist.

Why was she here? Then it hit me. Edison and Claire's wedding. It was probably this weekend. Was he her date for the wedding? From home? Or did she meet him here? *Fuck.*

I couldn't help but stare. Darci was tipsy, giggling, her smile loose and carefree—and he was drinking her in like he'd earned it. That smug, predatory grin twisted something in my chest. Every instinct told me to step in, pull her away, do something—but I stayed glued to my barstool. Instead, I turned back around, lifted two fingers, and signaled the bartender for another boilermaker.

I looked over again, unable to tear my eyes away. She was all I could see. *That fucking dress*—her breasts were practically spilling over the top. I flinched as a memory hit me—taking it off of her, tasting her, the softness of her skin against me.

I forced myself to face forward, not wanting to see whatever that was between them. Life was taunting me once again. I growled in frustration. Could this night get any worse?

"Hey… um, Alex… Everything okay?" Sarah tried to catch my attention, and I glanced her way. Her eyebrows rose as she gave me a little wave. "Do you know them?"

I grimaced and opened my mouth to apologize. But something caught my attention, and my head snapped toward Darci again. She nearly fell off the barstool, giggling as he lifted her back on as one of her heels slipped off with a loud click to the floor. I clenched my fists. He needed to quit touching her.

"Oops." She giggled.

I turned my entire body their way when I heard Sasquatch laugh. He scooted his barstool closer, wrapping his arm around the back of her chair. He couldn't stop pawing at her. A surge of anger bubbled as I watched the guy lean in too close, whispering something into her ear before standing up and sauntering away, leaving her alone.

I hesitated for a fraction of a second, but couldn't stop myself. I was drawn to her like a moth to a flame. She was... mine.

"I'll be right back," I muttered to Sarah as she watched me with a questioning gaze. I didn't even care if she saw where I was headed.

As I approached, she blinked, startled, "Alex?"

I smirked, trying to act casual and hide the simmering rage beneath the surface. "Hey, Tink. Funny seeing you here."

"What are you doing here?"

I shrugged, my voice laced with sarcasm. "Just thought I'd say hello."

Darci slid off her barstool. With just one shoe, she teetered slightly, and before I could think, I reached out, catching her by the arm. My hand closed around her elbow.

The jolt hit—sharp, hot, undeniable. It pulsed straight

through me, the same way it always had when we touched, like something in my nervous system still hadn't gotten the memo that we were over.

And then I saw it. The flicker in her eyes. Just a breath of hesitation. The way her lips parted—not to speak, just... surprised. Like maybe she'd felt it too. She didn't pull away. Not immediately. And that one beat of too-long contact told me everything.

Then the spell broke. Her expression hardened, and she stepped back, blinking at me like I was a stranger who'd gotten too close. The scent of her shampoo clung in the air between us. Familiar. Intimate. But underneath it, I caught a trace of cologne. Someone else's. And suddenly, she felt miles away.

She asked, "Where... where's my shoe?"

After a moment of searching, she spotted it under the barstool. With a muttered curse, she bent down to retrieve it, her dress hitching around her thighs.

As she straightened, I couldn't help but admire the view. Her legs were toned, and that dress still hugged her curves in all the right places.

She smoothed down her skirt, facing me, her eyes sparkling with a fiery glow, making them almost glow golden in color. "You don't get to look at me like that," she said.

I wasn't sure if she was threatening me or flirting, and I didn't care. I broke out in a smile, missing our banter and how I always got under her skin. I wrapped my hand around hers, and she shuddered.

"What are you doing here... with him?" I hissed.

She poked me in the chest, a playful glint in her eye as she slurred, "I could ask you the same damn thing, Alexxxxx..."

"Tink..." My eyes softened as they lingered on her face.

She poked me in the chest again, her playful demeanor melting away. "It's Claire's wedding weekend."

Please tell me you just met him here. But before I could ask, Sasquatch came up behind her, wrapping his arm around her waist, settling his hand on her belly. He towered over both of us and looked a little scary, but I wasn't about to back down.

He thrust out his other hand. "Hey, I'm Blue. Darci's..." He looked at her, then back at me with a slow, smug grin. "Husband."

The word hit me like a hammer to the chest. My stomach dropped so fast I felt sick.

Husband?

No. No, no, no. I couldn't have heard that right. My vision narrowed, the rest of the bar going blurry around the edges. The air thinned, and all I could hear was the rush of blood pounding in my ears. I took a step forward, my fists clenching so tight my nails dug into my palms. My throat burned with the words I didn't even know how to form.

I barely managed to get them out. "What? You—? You married *him*?"

I looked at her like I didn't recognize the person standing in front of me—like I was watching something precious fall right through my hands and there wasn't a damn thing I could do to stop it. I searched her face like I was begging her to take it back, to tell me he was lying, to tell me I wasn't already too fucking late.

But she didn't.

She rolled her eyes. Like it wasn't the end of my

goddamn world unraveling in front of me.

She slapped his chest lightly, her body language way too familiar, and muttered, "EX-husband."

I could barely hear her over the sound of my own breath, jagged and uneven.

I blinked. "What?"

She finally met my eyes, that old spark there but weighed down with something else. Something tired.

"We were drunk... stupid. We got it annulled as soon as we sobered up."

When? The word screamed through my head, but it came out strangled and desperate.

"When?"

She flinched. Looked away. As her cheeks turned red.

"A while ago..."

My throat tightened, breath catching somewhere between disbelief and hope.

"So... you're not married?"

It came out rough and quiet.

She pressed her lips into a tight line and shook her head.

I let out a shaky breath and dragged my hand down my face, trying to process, trying to breathe. But I *couldn't*—because Blue's hand was sliding down her thigh like he had any fucking right to touch her at all. I stared at his hand like I could set it on fire with just my glare.

He smirked, cocky and unbothered, like he knew he had the upper hand—and god, it made me want to put my fist through something. Through him.

Darci sighed and glanced between us. "Boys, we don't need a pissing contest right now."

She tried to defuse it, but I couldn't unclench my jaw.

Couldn't make my heart stop racing. I felt like I was standing outside my body, watching my last shot with her slip away.

And it wrecked me. And all I could do was stare at her. Like a man standing in a burning house, knowing full well he was going to let it all burn down around him... because he couldn't move. I just stood there—watching her, wanting her, already losing her all over again.

She looked past me at Sarah, and I followed her gaze to see that Sarah was now staring at both of us with confusion and annoyance.

Darci inclined her head. "So... who's that?"

I gave a slight head shake, turning to fully face Darci. "No one."

"Okay," Darci stepped out of Blue's reach, tilting her head, and said, "But why are you here?"

I cleared my throat. "A conference for work."

She nodded, her attempt to climb back onto the barstool ending in a clumsy tumble. I lifted her before Blue could touch her again, my hands lingering a moment too long before sliding down to steady her hips. A knot tightened in my stomach as our bodies brushed together.

I had this insatiable desire to lean in and kiss her. I didn't give a shit if Blue was right there or if he was a foot taller and a wall of muscle. But I backed off and sat on the stool next to her, gently pushing her handbag and drink closer to her. Blue sat on the stool on her opposite side, eyeing me suspiciously.

I leaned down, grabbing her foot, probably harder than I should, and she jumped as I slipped the shoe back on a second time.

The noise and movement of the room faded into nothing as she turned toward me, both our dates forgotten. Her focus locked on me, as if we were the only two people in the world.

"Claire and Edison are getting married tomorrow. Tonight was the rehearsal dinner and bachelorette party."

"Congrats," I said dryly.

She shrugged with a small smile on her lips. "I'm really happy for her." But something like sadness flashed in her eyes, "I've never known anyone more meant to be than those two."

I slowly nodded, not sure what she wanted me to say. I signaled the bartender and ordered two shots and another boilermaker. A moment later, he set them down in front of us.

I picked up a shot, holding it out to her. She took it as I grabbed my own, knocking it against hers. "To the bride and groom, may their love last a lifetime."

She knocked her shot against mine, and we glanced at each other as we downed them both before flipping the shot glasses down on the bar.

She swallowed hard. "I don't think I'm ever gonna find what they have. God knows I've tried."

I nodded as I dropped the shot of whiskey into my beer and watched it fall. I took a long drink, glancing toward Blue before finding her eyes again.

"Sasquatch not doing it for you?"

She gave me an incredulous look, "What?"

I jutted my chin toward Blue, his eyes narrowing at me. "Your... ex?" I couldn't bring myself to say *husband*.

"Blue?" Confusion in her eyes.

"Yeah?" I drawled out the word.

She leaned closer, her voice low. "I told you, he's just a… friend." She lifted a shoulder.

That guy was definitely not looking for friendship.

She shifted her weight, tucking her hair behind her ear like she couldn't quite meet my eyes. Her fingers toyed with the hem of her dress, like she was working up the courage to say it. Then she let out a breath, her shoulders curling in just a little—small, like she was bracing for how it might sound.

"I ran into him tonight, and I just… didn't want to go to the wedding alone."

Her voice was soft. Almost apologetic.

And damn it if it didn't feel like she'd just cracked my chest wide open.

"You could have…" I shrugged. "Asked me."

"Alex…"

I took a drink. "What?"

"I thought…"

"Yeah?"

Her cheeks reddened. "I don't know. After how we left things, I just…" She trailed off with a sigh, not finishing her thought.

She stared down at the bar, fidgeting with the sequins on her bag like she was trying to make herself smaller. Like she didn't want to give me too much to hold on to. But God, I wanted to hold on. I wanted to shake off every mile, every misunderstanding, every wasted day and start over.

I couldn't do this sitting here with Sasquatch breathing down our necks. Couldn't take another second of watching her pretend this didn't mean something—didn't still wreck both of us. I leaned in, dropping my voice low enough that only she could hear it.

"Can we go somewhere and talk?"

I glanced around, searching for anything—a booth, a corner, anywhere we could get some space. But every table was full, loud and crowded, like the whole damn world was conspiring to keep us sitting at this fucking crowded bar. I swallowed hard and shifted my body closer, lowering my voice even more as I slid my gaze past her to the man at her side.

I didn't bother hiding the disdain in my voice when I added, "Alone?"

I locked eyes with Blue, letting the word hang in the air between us like a loaded gun. I dared him to make it a problem.

Without hesitation, she looked up and nodded. "Um…yeah, okay. Where?"

I stood. "I have a room upstairs?"

"Your… hotel room?" She bit her lip, looking over where Sarah and I had sat.

"Yeah."

She nodded slowly. "Just let me… tell Blue goodbye."

I turned to Sarah, but her seat was empty, and a few bills were next to her plate. I should have felt guilty, but there was just relief. When I turned back, Darci was texting on her phone.

Blue stood up and walked over to me. He leaned over and shook my hand, hard. "I should say it was nice meeting you, but it really wasn't." He chuckled, "Take care of her." He gave Darci a grin and a salute before leaving the bar.

"Okay, let's go talk." She hopped off her stool, stumbling again. "Ugh, I hate these shoes."

I shrugged. "So, take them off."

She quirked her eyebrow, looking around. "Here?"

I grinned. "Who's going to stop you?"

Without waiting for a reply, I held out my arm to steady her and leaned down, sliding her shoes off as she chuckled. I picked them up, and with my free hand, I grabbed her other hand and led her out of the bar.

We arrived at the elevator bank just as one opened, and six other people followed us inside. There was barely any breathing room. Darci and I were pressed together at the back as the doors closed. My eyes trailed down her body, and I couldn't help but notice the way her pulse raced beneath her skin, a flush creeping up her neck.

A wave of desire washed over me. I leaned closer, my eyes fixed on her lips. She licked them, a nervous gesture that only fueled the fire within me.

The elevator lurched, a jolt that sent us stumbling against each other before it abruptly stopped. People panicked. Darci's hands shot out, catching my upper arms. Her eyes were wide with fear. The lights flickered twice and died, plunging us into darkness. Her hands tightened.

"Alex?" Her breath quickened.

I leaned in and murmured against her lips, "It'll be okay, Sweetheart," as my hands raised, cupping her face.

I took a deep breath, the darkness a cloak of privacy. My lips brushed against hers. She kissed me back, her hands grabbing my shirt as she let out a soft sigh, melting into me. The people around us faded away as we surrendered to the moment, a desperate hunger driving us.

Her hands tangled in my hair. A whirlwind of

emotion raced through me, and I didn't want to stop. But I pulled back, my breath coming in ragged gasps.

"Darci...," I whispered, my voice hoarse.

"I've missed you," she said so low I thought I might have imagined it.

The lights flickered back on, revealing six pairs of eyes staring at us. Darci's cheeks flushed a deep red as she quickly pulled away, her eyes darting to the floor.

A voice crackled over the intercom, "Apologies for the delay, folks. The elevator is back online."

As the doors slid open, I couldn't help but smile as I laced our fingers together, "Come on, Tink."

CHAPTER THIRTY-THREE

Darci

My heart pounded as he unlocked the door, holding it open for me to enter his hotel room. His familiar scent surrounded me, a reminder of our kiss in the elevator, but I was nervous. I tried to focus on the surroundings —the plush furniture, the mini-bar gleaming in the corner—but all I could think about was how his hands felt against my body.

He gestured towards the sitting area, a knowing smile on his lips. "Make yourself comfortable."

I nodded, sinking into the soft cushions of the couch. I tucked one leg underneath me, smoothing down my dress. I took in a deep breath, trying to regain my composure. He dropped my shoes next to me on the floor.

"Can I get you a drink?" he asked, his voice low and husky as he glanced at me.

I shook my head, a wry smile tugging at my lips. "Maybe some water?"

He nodded and walked over to the mini-bar,

grabbing two water bottles. He slid in next to me, his thigh brushing my knee as he handed me one.

"You do look a little flushed."

I took a long drink as we sat in silence, him watching me. I couldn't break eye contact. His gaze held me captive, a magnetic force pulling me closer.

"Darci," he began, his voice husky.

"Alex," I replied, my heart pounding in my ears.

He reached out, his fingers brushing against mine. I shivered and wondered how he always affected me like this when it felt like we were always at each other's throats.

"We need to talk," he said, his voice serious.

I nodded, my throat dry. "Okay."

He hesitated, his eyes searching my face. "About us."

My breath caught in my throat. Was there an 'us'? We hadn't spoken in weeks, two months now.

It secretly thrilled me at the bar when he got possessive. And then it clicked... that's what I needed, what I wanted. I wanted to be his—more than anything. But I didn't know what to say, so I picked up my water, hoping he wouldn't notice how my hands trembled. I drank to keep myself occupied in the awkward silence.

He searched my eyes before he finally spoke. "About Matteo's..." His eyes filled with regret. "I'm so sorry, Darci."

I nodded, my heart aching for him. "It's okay," I replied, trying to sound reassuring.

He shook his head. "No, it's not. You did this sweet thing for me, and I should have been..." He paused, searching for the right words. "More in control of my emotions."

I waited patiently, my eyes fixed on him. He took a

deep breath, his Adam's apple bobbing nervously.

"I went back to therapy. I called my therapist that same night," he confessed, his voice barely a whisper. "Twice a week for eight weeks now."

My eyebrows shot up. "Really?"

He nodded, a flicker of pride in his eyes. "It's been helping."

"That's so great," I said, my voice filled with genuine warmth.

He hesitated, a thoughtful expression on his face. "But I also had this dream..."

My curiosity was piqued. "A dream?"

Most people would probably think I was crazy, but there was more to the world than we could see. There were unexplainable things, and dreams were part of that. Something that could offer a glimpse into the unknown, a chance to find clarity.

He nodded, his gaze softening. "At first, I didn't even know it was a dream. I suddenly became aware I was driving to Patterdale, to the cemetery. It had felt so real, and I fell asleep against Jenna's gravestone. When I woke up, Jenna was sitting on the bench across from me," he continued, his voice trembling slightly. "She was holding the baby in her arms. She looked just the same."

A ghost of a smile went across his face as a lump formed in my throat.

"Savannah was cooing, and I just..." He heaved a heavy sigh. "I wanted to take them both in my arms," he confessed, his voice filled with longing. "But then, Jenna said..."

My eyes widened. "What did she say?"

A small smile played on his lips as he shook his head. "She said she had been waiting for me to tell her I met someone."

I blinked, trying to process the information. "She did?"

He nodded. Briefly, his eyes clouded with sadness, but they turned to hope. "She said she knew when I brought you there that you were the one who could..." His voice trailed off as a smile tugged at his lips. "The one who could give me the life she couldn't."

My heart pounded as I shifted, leaning closer. I tried and failed to blink back tears as one escaped down my cheek.

"Don't cry, Tink." He leaned in, giving me a sad smile as he wiped the tear away. "When Jenna said she wanted me to be happy, something changed. Something I hadn't been able to get past in all my therapy sessions. I felt like a weight had finally been lifted when I woke up."

His voice was quiet, hopeful.

I swallowed, my heart thudding. "It's just..." I hesitated, then let the words tumble out before I could second-guess them. "I was scared, Alex. Scared that no matter what we had... I'd always be standing in the shadow of what you lost. That I'd never be *her*, and I'd never measure up."

I glanced at him, eyes burning. "I didn't want to be the other woman—not to someone else, and definitely not to a memory."

He didn't speak right away. Just looked at me like he was seeing all the cracks I'd tried to patch over with sarcasm and sass. Then slowly, deliberately, he reached for my hand. He didn't speak right away. Just looked at me like he was finally seeing all the pieces of me I'd kept hidden, even from myself. Then he reached for my hand, his touch steady despite the tremble in his voice.

"I never wanted you to feel like you were in a contest with the past," he said. "But I thought loving you was betraying it… betraying them."

He paused, eyes searching mine like the words might undo him. "But I realized I'd hate myself more if I denied what we are together."

My breath caught.

He… he loved me? Oh my god.

In a whisper, I asked, "What're we together?"

He gently cupped my chin, turning my face as our eyes locked. A serious look came over him as he said, "We're the next chapter that I didn't think I'd ever get to write, Tink."

"You think so?" I couldn't believe what I was hearing. I looked down.

"How do you explain it all—the books, the dream, the random chance of me moving to the same apartment complex, living directly across from you?"

"I… I don't know." I shook my head.

Before Alex, I'd never made it past a second date with anyone. Sure, we drove each other crazy, but something clicked into place with him, something I couldn't explain, and it felt right.

This whole time we'd been apart, just the briefest glimpse of him sent a thrill coursing through me, igniting something. I craved the warmth of his touch, the familiar comfort of his scent. Being apart from him felt unbearable. Was this love? This aching need to be near him, this unspoken certainty that we were in this together.

He choked out the first few words, "I don't want to be without you—seeing you with that guy tonight. I want you to be mine. Only mine, Tink."

My eyes locked onto his in surprise. "Me?"

He broke out in a big grin that went clear up to his eyes as he gently took my hands in his.

"Yes, you, Darci. Without a doubt. I want you." He dipped his head, his lips right at mine as he whispered, "All that time we spent together, those were some of the happiest days of my life." He brushed his lips against mine before whispering against my mouth, "I want that. With you."

Our mouths crashed into one another, frantic, desperate, teeth clashing. My hands rose to his neck, my fingers tangling in his hair. In one swift move, he pulled me over his lap so I was straddling him, our lips never parting. His hands were all over me—my shoulders, my arms, my back, squeezing my ass and pulling me into him—like he couldn't believe I was here. He sucked my bottom lip, nipping it with his teeth before plunging his tongue into my mouth, tasting me.

He pulled back, his hands stilling on my hips, his breath ragged. "I can't believe you wore this dress… for him."

I chuckled, shaking my head. "I didn't wear this dress for him. I wore it for the rehearsal and the bachelorette party. I love this dress, and I look damn good. I just… ran into him at Hunk-O-Licious."

"Hunk O'what?"

I rolled my eyes. "It's a bachelorette party. What did you expect?"

He put his hands up in surrender, grinning sheepishly, "You're right, you're right."

"And speaking of which, I kind of left the girls hanging in the casino." I climbed off Alex's lap, slipping my shoes back on.

I let out a sigh, "I have to get back. Claire is probably imagining I ran off and got married again."

Alex raised an eyebrow, amused.

I smirked. "Can't really blame her. Last time I went rogue in Vegas, I came back with a husband and a hangover."

He followed me to the elevator, trailing his fingers lightly down my arm before I pressed the button.

"You'll come back after?" he asked, voice low, coaxing. "To my room?"

I bit back a smile. "That depends. You asking nicely?"

He stepped closer, all warmth and want as he pressed his hardening length against my hip. "Darci… I'm asking very nicely."

I leaned in, just enough to let my perfume hit him. "Then yes. After we go dancing at the Moonlit Lounge."

His mouth curved, but there was an edge of mischief. "And who will you be dancing with?"

I shrugged, already walking backward toward the elevator as the doors opened. "With the girls. But hypothetically… if some guy asked me to dance, I might say yes."

He gave a low chuckle, following me with his gaze. "Hypothetically, this guy—is he handsome? Deeply threatened by anyone else touching you?"

I tilted my head, playing innocent. "Hmm. Hypothetically, yes. Trouble, definitely. And very good with his hands."

"Tell him to keep them to himself," he said, stepping back as the doors started to close.

I smiled sweetly. "That's up to me, isn't it?"

The last thing I saw before the doors slid shut was his wicked grin.

I texted Claire to let her know I was on my way. She replied that I could find them at the tables. Apparently, Mallory was on some kind of hot streak at the roulette table.

A few minutes later, I spotted her and Mallory in their trucker hats amidst a crowd gathered around a roulette table. Their faces were flushed with excitement as they watched the ball spin. Mallory was having some ridiculous luck, her bets consistently landing on the winning color and number.

I slipped between them, squeezing into the tight space. "You're on fire," I whispered to her, my voice barely heard over the noise of the casino.

She grinned, her eyes sparkling with excitement. "I know, right? I can't believe it. I'm up two thousand bucks."

"Woah!"

I watched as she placed another bet, her fingers hovering over the chips. The ball spun, a blur of red and black, and landed. A collective gasp rose from the crowd as Mallory's number came up.

"Another win!" Claire shouted, her voice filled with disbelief. I couldn't help but smile.

Claire leaned to my ear as Mallory chose her next guess, "So... how'd it go? With Blue? Is he coming tomorrow?"

I gave her a mysterious smile and shrugged as I said, "Plans change."

She gave me a quizzical look. "What?"

I cleared my throat, "I, um, kind of ran into Alex in The Sapphire Room when I was with Blue."

"Alex is here? In Vegas?"

I chuckled, "I know, right? It's crazy, but... It all

worked out in the end. Long story short, Alex told me he loved me."

Claire's eyes widened. "What?"

I waved my hand dismissively. "We'll talk about it later. Right now, I want to dance the night away with you before you become an old married lady."

"I don't think I can wait to hear this one," Claire said, practically vibrating with anticipation.

I gave her a look. "Well, it started with Alex and Blue circling each other, and there was a moment when I thought they might pull their dicks out and start measuring."

"Darci!"

"Everything is fine now," I said reassuringly.

I leaned over to Mallory and said, "Hey, you ready to quit while you're still ahead and go party it up in the Moonlit Lounge? Mama needs to dance and free her soul."

She giggled as she stood up and gathered all her chips. "Yes! Let's go turn these in first."

When we got to the lounge, the dance floor was packed, and most tables were full, but we found a small one that would fit the three of us.

Claire leaned toward Mallory, "I can't believe you turned twenty dollars into two thousand. What a night!"

Mallory shrugged. "I guess I'm just lucky." She stood up and said, "I'll go get the drinks. Fruity cocktails all around?"

Claire and I nodded enthusiastically.

Claire's hand was on the table, and I put mine over hers. "Cold feet?"

She drew in a soft breath, eyes shining. "Not even a

little. I've never been more sure."

I grinned. "Well, if you change your mind, just let me know because I will be there with the getaway car. And we'll drive off into the sunset like Thelma and Louise."

We were still laughing when Mallory returned to the table with a tray of three very large, very pink drinks with flamingo swizzle sticks sticking out of them and six shots of god knows what.

"Look what I got! Three Pink Paradises and some tequila shots."

I slapped the table with my palm and said, "Let's get this party started!"

Twenty minutes later, we were a sweaty, giggling mess, our voices hoarse from shout-singing along to "Pink Pony Club." Claire and Mallory had abandoned the dance floor to freshen up, leaving me alone as I continued to dance in the crowd.

Heat pressed against my back just before the faintest hint of cedar and pine curled around me—unmistakable. My breath hitched as I turned, pulse drumming low in my throat.

There he was—Alex, standing a little too close, dark pants creased, and that white button-down tugged just slightly loose at the collar like he'd been wrestling with his thoughts.

"Wanna dance?" he asked, his voice low and husky.

I nodded, already moving to the rhythm of the music. He stood behind me, his arm around my waist, and pulled my body snug against him. Our bodies pressed together, and I ground my ass against him, a familiar heat igniting between us. I reached back, my fingers tangling in his hair. He groaned, his grip tightening around my waist as he pressed against me.

The music thumped beneath my skin, the kind of beat you didn't just hear—you felt. I let it carry me, shaking off the last of my self-consciousness, hips swaying, my heartbeat syncing to the rhythm as we gyrated against each other.

Out of the corner of my eye, Claire and Mallory burst back onto the dance floor, breathless and glowing, glitter catching the light on their cheeks. Claire scanned the crowd, then caught on us. She paused. Just a flicker. Her eyes darted between me and Alex, a tiny hitch in her smile before she smoothed it out. Alex and I took a half-step apart, like the music had suddenly changed tempo.

"Hey, uh… Dr. Alex," Claire said, a little too brightly as she approached.

He gave her a grin. "Claire. Nice to see you again. How's Edison doing with the whole… bee situation?"

She laughed, the kind that comes easily when you're happy. "A lot more careful these days. He carries his epi-pen now like it's a fashion statement."

"Smart man."

Claire nodded, her eyes flicking once more between us, curiosity behind her lashes. "I think we're gonna head out," she said, tone light but knowing, the corner of her mouth lifting.

I couldn't help but wonder what she saw when she looked at us.

I hesitated, glancing at Alex. "I should go with you," I offered to Claire.

She waved me off. "No, it's okay." She hugged me and whispered, "This was so much fun. It's fine. Really. I'll see you in the morning."

When she pulled away from the hug, I couldn't help

but notice the way her eyes lingered on Alex. She gave him a knowing smirk.

She leaned over and said in my ear, "Plus, I think you have something a little more important right here."

My cheeks heated as I glanced over at Alex. I turned back to him as Claire and Mallory headed towards the exit.

"So... wanna dance some more?" I asked, a playful smile on my lips.

He pulled me closer, his body pressed against mine, his hard length pressed into my stomach.

"Tink, does that feel like I want to dance?" he asked, his voice low and husky.

He intertwined our fingers and led me out of the nightclub. Even at this late hour, the casino floor was still bustling with activity. Just as we arrived at the elevator bank, the doors to one slid open, revealing an empty and dimly lit interior. We stepped inside.

Alex turned, a lazy smile pulling up one corner of his mouth. His pupils swallowed nearly all of his light blue irises. He pressed me against the mirrored wall, his body heat radiating through my thin dress. His fingers tangled in my hair, pulling me closer. I leaned into him, my lips parting slightly. His lips brushed against mine, a soft, tentative touch that stoked the fire that had been burning since we'd been in his room earlier.

Our kiss deepened, our tongues dancing together, building slowly. His arousal pressed against me as I slid my hand down to the button of his pants. His mouth found that spot where my neck connected to my shoulder, and he kissed, licked, and bit me, working his way up the column of my neck. My core was now molten as his lips made their way to the shell of my ear.

The elevator dinged, the doors sliding open. We broke apart, our breath ragged. I glanced around, relieved to see that we were alone.

"Let's continue this inside," He said as he grabbed my hand and pulled me toward his room.

I followed, my stomach flipping as he opened the door and waited for me to enter.

CHAPTER THIRTY-FOUR

Alex

As soon as I shut the door, I couldn't wait another second. I needed her like I was a dying man needing water. I pushed her against the door, kissing her hard. Her hands went to my shirt, yanking me against her as her leg wrapped around my body.

I pulled back, smirking. "If you keep doing things like that, we aren't making it to the bed."

"Shut up," She said through a giggle as she licked my neck. "God, I've... missed this. I've missed you."

"Fuck. Me too, Sweetheart."

This time I knew where that damn zipper was. I pushed her hands up against the door, holding them in one of mine as I unzipped her dress. I dropped them, and she helped me push the dress to the floor. She kicked it somewhere, along with her shoes.

She was in sheer green lace underwear that left absolutely nothing to the imagination with a matching strapless bra, her peaked nipples on prominent display. Was she wearing this for *him*?

I dipped my head, biting her neck and rasped next to her ear as I snapped the elastic of her underwear, "Was this for… Blue?"

"No." She let out a breathy laugh. "Sometimes a girl just wants to feel pretty. Now shut up and fuck me."

I kissed her again, turning with her against me, and walked her backward towards the bedroom. As soon as we were inside, I kicked the door shut and walked her to the bed. Lording over her, I laid her back.

I stood, drinking her in. Her golden-brown eyes locked on mine, full of heat, that smirk daring me to lose control. Fuck—she was a walking sin, and I wanted to break every rule for her.

She attempted to crawl to the pillows, but I wrapped my hand around her calf, holding her still.

"Stay," I commanded as I quickly unbuttoned my shirt, letting it fall to the ground.

I kneeled, grabbing her hips and pulling her towards me. I ran my fingers delicately over her panties, teasing her clit as I considered if I wanted to keep them on or yank them off. I leaned down, settling between her legs, pressing my nose to her core, and breathed her in.

"Fuck, so sweet, Tink. I need to taste you."

I couldn't wait. I ripped her panties clean off, pocketing them, and then raised her legs, putting them over my shoulders as I kissed and licked and nipped her inner thighs until I made my way right to her glistening center. My mouth watered as she squirmed in anticipation, whimpering.

"Please, Alex." She swallowed audibly, "Oh, god, please."

I pulled back and smirked. "I want to hear you say it. Tell me you want me to feast on your pussy."

She reached out, her fingers raking through my hair, and I leaned back as I said, "Nope. Say what you want."

Her breath was ragged. "I... I want..."

"Yes?" I teased her with my fingers, running a circle around her clit, but never touching it as she flexed her hips against my hand.

"I want you to..." She blushed and closed her eyes as she let out a soft sigh, "to feast on my fucking pussy... please."

"Good girl."

I leaned over sucking her clit into my mouth, feeling her pulse before letting go and running my tongue flat from her ass back up to that little bundle of nerves. I switched between teasing it with soft downward licks and swirling my tongue around her entrance before tongue fucking her again and again.

She moaned, "Holy fuck," reaching for me, her fingers running through my hair as her back arched off the bed. I pressed my other hand down on her pubic bone, holding her in place as I ran my fingers through her folds before plunging two deep inside.

I curled them in a come hither way, reaching her g-spot. The way she moaned my name was music to my ears as I leaned back down and sucked her clit.

Her breath ragged, she whimpered, "Fuck, baby. Right there. Right. There. Don't... don't stop. Please. God, please..." She was practically begging me to make her come.

My dick strained against my zipper, but I wanted.... No, I needed her to come from just my tongue and fingers. "Not stopping, Tink. Let yourself go... come for me."

Moments later, she screamed my name. Her juices

dripped down to her ass, coating my face, as I continued pumping my fingers and suckling her clit through her orgasm. I slowed my ministrations as she came down, out of breath.

I sat back on my knees, wiping the back of my hand across my face, "Fuck, baby. That was hot," before rising and dropping my pants and boxers to the floor.

She reached for me. "Come here," she said with a dark smile. "I need so much more of you."

She didn't need to ask twice. I climbed up the bed, but she flipped things and sat up, straddling me as I got to the head of the bed.

She settled between my legs and said, "Now, I need a taste of you."

My cock throbbed heavy between my legs. Her hand went straight to it, rubbing the bead of pre-cum before she sucked me into her mouth.

I leaned back, groaning as she stroked and sucked at the same time.

"Darci, baby." I moaned, reaching for her.

One of her hands tugged my balls down, and I groaned. Any blood in my body went straight to my cock. I could barely remember my name, but if she kept this up, I was going to cum straight down her throat. My hands went to her head as I bucked my hips in time with her mouth.

"Is… is this okay?"

She answered by reaching around, grabbing my ass, and pulling me deeper into her mouth. My eyes rolled back into my head as a moan escaped my lips.

"So fucking good, baby."

It was too much. I couldn't finish my thought. I reached down and hauled her up on top of me.

"I want to feel you from the inside, Tink."

She inhaled, and a slow grin spread on her face as she sat up, slowly sliding down, taking all of me inside her. I groaned, her tight pussy fitting me like a glove. My hands went to her hips, lifting her and grinding us together in a slow dance. She felt like heaven. Her wet heat alone was enough to send me over the edge.

I bucked against her, bending forward to take her mouth with mine in a slow kiss that I wished could last forever. I didn't want to let her go.

She sat up, grinding against my pubic bone as my balls began to tighten. My hands left her hips to caress her breasts, my thumbs rubbing her nipples. She threw her head back, her hips moving faster. I was close, but I wanted and needed her to come again.

One of my hands migrated down between us, circling her clit as she fucked me. I pinched her nipple with my other hand, pulling it. She whimpered as her eyes widened, staring down at me. Our gazes locked, and my hand went to her chin, holding her in place.

"That's it, Tink. Look at me when you come. I want to see it in your eyes."

I pressed the heel of my hand against her clit, my fingers feeling the friction between us as she rode me. Her breath became more ragged, and she screamed as she crested over the edge, her juices leaking down my balls like a waterfall.

God, the ecstasy that went through me as her scent filled the room. We needed to do that again and again.

I was nearly there, the coiling pulling taut in my belly as my cock pulsed, begging to spill. I couldn't hold it anymore.

My voice dropped an octave as I moaned through my

release, "Darci... Fuck." My heart felt like it would burst through my chest, and then the words just came out without thought, "I... I love you."

Still breathless, she leaned down, my face in her hands, kissing me slowly, tenderly, like she... loved me, too. We broke apart, nose to nose, sharing one breath. I felt a drop of wetness hit my cheek and then another. She was crying, her eyes tightly closed.

I breathed out. "Darci?"

More tears came. I ran my hands down her back before wrapping my arms around her, rolling us to face each other on the bed, still connected. I swiped away her tears.

"Don't cry."

I tried to soothe her, stroking her arms, her back, and her hair as she pulled herself into my neck and cried harder. I waited, kissing her softly on her forehead, on her cheek, in her hair until her cries calmed into quiet shuddering inhales.

I smiled, stroking her hair, "It's okay. I love you, but you don't have to say back if you're not there yet."

She sniffled, nuzzling my neck. Her hands came up to my chest, and she pressed her hand over my heart, feeling the frantic beat. She leaned back and opened her eyes, and it was like she was looking at me for the first time. Something had changed in her eyes, and I wasn't sure what it meant.

She smiled through her tears, "You said..." She looked away, her smile faltering. "You said you loved me."

"I did."

"How do you know?" She swallowed thickly.

Without hesitation, I said, "Because I can't live without you. Because I think about you all the time.

Because I think about us creating a life together. And... I want that. With you."

Shaking her head, whispering, "No one's ever said they loved me."

I searched her eyes, sadness washing over me. "You've never been in love?"

She shrugged, shaking her head. "I thought..." She trailed off with a sigh.

I brushed some hair out of her face. "Tell me."

She took a deep breath and let it out slowly. "I thought maybe... I was just..." Her voice dropped to an almost imperceptible whisper as a tear traced down her cheek. "Unlovable."

Her eyes filled with tears again, and I kissed her tenderly, shaking my head. "Never." My heart pounded in my chest as I watched her struggle. "Darci," I whispered, soft and gentle, "You're loved."

She looked up, her eyes filled with a raw vulnerability. "I love you, too," she confessed, her voice soft.

My stomach flipped. I dipped my head, lips pressing against hers in a soft kiss. When we pulled back, our foreheads pressed together.

"You're loved, Tink... so much," my voice filled with emotion.

When I pulled back, she offered a shy smile, her cheeks flushed. I couldn't help myself when I leaned back in and kissed her slowly, lazily, like we had all the time in the world.

I pulled her against my chest and begged, "Stay with me."

Softly, she said, "Okay," against my chest.

I didn't want to let go of her, not even for one second.

We only parted when I grabbed the covers and pulled them over us. She nestled against me, throwing her arm around my body, her lips against my collarbone. Our legs tangled as I kissed her forehead, and we settled together.

I stroked her hair and murmured, "I don't think I've ever felt this… happy."

She let out a soft sigh against me as I continued running my fingers through her hair, and it wasn't too long before her breathing slowed, becoming rhythmic. I let my eyes close. My last thought was that I was exactly where I needed to be.

I woke in a panic, a shiver running down my spine. *Where was she? Had I imagined the whole thing?*

I swung my legs over the side of the bed, the cool air chilling me. Outside, the sky was overcast, and the sun was peeking behind a cloud.

"Darci?" I called softly, my voice carrying through the stillness of the room.

"In here," she replied from behind the bathroom door.

A moment later, the door opened, and she stepped out, her dress gliding gracefully over her shoulders as she adjusted it into place.

"What's going on?" I asked, my voice hoarse from sleep.

She smiled, her eyes sparkling. "I have to get back to the ranch. Claire, Mallory, and I have hair and nail appointments this morning."

"Oh," I nodded, a pang of disappointment shot through me.

I glanced at the clock, realizing it was already well into the morning. I'd already missed the first sessions of the conference.

She sat down on the bed next to me and smiled. "Come to the wedding. Be my date?"

I gave her a quizzical look. "What about Blue?"

She chuckled, "Who?"

I wrinkled my brow. "Didn't you already ask him?"

Her lips curved into a sly smirk, one brow arching in playful defiance as her eyes sparkled. "You know, when a man tells you he loves you, you sure hope he's your date to your best friend's wedding," she quipped, her tone light but edged with teasing. Then, her expression softened, and she leaned down, kissing me sweetly before adding with a casual shrug, "Besides, I canceled on him at the bar."

I smiled against her lips, "You did?"

She let out a breathy "Yeah" before kissing me again.

I wrapped my hand around her waist. "I'd be honored to be there."

I stood up and grabbed a pair of athletic shorts from my suitcase. "Let me walk you down and get you a car," I said.

I looked up at the sky as we waited outside for her rideshare. "Is the wedding outside?"

"It's in a fruit orchard."

"I hope it doesn't rain."

"That would suck, but I've always heard it's good luck when it rains on your wedding day."

A black sedan pulled up, and I wrapped my arms around her and gave her one last kiss. I pulled back and said, "I love you."

Her smile lit up her face, a soft, radiant glow that seemed to emanate from within. "I love you, too."

Before I shut the door, I said, "I'll see you this afternoon."

I watched as they drove off and immediately felt a tug to follow her. I was dreading sitting through the sessions today until I could be with her again.

CHAPTER THIRTY-FIVE

Darci

I rushed back to my hotel room, my heart pounding with excitement. After a quick shower, I slipped on a pair of leggings and a T-shirt, eager to prepare for the wedding.

Just as I was sliding on my clogs, I heard a knock at the door. My stomach fluttered. I knew the questions were coming.

I swung open the door, revealing Claire and Mallory standing on the other side, grinning like two idiots.

"Well?" Claire demanded, her voice filled with excitement. "What happened with Alex? And don't even deny it, girl. We know you just got back."

I grinned, unable to hide my excitement. "He told me he loved me," I blurted out.

Claire's jaw dropped, her eyes wide with disbelief.

"No way!" Mallory exclaimed.

I nodded, my heart still racing. "I kind of can't believe it."

Claire grabbed both my hands and whispered, "And?

Then what happened?" She searched my eyes.

I looked down, feeling the heat in my cheeks, "We said a lot, but I told him I loved him, too."

Her eyes widened again, "Oh my god, Darci! I'm so happy for you! Is he coming to the wedding?"

I grinned. "Of course he is."

Mallory came over, wrapping her arms around us, "Darci, I'm so happy for you. But, we gotta get up to the bridal suite. Francoise is probably already waiting for us."

"Oh, shit!" Claire looked at her watch.

Mallory shrugged, "Yeah… chop, chop. Darce, grab your stuff, dress, makeup, shoes, whatever. Everyone meet in the hallway, pronto."

A few minutes later, a large man with a gray faux hawk opened the bridal suite door. He wore a flowing caftan in pinks and reds, beautiful bangle bracelets, and thick red glasses.

"Ladies! Who's ready to get beautiful?"

Francoise was a local stylist known for his impeccable taste and gentle touch. The ranch staff had recommended him when Claire booked the wedding. We exchanged nervous glances as he surveyed each of us.

"Now… who is the blushing bride?"

Claire shyly raised her hand. "That would be me."

"Oh my goodness, your hair is exquisite." He picked up a strand of her curls, "The color… the curls. I'm already getting visions. How do you feel about keeping it down and letting those curls shine with a crown of flowers?"

"That sounds perfect. The florist should have left some small flowers with our bouquets."

"Ah…yes. I saw those. Red poppies and baby's breath?"

She nodded enthusiastically.

He put his hand over his heart. "You are going to take your man's breath away when you walk down that aisle."

He scanned Mallory and me, rubbing his hands together, "Why don't we do a similar thing with the bridesmaids with just the baby's breath?"

We all exchanged glances, everyone looking at Claire. She grinned, "I think it sounds fabulous. Mallory? Darci?"

We both nodded.

Francoise clapped his hands. "Wonderful! It's settled. Let's get started."

A moment later, Claire's mom and a woman from the spa came in. The woman set Mallory up for a manicure while I went to the ornate bathroom and got to work on my makeup. When she was done, we switched places.

As soon as my nails were done, Francoise was finishing the last touches to Claire's mom and called me over.

Trading seats, Claire's mom settled down in front of the manicurist. Claire was in the chair beside me, wrapped in a silk robe. The front of her hair was pulled loosely back in waves. I motioned for her to turn so I could see the back. She stood up, turning her head left and right. Francoise had added poppies and baby's breath along the back in a half-up twist, her curls in full display.

I gasped, "Oh Claire, your hair… it's just gorgeous."

With my hair on the shorter side, I wasn't sure how much Francoise could do, but he got to work on my hair.

He added waves, fluffing and spraying, and a few moments later, he tucked and pinned one side of my hair behind my ear and carefully placed baby's breath through it. When he was done, he turned me towards the mirror, handing me a hand mirror to see the back.

"What do you think?"

I leaned towards the mirror, my eyes widened, "Oh, Francoise, I can't believe it. It's lovely. Thank you so much."

He beamed.

We sat in the lounge with glasses of champagne as Francoise cleaned up and wished Claire well. Claire asked me to do her makeup, so I flitted around her as we chatted.

A little while later, a staff member walked in, wheeling a cart with a large charcuterie tray full of meats, cheeses, fruits, and nuts. When my stomach grumbled, I realized I had never thought about breakfast today. It didn't take long for us to dig in and devour it.

Mallory cleared her throat, "So... I think it's time to get dressed."

I raised my eyebrows at Claire, "It's almost time! Still feeling it?"

She giggled, "You have no idea. I'm so ready."

"Aww..."

I said, "We'll get our dresses on and then help you."

Claire nodded, sipping her champagne. Her mom was beside her, already dressed in a romantic, vintage-inspired gown in pale green with delicate ivory flowers scattered across the flowing fabric. It was beautiful with her hair and made her look like she just stepped out of an old love story.

Mallory grabbed her garment bag and went to the bathroom to change into her bridesmaid dress. Our dresses were the same sage green color, but completely different styles. My dress was sleeveless with a high neck that gathered in the front and opened in the back. It had an empire waist with a high-low skirt that fluttered. It was very lovely. I hoped to wear it again sometime. But, I was curious to see Mallory's dress.

It was just us girls, and I wasn't shy, so I yanked off my leggings and T-shirt. I was already in my longline bra. I slid the dress up my body, sliding my arms into the straps. Claire stood up and tied the bow at the back of my neck. I grabbed my gold heels from the duffel bag and slipped into them just as Mallory emerged from the bathroom. Her dress was strapless, with a high waist and a flowing skirt to the floor. She had gold peep-toe heels on.

"Mallory, you look gorgeous."

"Thanks. I love yours, too."

"Mal," Claire said, "Would you go check and ensure everything is going okay with Sonny and the boys?"

Mallory's eyes brightened. "I'd be happy to."

As she left the room, I asked Claire, "Nervous?"

She took in a deep breath and laughed. "A little. I'm just ready for the honeymoon."

Claire's mom followed with the garment bag as we headed to the bathroom dressing area. She hung it on a hook on the wall. Claire stripped down to her strapless bra and panties, the palest pink to match her dress. I unzipped the garment bag and pulled out her dress. It had been a while since I'd seen it, and I'd forgotten how beautiful it was.

It was soft and romantic in delicate pale pink fabrics.

Floral lace appliqués embellished the bodice and cascaded down the skirt. The fitted bodice had a plunging V-neckline with off-the-shoulder sleeves that showed off her freckled shoulders.

I held it out, and she stepped in, helping me work it up her body. She slid her arms into the sleeves, and the skirt unfurled as I let it go. Her mother slowly worked the zipper up, a smile on her face.

Claire turned, looking at herself in the full-length mirror, smoothing the skirt. I looked over her shoulder and couldn't help but gasp.

"Claire... You are absolutely stunning. Edison is going to die when he sees you."

She grinned, a giggle escaping. She turned from side to side, trying to view it. "You think so?"

"It's beautiful, darling." Her mother cooed.

"Oh yeah," I chuckled and nodded. "You look ethereal. When you walk down that aisle, it'll be like the queen of the fairies fluttering down it."

With a grin, she shooed us out of the bathroom. "I have to pee."

"Oh, Claire Bear, why didn't you do that before you put the dress on?" Her mother's lips pressed together in a white line. "Be careful."

I took her mom's arm and gently led her away. "Come on, Mrs. Montague. We'll wait outside."

I arched an eyebrow at Claire as she rolled her eyes at me before we walked out, shutting the door behind us. This place was old, and the bathroom door stuck a little, so you had to really pull it shut. I let go of her mom's arm, but when I pulled the door shut this time, the doorknob came off in my hand.

My eyes widened as I looked at the doorknob in my

hand and then back at the door.

I muttered, "What the fuck?"

I tried pushing it back on, but it just fell off on to the plush carpet.

What was I going to do? I looked around the room. I didn't want to panic Claire or her mom, so I leaned into the door.

"Hey Claire, don't come out here. Um… Edison was headed this way, and you don't want him to see your dress."

She hollered back, "Okay. Let me know when I come out."

I held the doorknob behind my back and said, "Hey, Mrs. Montague, why don't you go to the ceremony and see if everything is on time?"

She nodded and headed downstairs.

I sighed and turned around, carefully trying to push my finger into the hole, seeing if I could jiggle something to open the door as delicately as possible. But it wasn't working.

Mallory walked in and gasped when she saw the doorknob in my hand.

She put her hands on her hips and said, "What happened?"

I looked at her and grimaced. I whispered, "The doorknob fell off in my hand. I haven't told Claire yet. Don't want to freak her out."

She nodded, taking a deep breath, "That's the last thing we need."

"How's the groom?"

She waved dismissively, "Cool as a cucumber. About to head outside."

I nodded as I made a decision. "Okay, we have to tell

her."

"Yeah, you do that." She walked backward to the door, "I'll go downstairs and… get some help."

"Good idea." I huffed out a breath, preparing myself, "Um… Claire, babe?"

"Yeah?"

"The, um, doorknob to the bathroom came off in my hand. Can you see if you can open it from your end?"

"What?!" Claire exclaimed. "I'm trapped in here?"

"Um… no, of course not. But could you try and see if it opens on that side?"

I could hear the door jiggling, but it didn't budge.

"Fuck." I heard through the door.

"Don't panic. Mallory went to get help. We're going to get you out of there."

I bit my lip as I thought about what we could do.

"Darci?"

"Yeah?"

"Uh, there's a window in here. What if I climb down it? It's just two stories."

"Are you fucking kidding me, Claire? No, absolutely not. That will ruin your wedding dress."

"Well… I can see Sonny and the guys are all lined up. Carole is standing there looking at her watch. They're all waiting, and I'm stuck here."

"The wedding doesn't start until you show up, so… they can just hang tight." I thought for a minute, "What if… Let me try kicking the door."

"Are you sure?"

"Just…" I stared at the door, trying to figure out the best place to kick the shit out of it, "Stand back."

"Okay."

I kicked off my shoes, picked up my skirt in both

hands, and gave the door a good kick, but it didn't budge.

"Damn, that looked easier in the movies."

Claire laughed through the door, but it quickly turned into a groan.

"How am I going to get out of here?"

"I don't know, but stay calm. We don't need you all blotchy and stressed. This is just a little hiccup. We're getting you out, and you are marrying the man of your dreams today even if I have to find an axe and hack the door down."

I looked around the room and saw the wooden chair at the vanity. I dragged it over. I was going to beat that fucking door down if it was the last thing I did.

"Claire?"

"Yeah?"

"Stand back... far back."

"Oh god, Darci, don't hurt yourself."

I hefted the chair high over my head and was just about to hurl it against the door when a familiar voice asked, "Darci? What the hell are you doing?"

I startled and lowered the chair. Alex.

"What're you doing up here?"

He chuckled as he walked in, looking fabulous in a charcoal suit. "I should ask you the same thing."

"This is the bridal suite and... Claire's trapped in the bathroom. The doorknob fell off, and we can't open the door."

"Let me give it a try."

I let out a deep breath, "Okay..."

He went over to the door, stuck his fingers inside the hole, jiggled a few things, and suddenly, the door opened. Claire immediately came out, flushed but with a look of relief on her face.

"Oh, thank god, Dr. Alex." She squeezed his forearms.

He grinned. "My pleasure."

I slipped on my shoes. "Time to go down."

I grabbed the bouquets for me and Mallory, and Claire grabbed hers. We flew out of the room, Alex grabbing my hand as we ran down the stairs. Claire's dad was coming up at the same time.

"Claire Bear, there you are!" He said brightly. "Ready to go down?"

Claire, slightly out of breath, said, "Hey Dad. I'm so ready." She grinned.

He smiled, "Let's do this."

When we got to the lobby, Mallory was at the front desk. She let out a visible breath when she saw us. "Oh, thank god!"

I hooked my thumb to Alex. "It was all him and his magic fingers. But come on, we need to go!"

She joined us. I handed her a bouquet as we followed Claire and her dad, taking the path into the fruit orchard and lining up in the trees.

Alex gave me a tender kiss and whispered, "I love you," before he walked backward towards the ceremony and said, "I'll let them know you're ready."

He walked out of the trees, giving the officiant a grin and two thumbs-up that things were ready to start before he sat near the aisle in the back pew.

Mallory and I hovered around Claire, fluffing her dress, ensuring every hair was in place, and her lipstick was on point.

I squeezed her hand and whispered, "You make a stunning bride."

A shy smile flashed across her face as she squeezed

my hand back. "Darci, I would have never gotten here without you."

I grinned as I lined up behind Mallory clutching my bouquet. And before I knew it, the music swelled and the ceremony began.

I whispered, "Break a leg," as Mallory took her first steps, making her way down the aisle, her movements graceful and sure as her sage green dress caught in the breeze.

I reached back, grabbed Claire's hand one last time, and squeezed as I whispered, "You deserve this," my voice full of everything I couldn't quite say. "More than you know."

Then, I let go and stepped forward. The music seemed to rise around me, through the trees themselves. I looked up, and I swear birds in the branches trilled along with the melody, soft, sweet notes that seemed too perfectly timed to be coincidental.

The petals beneath my feet were a trail of blush and cream, fluttering in the breeze like they were dancing me forward. And just as I passed the halfway point, a rush of blue butterflies swept across the aisle—dozens of them, shimmering and wild, as if the air itself had turned to color.

I felt something I couldn't explain then—a tug at the center of me, and my eyes went toward the end of the aisle... and I found him. Alex.

He was already looking at me, like he'd been waiting for this exact moment. Not the wedding. *Me*. His expression softened in a quiet way that always undid me, like he was remembering everything we still hadn't said.

And just for a breath, I let myself imagine it. Walking

down the aisle toward *him*. Wearing white instead of green. Him reaching for me. My hand in his, not because I was falling, but because I wanted to stay forever. The thought wrapped around my heart before I could push it away. It was foolish. Reckless. But God, it was beautiful, and I wanted it.

I kept walking, smiled at Edison as I passed, but that quiet, impossible daydream nestled deep in my chest like a prayer I hadn't meant to say out loud.

After I made my way up to the front between Carole and Mallory, I turned to face the aisle, and Carole gave the call for everyone to stand as the music changed to Fur Elise. I scanned the guests and was surprised at how many people came all the way to Vegas. Anna and Melody were here seated next to Tate and Noelle. Bert had even made the trip.

But one person caught my attention. I didn't know who he was. Some dark-haired mystery guy with wavy hair down to his shoulders stood at the back, but he only had eyes for Mallory. *Who was that?*

But he was forgotten when my eyes locked with Alex's again, and he gave me a secret smile that made me melt.

A few seconds later, Claire and her father emerged between two trees, and I heard audible gasps. She truly looked like some otherworldly creature walking through the forest. I glanced at Edison, his eyes shimmering with unshed tears, his expression filled with awe and overwhelming emotion. I couldn't help my grin as I watched him fidget, flexing his hands, like he wanted to run toward her.

When she reached the altar, her father kissed her cheek, and Edison held out his hand.

His voice was low as he pulled her close, "You take my breath away."

She dipped her head with a shy smile.

He asked with a grin, "Ready for this?"

She nodded, her eyes sparkling, as they took their places in front of the officiant, and the ceremony began.

A few minutes later, it was time for the vows. Claire handed me her bouquet of poppies, and they turned to face each other, holding hands.

Edison was first. "In a world where time never stands still, you are my constant. From this moment until my last, I will love you through all the days and years we are given.

I promise to stay by your side, never wavering in my commitment. I will honor you in moments of joy, and lift you in moments of challenge, for as long as I breathe.

Though time may test us, it will never weaken our bond, for our love is timeless. I am yours—today, tomorrow, and always."

She watched as he slipped a white gold filigree band circled in small diamonds, matching her engagement ring, on her finger. She raised her eyes to his and looked up at him with such love.

Carole indicated to Claire it was her turn.

She took a deep breath and began, "From the first moment our paths crossed, it felt as though time slowed just for us. You are my past, my present, and my future.

I vow to stand with you through every sunrise and sunset, to cherish the moments we create and the memories we'll look back on. Everyday, my love for you will only deepen, for it is not bound by hours or minutes but by a promise.

I promise to be your partner, your lover, and your

anchor until the last stars fades from the sky."

She slid a thick black titanium ring on his finger, and they both turned to the officiant. Edison raised an eyebrow, ready to seal the deal.

Carole grinned, "You may now kiss your bride."

He turned to Claire with that crooked smile as he wrapped his arms around her and leaned in, bending her back and kissing her like he was a dying man and she was the cure. She held onto his shoulders, kissing him just as fiercely.

Everyone hooted and hollered before they broke apart.

They turned to face the crowd, and Claire looked back at me, beaming, as I handed her back her bouquet.

Carole announced, "May I introduce, for the first time, Mr. and Mrs. Edison Wright."

They both grinned, hands clasped and eyes only for each other, as they walked back down the aisle to applause. I followed behind, meeting Avery in the middle as he held his arm for me to take. As I passed by, I smirked at Alex, but his eyes were on my hand, holding Avery's arm. Once we made it back to the tree line, we all broke apart.

I turned to Claire and Edison. "Congratulations, you guys."

He leaned down and kissed her forehead. "Thanks, Darce."

I did a little shimmy and said, "Now, who's ready to party!"

Claire giggled when Edison said, "Let's go make an announcement for everyone to return to the hotel bar for the reception."

He led the way back down the aisle, Claire's hand

intertwined with his and invited the guests to follow the wedding party back to the reception.

Seconds later, Alex found me and walked me back to the hotel. When we entered the bar, he grabbed two glasses of champagne off a tray, and we found an empty table. Within minutes, the party was in full swing as the photographer stole Claire and Edison for some shots around the property.

Shortly after, Anna and Melody found me and sat down at the table.

Anna gushed, "Darci, Claire's dress was simply amazing."

I nodded, "She looks like a fairy queen."

They glanced at Alex, and I realized I hadn't introduced him.

"Melody, Anna, this is Alex, my…" I trailed off, looking at him, not sure what we were.

He stuck his hand out, grinning, "Her boyfriend."

I gave a hesitant smile as Alex greeted each of them.

They both gave me a quick glance when I said, "Sorry, it's, uh, new. Very new."

Anna immediately whispered, glancing at Alex as she asked, "So… how was the bachelorette party? Weren't you guys going to that male stripper place?"

I laughed, "Hunk-O-Licious? Yep, we did, and they pulled Claire up on stage and gyrated all over her."

"Oh my god," Melody whispered. "I would have died."

"Claire went right along with it." I smirked at Melody, "I have a feeling that you'd have done the same thing." I chuckled. "They say it's always the quiet ones."

She covered her mouth as she blushed and giggled.

Suddenly, the DJ's voice boomed through the

speakers, "And now, let's welcome Mr. and Mrs. Edison Wright as they share their first dance as husband and wife!"

As the melody of "Speechless" filled the room, Edison and Claire stepped onto the dance floor, their faces aglow with happiness. They moved across the room like they were the only two people in the world. He spun her, drew her close, sang into her ear with that dopey grin he always saved just for her. She looked up at him like she'd never looked at anyone else.

Then I felt it—Alex's heated gaze on me. When I turned, he was already leaning in, close enough that his breath brushed warm against my cheek.

"You look so beautiful, I could…" he murmured.

My breath caught. Just for a second, the air in my lungs refused to move, like maybe I'd been waiting to hear those words my whole life.

I leaned in before he could finish, kissing him. When we parted, I whispered, "I think I could too."

I blushed, tucking a hair behind my ear, wondering if we might end up where Edison and Claire were someday.

The afternoon passed in a blur. The cake had been cut, toasts had been given, and Edison and Claire were preparing to leave on their honeymoon. Alex sat in the bar while I went with Claire to change.

I helped her out of her dress and asked, "Well… how does it feel to be officially married to the man of your literal dreams?"

She grinned, more to herself, as she said, "Like it all finally came true."

I grabbed my chest dramatically and said, "Be still, my heart."

She swatted me and giggled before she said, "Did you see Mallory's date?"

"Her date? Wait… sexy black suit guy?"

Claire nodded. "He's in a band, and apparently, they just exploded, got some song on a Netflix movie or something."

I arched an eyebrow. "Where'd she meet him?"

"Some club show. She goes to them all the time by herself."

"Brave girl." I chuckled.

"I know. I don't know if I could ever do that. She told me she met him at the merch table. Held up the line for 20 minutes until one of his band members took over the table for him. I don't think she got home until the next morning. Sonny was up all night worrying."

I twisted my lips, "Well, that's definitely a meet-cute if I ever heard one."

Claire chuckled, "I know. It's something. I can tell you that. They've been flying back and forth to see each other for weeks now."

"She told you all this?"

"Not really," Claire hissed, "Sonny told me. He confronted her, worried she was up to something, and she told him everything."

Claire looked like she wanted to say more, but instead just shrugged.

"Well, well, well. That girl is good at keeping secrets. She hasn't said a damn word to either of us."

I hung up her wedding dress and took another from the back of the garment bag off its hanger. It was a romantic baby doll dress in light blue with delicate eyelet trim on the skirt edge and the fluttery sleeves.

"This is so cute, Claire. When did you get it?"

She smiled as she took it from me and slid it on, "Oh, I picked it up a few weeks ago at the store."

She slipped on a pair of wedge sandals and looked over at me. "You'll get our stuff back home?"

I smiled, "I'll take care of everything."

She hugged me tightly, "I'll see you in a couple of weeks."

I grinned, "I hope you have a wonderful time in Greece—channel your inner Aphrodite, drink all the wine, and tell Edison if he's not worshipping you like a goddess every night, he's doing it wrong. Now, let's go find that husband of yours."

CHAPTER THIRTY-SIX

Alex

The final notes of a love song lingered in the air as the crowd spilled outside. Each person was holding a tiny bottle, sending bubbles floating up into the sky as Claire and Edison, both grinning with joy, disappeared into the back of a black car bound for the airport for their Greek honeymoon.

Darci and I laughed as we blew bubbles at each other as we watched them drive away. On our way back inside, I couldn't help but glance at all the familiar faces. Darci had made sure she introduced me to everyone, wanting me to feel included.

But... there was this one guy I was curious about. He held back from the crowd. He seemed like a stranger to everyone. He exuded an air of mystery, dressed in an impeccably tailored all-black suit. I didn't know a lot about fashion, but his clothes suggested a man of refined taste, as did the silver chain that dangled from his suit pocket.

His eyes, hidden behind dark lenses, seemed to pierce

through the crowd. But even in the bar, he didn't take them off. *Who was he?*

I leaned over to Darci as she grabbed another slice of cake, offering me one. "Who's that guy?"

She slid her eyes to mine, "The one in all black?"

I took the plate and cut a bite. "Yeah, he seems to be hanging back from everyone."

She leaned closer, her breath against my ear, "I think the mystery man is Mallory's date. She was the bridesmaid. Edison's sister?"

"Oh yeah, you introduced us earlier."

Darci raised her eyebrows with a conspiratorial smile and said, "Claire told me all about her little tryst. He's in a band. They met at his concert, and apparently, they take turns flying out to see each other. I think he lives in L.A."

"Wow. Long distance takes some serious dedication."

She set her plate on a table and nodded, "Yeah." Then, she grabbed my forearm and began leading me over to him, saying, "We should go over and introduce ourselves."

I raised an eyebrow at her, "You want to?"

Without batting an eye, she dragged me along and whispered, "Yes, we're doing it."

We had just made it to his table when Mallory walked up. "Hey, Darce. Fancy seeing you here." She giggled.

The mystery man caught her around the waist and pulled her down beside him.

He grinned, a dimple in his cheek. "Hey, I'm Jameson."

Darci immediately said, "Darci, maid of honor and best friend of the bride." She hiked her thumb my way, "And this is Alex, my boyfriend."

Jameson stood up, holding his hand out for each of us to shake, a big grin on his face. His hand was rough with calluses, but his grip was firm. "I'm with Mallory here."

She grinned, laying her head on his shoulder.

A second later, his phone rang, and he looked at it with a frown. "I'm sorry. I have to take this. I'll be right back."

We sat down with Mallory, who seemed a little tipsy.

"So... Mal, where'd you two meet?" Darci asked, her curiosity barely disguised, but Mallory just grinned at the question.

"Jace?" She waved toward Jameson, who was hovering just outside the bar, doing a terrible job pretending not to stare at her as he talked on the phone.

"We met at his show," she said, glowing. "At the merch table." She giggled. "But we knew each other as kids—our families used to share a beach house every summer."

She lifted her hands in a little flourish, eyes dancing. "And now here we are, all these years later, like the universe hit shuffle and threw us back together. He even remembered the name of the floaty I wouldn't let him touch."

I raised an eyebrow. "Your great love story started with a pool toy?"

"Mr. Bubbles," she said, completely unashamed.

Just then, Anna—one of Darci's colleagues—appeared beside us, clutching a glass of sparkling something and a look like she'd walked in at precisely the right time.

"Oh, I love that," she breathed. "It's like childhood sweethearts reuniting on the road to happily ever after.

Darci laughed. "Okay, Nicholas Sparks."

Something inside me tugged and made me look over

at Darci. A quiet voice whispering that maybe, fate did weave people back into your path for a reason.

I sipped my drink, trying not to smile.

Darci offered, "He seems really into you."

Her eyes widened, "You think?" Darci nodded, but Mallory frowned a little. "The only sucky thing is that he lives in L.A., and I live here. I wish we lived closer. Sonny's probably sick of me constantly flying off to see him."

Darci threw me a quick glance before saying, "Just… don't do anything impulsive. Like moving away. We'd miss you, especially on Murder Nights. You're an official Crimebrarian now, remember?"

I chuckled, but Mallory suddenly looked serious.

"Aww, Darci," she said, pulling her into a hug. When she let go, her tone was playful but firm. "Relax. I'm not going anywhere. I'm probably the *last* person who'd make an impulsive move. I traveled the world for three years because I planned that trip down to the *molar*."

I leaned over, kissed Darci's temple, and whispered, "Why do I feel like she just dared the universe?"

She covered her mouth and looked away, trying to contain a laugh as I chuckled.

Jameson returned to the table and looked at all of us. "What's everyone laughing at?"

Darci quickly pointed to the dance floor and said, "Oh, you know, just Claire's mom out there trying to do the Cha-Cha-Slide."

Jameson raised his eyebrows, his lips twitching as we all tried to hide our laughter.

"Well, it was good to meet you two, but I must steal Mallie away before I go."

He held his hand out for Mallory and quickly whisked

her out of the bar.

Darci and I said our goodbyes to several guests and headed upstairs. Tomorrow was the last day of my conference, and we were checking her out of her room so she could stay with me. We would change our flights so we could fly home together.

I ordered a rideshare as Darci haphazardly threw things in her bag. But she carefully folded Claire and Edison's wedding attire before putting it all in another duffel.

When the car arrived at the ranch, I piled all her belongings into the trunk and slid into the seat beside her. I shrugged off my suit jacket and rolled up my sleeves, feeling relieved as the formality of the day was finally over. Darci leaned against me, her head resting on my shoulder, and my arm instinctively wrapped around her.

The ceremony played on a loop in my mind—Darci, stepping into the sunlight, her dress swaying as she moved down the aisle—eyes bright with nerves and something else. Hope, maybe. Or possibility.

And then Claire, walking toward Edison like gravity itself was pulling her forward. His expression when he saw her... it wasn't just love. It was awe. Like the kind of devotion that doesn't fade, no matter how many years pass.

I'd felt that once, with Jenna. And when I looked at Darci, I didn't just feel the echo of it. I felt the beginning of something real. Something that could grow, if I were brave enough to reach for it.

That question lingered in the back of my mind. Was I brave enough? Being with her now, the thought of being apart was almost unbearable, and I realized that I couldn't imagine my life without her.

The plush carpet of the suite muted our footsteps as we shuffled inside, tired and a little tipsy, dragging our bags behind us like afterthoughts. We peeled off the layers of our formalwear—me down to just my boxers, Darci swallowed up in one of my t-shirts, the hem nearly reaching her knees—and collapsed onto the bed.

She curled up beside me, warm and quiet, her breath soft against my shoulder. Just as sleep began to tug at the edges of my mind, I felt her fingers reach for mine, slow, searching, and gently intertwined. No words. Just that small touch. And the comfort of knowing she was right beside me.

I woke to the comforting warmth of her hand still clasped in mine around midnight. Gently untangling our fingers, I went to the bathroom. When I returned, she was perched on the chair by the window, her gaze lost in the sparkling city below.

"Do you think we'll ever have what they do?" she asked softly.

She didn't have to explain—Edison and Claire. Between Darci telling me about them and seeing their love story as a fairy tale come to life, I knew. It was the kind of love that seemed almost tangible. Anyone who witnessed it would want a piece of it, myself included. Darci wasn't jealous, but I could see the longing in her eyes. She wanted it, too.

She scooted over, making room for me in the chair. I sat down, pulling her into my lap. She leaned against me, letting out a soft sigh.

"I don't know," I admitted, my voice quiet.

Her smile faltered, worry flickering across her face.

"What I mean is... we're not them. Our story is

different. It's ours."

She tilted her head, listening intently.

"But I love you, and those weeks apart from you felt like I was missing a piece of myself."

She cupped my face, giving me a small smile, "Sometimes you know exactly what to say."

She grazed my mouth with hers, slow and deliberate, and heat licked up my spine. I pulled her to straddle me, wrapping my arms around her waist and dropping my hands down to her ass. I pressed her hard against me, grinding her against my thickening length. I stood up, lifting her with me, and she locked her legs around my body as I walked her to the bed, where I gently laid her down and stripped her bare to make passionate love to her. It was slow. Unhurried. And my lips never left hers.

When we were both satiated, I lay on my side, pulling her back into me and draping the sheet over us. The future was uncertain, but one thing was clear—I needed her. She had brought me the peace I'd been searching for, and I had finally found my home.

CHAPTER THIRTY-SEVEN

Epilogue- Mallory

One year later

We'd been sitting here for hours, and each minute felt like an eternity. The waiting room was tense. Nobody was saying much. We were mostly drinking coffee and eating candy bars from the vending machine. Everyone was anxious with anticipation.

Darci and Alex burst through the doors, their faces flushed with excitement.

"Did we miss it?" Darci gasped, her eyes scanning the room.

Jace, ever the laid-back one, sprawled out in his chair in a sweatshirt and jeans, stretched his body, and grinned as he said, "Nope, still waiting."

Darci collapsed beside me, her hand clutching her chest as she let out a dramatic sigh. "*Oh, thank god.* We came as fast as we could. I ran from the parking lot. Like, actually *ran*. On purpose." She turned to Alex, deadpan. "If this baby's first word isn't Darci, I'll be personally offended."

I glanced at Alex, leaning back in his chair with a calm smile. He seemed completely unaffected by the tension in the room.

I turned to her, ready to catch up as we waited. "How was the honeymoon?"

Her face lit up, a wide grin spreading across her features. "It was amazing," she exclaimed, her eyes sparkling. "The water was the most beautiful shade of turquoise I've ever seen. We had such a great time. We'd sit on the beach at night. The stars, oh my god, were amazing. You can see millions of them, the Milky Way. It was breathtaking."

I couldn't help but feel a pang of sadness. "I'm sorry you had to cut it short," I said, my voice filled with sympathy.

She rolled her eyes, a playful smile on her face. "What? You think I'd miss this? We'd already been there for a week and a half. Leaving a day or two early wasn't going to kill us."

Just then, the double doors swung open, and Sonny emerged in paper scrubs with a look of pure joy.

"I'm a daddy!" he announced, his voice filled with excitement as he pulled off his disposable surgical cap.

The room erupted in cheers and applause.

I stood up and hugged him, my heart pounding in my chest.

"Can we see her?" I asked.

Sonny nodded as his arm wrapped around me, and a warm smile was on his face.

"Claire's feeding the baby right now. I just wanted to let y'all know she's here, and they're both fine. I'll be back soon."

As the double doors swung shut behind him, I sat back down and turned to my boyfriend, squeezing his hand. "I can't believe it! I'm an aunt!" I exclaimed, my voice filled with excitement.

He grinned, his eyes sparkling with pride as he reached for my hand and kissed my knuckles. "You're going to make an amazing one."

He always said the sweetest things to me. We sat in silence, my gaze fixed on the doors, waiting for Sonny's return.

Jace leaned in, his breath tickling my ear. "Do you ever think about doing all this someday?" he asked, his voice low and husky.

I turned to face him, my heart skipping a beat. "Of course I do," I admitted, my voice low. "I want to settle down—Marriage. Babies. A family."

His eyes softened, and a tender expression crossed his face. "With me?"

I nodded, my heart pounding in my chest. "Well... yeah, of course I do. But... I wasn't sure if you wanted that."

He took a deep breath, his eyes filled with hope. "Only with you. I knew that back when we were just kids."

My eyes widened, and a wave of emotion washed over me. I didn't know what to say. I never expected him to say anything like this.

"Really? But after... everything?"

He nodded, leaning over and brushing his lips against mine. "Yes, after everything, I still want it. With you." Pulling back, he lifted a shoulder, "So... let's do it."

I raised an eyebrow, "Have a baby?"

He grinned, "All of it. Let's get married, have some babies, and live happily ever after."

"You're serious."

He smirked, "Why wouldn't I be?"

"Are you... Are you asking me to marry you right here in the middle of a hospital waiting room?"

He shifted in his seat thoughtfully, slowly nodding and grinning at me, "Yeah... yeah, I am, Mallie. I want to marry you."

Our eyes locked as I whispered, "Okay."

His head dipped as he asked, "Is that a yes?"

I laughed. "Yes, absolutely yes. Of course, I want to marry you."

Before we could say anything else, the double doors swung open, and Sonny walked out, no longer in the scrubs. All eyes went to him.

"Who wants to meet my baby girl first?"

I jumped up immediately and ran towards him. "Oh, me! Me!"

He grinned. "Of course, Mal."

He looked at Jace, raising his eyebrows. "Coming?"

I swore sometimes it felt like Sonny just tolerated him. I don't know why he was so protective. I was 29 years old, and I could make my own decisions on who I dated.

I held my hand out as my boyfriend stood up. He stretched his long limbs and reached for my hand, intertwining our fingers as we followed Sonny and headed to Claire's hospital room.

I nudged my brother's shoulder. "So... how was it? Everything go okay?"

He rubbed the back of his neck, letting out a heavy sigh. "It got a little hairy there for a minute. The baby's heart rate started dropping at each contraction. The doctor wanted to prep Claire for a c-section, which is why I had those scrubs on earlier. But Claire..." He shook his head, "She was determined. She begged for one more try, and within five minutes, she pushed her out."

I held my breath, listening to him. "But everything's okay now?"

He grinned as we slowed down and stopped at one particular hospital room. "Yeah, they're both doing great."

Sonny pushed the door open slowly, "Knock, knock? We're coming in."

Claire's tired face lit up when her gaze caught mine. I immediately went to her, standing by the side of the bed, peeking at the little bundle in her arms.

"Oh my god," I gasped, "She's just... beautiful. Look at that red hair."

Claire shook her head as she chuckled. "I know. I can't believe she's finally here."

One of the baby's hands had escaped her swaddling blanket, and I brushed it with my index finger. She gripped my finger tightly. And that was when I fell in love with this tiny angel.

I gushed, "You're just the cutest thing ever. Aunt Mallie is going to spoil you rotten."

Sonny and Jace were off in the corner whispering, but I noticed Sonny was constantly watching his wife and child.

Claire and I both stared in awe as the baby yawned, her tiny mouth opening like a perfect little O before she wiggled deeper into the swaddle.

I leaned in, asking quietly, "Does she have a name yet?"

Claire smiled, soft and glowing. "She does. Amelia

Rose."

Amelia Rose.

The name bloomed in my chest—simple, elegant, and meaningful. I loved that they'd given her our mom's name as a middle name. A quiet thread tying the past to the future.

My throat tightened as I said, "Mom would've loved being a grandma."

Claire's smile wavered. She reached for my hand, squeezing gently as grief and joy passed between us like a current.

My brother came up, his hand on my back as I slid my eyes to him.

He grinned and asked, "Want to hold her?"

I looked at Claire, my eyes wide. "I can hold her?"

Claire laughed, "Of course, you can hold your niece."

I gently rocked her in my arms as she watched me with those curious newborn eyes—still blue for now, but I had a feeling they'd settle into that familiar tri-colored mix, just like mine and my brother's.

I cooed at her, "You are just the prettiest baby."

She replied with a big yawn and closed her eyes. I continued gently rocking. When I looked up, both Claire and Sonny were watching me, small smiles on their faces.

I asked Claire, "How are you doing?"

She gave me a tired smile. "I'm exhausted but so happy. Also, no one warns you that postpartum glam includes disposable mesh panties and a pad big enough to double as a mattress topper."

I laughed, "Sounds fun."

She chuckled, "Definitely worth it, though. I never knew I could love someone so much."

I looked at Jace, "Get over here and see this beautiful baby."

He smirked but came immediately, leaning over my shoulder. Seeing the tiny, sleepy baby, he cracked a genuine smile.

Sonny had moved to the other side of Claire's bed, offering her water.

He jutted his chin at his daughter in my arms and with a twinkle in his eye asked Jace, "You ready for one of these?"

We exchanged a glance. I felt the heat in my cheeks and saw the flush rising up his neck.

"Well…" He started as he tilted his head.

Sonny wrinkled his brow, looking between us.

I swear his voice dropped an octave, "Well, what? Is my sister pregnant?"

I laughed a little too loudly, making the baby stir. "No, no, no. Nothing like that." I swallowed, raising my eyebrows as I glanced at Jace again before I looked at Sonny, preparing for whatever lecture he would throw at me.

I smiled as I said, "He actually proposed out in the waiting room, and I said yes."

Sonny's eyes flicked first toward Jace and then me.

He piped up, "It was kind of spur of the moment, but I meant every word. I have been in love with your sister since we were kids."

Sonny was utterly silent, just staring at the two of us. We stayed that way for a few minutes until Amelia started to fuss and wiggle.

Claire broke the stalemate, "Sonny, quit staring at Jameson like you're some alphahole. Mallory's a grown woman. Now, take Amelia. I think she might need a diaper change."

His lips pressed into a tight line as he let out a breath, rubbing the back of his neck like he'd been caught doing something wrong. But then he stepped forward, carefully taking the baby from my arms. He cooed softly as he carried her to the bassinet, already crouching to grab the supplies. In seconds, he had her unwrapped and was changing her like a total pro.

I couldn't help myself when I came over and asked, "So, how many diapers have you changed?"

His voice softened as he chuckled, "This will be my second one ever."

When he was done, he expertly swaddled her and then cradled her in his arms.

"Wow, bro, expert dad level." I grinned, "I'm impressed."

His cheeks reddened as he looked down at his little girl, a smile playing on his lips as he muttered, "Thanks, and I'm sorry. If you and Jameson want to get married, it's none of my business. I just want you to be happy, Mal. That's all I care about."

"I know." I breathed out.

We watched as his little girl scrunched her nose and twisted in her swaddle, already full of personality.

I smiled and said, "I think we need to give someone else a turn. There's a whole waiting room ready to see sweet little Amelia."

I leaned in slowly, pressing a soft kiss to her forehead. She was so impossibly small, all wrapped up like a little burrito with cheeks that could stop traffic.

"Welcome to the world, little love," I whispered. "You have no idea how lucky you are.

I lingered for a second, then glanced up, back at my

big brother.

Sonny was watching us, eyes full, smile soft. Not the teasing, lopsided one I'd grown up with. This one was different—quieter, warmer. The kind that said *this* was everything. For a second, he didn't look like my big brother. He looked like a dad. And it broke me in the best way.

I went over and squeezed Claire's shoulder. When I looked back, my brother was still cradling his new daughter with a look of awe.

"Congrats, you two." I turned to Claire, "You did an amazing job."

Claire's cheeks blushed as she said, "Thanks."

Sonny lifted his head, pinning his eyes on Jace as we left.

I chuckled when we walked out the door and heard Claire say, "Sonny… what the hell?"

When we returned to the waiting room, several pairs of eyes went right to us, and I couldn't help but gush, "Oh my god, she's beautiful, just precious. She's got a tuft of Claire's hair color, and I have a feeling she'll have me and Sonny's eyes."

Darci piped up, "Aww… I can't wait to see her."

I said, "We're going to head out. We've been here for hours. I'm exhausted, and I didn't even have a baby." I grinned, "But Sonny said he'd be back in a minute to get whoever's next, so be ready."

Darci sat up straight. "It's me. I've been mentally preparing like it's a baby-holding Hunger Games."

Claire's mom raised a perfectly arched brow. "Excuse me? What about the grandma?"

Darci sighed, flopping back dramatically, "Ugh, fine. First dibs to the woman who literally made the mom. I guess that's fair."

She shot a grin at Claire's mom.

Claire's mom grinned right back, clearly delighted. "Good instincts, sweetheart."

Honestly, I should've brought popcorn. I hid my smirk as I headed for the door. But under all that sass, I knew Darci'd been counting down the seconds to meet that baby.

We said our goodbyes to the cluster of family still waiting their turn to meet the newest addition. The waiting room was full of love and soft chaos, and I left it behind like music trailing in our wake.

Jace's hand found mine as we slipped into the quiet hallway, fingers threading together like a secret. I squeezed once, and he didn't let go. The elevator was waiting for us, doors already open like it knew. We stepped in, the lights humming low overhead, and everything felt still for the first time all night.

I leaned into him, pressing my shoulder gently to his chest. He drew me closer, one arm around my waist, his chin brushing the top of my head. No words—just the slow cadence of his heartbeat and the safety of his arms feeling like home.

I let out a breath I didn't realize I'd been holding, my heart full and flickering with everything we'd witnessed tonight. Love. Life. A little miracle wrapped in a hospital blanket.

He looked down at me, and I didn't need to see his face to feel his smile. It moved through me like a promise. And for once, I didn't rush the moment or try to name it. I didn't need to. I just stood there, wrapped in him, quietly believing that maybe this was what forever could feel like.

THE END

Thank you so much for reading SOMETIME AROUND MIDNIGHT, Book 2 in The Enchanted Heart Series, a magical realism romance series.

I hope you enjoyed it! If you did…

1. Help other people find this book by writing a review.
2. Sign up for my email list so you can know when the next book is coming out.
3. Come follow me on Instagram, TikTok, or Facebook.
4. Use the QR code below to visit my website:

Keep reading to get a sneak peek of Mallory's story in THE BEACH HOUSE, coming September 2025!

Sneak Peek
THE BEACH HOUSE

Mallory

The plane touched down with a jolt, dragging me out of the half-sleep I'd fallen into somewhere over the Pacific. My head throbbed dully from crying, and my back ached from sitting for nearly sixteen hours. I blinked at the harsh overhead light, sluggishly reaching down to grab my bag from beneath the seat.

Thailand already felt like a different lifetime—even though it had only been a day since I walked out of that bungalow and slammed the door on Devin and the girl he swore was "just a friend."

Three years together. Two years of bouncing around the world like we were the stars of some bohemian travel blog. And now I was back in Dallas with nothing but a broken heart and a suitcase full of clothes that felt like they belonged to someone else.

I still couldn't believe I'd finally dumped him for good. It just took me finally calling Sonny, even if my fingers were trembling.

My big brother hadn't even hesitated. "Let me buy you a ticket home. Come stay with us."

Claire. That tugged at my nerves more than anything. I'd met her once, years ago, back when Sonny brought her to Pizza Verona that one night. We'd barely exchanged words. She seemed kind. Warm. But this wasn't the same. This wasn't polite small talk and passing smiles. This was living with her. Being the emotional wreck on her guest bed. Me, the girl with no job, no plan, no clue.

I followed the slow-moving line of passengers off the plane, rolling my shoulders under my sweatshirt and trying to keep my breath steady. The hum of the airport hit me all at once—conversations overlapping, carts beeping, the sharp scent of coffee and fried food tangling in the air.

As I made my way toward baggage claim, my mind wandered the way it always did when I was this tired, this hollowed out —straight back to the past.

To Rockport.

Every summer since I was five, our families rented the same beach house on the Texas coast. It was one of those traditions that didn't seem all that special at the time —just something that happened, expected and reliable. I didn't realize how much I'd come to cherish those summers until they were gone.

And every year, without fail, he was there. Jameson. But I never called him that. To me, he was always Jace.

A soft smile tugged at my lips as I pictured the first time we met—me, a quiet, wide-eyed five-year-old clinging to my mom's hand, and him, a boy with sun-kissed skin, wild curls, and a plastic sand bucket in one hand, asking if I wanted to help him dig for crabs.

From that moment on, we were a pair. A summer duo. Peanut butter and jelly, sunburns and popsicles. We chased waves until our legs gave out, built lopsided sandcastles with seashell flags, and shared freezer pops on the porch until our tongues turned ridiculous shades of red and blue.

He called me Mallie from day one, mispronouncing it at first and then deciding he liked it better that way. I pretended to hate it—but I never corrected him.

Looking back, those summers were some of the sweetest moments of my life. Simple. Golden. Untouched by the messiness that would come later.

And come it did.

But for a while, it was just Jace and Mallie, sun and salt, and the kind of friendship that made everything else in the world feel like background noise.

Things changed when we were thirteen. The games slowed. The glances lasted a beat too long. My heart felt different around him —faster, fuller. He kissed me for the first time that summer, awkward and sweet. I memorized the feel of his lips.

And by fifteen, everything had shifted. That summer was full of secret kisses and whispered I love yous. Late-night walks on the beach. Quiet moments that felt like the entire world had narrowed to just the two of us.

And then... our last night there. Our first time. My first everything. It was beautiful. It should've stayed beautiful. Instead, it ended everything in the worst possible way.

I never saw him again after that summer.

The memory hit like saltwater in an old wound. I pushed my hair back and kept walking, eyes fixed on the baggage claim signs ahead.

Where are you now, Jace? Was he still in Texas? Did he ever think about me? Had he moved on? Gotten married? Built a life that had no room for the ghost of that beach house or the girl who left without a choice?

I bit my lip, chest tightening with questions I didn't dare speak aloud.

Still, even with the ache in my back, the

buzz of the terminal around me, and the whirring of the baggage carousel spinning to life, my mind stayed stuck in the past.

In Rockport. In that house by the sea. In the boy who once looked at me like I was the only girl in the world.

The clink of ice in my glass and the low hum of chatter offered a strange kind of comfort as I sank into a barstool just past security. I'd made it through customs, picked up my bag, and wandered aimlessly until the dull ache in my back reminded me I'd been sitting down for nearly twenty hours. My hair was a mess, my skin felt dry and gritty from recycled plane air, and I hadn't slept more than thirty minutes straight—but I was home. Or something like it.

I pulled out my phone and dialed Sonny. He picked up on the second ring.

"Hey, Mal," he said, slightly breathless. "You back in Texas?"

"Yeah, just landed. I'm still at the airport. Thought I'd grab a drink before I try to figure out how to Uber with three bags and a carry-on."

There was a rustle of papers, and what sounded like furious typing. "I was just about to take a break—I'm knee-deep in a scene, big plot twist, my detective's finally figuring it out a suspect after 200 pages of being an idiot. I thought I'd send Claire to come get you? I checked your flight, and she's already on the way. She's not far."

I hesitated, just for a second, but then guilt crept in. I was already imposing. The last thing I wanted was to make Sonny feel like he had to drop everything for me. "Yeah, that's totally fine. Don't stop writing on my account."

"Thanks, Mal. You're the best. Claire should be there in, like, thirty minutes. She's excited to see you."

I smiled faintly. "Me too."

We hung up, and I sipped my watered-down vodka soda, watching travelers rush past, everyone headed somewhere with a purpose. I'd had purpose. Once. Now it felt like I was starting from zero, building something new out of what was left.

Thirty minutes later, Claire called to let me know she was pulled up outside. I paid my bill and headed outside, spotting two women weaving through the crowd toward me. Claire hadn't changed much—still glowing with that effortless warmth I remembered from years ago, her arms outstretched the moment she saw me. "Mallory! Welcome home!"

And next to her was someone I didn't know yet, but felt like maybe I had. Petite, with bright eyes and a dark brown pixie cut, wearing a Murderino sweatshirt and balancing two iced coffees in one hand.

"You must be Mallory," she said. "I'm Darci. We brought you caffeine and zero judgment."

"God bless you," I said, taking the cup and laughing, the tightness in my chest easing a little.

They talked a mile a minute as they helped me load my bags into Claire's trunk—Claire asking about the flight, Darci already telling me about the wild true crime documentary they were planning to watch that night, something about a yoga cult and fake retreats in Costa Rica.

"You have to watch it with us," Claire said, sliding into the driver's seat. "Murder Night is sacred. Cocktails, Thai food, and us yelling at the TV about bad life choices."

"Yeah, and if that's not therapy, I don't know what is," Darci added, twisting in her seat to grin at me. "You're officially adopted."

I laughed, really laughed, and for the first time in what felt like years, I didn't feel like I was intruding. I felt... included.

When we got to the house, Sonny opened the front door before we'd even made it up the walk. "There's my baby sister," he said with a grin, pulling me into a hug and ruffling my hair before grabbing two of my suitcases like they weighed nothing.

Claire and Darci whisked me into the living room like I'd always been there, handing me a plate of Thai food and a strawberry margarita.

Once we were settled on the couch, he said, "Don't let these two corrupt you."

I rolled my eyes, smiling. "Sonny, I'm twenty-eight. If I'm corrupted, that ship sailed a long time ago." He smirked and disappeared down the hall with my bags.

The next three hours flew by in a blur of laughter, green curry, and a truly disturbing documentary about a serial killer who'd evaded capture for over a decade by pretending to be a traveling handyman. We curled up on the couch in leggings and mismatched socks, sipping cocktails and yelling at the screen every time someone ignored an obvious red flag.

"He literally said, 'I'm great with rope knots,'" Darci shouted, tossing popcorn at the TV. "How is that not a red flag?!"

"Honestly, how do people like this find dates so easily?" Claire added, sipping her drink.

I laughed so hard I almost choked on a spring roll.

Somewhere between the second cocktail and a deep dive into unsolved cases, I found myself opening up. Really opening up. I told them about Thailand. About Devin. About the life I thought I wanted and the person I thought he was—and how it all came crashing down the moment I walked into our shared room and saw him with someone else in our bed.

Claire reached over and gently squeezed my hand. "I'm so glad you left."

Darci gave me a sideways smile. "And now you're here. You've survived a manipulative man and international customs. That makes you basically unstoppable."

I smiled through the tightness in my throat, tears welling without warning. For the first time in a long time, I didn't feel like I was falling apart. I felt like I'd landed in the right place, with the right people. And I felt like I could breathe again for the first time in forever.

Over the next few weeks, I started piecing together a version of myself that wasn't built around someone else's choices. Claire had become a true friend—the kind who never made me feel like a burden, only like someone worth rooting for. And her best friend Darci? Darci reminded me how to laugh at dumb reality shows, how to sit cross-legged on the couch with popcorn and forget the world for an hour or two.

I unpacked. I slept through the night. I remembered how I like my coffee and how silence doesn't always mean something's wrong. So when I got an email for a small venue show across town with one of my favorite bands, I didn't think twice. I bought a ticket, put on mascara for no one but me, and went alone. I wasn't looking for anything. I just needed to feel like I was moving forward.

I came for the headliner.

That's what I told myself as I stood in the back of the crowded venue, sipping a lukewarm cider and pretending not to feel wildly out of place among the sea of younger twenty-somethings swaying to the music. I wasn't here for the opening acts. I didn't even catch the name of the next one when it was announced over the speakers.

The band took the stage. They opened in near darkness, just a haze of silhouettes and flashing red lights. I could barely make out their faces, but the crowd around me was buzzing, like maybe they already knew who these guys were. By the second song, the lights came up, blinding and bright, and I got a better look at the lead singer.

He had a guitar strapped across his body, the kind of presence that made you pay attention even before he opened his mouth. And then he did.

By the third song, he stepped up to the mic and ran a hand through his hair. "Hey, Dallas," he said, voice rough around the edges. "We're The Midnight Run. Thanks for showing up early. We've been working on a new album," he said, voice warm and steady, "and we just cut this next track a couple days ago. It's called Real You."

Then he started to sing. And something in my chest cracked open.

That voice. That tone. That song.

I stared at him, heart racing, trying to tell myself I was imagining it. But I wasn't.

He looked familiar. So familiar. The way he moved. The way he sang like every word still hurt. My breath caught in my throat.

Wait a minute... Jace?

As the song continued, a sick, twisting feeling settled in my stomach. The lyrics hit too close. The words were raw, honest— aching in that specific way only the truth can.

It wasn't just a love song. It was my story. Our story.

The way he sang about promises under stars, about being seen and then erased, about losing someone not because they left, but because they were taken. My mother's voice echoed in the back of my mind—sharp, unwavering, cruel. He forced himself on her.

That was the lie that shattered everything. And now, years later, he was standing twenty feet away, singing the broken truth of it into a microphone.

I felt frozen in place, my eyes locked on him, the noise of the crowd fading around me. He looked out over the crowd like performers do, scanning faces—until his gaze landed on me.

It was like something passed between us in that split second.

His voice faltered—just slightly. His eyes widened. He did a double-take, eyebrows pulling together as his gaze stayed fixed on mine.

Recognition. Confusion. Maybe even pain.

But he didn't stop playing. He didn't miss a word. He just closed his eyes and pushed through the rest of the song like it physically hurt to keep going.

When it ended, the crowd erupted. He gave a tight smile and moved on to the next track without saying a word. He sang three more songs after that—each one louder, more electric—but he never looked in my direction again. Not once.

And I stood there, heart pounding, trying to keep my knees from buckling, while the girl next to me kept dancing like the world hadn't just cracked wide open.

The Midnight Run—the name hadn't registered because I hadn't followed his career. I couldn't. I knew he was in music. I'd heard whispers, seen a tagged photo here and there—but I never looked deeper. I couldn't bear to. Not when he had no idea what I gave up.

I told myself he didn't recognize me. It had been more than a decade. But when the set ended, and I dared to wander over to the merch table, telling myself I just wanted a better look at the shirts, he looked up. And froze.

His eyes widened for the briefest second —barely more than a blink—but I saw it. Felt it. Recognition. Surprise. Something like hope.

"Mallie?" he said more than asked, with that same crooked grin that used to melt me. "I thought..." He let out a sigh, "I thought I'd never see you again."

And just like that, I was a teenage Mallory. Only this time, I had a secret.

THE BEACH HOUSE

First loves never really let go...

Every summer since they were five, Mallory and Jace spent their days chasing waves and whispering dreams inside the walls of their families' beach house. The summer they were fifteen, they made promises they were too young to understand—promises that shattered when Mallory disappeared without a word.

He never knew why she left. She never stopped carrying the secret.

Years later, Mallory's trying to piece together a life she no longer recognizes. But when she spots Jace onstage at a small venue concert, the years fall away in a single heartbeat. One look, one smile, and she's back in the pull of the only boy she ever loved.

Jace is all in—ready to pick up where they left off. But Mallory's past is about to knock on her door in the most unexpected way... and telling him the truth might cost her everything all over again.

A story of first love, second chances, and the one secret that could ruin it all.

Coming September 2025!

* * *

Acknowledgments

To my incredible beta readers—thank you for reading early, reading fast, and never hesitating to tell me when something wasn't working (or when something very much was). Your thoughtful feedback helped shape this book into something I'm proud of. To my ARC readers—thank you for championing these characters before they even had their final polish. Your love, enthusiasm, and support gave this story its first wings.

To every single reader who fell in love with this world, these messy hearts, and all the imperfect ways they find their way to each other—thank you. It means more than I can ever express that you see them the way I do.

To those who adore Darci (and especially those who are Darci)—you should know many of her most unhinged, hilarious, and big-hearted moments are rooted in real life. My daughter, Emma, unknowingly gave me so much gold. I will never forget the day we discovered that cigarette-infused couch, and she was frantic to get rid of the smell—until she called me two days later to tell me she'd taken that thing down to the frame. I laughed so hard I peed myself. No lie. To this day, if one of us even mentions that couch, we both end up in tears from laughing so hard. Darci would be proud.

And finally, to anyone who's ever loved these characters as fiercely as I have—thank you for making room in your heart for them. They live because you let them.

With gratitude,
Stephanie

About the Author

Stephanie Pass hails from a tiny Texas town where she lives with her husband, children, and a Boxer dog who talks more than she does. She writes contemporary romance with magical realism and romantasy. Soon, she will dip her toe into some sci-fi romance. She loves books about love, magic, and high fae. She had her own real-life romance story come true when a chance encounter led her to meet her now husband. When she's not writing romance stories, Stephanie is a mom blogger dancing to Taylor Swift at https:// thetiptoefairy.com. But you can often find her at the roller skating rink or dancing at the goth nightclub.

To learn more join Stephanie's email list - https://thetiptoefairy.myflodesk.com/join-romance-list

9 7 9 8 9 9 9 2 4 7 7 6 4 1